Gold

by Andrejs Upīts

translated by Uldis Balodis

Vagabond Voices
Glasgow

First published in 1914 as *Zilts* © Andrejs Upīts

This translation first published in September 2024 by
Vagabond Voices Publishing Ltd.,
Glasgow,
Scotland.

Translation © Vagabond Voices 2024

ISBN 978-1-913212-37-7

The author's right to be identified as author of this book under the Copyright, Designs and Patents Act 1988 has been asserted.

Printed and bound in Poland

Cover design by Mark Mechan

Typeset by Park Productions

The publisher acknowledges subsidy towards the translation and publication from Latvian Literature

The publisher acknowledges subsidy towards this publication from Creative Scotland

For further information on Vagabond Voices, see the website, www.vagabondvoices.co.uk

Changeling Twenty Changeling Twenty

Contents

Introduction	vii
Part One	3
Part Two	65
Part Three	411

Introduction

Just before the First World War, the Latvian writer and translator, Andrejs Upīts, completed his fifth and highly original novel, Gold, which examines the essence and extremes of capitalism and materialism in the early twentieth century – and beyond, it should be said, because his Edwardian world is not so different from the neoliberal societies we live in today. The novel is both a classic family saga and a scathing satire. The structure unusually consists of three parts of very different lengths, the first part of about fifty pages, the second of about two hundred and fifty and the last of only twenty-five pages. Part One describes the bleak world of the old tailor Augusts Sveilis and his family, in which every member but one is struggling to make ends meet and yet driven by the will to survive however much it wears them down. In spite of their conditions, old Sveilis lives in accordance with an idealistic work ethic and he holds his dignity dear.

Sveilis and his wife are concerned about their son Roberts, who is a student, and they are not convinced that his studies will be much help, but they don't want him to go the same way as their oldest son, also called Augusts, who in their opinion has gone astray. However, it is this other son who changes all their fortunes and takes them away to a life of luxury and the absence of work – a world in which work is despised and they need to get others to run their errands. It is a difficult transition for the old couple. This device – the sudden shift from poverty to wealth – underscores the enormity of the change: the before and the after. They do not return to the "before" although the reader may expect this, and yet it would be difficult to say that the "after" brought them much happiness following the initial exhilaration.

The novel is set in Latvia, when it was part of Tsarist Russia, which was still using the gold standard, so gold represents money and wealth, and comes to symbolise their corrosive consequences. The author uses the physicality of the precious metal to great literary effect, as if the metal itself had some metaphysical power over human beings.

In Part Two, Augusts Sveilis Junior emerges as the protagonist, and although he is on the road to depravity, he is initially a well-intended young man capable of genuine generosity and yet also quickly learning to use wealth to manipulate other people and not only his own family. Upīts also follows the trajectories of the other family members, which are distinct. Augusts Sveilis Senior is hollowed out, no longer the real head of the household and without a replacement role. His wife is the least changed by the experience and retains her inferior position which society demanded of her and to which she long been accustomed. Roberts, who had been working fairly hard at his studies, completely loses his way and even his innocent love affair is pushed aside by his older brother, and whatever had been honest in him is destroyed. The most tragic figure is Made, the daughter who is older than Roberts, and already worn out by hard work when they come into money. The reader may believe that Augusts is going to pay a price for his evil behaviour, either by going bankrupt – which he almost does – or by some dramatic accident, but Upīts is not that predictable. Like Zola, he has to demonstrate that the ineluctable economic machine has no moral content. It crushes lives in the same manner of some natural calamity like a tidal wave or the eruption of a volcano. It moves on and the only person completely destroyed is Made, the most important female figure in the novel, whose psychological vicissitudes are carefully observed. It's true that almost all characters are humiliated and degraded, but all of them can bend and adapt to this merciless and broken environment, in which the old morality has died but a new morality has not replaced it.

But let me be clear: this novel is certainly about morality, but it is not moralistic. It follows the methodology of French naturalism and, in my opinion, improves on it, as all good authors want to do. Too often great novels are hidden in the literatures of small nations, and this is certainly one of them for many reasons, but I will only mention here the brilliance of the dialogue which is both utterly plausible in terms of the characters but also full of profound insights into human behaviour. There is also a degree of lyricism in the descriptions often of the countryside, which to some extent is the pool of normality but mainly absent from the novel except in Part Three. However this is also true of the cityscapes and the descriptions around the city, and yet in this case there is also a sense of menace that matches the real dangers it contains.

Alcohol and the shallowness of human relationships are also important themes in this book. Business in Riga appears to be fuelled by alcohol, which also provides material for less important but often entertaining character studies. Alcohol is related to sexual violence which becomes increasingly evident as the novel progresses. Towards the end of Part Two, Upīts accelerates the process of decay, precisely the thing that makes the reader think that they are doomed. But this is not before the author has thoroughly described the workings of shareholders' meetings and their internal and interminable disputes. This should be dull, but not in Upīts's hands. The rhetoric and argumentation are both cunningly persuasive and examples of the horrendous venality of these earnest and passionate businessmen – passionate about gold, that is.

Aina Zvaigzne has a relatively small part in the novel, but she is the moral foil for the immorality and spinelessness that surround her. She is an activist and wants to set up a socialist school to teach children to change the world. She is unbending and believes that marriage is a dishonest farce, which causes serious problems with her parents and her lover (clearly she had been reading her Engels). Upīts very wisely restricts her presence, as I have already suggested, and we never know what happens to her. She leaves to pursue her unlikely enterprise which is probably fated to fail, but the concept that human probity is possible but very fragile remains in the air.

I have been told that Gold was neglected in Latvia for a long, but became more prominent shortly after the republication of one of his other novels in 1985. Gold was reprinted on the 120th anniversary of his birth in 1997, and the ideas of Andrejs Upīts began to be reappraised in light of the "nouveau riche" behaviour in post-soviet Latvia during the 1990s and possible parallels with Augusts Sveilis's extreme lifestyle.

Gold is a socialist novel and a realist novel, but it is most definitely not a Socialist-Realist novel; in fact Upīts would later claim that there was no place for Socialist Realism in literature, when that particular credo came into fashion after the Second World War. Gold predated and outshined Upton Sinclair's The Jungle, which has been essential reading for socialists everywhere, and Gold is at least as great a work of literature as Émile Zola's Germinal (1884), whose observational and pessimistic approach is similar to Upīts's. But Gold's particular originality lies in his decision not to critique capitalism principally for the harm it inflicts on the working class, but for the harm it inflicts on the rich – the supposed beneficiaries of the economic system.

*

Andrejs Upīts was born in 1877 in Skrīveri, a small rural town in Latvia, where he completed his studies but still pursued his self-education which included studying German and Russian, both culturally significant in his country at the time, and also English, French and Italian. He did get into print in his teenage years – in 1892 to be precise – and in the late 1890s he began to be known for his journalism. Later in life he would go on to work as a teacher, translator and civil servant, but of more interest to us is his shift towards literary criticism in 1904.

Because Latvia was still part of the Tsarist Empire in 1905, the country was caught up in the 1905 Revolution, and this affected Upīts's thinking and introduced him to Marxism. He wrote his first play in that same year, and his first novel was published in 1909. This was quickly followed by three more novels in 1910, 1912 and 1913, before the publication of Gold in early 1914.

Following the two revolutions in 1917, the country entered a period of considerable disruption with armies going back and forth, factions within the country and outside influences from Germany and Russia. Upīts was arrested by the Germans in 1918 during their occupation of the country, and in 1919 he was appointed head of the arts department at the Education Commission of the short-lived Latvian Socialist Soviet Republic.

On returning secretly to Latvia from Russia in 1920, he was arrested twice and sentenced to death, but other artists and writers intervened and the sentence was not implemented. He continued to live and work in Riga and Skrīveri during the interwar years and wrote six more novels during this period. It became difficult for him to publish his literary works following the coup in 1934 which created Kārlis Ulmanis's dictatorial right-wing regime, and he was obliged to adopt various ploys, such as using a pseudonym or self-publishing.

Upīts supported the Russian occupation of Latvia in 1940 and was a member of the People's Seimas, which only lasted a month or two. After the Second World War when Latvia was forced into annexation by the Soviet Union, his career improved and he won the USSR State Prize in 1946 for his novel, Verdant Land, and in 1957 he won the Latvian SSR State Prize for Problems of Socialist Realism in Literature, a non-fiction work which expressed his reservations about Socialist Realism I have already mentioned. However, he must have had problems with the Soviet regime as well, because the performance of his play, The Blooming Desert, was banned and the censors would not allow distribution of his History of Literature.

He died in 1970 at the age of ninety-three, and a museum was opened in his name.

*

I wish to thank Arnis Koroševskis for his invaluable assistance in writing this introduction.

Allan Cameron, Glasgow, May 2024

Gold

PART ONE

During the night a powerful gale had almost torn the tailor's shop sign from its lower supporting beam. For some time its boards had been rotting and the screws had begun to loosen and give way. The larger, upper beam couldn't take all the weight and was sagging downwards. Before the sun could rise, Sveilis was out in the street with a chair ready to repair the sign with a few nails.

It wasn't very high up, but he still had to stretch to reach it. His clothes were wearing thin, his shoes slipping off his feet, and the chair wobbled on the uneven cobblestones. But Sveilis persevered, pressing his knees into the door frame and straining to secure the sign. He hammered in the second nail, with the third one still in his mouth. Two children watched him from the top floor flat: first through one window, then the other. They pressed their grubby faces right up against the glass as they looked down at him.

The nails went into the wood without resistance. Once he had hammered them all in, Sveilis climbed down and looked at the sign. It wasn't going to last long like that. The plaster covering the whole house was looking pretty shabby, crumbling in some places, and the locks on both windows were crooked. The front step had worn down completely, leaving a large gap underneath the door. But at least the signboard was now straight and creaking gently in the wind. It read "Portnoy" above and "Schneider" below – the Russian and the German for "tailor". In the middle there was a picture of a faded coat: an army uniform with a sword belt hanging diagonally across it. Sveilis walked around to look at the other side, and saw the same coat but different words: "Tailor Augusts Sveile". At that moment he noticed the children above were sticking out their tongues at him. Visibly annoyed, he waved his hammer at them threateningly, grabbed the chair and went back inside.

"Well, did it fall down?" his wife asked as she crouched over the stove where the pan for the coffee was beginning to steam.

Sveilis felt no need to respond. He shook off the chill he'd got from working outside, cleared his throat, spat on the floor and rubbed it with his foot. His hands were frozen, so he rubbed them together and got to work. Juškans, who owned the local tavern, needed to have the button holes on his coat whipstitched – and it had to be ready by lunchtime.

The fire crackled reassuringly in the stove. The warmth kept misting up Sveilis's his glasses and when he occasionally looked over to the fire he saw it flickering in duplicate. The welcome warmth that came from its long, red tendrils suffused the entire room. Sveilis cleared his throat and scratched his thinning grey beard.

The pan on the stove started to hiss. His wife filled the iron with embers, then cleared the corner of the table and began to bring everything out for breakfast. As he stitched the button holes, Sveilis stared critically at each object being placed on the table. Two coffee cups and two glasses. Both cups had matching saucers with a floral pattern. One of which was white with a chip in its rim and the other, which was at the end of the table, didn't have a saucer. Mrs. Sveilis stood at the head of the table and was observing her handiwork. Sveilis looked down, but could still see the table out of the corner of his eye as he stitched the button holes on Juškans's coat. He saw that the sugar bowl and the knives were missing. His wife was looking at it too, but it felt like she was seeing a completely different table than he was. As his thimble bumped against the needle, his large nose flushed visibly – but, as was his habit, Sveilis didn't say a word. Then, his wife suddenly remembered the missing items, and rushed off to retrieve them from the cabinet behind the door.

The pan on the stove began to rattle. Mrs. Sveilis lifted it off the stovetop and returned it several times. She rekindled the fire, knocking the logs against each other and prodding them into ashes. The pan slowly settled down, its hissing getting quieter and quieter. Mrs. Sveilis poured the black liquid into a battered old blue, flowered-patterned tin pot. A gentle cosiness permeated the room as the smell of coffee mingled with the warm glow of the cast iron pot.

Sveilis was delighted and leant back in his chair as he threaded a needle with a new silk thread. He crossed his legs and kept on sewing, while his wife continued to fuss over the iron.

"It's not ready yet," she said. Her voice seemed to alternate between shrill and sullen, but her face – old before its time with its foggy blue eyes and sharp nose – remained tired and indifferent.

"It'll cool down..." Sveilis answered and cast a quick glance through his long grey eyelashes in the direction of the door. "Don't bring it over yet."

"No, of course not." Mrs. Sveilis pushed the coffee pot over to the hottest spot on the stove. She leaned down over the iron again. "It just doesn't want to heat up..."

Sveilis stopped his needle in mid stitch and leaned back abruptly.

"Get on with it!" he called out angrily. The tips of his ears were bright red. "Is this the first time you've ever picked up an iron?"

Mrs. Sveilis did get on with it. Puffs of white ash escaped from the curved front of the iron. The room seemed to fill with a thin, grey, steam that stank of cinders. The iron began to heat up: with every swing, its heart-shaped opening grew redder and redder.

A group of Jewish children walked by, chatting loudly with each other. A face, smudged with dirt, pressed itself against the glass of the door. With flashes of bright white teeth, the face was set beneath an oversized cap – the front of which was drooping low over its owner's eyes. The face disappeared and then a hand reached out from a tattered sleeve. There was a loud knock and, moments later, a chant of "Sveile! Sveile! oo-ooh!" Then the carefree group drifted by, laughing and talking all the way. Sveilis didn't look up, though he'd seen and heard them. He hunched down even further over Juškans's coat and kept sewing fretfully.

The door swung open and a teenage boy came in wearing a school cap and a homespun shirt bound by a leather belt.

He slammed the door and talked loudly as he walked to the window at the back of the room, where he cleared away the rags thrown on top of his books and sat down at the table opposite Sveilis. He threw down his cap and took out his notebook.

Mrs. Sveilis came over with the coffee pot.

"Damn peddler!" the boy muttered, scornfully taking a drawing out of his notebook and turning it over in his fingers. "It gets tougher every day."

Sveilis shifted in his seat.

"What good will come from drawing like that! You'd be better off going over to Pētersons – he makes pens."

The boy stuffed the drawing behind the book's dust jacket.

"You can make a lot of money from a drawing like that…"

Mrs. Sveilis stood at the end of the table holding the coffee pot.

"Of course you can, dear Roberts! But doesn't a pen also bring in some money?"

"Do the pens Pētersons makes actually work properly?" The boy uncorked a round ink bottle. "Pens for a pittance – he sells a dozen for three kopecks. You can write with them, but never try using them for calligraphy."

Sveilis would have liked to say something else, but didn't react quickly enough. He just stared at Roberts for a moment and then went back to his sewing. Mrs. Sveilis sighed. Then she wiped the bottom of the coffee pot with the corner of her apron and topped up the cup at the far end. Leaning over the table, Roberts wrote his name in the new notebooks, moving his lips along with the pen as he did so. Sveilis sewed for a few more minutes then stopped, and without lifting his head, began to watch every movement of his son's pen.

Roberts craned his neck to see it from both sides and began to blot what he had written. When her son had finished writing, his mother said, "Drink your coffee now. Made won't be getting home until later."

Recorking the bottle, Roberts lifted it up to the window

and observed, "Made has been writing again. She always uses up my ink."

Sveilis stared angrily at his wife, which put her on edge. "No she hasn't, my dear Roberts. She couldn't have written anything yesterday or I would have seen it."

"That's not true!" Roberts retorted. "I know it for a fact. Yesterday morning the ink was just up to this groove. And look at it now! She's always using up my ink." He opened the drawer in the table and after rummaging around amongst the odds and ends, he took out a tattered notebook. He leafed through it roughly, flicking from the front to the back then the back to the front, until he found what he was looking for. "Look at this: 'By the gates of Plevna, the battlements. We fought there...' That wasn't there yesterday – so this has obviously been written since then." He turned one page after another, adding something up in his head. "Thirty-seven verses... What a waste of my ink!"

His mother shifted her weight from one foot to the other. "I don't know. Maybe she did but I didn't see her. Drink your coffee now, dear Roberts, you don't have much time."

Sveilis shifted the thimble to his other finger, and commented, "Just keep babbling, the lot of you."

Roberts sugared his coffee, but instead of putting the song book away, he pulled it closer so that he could read it while he stirred his drink. At first he read it with a smirk, then his face changed as he became more interested. He turned to a different section of the book and began reading again. His mother was busying herself at the stove, and his father kept glancing across the table as he continued to sew.

"Mum, where's the milk?" Roberts asked abruptly.

His mother reacted as if she'd been stung, clapping her hands and rushing over to the cabinet behind the door.

"Isn't there anything more interesting to read than that nonsense?" his father interjected, but he continued working when Roberts didn't answer or lift his eyes from Made's song book.

"Eat those rolls, son," his mother urged, as she filled his cup with milk. "The pretzels went completely stale overnight. It wouldn't have happened if we had a cool place to put them in." She pushed the jug of milk closer to him and moved the knife so it would be easier to reach.

"Bread dries out even faster in a cool place," Roberts mumbled. Sveilis pulled on his new thread with such force that the knot shot right through the cloth with a crack. Each time he pulled it through, Sveilis's eyes widened behind his glasses. He watched as his son coated a piece of white bread with a layer of butter, while ignoring the milk his mother had brought. He watched his son's white teeth bite off large chunks of bread, and he watched how the youth gulped down steaming brown coffee after each bite. He noted the semi-circle shapes made by each bite in the soft, slightly yellow bread, and observed the way the tiny white crumbs that fell from the hand that held it onto the threadbare sleeve of his son's shirt – a hand propped up by the forearm and elbow beneath it. The shiny, black cloth he was working on seemed to have been covered in frost and his teeth chattered at the thought of touching the next spot. His tongue sensed the sweet smell that makes one's mouth water. Sveilis cleared his throat and tried not to look, but he couldn't help it – he had to, he had to look. As he lowered his head, his needle pierced more skilfully and he pulled the thread more briskly. His lips were tightly pressed together, giving his face a strangely malevolent expression.

Both of the rolls had now been consumed, and Mrs. Sveilis who had been tinkering with something and had dropped her cloth, pushed a piece of dark bread over to her son.

"Take a few slices and dip them in milk. Mrs. Baumanis pulled it off this time: it's nice and yellow – made from new wheat. And such a pretty crust..." she stopped talking when Sveilis coughed loudly and gritted his teeth, deep furrows appearing down the sides of his cheeks. And then she said, more sharply this time, almost as if she were arguing with someone: "You'll not get another bite to eat until the evening, except what's left of that stale pretzel you stuck in your bag for lunch!"

Roberts broke off a piece of the black bread. He ate more slowly taking smaller bites, while his father moved on to the final button hole. His mother was standing behind him at the sewing machine.

"Sveile, Sveile!" echoed somewhere from down the street with the same mocking tone as earlier.

Only the occasional hair in his grey beard seemed to tremble a little. Mrs. Sveilis stepped on the sewing machine pedal, which resulted in a rattling noise. But Roberts remained completely still for a moment with the piece of bread at his lips. He seemed confused, suddenly blushed and, leaning over his coffee cup, began to eat quickly again. When he looked over at his father across the table, he saw that his eyes were full of tears, and suddenly he no longer wanted the bread. He placed what was left back on the table. He leaned back and took his time over drinking the last of his coffee, savouring each mouthful.

He glanced at the old wall-clock above the bed. It was time to go. He piled the books back up at the end of the table, blowing off ash, wool and cotton fluff. Finally, he went over to his father and said, "We have to pay for the German classes this week."

His father stuck the needle into the fabric and lifted his head. His mother also came back into the room.

"This week? ... But I just ... you just..." This unwelcome news came as a shock he was unable to digest. He couldn't think of what to say and his eyes blinked helplessly behind his glasses.

"Everybody else has already paid. Yesterday the teacher had to remind me once again. This is the last week."

His mother clutched her apron and looked at them both anxiously, but she nodded in agreement with her son.

"Well, then we'll just have to pay...There's no other option..."

"Dammit with your fees!" His father sewed angrily, his needle glinting. "I just paid your school fees. Thirty roubles... And now there's more!"

"Well, it's time to pay them again." Roberts had put on his cap and pulled it down over his eyes.

"It's only five roubles," his mother added quietly, "we'll make sure that we get Juškans's suit ready today."

"Ten roubles!" Sveilis interrupted angrily. "Dammit! We still need the linings, all the accessories...We have to buy firewood. How much does a cord of wood cost! And the week after next, the rent will be due again..."

Roberts stormed out of the room, stamping his feet to show he was offended. At the end of the table his mother stood motionless as if on a knife-edge.

"You always act this way when it's time to pay up. Is any of this Roberts's fault? You were the one who wanted those German classes. You didn't mind last year, or the year before that, because you had enough money to pay for them. But now you don't...Actually, that's not true at all. I forgot to tell you, the other day Mrs. Skrastiņš said that her husband and son are going to be needing new suits for the society bazaar."

Sveilis gave his wife a long, sceptical look.

"They'll both need one...I remember when they had to play for the society ball for Pentecost, and they needed those suits. And Springers did too, and that other one – all of them acquaintances! When it's just talk, they're all good friends, but when it comes time to make a commitment, then nothing." Despite all the commotion, Sveilis's hunger hadn't passed. With every passing second the food seemed to smell even more delicious. The piece of bread sat temptingly next to the bowl of cottage cheese... Sveilis couldn't carry on anymore. He pinned his needle to the fabric, put Juškans's coat on the table, and his long bony fingers grabbed the piece of bread with one hand and the knife with the other. With a single motion he split the piece of bread into two equal pieces. "Pour me some coffee. Let's eat. Maybe Made won't come home today."

Mrs. Sveilis poured the coffee for her husband, and looked back towards the door before pouring, then poured some for herself as well. Then she sat down on the edge of the chair at the end of the table, and cut half of a slice for herself, while carefully sprinkling the crumbs over the dry cottage cheese. She nibbled at the bread so as not to make noise with her toothless mouth.

Sveilis took huge bites and slurped his coffee loudly. His forehead was covered in wrinkles, and his sparse grey beard quivered as he ate and snorted loudly. He didn't say a word for a long time and his eyes shifted from the cup to the bowl of milk and back again. He didn't fully submerge the bread but only dipped each piece part way into the bowl. He put his index finger around the piece of bread but kept it slightly raised, scraping it along the tip of the knife where there was still a bit of butter and a clump of cottage cheese. He licked his lips and the underside of his finger, which was wet and shiny. Not a single crumb fell to the ground.

"Pour me another cup." Sveilis pushed his cup towards his wife. "Made probably won't come home today."

Mrs. Sveilis poured the coffee slowly. You could tell what she was thinking just by looking at her: there's still plenty left – there'll be enough for Made too. But after filling up her husband's cup, she shot a worried glance at the bottom of the clay pot.

"Disobedient girl," Sveilis started up again after a moment. "Who knows what she's up to! I'm certain she won't bring back one single button, and Juškans's suit has to be ready by lunchtime."

"She's not up to anything around anywhere." Mrs. Sveilis said.

"What do you mean she's not up to anything? Then why did she have to go to that dance last Sunday? Thirty kopecks thrown away just like that. Her boots need to be repaired, a new buckle for her belt...How are we supposed to manage that!"

By now, Mrs. Sveilis was starting to get worked up.

"Oh, come on! Doesn't she spend enough time with your rags all week long? A young person needs to have fun too..."

"Fun!" Sveilis twisted his mouth mockingly. His wife had stopped listening.

"Who else's daughter has to walk around in patched up boots like that! Her only skirt is two years old – who knows how many times it's been washed!" Mrs. Sveilis was now extremely agitated. She pushed away her glass so that it clanked against the coffee pot, and started nervously rolling a small bit of bread into a ball with her fingers. "Couldn't Augusts have helped us out just a little?"

Sveilis dismissed her with a wave of his hand. He knocked his wife's knife onto the floor with his elbow. While she was busy picking it up, he quickly ate the piece he'd bitten off. After swallowing it, he didn't say anything at all. Only after a long silence did he begin to speak again.

"Nothing is going to come of those German lessons. Nothing at all. It's just like what happened to Skrastiņš's son. He finished that district school, and it came to nothing. Now he's in exactly the same position as his father, who never went to school at all. He just plays the fiddle at dances. What an achievement! Who knows what will become of our children. If one of them has already turned out like...that, what are the chances that the other ones will turn out any better?"

Mrs. Sveilis held her silence for a moment, and then said, "What happened to Augusts was our fault too. We sent him out into the world too soon. If we'd put him to work, he wouldn't have learned to drink, and he wouldn't have become such a good-for-nothing. Though he does say that he's in a good place now."

"Him – in a good place!" Sveilis sneered. "Good places are for good people, not for people who don't know how to behave. A coachman? A stable lad more likely, but I don't believe that: he's probably never even seen a horse, and if so, it will have only been from a distance – a coachman!" For a while he continued to sew, and the silk thread squealed faintly as it brushed through the soft cloth. Then, all of a sudden, he stuck his needle into the cloth and rested his hands on his knees. "It's our fault – our own fault! Didn't I try putting him to work, didn't I keep trying to help him in every way I could! Ever since he was a baby he's had the devil inside him. A whirlwind, not a person! And you were always his biggest defender! I was an idiot. I should've skinned him alive..."

Mrs. Sveilis crouched over the sewing machine, and wound thread onto the spools. She had her back to him, but it was clear she felt guilty. Sveilis began to sew again.

"That's why I'm worried about Roberts, too. He goes to school every day, but that's all we know. He's there, and we're paying all this money, but will we ever see a penny of it back?"

"Roberts isn't like that," Mrs. Sveilis objected.

"What do you know! They're not children anymore – they're animals! The world is raising them now, not us. Made, too. She's wasting her time on that nonsense – burning kerosene for nothing, wasting that boy's ink...on songs – complete rubbish, damn it!" He spat angrily on the floor.

Mrs. Sveilis was crouching even lower. "Roberts isn't like that. All his teachers praise him, after all. He's always carrying around those books of his, always with those books. I just hope he doesn't ruin his eyes – what with the poor lighting in here. He'll finish next year, then it'll be easier for us..."

"Easier..." Sveilis sneered, lingering on the word, but he turned towards his wife anyway, waiting to hear what else she had to say. His wife knew him well, and so she continued.

"He'll finish – and then he just needs to find some little position, maybe there'll even be one around here, close to home. The notary needs a clerk, and there are three or four positions at the police precinct, two note-takers at the wood-yard..."

"The examining magistrate has a clerk; the justice of the peace has a clerk..." Sveilis continued briskly, as if it had all just occurred to him, as if they didn't say these same things to each other every single day. Both of them had started to become gentler and kinder towards each other. Hope for the future shined like a beam of sunlight through a crack in the wall of the dimly lit room.

"Then it'll be easier for us," Mrs. Sveilis repeated her favourite thought and Sveilis nodded in agreement. His short-sighted eyes peered through his spectacles across the table, as if he were trying to catch sight of something mysterious in the distance, barely visible and strangely alluring. His inner smile was given away by countless tiny wrinkles which extended in a fan shape from the outer corners of his eyes and stretched right across his temples.

"If only he'd just study and not let himself be led astray," he added pensively. "All kinds of things can happen in the city. We can't be there to guide him all the time."

"Roberts isn't like that." Mrs. Sveilis comforted him.

"No, that's true," Sveilis kept to his point, "although we can't really know for certain. Augusts wasn't like that at first. Nobody can teach you how to be good, if you don't have it in you."

"But he's not as bad as all that," Mrs. Sveilis tried to say in defence of her son, "Augusts hasn't killed or robbed anyone..."

Sveilis interrupted her with a nervous motion.

"It's better not to say that! Why didn't he finish his apprenticeship as a bricklayer, once he'd started? Why couldn't he live at Vulfsons's shop? No, no, it's got to be a coachman! A vagrant, I would call it. That's all he is..."

He tried to start sewing again, but the needle seemed almost completely blunt. It kept catching on the cloth and wouldn't go through, so he put it aside and turned towards his wife again. She tried to move the conversation on to a happier topic.

"The crown forest surveyor needs assistants every summer. He could stay right here with the district foresters. Last year, when Made and I brought their clean laundry over to them, I asked the forester's wife about it. She's a good person, and she promised to put in a good word for him. But it's still too early, there's no way of knowing yet."

"Thirty roubles – well, even if it's just twenty a month. He'll get about that much, I guess..." Sveilis started counting with his fingers, folding them down as he said each number, "Ten roubles for supplies, five for expenses...and five...We don't need any more than that. Just enough to pay the rent. We'll earn enough on our own to support ourselves."

Mrs. Sveilis let out a long and heavy sigh before speaking, "But we don't earn all that much... I earn almost nothing. And it's not easy for Made! She'll wear her fingers down to the bone with all that laundry. And will it be worth it? She'll be out collecting it and delivering it all over again, meanwhile that old dress of hers is hardly ever washed ..."

Sveilis coughed dryly. "You're right...but it won't always be that way. The notary said last year he might need a coat. I reckon there'll be more sewing work when it gets nearer to winter. Even without the laundry, there'll be plenty for all of us to do."

"You reckon..." Mrs. Sveilis repeated. "You're always reckoning, but it never gets us anywhere. The notary will ask you to mend his coat. We'll be lucky if anyone brings us an old pair of trousers. The more delicate items – everyone always takes those to Vulfsons. A Jew will always stand up for a Jew, but a Latvian barely recognises another Latvian!" She sighed again heavily. "You should think about paying for those new tailor's classes.".

"Damn it!" Sveilis twisted to one side to grab the needle, but threw it straight back down again. "Six and a half roubles!" He stooped under the weight of his tiredness, "and besides nothing would come of those classes. My eyes are getting dimmer by the day. When I can no longer see anything, that'll be it. If Made hasn't learned the trade by then, I don't know what we'll do."

He carried on sitting there, hunched over. Blinking behind his spectacles, he looked across the table with such intensity that it seemed as if they were trying to pierce the wall. Mrs. Sveilis kept tinkering with the sewing machine without any particular purpose.

Outside, traders were riding down the street on their way

to the market. The walls and floor shook, and the window panes rattled as they passed. The oil container on the sewing machine clinked lightly as it bounced around. The window facing the street and the glass above the door were so covered in condensation that the people moving past appeared to be nothing more than grey shadows. The back window was almost completely clear. Behind it was a narrow yard, surrounded by a rotten half-collapsed fence on one side and a broken-down wooden shack on the other. Next to the woodshed, the upstairs neighbour was hauling something around. A grey, bony cat was walking along the edge of the well with chicks squawking and scurrying around behind him. Sveilis looked out at the yard, but immediately shrank back in his chair. The strain typical of his long working days was so great that the surroundings couldn't hold his attention for very long.

"As long as he finishes and gets good grades..." Sveilis started up again, though he was unsure as to what his point was.

Mrs. Sveilis stirred. "Are you really going to start picking on that boy... again!"

Sveilis would usually have responded angrily when his wife raised her voice, but today his brooding seemed to calm him.

"Just think about it for a moment. Why do we have all these high hopes? Augusts is..." But then he dismissed his son with a wave of his hand. "And nothing will come of Made either. Skrastiņš's son was sniffing around here for a while, but now there's no sign of him."

A red-faced Mrs. Sveilis tore herself away from her sewing machine. "Doesn't it matter that she doesn't want to! If she'd married him, she would be just like the rest of them. But she says that if it's not who she wants, then it's better to have no one at all..."

It was unclear from his expression whether Sveilis had heard her or not. He just sighed heavily and carried on talking, "Well then, there'll be nothing for it when we're older other than walking around with a begging bowl! You can defend him all you like, but Roberts isn't perfect either. Remember what he used to be like compared to who he is now: his nose in his books all day long; he even falls asleep with them. Every Sunday it's those black ones... with the numbers on the back. I once said: 'Son, get that song book, and why don't all four of us have a sing-song? It has been too long since the last one. You know that my sight is fading.' He didn't even reply; he just took his hat and walked out."

"Well why do you always have to force your songs on everybody? The boy has to study..."

Sveilis shook his head vigorously.

"If only he'd had no other problems apart from his studying! But it's those books with the little numbers in them... And then he has started telling Made about them... Didn't you hear? Rubbish! Just total nonsense! Is any of that going to help him when it comes to his exams? He's up all night, burns through half a quart of kerosene. All that sitting around can't be doing him any good."

He sighed and began to sew again. Mrs. Sveilis also sighed and glanced at the clock. It was just about ten. She looked into the coffee pot, now only lukewarm. It was strange that Made had been gone for so long. She sat down to work again and began working on the coat belonging to Juškans, the owner of the tavern.

The traders were still riding down the street. Once the wind had abated, the footsteps of passers-by could be heard from inside the house: they were talking as they walked – some laughing, others coughing and spitting. Then a fresh gust of wind blew and drowned out their noise again. The wind also found its way underneath the door and into the room, rustling the strips of yellow-brown wallpaper which were peeling off the wall. Sveilis pulled his feet under his chair, closed his top coat pocket and folded up his collar. This kept him warm, and also hid his worn and dirty shirt front.

The clock struck ten.

They heard the sound of footsteps stopping in front of their door, and a shadow blocked the light from the window above. Neither Sveilis nor his wife looked up, but they both knew it was Made. They could tell it was her from her footsteps. They knew that, any second now, she would dust off her shoes and come inside.

But this time she didn't dust off her shoes. She just stopped for an instant – probably to free her hand so she could open the door – and immediately came in. The door opened and a gust of wet, icy-cold air surged into the room and drove out the warmth. She slammed the door so heavily that the whole house shook: tiny flecks of plaster rained down from the ceiling onto the table and all over the tavern owner's coat.

Mr. and Mrs. Sveilis looked up at Made, then looked down at their work again. Made's entrance was too unusual, her countenance too odd for them to ask her anything. If something was wrong – and it clearly was – then she would be sure to tell them anyway, whether they asked her or not.

Made threw down a tangle of dirty laundry, wrapped in a striped flannel cloth, next to the stove, and then came over to the table. She tossed in front of her father a small bundle that tinkled. "Buttons." And she didn't say anything else.

She took off her shabby padded coat and flung it onto her bed. Then, she untied the black, fringed scarf from around her head and tossed it onto her parents' bed, which was almost placed right against the stove. She bent down over the stove and rubbed her hands as she warmed them.

When she stood up straight again, her mother and father quickly dropped their eyes back towards their work. They both had exactly the same thought: now she'll come over to the table to eat. She'll eat and tell us what has happened. But Made didn't sit down to eat. Instead, she walked over to the door, wiped a patch of the window with the corner of her apron, and stood looking out at the street.

Her father was sewing at a furious pace. His thimble scratched the end of the needle again and again. Her mother snipped the ends of the thread for the loop sewn into the neck of the coat so it could be hung up.

At that moment Made walked outside. Her father and mother stirred, but still neither of them would speak. Made's behaviour was so unusual because it seemed that she didn't want to talk about anything. They were both afraid of saying the wrong thing, which could jab like a pointed finger at a sensitive spot. And yet they had to say something. Their curiosity grew, and a peculiar and somewhat unsettling feeling began to weigh heavily on them both. They couldn't sit calmly for much longer.

Made reappeared carrying a tub of laundry from the storage shed across the yard, and was clearly planning to soak the laundry. Meanwhile, the coffee on the table remained untouched. Sveilis's long, bony fingers nervously smoothed out some creased fabric. She brought in the tub and put it in its usual spot. She should have heated up the water first, but today she hadn't thought of that. She turned towards the door again, but her mother had finally lost her patience. She jumped up and suddenly sat back down again. "Well come on, have some coffee!" Her voice sounded concerned and nervous. It was clear from his facial expression that Made's father wholeheartedly agreed with this invitation.

Made walked over slowly, and when she had got to the end of the table, she turned her face to the window and looked out into the yard. It was striking how similar she looked to her mother. She was a little larger – and of course younger – but with that same thickset, slightly round-shouldered body and that same face, which had aged from hard work. Poverty and endless worries had reduced her to weariness and a constant frown. Only her lovely, flowing ash-brown hair could have brightened up her appearance. But instead it was unkempt, hastily arranged into braids, serving only to accentuate her resemblance to a withered old maid.

She poured the coffee unthinkingly, broke off a piece of bread, and scraped some butter onto the end of her knife.

Just like that and still standing, she took a bite and a sip. She took three or four more bites – and no more. She put the rest down on the table, but then she picked it up again and carried it over to the cabinet to put it away. Afterwards, she wiped the crumbs off the table with the corner of her striped apron. Her mother stood watching her the whole time.

"What's wrong with you? Why aren't you eating? Are you sick?"

Made was working with the iron without paying much attention to she was doing. "No... it's nothing. I'm just... not hungry."

"What do you mean you're not hungry! You can't work on an empty stomach." She walked over and took the iron away from her daughter. She waved it around, blew on it, and then placed it in the wire holder on top of the stove, continuing to speak in bursts as she did all of this. "Running around all morning – and without a bite to eat! Your father was worried there wouldn't be any buttons... Did you get the laundry from the foresters?"

"Yes. There isn't as much as usual, only eight sheets. The scullery maids working in the kitchen are going to start washing the kitchen laundry themselves." She sat down heavily on her bed and put her hands in her lap.

"I can see that it's a smaller load," her mother added and began to lift the pots up onto the stove to heat some water.

The cast iron rings clanked and then the room grew quiet again. Her father pulled a button out from the package made of stiff, shiny paper, coughed dryly and stared in his daughter's direction.

Made moved her hands, then clenched them tighter and began to speak in a strange, deep voice: "Augusts is here."

The news in itself would not have upset her parents. The manor house where he was said to be living wasn't too far away – sixty or seventy versts. It was Made's voice and her behaviour that they found profoundly disconcerting.

"So, he's riding along with the gentlemen?" her father asked sarcastically, though there was an intense curiosity masked by his sarcasm.

"No, just on his own," Made answered.

"Then he must have been thrown out again." Sveilis sounded almost happy about his son's possible misfortune. Made was barely listening to him at all. She got up and nervously held on to the side of the bed.

"He arrived last night... After I left this morning, the pharmacist called me over to her door: is it true that your brother, the one from that manor, has come back? I - don't know anything about it. I'm coming from the foresters and that other woman had been at the market with the piglets. Is it true? Everyone at the market was talking about it."

She was interrupted by her father's sardonic laughter.

"Well, there's plenty to talk about! Quite the gentleman! What a joke!"

Made wasn't listening to her father's laughter or his comments.

"I don't know anything about it. But yes, everybody was talking at the market. He came back last night. They spent the whole night drinking at the hotel. They ran out of beer - this morning a boy had to run over to Vītiņš's to refill a large basket with more drink."

"That's right," her father interrupted again. "Thrown out - and whatever he managed to get, he's drunk it all away by now. If he happens to have a spare rouble - well, he'll keep going until he's lost the shirt off his back."

"No, it's something else," Made answered. "Wherever I went, people were standing in their doorway. They were talking and pointing, everyone was looking at me. Three boys muttered something but I couldn't quite hear, and then they ran after me all the way down the street. And when I got to the corner, I ran into Mrs. Juškans..."

"Oh, Mrs. Juškans!" her mother called out without taking her eyes off of Made, and then rushed over to the door.

"She was asking about Augusts and want to know if he'd been over to see us too," Made continued, "They'd been drinking and carousing all night. They ran out of beer. This morning they'd sent for her husband, too. Once he had dragged himself over there, he never came back. She had to go to the market, and there wasn't anyone left to stay at home. The tavern had to be closed. Such a mess that it's hard to bear; there are always more people coming in on market day... As long as that devil doesn't get completely drunk – after lunch there's beer to be sold..."

There was an uncomfortable silence in the room, then Made started up again, "He's tossing around hundred-rouble notes as though they were old rags."

"Who – Augusts?" her father and mother called out at the same time. Her father even bounced up a little on his chair and laughed again, but then stopped and angrily spat off to the side. "Damn it! Why are you telling us these tales?"

"They're not tales. I didn't believe it at first, but that's what everyone is saying... I thought I'd go by the hotel, then maybe I'd hear more. And as I was walking... the street was full of Jews, mostly young boys but also some older ones. The crowd stretched down the street along the entire front of the hotel – everybody gossiping with each other and looking in through the windows. I couldn't see anything through the bottom windows, only the women working at the buffet standing inside and grinning. But upstairs one of the windows was open, and there was a hellish racket coming from it. Yelling but also singing; I couldn't make sense of it. But there were a great many people up there; you could hear that. Glasses kept clinking, billiard balls were knocking against each other, and now and again the accordion would start up again... The window was open, and downstairs in the middle of the street, there was a whole pile of broken glass: bottles, tumblers and carafes, as well as broken plates sticky with scraps of meat, a couple of trampled buns... And a hellish racket coming from that window: singing, shouting, the accordion playing... The policeman was there too – his eyes glazed over, he must have been there the whole night: standing, smiling and not saying a thing..."

Clearly distressed, she grabbed her scarf, threw it on, but then removed it immediately. She walked over to the tub and upended it. She stood there for a moment, then walked to the door and looked outside, over her mother's shoulder.

But there wasn't much to see there. The traders had already gone home. Occasionally someone walked by sullenly as they headed into the wind. A stray dog moved past the door whimpering and sniffing at the lamppost. The odd plump raindrop fell heavily against the window of the hat shop across the street.

The upstairs neighbour's children were playing with something heavy, clattering across the ceiling. Flecks of plaster rained down onto the table again.

"Dammit!" Sveilis growled under his breath, "I hope he hasn't murdered or robbed somebody..."

Made and her mother stepped away from the door to let someone in: Rozentals, the master carpenter.

Out of habit, Sveilis put his needle and thread down on the table. He felt underneath his coat for the ends of the tape measure around his neck and pulled it out. Then, he opened the drawer underneath his sewing machine where he kept his notebook for writing down measurements.

But Rozentals hadn't come to have a jacket measured. He greeted all three of them and expressed the usual meaningless phrases about the weather and similar subjects. Then he just stood there; he seemed to be searching for the right words, while everyone waited in awkward silence.

"Sit down, Rozentals," Mrs. Sveilis eventually offered. But Rozentals didn't want to sit.

"No, thank you. I won't be staying long, I was just passing by... I had to get nails from Kacs. So, I just dropped by... Have you heard the news?"

But nobody responded to his inquisitive gaze. All three Sveilises were staring at the floor. Rozentals continued on his own.

"Your Augusts... They say he's hit the jackpot... Some say

he found some money and was able to keep a third of it, and they're talking about huge sums of money."

But the Sveilises had nothing to say.

"The whole city is talking about it," Rozentals began again more energetically and moved towards the door, closer to the women. "Saying crazy things... but anyway, whatever it is, it's no business of mine! Though, as your neighbour, I'll tell you one thing: it's not a good sign. How can a person suddenly get so much money! Lighting cigars with five-rouble notes!" Their neighbour laughed sourly. "Of course, it's no business of ours. Everybody is free to do what they like with their own money. But what he's doing is too much! No matter what kind of a banker someone is – money doesn't grow on trees! No one should live like that."

Rozentals couldn't stand still; he kept fidgeting and shifting around. It was obvious to Made, from his restlessness and voice, that it did matter to him, greatly. Their good neighbour was racked with jealousy. She turned and straightening her back, she said, "Hey Rozentals, you shouldn't listen to idle gossip. If somebody has money, they can do what they please, and those who don't are always going to feel bad about it. That's just how it is."

"Me – feel bad?" Rozentals spread his arms out and tried to smile contemptuously. "Made, I wish that even now you would..."

"Oh, what does it matter what we wish or don't wish for each other!" Made snapped back sharply. Every moment a new thought popped into her head: she had to stitch a suit, then she'd need to take it to Vulfsons. And who was it that put Skrastiņš's son off, and who did they think he was going to get. She knew how to cough dryly just like her father, and say, "Everyone should look after themselves and not meddle in other people's business. That's a fact."

Her mother wished she could say something to make up for Made's ill-considered harshness. But Rozentals realised that he didn't have anything else to say, and he went on his way, almost bumping into Mrs. Skrastiņš coming the other way.

As she passed through the door, Mrs. Skrastiņš shot a shy glance at each of the Sveilises. She looked most intently of all at Mrs. Sveilis, but could gather the least from her. Sveilis was staring at the floor, his brow drawn into countless furrows. While he sat there attaching buttons, he stabbed the needle angrily into the cloth and pulled forcefully at the silk thread which squeaked slightly as it went. Over and over again the needle with the thick, soft thread was launched towards a button, and yet the experienced fingers slid effortlessly over its steel tip. The tailor's teeth were clenched so tightly that deep hollows appeared on both cheeks, his thumb curved like a hawk's talon as he pressed the needle against the side of his index finger. Made, still upset by Rozentals, was standing proudly with her straight back. Around her thin, bluish, tightly pinched lips it looked as if a haughty smile was in the making. The realisation of a great and beautiful future flickered in her eyes. Her mother was the only one who appeared unchanged. Stunned and confused, she shuffled about staring at the floor, not knowing whether to go or stay, smile or sigh.

She greeted Mrs. Skrastiņš kindly, and the guest was diplomatically avoiding the subject for the moment.

"Terrible weather!" she declared, while she continued to smile and shook out her headscarf, dampened by rain. Her eyes darted mouselike from one person to another. "Wind and rain. And there's some snow on the way."

No one else said a word. Sveilis pulled out a new button from the paper pouch. Made sat down on the bed. Mrs. Sveilis started fussing with the iron. They all looked at their guest and waited. But Mrs. Skrastiņš was a born diplomat. She smiled and shook off more rain drops.

"The mud on the street is so thick that you can't even wade through it. If it keeps up like this for another couple of days, we'll have to get a boat. Water is just sloshing about in those potholes where the cobblestones are broken."

Made had collected herself and knew exactly how she was going to deal with their guest.

"Oh, my dear Mrs. Skrastiņš!" she responded loudly and subtle mockery was unmistakable in her voice. "You don't need to wade! Just walk up along the pavement."

Mrs. Skrastiņš waved her off. "Don't be silly, my dear, the pavements are no better. On the lower streets you can't even wade. Where you're living, there are lampposts, but on the smaller streets you have to almost swim to get across the mud. Earlier, we went to buy a pound or two of starch from Volkovs... We wanted to make some cranberry jelly for lunch, but we couldn't get through! We had to go the long way, along Central Avenue..."

There was a hotel on Central Avenue. The Sveilises started to feel nervous, which was made most obvious by the way all of them did their best not to show it. Mrs. Skrastiņš waited for a moment, but when it became clear that no one else was going to say anything, she carefully steered the conversation towards her intended topic.

"Rain or shine – it's always dry there. Cobblestones as flat as a tabletop, electric lights...Well! Anybody with a home there wants for nothing. There's a hotel..." She paused again for a moment, and the silence that fell on the Sveilis family was even tenser than before. She started off again as if, by coincidence, something else had just occurred to her. "Well, what I wanted to say... You see, my dears... As I was walking past, I saw a whole crowd of people on the street outside the hotel. A whole sea of people – big and small, Jews and Latvians – there were open windows, music playing, shouting, singing, bottles falling to the ground like rotten apples, platefuls of food! It's a wonder someone didn't get into trouble over there..."

At first, it had seemed as if her audience might have had to say something here, but when it appeared that they didn't, Mrs. Skrastiņš was suddenly unsure of what to do next. Only her face and its nervous tics showed how anxious and wildly curious she really was.

Made found it difficult to restrain herself if she had to say something. She got up from the bed and straightened out the blanket. "Oh, well! We know all about that, too. Everyone has started gossiping about it. One person has barely left before the next is running over to tell us all about it. Nobody seems to be concerned about their own lives as much as they are about other people's."

"My dears, you should know that it's nothing to me, nothing at all!" Mrs. Skrastiņš waved it all off with a grand motion. "What's it to me? But others are saying that he found half a million. It was stolen from a Russian gentleman, and he found it..."

"Damn it!" Sveilis muttered into his beard.

Made laughed, and, if you had listened closely, you would have heard that it was tinged with both excitement and annoyance at knowing less about her brother's deeds than these nosey strangers. "Well, well," she said, "they do say: that those with good eyes find what they're looking for, while others can trip right over it and not see a thing!"

Mrs. Skrastiņš kept trying to get something out of them, but eventually realised that the Sveilises didn't know anything themselves. After that, her flood of words began to ebb, and driven by sheer curiosity, she rushed off barely stopping to say goodbye.

But there was no peace for the Sveilises. More visitors started appearing one after the other – sometimes two or three at a time. They'd tell them what they'd heard and ask them questions. A small crowd of unemployed neighbours began to gather outside their door. There was no time for cooking lunch or boiling water for the laundry.

The stories these people told! He'd found half a million... He'd won the big jackpot... He'd won a wager... He'd won it playing cards... He'd murdered and robbed a shopkeeper... He'd given a boy a three-rouble tip for bringing him beer... He'd been slipping hundred-rouble notes into the stockings of young ladies at the hotel... He'd tossed a handful of small silver coins out the window... Sveilis looked increasingly grey and glum, and his nose became redder. Made was becoming nervous and agitated; she couldn't work anymore, but couldn't sit still either. She got up from the bed, walked over to the door, and with her eyes flashing she looked out the window at the crowd that had huddled meekly on the other side of the street. Her breasts, which earlier had been practically imperceptible, now rose higher. Her mother, fidgeting with this and that, clenching her apron and sighing, now and then glanced at her husband and daughter without their noticing.

As he ironed, Sveilis was so transfixed with what their guests were saying and with fighting off his own dark thoughts, that he forgot what he was doing and singed the back of Juškans's waistcoat. Shaken by this, he pulled himself together and drove off those unnecessary distractions. He brushed everything, folded and tied it into a package using a black cloth, put on his waders, his shirt front without a collar and his coat, and took the suit over to Juškans. By then, it was half past two.

As Sveilis came outside, a hush fell over the crowd and they parted to let him through. It was hard to hear much of anything because the wind was howling like crazy and rattling everything it could grab hold of. And there was much to be grabbed and rattled here: the shutters on the small wooden houses, open and unhooked doors, loose sheets of tin on roofs, shop signs, strips of leather for making pastalas hanging outside of shops, trees, bundles of chains, tangles of wool, strings for hanging pretzels. It was hardly raining now, but the cobblestones were still awash in a sea of mud.

In the crowd, Sveilis noticed some of the boys who would usually taunt him and whom he usually tried to avoid. Pulling at the skin under their chins and warbling their voices, they would follow him with their jeers. As if instinctively protecting himself from blows he couldn't deflect, he pulled his head down deep into his coat collar and quickly crossed the street. As if by some miracle, this time he didn't hear any of those rude and mocking jeers. An awkward cough came from one, and another even lifted up his cap as Sveilis passed by. Sveilis felt so strange that he wanted to turn right around and head home again. But he couldn't. Juškans was waiting for his suit.

Three farmers – two older ones with beards, one still just a boy – came staggering out of the tavern. Mrs. Juškans could be seen standing inside. The farmers looked back laughing, but Mrs. Juškans, red as a beetroot, was waving her arms and scolding them.

"I can't believe it – utterly shameless!" she complained as she followed Sveilis into the tavern. "Crooks! I was sitting there drinking with them, then they said – Split the cost! A quarter of it! Do you think I sat down with them because I wanted to, when it was them who invited me? Absolute crooks! Sitting around here for three hours and the bill only comes to two roubles sixty – just swilling their vodka and gobbling down herring. And just look at these filthy dishes!" She grabbed a plate piled high with fish heads and three dirty knives from the little table by the wall, carried it over to the counter, and threw it down with a crash onto the shelf. She gave one more angry look at the men through the window. "They invited me! Then all of a sudden they had mouths wide as feed-lots. And that little so-and-so was touching me and flirting – oh yes he was. But when it's time to pay up..." So frustrated was she that she stood at the window shaking her fist after the men and breathing heavily.

"Is Mr. Juškans not home?" Sveilis asked.

With a heavy sigh Mrs. Juškans fell back onto a bench, causing the floor to sag noticeably. "At home! Why would he be at home! There's been no sign of him since he went off this morning." She searched for her handkerchief, but not finding it wiped the sweat from her forehead with her apron. "He's out drinking with that son of yours. He'll have frittered away all his money by now. He can't help it, once he gets started. He'll probably start up with those hussies too... What can you do with men like that? They'll throw away their last kopeck." Completely out of breath, she tried to calm down, but couldn't help herself. She stood up, supporting herself by holding on to the edge of the counter. "All day long, since he left the house this morning, I'm left here all by myself, fighting with these crooks! If I'd known what would happen, there's no way I would have let him go..."

And all of a sudden, she laid into Sveilis as if he were the guilty one. "It's that son of yours and his aimless lifestyle! A big banker now! From one day to the next! I'm telling you, anybody who dares to drink with him will go down with him in the end. A millionaire! What a joke. All I have to do is say one word to the police and they would take him in and grill him within an inch of his life. How can a pauper like that suddenly afford to be squandering money? It doesn't grow on trees for anybody. If he hasn't killed or robbed somebody, then he must have been dipping into the till. Something dodgy is going on, that's for sure!"

Sveilis shrugged. "I don't know. All I know is what other people have told me. I just came here to bring Mr. Juškans his suit." He put the package on the counter and undid the black cloth wrapping.

Mrs. Juškans took out each piece of the suit and carefully examined it. She hung it up on a nail in the wall, on top of the jumble of keys already hanging there, and examined it one more time in the light, breathing heavily as she did so.

"There's another spot that's been singed into it with the iron," she pointed with her finger as she stared angrily at Sveilis. "It's like that every time with you."

"It's nothing," Sveilis said. "Just where a little bit of water splashed onto it."

"It's nothing to you," Mrs. Juškans shouted back. "But we have to pay for it. And it's right on the front of the jacket! How could anybody wear something like that! And there's a white chalk mark here too!" She ripped the suit off of the nail and threw it onto the chair. She examined the waistcoat and trousers, poking angrily at the trouser buttons. "What kind of buttons are these! How long will they stay on! Nowadays you can get the ones with little clasps so you don't need to make any holes – but you always have to use the tackiest and cheapest materials, don't you? Is it that you don't want to use good materials or that you just don't know how to? Please, tell me! Because there's no shortage of tailors – my goodness! They're on every corner..."

Sveilis bit his lip so that the trembling of his beard wouldn't be so obvious. It was always the same, every time, but he just couldn't get used to it. It would be different if she got angry about the things that were actually wrong with the suit: that there wasn't enough horsehair fabric, that the lapels were lined with worn flax cloth. But she didn't notice these things. And yet she sensed that it wasn't good enough, so she looked for new problems where there was nothing to find. This deeply offended Sveilis. His blood boiled every time he caught sight of the tavern owner's fat wife. But he couldn't say anything: Juškans was the only one who still gave him work. His wife's scolding was just something he had to endure.

"It's nothing... It's nothing..." he muttered quietly.

Then the door opened and Juškans himself burst in. A heavyset, middle-aged man with a pale, pockmarked, smiling face, completely free of stubble.

Quite clearly drunk, he was swaying and laughing before he even came in, showing his white teeth and wrinkling his already small, kind eyes. In his giddiness he failed to notice his wife's anger.

"Greetings, maestro!" He shook Sveilis's hand warmly and didn't let go of it afterwards. He put his other hand heavily on Sveilis's shoulder and looked at him with blinking eyes. "Well, quite the bash for once, right?" He shook Sveilis so hard that the black folded cloth became completely unravelled. Sveilis laughed reluctantly in agreement and looked over at Mrs. Juškans. She was tossing all of the suit pieces onto the bench.

"Half-wit!" she muttered spitefully. "You – as soon you walk out that door you don't give one thought to this house. Take a look at what this tailor did... Can't even be bothered to clean off chalk marks! And what kind of trouser buttons are these!"

Juškans, continuing to chuckle quietly, slowly lowered himself onto the nearest bench. It was clear that he'd been laughing like that for quite a long time, and was tired of it, but his mouth carried on cramping itself into endless laughter.

"Trouser buttons... mother!" He waved her off and couldn't stop giggling. His voice was huskier than usual from the laughter and drinking, as if every word he spoke had a metallic quality. "Now things are different! A new life starts now!" He tossed his head back and stared lovingly at his wife for a moment and then turned towards Sveilis. "Have you heard the news, old man? Well, don't just stand there blinking, come over here!" He pulled him closer. "A millionaire – believe it or not! Oh, you don't believe me? But I'm serious! Just think: Augusts, Au-gusts! Go take a look and see for yourself. Full pockets – however many times you stick your hand in, you come back with a handful. Handfuls of coins thrown out the window! A three-rouble tip to the boy for the beer basket, and for the young ladies at the buffet..." He laughed and laughed. "I could light a cigar with a hundred-rouble note, he says..."

"Swine!" Mrs. Juškans arched her shoulders angrily. "Then he must be completely drunk."

"Not at all!" Juškans responded. "I've had a bit to drink – sure. But it's true. Anyway, why shouldn't he be drunk! Full pockets!"

"Well, the police will sure have their work cut out for them," Mrs. Juškans sneered, but it was clear that she too was becoming interested in Augusts's mysterious wealth. She looked out the window at the clock.

Sveilis coughed. "We don't know anything; we're just taking it all in. But what do the finer gentlemen think about somebody creating this kind of havoc?"

Juškans waved him off.

"The gentlemen are right there next to him! They aren't going to say anything – he's one of them now! He can bathe in beer and wine! I had to sneak out of there. You – he said, you, Juškans, don't go anywhere. You'll come with me to Rīga. Why are you wasting your time in this shabby tavern! I have a house and a second-class hotel – you can work behind the buffet! You won't need to brawl with burly farmers; you'll be rubbing elbows with high society!"

"What are you babbling about!" Mrs. Juškans said, moving closer to him all the same.

"This is what I'm trying to tell you! It's practically a done deal. Why should I waste away here, when I could get fifty roubles a month, plus interest!"

Sveilis couldn't stay quiet any longer. "Maybe I could have that money... those ten roubles for your suit?"

"Nothing at all – ten roubles!" Just then Juškans seemed tremendously drunk. "Ten roubles is nothing compared to millions. I spit on ten roubles. If I've got fifty roubles, plus interest, why should I waste away here!" He started to sing, tapping out the rhythm with his foot: "Put on your shoes nightingale, let's go take the cows a grazin'..."

Sveilis just stood there, uncertain what to do. He needed the money. But it seemed strangely inappropriate to force a matter of ten roubles on a person who'd just been cheek to cheek with millions! A strange sort of glimmer, the glimmer of gold, seemed to be lighting up this pale, pockmarked face. And as a result, this person he knew so well suddenly seemed less familiar, more distant... unreachable and not to be disturbed. He had an involuntary feeling of reverence towards him – maybe even fear. Was there also hidden anger, a hint of jealousy, a smidgen of wicked greed? No – he couldn't approach somebody who'd just seen millions and ask for a measly ten roubles!

Sveilis left.

Outside the autumn wind grabbed a hold of him again with its moist, cold hands. It tore open his coat and groped at his skin with its stiff fingers. The blanket of clouds had been torn to shreds, and were now sliding along above the rooftops. Here and there a clear patch of blue shined through. Behind the buildings, red rays of the obscured late evening sun were streaming through every gap in the skyline. It was dazzling after the overcast daytime. Initially Sveilis had been deeply moved but afterwards he ask himself why he had been taken in by that trivial, deceitful glow. He became angry at his own cowardice. He wanted to turn around, go back and demand that he be paid what he was owed. But his feet kept on going of their own accord, carrying him on towards home as if he had no choice.

The crowd of people by the door had disappeared. As Sveilis approached, his wife tore herself away from the window, but when he walked in he found that she was confused. She couldn't look at him and started busying herself with the empty laundry tub without any clear purpose. All she could do was watch and wait! Sveilis pursed his lips and looked around the room. Made wasn't there. He was just about to speak when his wife started up.

"Did you bring it?" Though she could clearly see that he hadn't brought anything. "I told you: two pounds of barley, salt, and a pound of herring... I asked you to get them from Juškans... You always forget!"

His wife was unusually cross about something as trivial as a few groceries. It would only take a few minutes to go back for them! But Sveilis couldn't bring himself to tell her what had happened at Juškans's, that he had panicked and couldn't possibly go back. He turned around and walked back outside.

He wanted to go straight ahead, but on seeing Made in the distance, he decided to turn down a side street. He didn't know exactly why, but he didn't want to meet her. Relationships in the family had undergone some kind of change, and now there were things that he had to keep to himself. Sveilis lengthened his steps.

He had no particular destination in mind. He surprised himself by suddenly turning into Central Avenue. But it was no surprise at all to see that a lamplighter had already lit the lamp and, having turned the switch, was putting it back onto the lamppost, even though it was still light outside. The light seemed peculiarly dim against the bright red evening sky. It seemed absurd that this weak, little light had been lit, as if to demonstrate its feebleness compared to nature's grandeur. But it didn't look odd to Sveilis.

A few people were still standing on the street by the hotel doors. Sveilis noticed them, but didn't look closer. He didn't look around to see if there were any broken plates or glasses lying discarded on the street. The first thing he did notice was that all of the shutters along the bottom floor of the two-storey building had been closed, and on the top floor all of the curtains had been drawn, obscuring all of the windows there. Lamplight was shining faintly through them. Sveilis wondered why he hadn't gone to where needed to go – back to Juškans – and instead had come here, a place he didn't need or want to visit.

Sveilis walked into the hotel. Despite never having been there before, he seemed to remember the layout of the building, possibly from stories he'd heard about it in the past. He began walking up the stairs. He could hear a woman's voice singing a light and gentle melody rising from somewhere downstairs – probably the buffet. He didn't need anything from there. He climbed up the creaking wooden stairs lit by a small kerosene lamp. Its flame was too high and smoke was billowing up from the top of the glass cylinder. Sveilis turned down the wick and then kept climbing.

Upstairs, practically all of the doors along the corridor were wide open. As far as he could see, all of the rooms were lit. He could hear the loud hubbub of a busy tavern, but couldn't tell which room it was coming from. The whole corridor echoed with the disorderly turmoil. It would dip for a moment and then rise up again into an even stronger wave of conversation, laughter, footsteps and clattering plates.

A young man in a long, well-worn coat with rounded tails burst out of one of the rooms and moved in the direction of another. When he noticed Sveilis, he hesitated before going into the room, and then walked over to him instead. He stood before him and looked at the intruder disdainfully.

"What do you want?" he asked sharply.

Sveilis himself didn't really know the answer either. He kept looking past the young man with the long coat, towards the light behind the open door.

"Nothing. I'm just..."

"There's no 'just nothing here'! There are gentlemen here..." He nodded his head towards the door and then pointed downwards. "The buffet is downstairs."

Sveilis shook his head. He hadn't come here to drink, and he kept his eyes on the door and listened until the young man began to move towards him menacingly.

"If you don't need anything, then... there are gentlemen here, you see."

Just then, Skrastiņš came out through the door. Smiling and slightly hunched over, parting his bushy beard down the centre, he saw Sveilis and hurried over immediately.

"Oh – hello, pops!" He squeezed Sveilis's hand with both of his. "How nice to see you! But why so late? We've been here since the crack of dawn." His face radiated absolute joy as he looked back towards the open door. "I saw Augusts, your son, and I said, 'Augusts,'" he looked over at Long Coat to make sure he'd heard him refer to a rich man by his first name, "'Augusts,' I said to him, 'You have to send for your old man. Your dad absolutely has to be here; it just wouldn't right if he weren't!' Would you have ever believed it, old man? Nobody could have! If anybody had ever dreamt it, they would have spat on it and said, 'What rubbish!' No more than that! But no one could come here now and say that it's rubbish once they've taken a look inside. Come on, old man!"

Taking him under the arm as if he were a fine lady, he led Sveilis over to the first open door. Even though he'd made the decision to come over on his own, he hesitated and didn't want to go in. Suddenly shyness overwhelmed him. He was scared of his own son, of this rich man with whom all these strangers were so friendly and smiling.

"Come on, old man!" Skrastiņš laughed as he slapped him on the shoulder with his free hand. "I told him: your dad has to be here, without him it's just not right!"

As he stood in the doorway, the white light coming off the prisms hung around the ceiling lamp hit Sveilis hard in the eyes and left him momentarily dazzled, and he flinched when a sudden burst of music filled the room with twanging string instruments and booming drums. He stayed on his feet, with his arms slightly bent, chin upturned, mouth open and eyes frozen behind his spectacles which had misted up again. In that one moment, he noticed a great deal: a semi-circular table covered with a table cloth reaching the floor was piled high with bottles, glasses and plates, strewn with cutlery, cigarette packets and corks. Cigarette butts were scattered everywhere and covered with yellow and brown stains. All manner of things had been dropped and spilled on the floor as far as the door. There were baskets along the walls and in the corners and rows of glass bottles – some standing and some on their sides. There were regular beer bottles and ones with labels and white and red colouring around their necks. A cap with a cockade was hanging off the stove door. There were people draped across each other in all kinds of positions on the randomly arranged chairs and a torn leather couch. Red-faced, laughing strangers and familiar faces... Smoke rising from cigars and cigarettes... Lifted glasses, some straight and others lopsided and spilling their contents.

Sveilis's gaze passed quickly over everything – making contact with it all only for an instant – but when it fell upon Augusts, it lingered a bit longer. He was sitting at the far end of the table with his face pointed directly towards the door. From the look on his relaxed, smiling face, and the way his hands lay spread out across the table – and from the slightly hunched over, subservient postures of everyone else in the room – it was clear that Augusts was running the show: the top dog. But he didn't get a chance to look at him longer than that. Next to him, a golden shoulder-sash flashed at Sveilis's eyes, and a yellow belt stretched across a chest glinted threateningly, and then his spectacles steamed up in an instant. He could only see what was happening through a fog of confusion, nor could he hear anything in all the chaos. He began to take a few steps backwards.

He couldn't tell whether somebody was holding him or calling him. With a huge effort he forced himself to rush away as fast as he could and he only came to his senses when he was opening the heavy oak doors downstairs and a sharp gust of wind hit him in the face. Only then did he notice that his back was soaked with sweat and his heart was thumping from the fright. What was he doing there? What had he walked into! Off he ran, only looking back when the doors slammed heavily behind him.

The gang of boys he knew all too well were waiting on the corner. Sveilis instinctively slouched down into his collar: any moment now he would hear their familiar jeers. These troublemakers had taunted him for fifteen years. When one generation had grown into adults, another one would take its place and keep up the tradition. Any moment now it would start again: "Svei-le! Svei-le!" But no, the boys stepped aside, and not one of them seemed ready to mock him!

Sveilis walked down the street, deeply confused. As he walked away he kept turning to look back until he felt that he was spinning and nearly walked right into two pine trees on the roadside in front of the last house on the edge of town. He shook himself together, turned around and started walking back, immediately sinking back into his profound confusion.

The sun had set. A few stars were beginning to twinkle in the vast, empty stretches of sky in between the cresting clouds. When Sveilis got home, Roberts was already back from school. He was sitting in his place by the window, hurriedly leafing through a book. Sveilis could instantly tell that he'd heard the news. Made was sitting on the other side of the table, holding her hands on her lap and pressing her lips together as she looked out of the window into the yard. Her mother was busying herself with something at the end of the bed. Sveilis's thoughts had not yet crystalised, but they were increasingly determining his mood. He tore off his coat, threw it down and slumped heavily onto his bed, interlocking his fingers behind his head and sniffing. He was getting more and more irate.

There was an unbearable silence in the room. The old clock ticked slowly – so very slowly! At other times it click-clacked far too quickly. Mrs. Sveilis sighed again and tried to mask it with a cough and a sniff. Sveilis on the other hand was getting angrier and angrier.

"Damn it! What are you sniffing about?" he finally called out.

Mrs. Sveilis didn't answer. But Roberts slammed his book shut and got up. "What rubbish!" he called out nervously. The expression on his slender face was constantly shifting. A red spot burned on each of his cheeks. "A thousand-rouble bill! He took ten roubles out of someone's pocket and is boozing it all away now."

"Roberts, dear..." his mother interrupted meekly, but Made pursed her lips in a mocking expression. "Who told you to speak, and what does a dumb boy like you know about these things?"

"You'll soon see! Well, I'm sure you'll get to see those things...," he retorted.

"No good will come of any of it," their father finally joined in. "I was there; I saw it all... They were behaving like animals. All the walls piled high with mountains of bottles. Handfuls of money being tossed around."

"And what about him?" Made's voice burned with curiosity.

"Sitting and drinking with the others. Half the city was there – both the upper-class and the lower. Juškans and Skrastiņš were there too."

"Them too, eh? Ah, so there are already some hangers-on!" Made said with a grin.

"I think that...," Sveilis was looking for the right word, "we should alert the police, but they were all there too and all at the same table!"

Roberts couldn't stay quiet any longer.

"I'm not staying here! I can't go to school anymore. Everybody will be gossiping and poking fun. They'll be chasing me down the street. What do I know? During the break a big crowd from the school run down to have a look. Everybody had to stay back after class, and the inspector interrogated me about it...What do I know! I can't take it anymore."

"Just ignore them!" Made said. "Jealousy, that's all it is. I don't care what they say – they make me sick!"

The door burst open and hit the wall with a crack. Outside in the street someone was leaning over and picking something up. He came inside, and it was a porter from the hotel who in one arm was carrying a large basket full of bottles, and in the other a heavy roll of grey paper. He silently placed the basket on the floor at the end of the table and the roll of paper on the ground. Sveilis recognised him immediately as the person he'd seen earlier in the long coat with rounded tails.

They could clearly hear the sound of familiar footsteps through the open door in spite of the howling wind. Augusts walked in on uncertain legs and as he did, he unbuttoned his coat.

The porter approached him, and as they passed each other, Augusts nimbly put two fingers into his waistcoat pockets, pulled something out and tossed it to him. "Take it and go!" He said and began hiccupping.

The porter bowed, thanked him and closed the door as he walked out, while Augusts came over to the table.

When he nearly tripped on the basket, he bent down as if to take something out, but then he suddenly stood up straight again, having remembered that he should probably greet all of his family first. Made was closest, so he gave her his hand first. Roberts was leaning against the edge of the window, half-turned away. Augusts stepped towards him.

"How's it going, student?" Augusts laughed as he tightly gripped Roberts's bony hand, which his brother was desperately trying to tear free. Augusts dropped it when he saw his father sitting on the bed and walked over to him. "Hello there, old man!" He energetically shook the tailor's hand. At first Augusts didn't notice his mother, who was standing behind him, and he never got round to greeting her. She brought over some chairs, wiping them with her apron.

"Sit down, son!" she said, before stepping back again and leaning over the stove.

Augusts sat down, his hands holding onto the curve of his cane. He leant back and stared up smiling with misty eyes at the small light set in a white globe, which had a missing part on one side. Then he turned back and looked with drunken casualness around the room. The fogged-up window, the peeling wallpaper on the walls... Three beds with striped, home-sewn blankets and hay-filled sacks for pillows... The tub by the stove and the pile of laundry next to it, a dirty shirt sleeve poking out... He turned back and shook his head.

Made hadn't taken her eyes off her brother from the moment he walked in. He had a lean, healthy build, and was wearing a stiff, round-brimmed hat, and a modern, chequered coat with an open collar. She'd only ever seen collars like that in the fashion pages. Where his fine black plush coat was hanging open, she could see a spotted, black and white, imitation fur lining and a shiny white polka-dotted waistcoat with a thick gold watch-chain stretching across his torso. His shirt front was creased, sticking out in a few places, but the head of the red-striped cravat pin was shining like a shard broken off of a rainbow. His pale hands lay gently on the engraved silver handle of his black cane adorned with three monograms. From the arrangement of his features it was only just possible to tell that he too was a Sveilis. If you looked closely you could see the characteristic features of their family, but his long blonde moustache, and especially his well-fed look, not to mention his complexion and the rosy tint of his face warmed by alcohol made him seem unfamiliar and strangely dignified. He gave off a strong stench of booze, mingled with large quantities of a fine cologne... Made's eyes gradually lit up – like the head of the cravat pin, like the stone set in the ring on her brother's pale finger...

Augusts hung his cane over his knee and threw back his head and the hat he was still wearing.

"What are we sitting around here for! We should have a little something in honour of our reunion." His voice cracked and his speech slurred from too much alcohol. As he spoke his full lips seemed to come together into a circle, but never closed. He tried to open up the bundle, but couldn't untie the knot, so he just rocked the basket to and fro.

"Here are the scissors!" Made hurried over to help and obligingly cut the string.

"Thank you!" Augusts smiled and bowed to his sister with gallantry. He cleared a bit of space on the table with his elbow and Made hurried over again to help in pushing everything left on the table over to the far end: Roberts's books, street clothes, strips of buckram, protractor and scissors, a centimetre measuring tape, an oil can, balls of wool, pieces of wax, soap, chalk, the paper Sveilis had just used for sewing on buttons and Sveilis's hat... And then she looked to see what her brother was piling up onto the table.

Tins big and small filled with chocolates and marmalade, canned sardines, mackerel and lamprey, a container of caviar, pieces of smoked salmon and eel, packages containing different types of cheese, a loaf of sourdough rye bread, a little basket of apple cake and a cigar box with a glass lid... He untied and unwrapped everything and threw it together in a pile. His fingers, awkward from intoxication, ripped and tore at it all. The entire end of the table was covered with packages and various types of sweet-smelling and delicious-looking food.

Surprised and confused, the Sveilises looked with wide eyes at these unseen and unexpected wonders. Mrs. Sveilis was looking at this cornucopia from the middle of the room where she could barely hold back her tears and couldn't bring herself to come closer. Sveilis smacked his lips and gulped. Roberts's hands were shaking visibly. Only Made was able to control herself and help her brother unwrap more of the packages.

Augusts smiled at his family's confusion. He understood their feelings and the delight on his face showed on his ever rosier cheeks. He commented briefly on every package, speaking with feigned exasperation.

"This is a real paupers' town; you can't get anything here!" The wheel of cheese rolled over and would've fallen off the table if Made hadn't caught it. "Is that cheese? Devil only knows what they shoved in here! But eat. You won't find anything better around here." He handed the little basket of apple cake to Made and then his mother. Made bit into it eagerly, while their mother bit off a smaller piece and, holding it gingerly with the tips of her fingers, sat down on the bed.

Augusts leaned over and began to rummage around in the basket, bottles clinking. He lifted them out two or three at a time, examined them by the light, and then tossed them back with contempt.

"What were they doing when they put that in?" he muttered crossly. Finally he picked a squat round bottle with a long neck. "Well, let's give this a try." He checked his pockets for a corkscrew, and spat, "God knows where I left it... or if someone at the hotel stole it?" He put the bottle on the table, and began to search with both hands, but couldn't find it. "You don't have one, do you?"

"A corkscrew? No, we don't..." Made shrugged and looked at her mother.

"You don't have one! Wonderful! Who would have thought it! Give me those scissors. I'll give it a try..."

He took the scissors from Made and began to remove the various labels and wax around the bottle's neck. As he did this, he noticed a cigar box, ripped it open, and took a cigar and handed it to his father.

"Here, smoke this."

Made laughed out loud. "You know he doesn't smoke!"

Augusts waved his hand, disregarding her comment. "Even a non-smoker can smoke these. They're very light. Take one!"

Sveilis stiffly removed a light brown cigar with a red paper ring around the middle. Augusts took out an engraved silver cigarette case with gold down the middle and put it on the table. While he was looking for his cigarette holder, everyone examined it in amazement. Then they were introduced to the yellow amber holder with its shiny metal rim on its fat end and the blue-enamelled rose in the centre. Then came the box of matches – a grey metal container, one side of which was engraved with a monogram and the other with an image of Bastion Hill. Augusts began to smoke, but forgot about his father. Aromatic swirls of smoke began to rise towards the ceiling and gradually filled the room.

On the table, amongst the packages and unwrapped, greasy paper, a bottle stood with the scissors rammed into its cork. Augusts was smoking contentedly and had forgotten all about it. He was clearly thinking about something very amusing; a smile was distinctly spreading across his rosy face. His full lips quivered as if he were about to say something, but then he caught sight of Roberts's distrustful face – perhaps even an expression of hatred – and Augusts's own face seemed to darken a bit.

"Student, why aren't you eating? Take some! Here!" He nudged the basket of cakes towards his brother.

Made licked her fingers and reached over to take another cake. But Roberts didn't take one. His body was turned towards the window, but his eyes – they were drilling straight into his brother.

"Thank you. I don't want any of your sweets."

Augusts forced a chuckle.

"What, do you have toothache? You know what, student, it's a bit too early for all this. I wonder, does that mean you've picked out a bride for yourself already?"

Roberts blushed and turned to face him. His hands were shoved nervously behind his leather belt. "I don't need your sweets. Why don't you go and leave them for the boys out on the street, so they can fight over them! Let Made eat as much as she wants. Here, have some more! Some more!" He pushed the basket back across the table towards her.

"Children!" their mother called out and moved forward as if she wanted to get between them.

"Yes, I do like them, and I am eating them!" Made snapped back obstinately and grabbed another cake, even though she hadn't even finished half of the first one. "Thank you, brother!" And she nodded to express demonstrably her appreciation of what Augusts was doing. He bit his lower lip with his white teeth and continued to stare at his brother. His misty and until then smiling and friendly eyes slowly narrowed, but he stopped himself from saying anything else.

Sveilis got up and straightened his back. His glasses glinted in the dim light, and his lips were tightly pursed together; he walked over slowly but with determination to the table. He carefully put his untouched cigar back into the box and closed the lid. He stared at Augusts: "Tell me, where did you get all this?" His voice was a little hoarse but firm, and it was clear that Sveilis's entire demeanour had visibly affected Augusts, who laughed loudly in response.

"What a funny question! From the store, of course, the store right there. Give it a try, smoke it, you'll see, it's not bad at all."

But his father appeared not to have even heard him.

"We need to know. Everyone we meet keeps asking these questions of us. You're tossing money around by the handful... carousing... turning the whole town upside down..." He spread his hands, but then quickly brought them together again and forcefully leaned closer in to his son. "Are you crazy? What's wrong with you?"

"Dad!" Made interrupted crossly. "What are you babbling on about?"

Augusts waved her off proudly. "Let him babble..."

His father continued, "Some are saying that you murdered and robbed someone... others that you won the lottery! Everyone is asking us, and we know nothing about it."

"Why do you need to know?" Augusts sneered back.

"Everyone should mind their own business and leave me alone. I have money, and I can do whatever I want with it. Who's going to stop me? Who - is - going - to - stop - me!" He slammed his fist on his knee, so that the cane with the monogram and silver handle crashed loudly to the floor. And then he moved his hand gently over the table. "Is this enough food for you? Isn't there plenty to drink? Don't worry: if it's not enough, we'll get some more!" He started to give the bottle another try with the scissors.

"I won't touch a single crumb, a single drop..." his father continued excitedly. "I don't know where it's come from or whose money bought it. Maybe it's stolen. Maybe someone's blood has been spilt all over of this. Don't eat any of it!" He ripped the cake from Made's hand and threw it down onto the table.

Augusts laughed hoarsely. But his laughter soon stopped. Despite his drunkenness, his considerable agitation was evident. He pulled himself together and turned his back scornfully to his father.

"There's no point trying to talk sense to fools... He thinks that everyone whose pockets are full of money earned it working with their own two hands! With a needle and an iron! You can sew and iron for seven hundred years and you'll still be naked, and nothing will ever change..." He cast a look of disgust around the room. "Is this living? Is this even a house! It's a pigsty not fit for humans... I could get you six rooms in Riga... and a hotel across the street on the corner. I'm not a dog, and I don't want any relatives of mine living in a place like this."

"We're not going anywhere!" his father yelled back angrily. "We'll make do, just as we always have, and we don't need a thing from you. Not a thing! You'd better be careful: that's not your property. Don't pretend, because you couldn't possibly have anything of your own."

Augusts sighed with resignation. But in his insincere sigh, in his loud forced laughter - behind all of his bravado something quite meek and timid and shy was hiding. When he puffed out his chest proudly, he never looked anyone directly in the eye. And when he lifted his head up provocatively, the corners of his eyes quivered ever so slightly, as if he wished he could fall through a hole in the floor. It seemed as if in his every movement, in his every expression, someone was holding onto him tightly from within and pulling him back. In his every gesture there was something forced, a kind of unwanted effort, which had to be kept hidden. And it was exactly because he tried so hard to hide it that it became so obvious to everyone. Made stared at her wealthy brother without even blinking. Let him carry on, she thought, let him shut everyone up with just one word.

But apparently he was having difficulty in finding that single, compelling word that would put his family in their place. Instead he started from somewhere very distant from their understanding and advanced in a roundabout fashion.

"What really is my property and what is someone else's? Not everyone can have money, only the people who know what to do with it. More intelligent people live better lives. That's a fact. In the whole world, there's only a handful of gold that gets passed around from hand to hand. Someone who doesn't want to let go of it, will have it knocked out of his hand and it gets scattered across the ground. Isn't it better to scatter it yourself, rather than waiting for someone else to force it from your hand?"

"Crazy!" his father interrupted and backed away with genuine fear. "How can you have enough to grab and scatter around like that?"

Augusts laughed again. "But I do have it! A person just needs to know what to do. You don't need to rob or steal or find it on the ground. Just grab it from those who don't need it, and then live it up so that the whole world keeps spinning! Eat!" He pushed the chocolate and marmalade tins towards Made. "If you like it, eat. If we run out, we'll buy more..." He stopped for a moment as if considering something. Then he began again, but slower, more quietly, and in a different voice. "She was never very healthy... the lady at our manor..." He interrupted himself with the loud laugh of a drunkard. "Sometimes of course she was...but mostly she had to be tended to and fed in bed. This summer she went on a trip abroad. She said she'd be gone all summer, but by midsummer she was already back home. 'I can't manage without you, Augusts. You're like a son to me,' she would say." He suppressed a desire to laugh. "She practically never got out of bed again. And I always had to be there with her. As for her daughters, it never occurred to them that they should do something. She poked one of them in the cheek with a hairpin – she did become a little crazy towards the end. I had to lift her. I had to warm her pillow. I had to sit with her. It was torture! We thought we would be stuck forever with her endless moods, but then suddenly a telegram was sent and three doctors arrived from Vilnius. They didn't leave her side, day and night. Then we knew it was serious. On the second day she called us all in to see her... She was lying in bed... We could hardly recognise her, and she was mumbling... She managed to say, 'That's for you, that's for you – and for you, Augusts, the package in the left-hand drawer of the desk... and a ring. You must take me down to my grave, and don't let the others near me.' And that very night, she passed away." His mouth was twisting into a laugh again, but realising that laughter would be out of place, he shook his head so vigorously that his hat slipped sideways onto one of his ears. He threw one leg over the other and fell back in his chair. "I lived for a month and a half in Riga. You can't get anything in a hurry... But that hotel is a good place. You just need to know what to do. There is an apartment nearby with six rooms – enough for everybody! Now have a drink, old man!" He grabbed his father by the corner of his coat and pulled him closer to the table.

Made's face was beaming with pride and happiness. "Come on!" she urged her father, then turned closer to her brother. "It'll be fine. Just don't worry... If you need any help – we can all chip in. As it is, living here is no life at all."

Augusts threw his head all the way back. His hat practically covered his eyes. He laughed warmly and a sharp stench of alcohol and tobacco flowed from his mouth. "Oh, so you think I need your help! Really, what could you possibly help me with? You, tailor, what could you do?" He shook the corner of his father's coat. "Maybe I'll open a first-rate clothing store – then you could watch over it. Readymade clothing for gentlemen and ladies... and toiletries." With his other hand he took Made by her jacket sleeve, "and you'll be able to work the cash register." Suddenly he had become serious and wasn't joking anymore. He let go of his father and sister, and straightened his hat. "A pastry shop is also a possibility... Modern equipment and the salesgirls in tailored suits... a ladies' orchestra... a midday and evening concert... Café Tirol or Café Mexico, what do you think of that...? Or a gentlemen and ladies' hairdresser doing all the latest styles."

Made put her hand gently on his shoulder. "No, brother, a pastry shop is the better idea... or a clothing store."

"Or a pilchard shop at the Daugava Market," Roberts interjected. Made and Augusts looked over at him. His mocking tone was a mixture of disbelief and curiosity.

Augusts straightened up. "Listen boy, don't fool around. If I wanted to, I could take you to Riga and enrol you in a high school of your choice. Don't you understand? Wherever you like, as long as you watch that big mouth. Why don't you just eat one of those cakes? Eat! Do you think I don't have enough money, that I don't have any money?"

Very theatrically he reached his hand into his coat and fiddled around with some buttons in order to produce a shiny new yellow wallet, which he threw down on the table. It fell with a heavy thud.

"Is this money or isn't it?" He looked scornfully at Robert, who stared in amazement at the wallet and was unable to say anything in reply. Augusts's performance had fully achieved the desired effect. This enthused Augusts even more, and he dug his hand into his trouser pocket and pulled out a handful.

"Is this money or isn't it?" With the practised manner of someone accustomed to handling money, he threw it onto an empty space on the table. The strange yet familiar clinking sound of money sent shivers of delight and fear through the bodies of everyone in the room.

Once he had lifted his soft, pale, chubby hand, they could see a sizeable sum of money on the worn deal table. One three-rouble note and a few silver coins. The rest were ten and five rouble gold coins.

The small lamp with the torn shade dimmed as if ashamed. The entire room grew darker, and all the worn and overused objects shrank and sought refuge in the semidarkness close to the walls. Absolutely nothing looked or felt like it did before. All that remained was the yellow metal radiating its mysterious glow on the scuffed table. Not a single breath could be heard, not a single eye blinked. The only presence was the yellow shine of the gold in the silent, twilit room.

Augusts grinned in silence, but even his grin had lost its usual flippancy and boastfulness. Even he felt a kind of reverence or respect for gold, which could be wrapped in rags and handled by filthy fingers or even thrown on the ground, but still remain the ruler of this planet.

The paper banknotes and the silver coins weren't fit to keep its company. Their presence only diminished the true metal's glory and detracted from its value. Augusts picked it up with clumsy fingers and stuffed it back into his waistcoat pocket. As he did so, one little silver disc slipped out and rolled away, spinning and hopping, jingling and tinkling its way across the floor. Like an unruly stray bee, it flitted around the dusty room, and came to rest somewhere near the door.

Mrs. Sveilis let out a loud, involuntary sigh – and the room came back to life. Everyone shifted around on their feet and looked at each other, with the exception of Roberts who didn't want to look at them but only at those gold coins. His father rubbed his glasses with a cloth, but couldn't get them clean enough. Augusts put his wallet back into his pocket.

Just at that moment, they heard the sound of footsteps outside the door, as well as a few stifled coughs. The door opened to reveal a policeman's uniform.

Made shuddered. A terrible thought struck her like a heavy blow. She grabbed the end of the table with both hands and looked wide-eyed at their guest. Her face became paler, almost white.

But there was no reason to be worried. The policeman stayed right there at the door and lifted his hand up to the visor of his cap. His yellow teeth shined through his long moustache.

"Excuse me... but the lord of the manor asked if you could come along."

"What?" said the wealthy man who leaned back proudly in his chair. "I'm supposed to come now?"

"Yes, he asked me to ask you to come now. He has business."

"Oh, he has business, does he!" Augusts laughed loudly. "I know his business... Well, tell him I'll be right there."

"Yes... But he asked me to ask you to come – right now!"

"Get out of here when you're told!" Augusts screamed at him and stamped his foot. Despite his servility, there was a hint of familiarity in the policeman's demeanour, and, at times, even a sense that he wasn't taking Augusts very seriously. This offended Augusts, who wanted his relatives to see that this policeman meant nothing to him.

When the door closed again, Made exhaled loudly. "Phew, that really scared me..."

Augusts got up. Though it was hard for him to stand without swaying, he puffed out his chest and laughed scornfully. "Scared of that little man; what's there to be afraid of? He'd dance for ten kopecks!" He went over and slapped Roberts on the shoulder in a half-friendly, half-joking manner. "Well then, now you just need to decide: high school, Realschule – or whatever you like... And your books, they've sure got plenty of bulk!" He lifted one of them up without concealing his disdain and dropped it back onto the table. "A boy has to study, it's the only way..."

And without bidding them farewell or even looking at any of them, he walked out the door. He didn't close the door tightly enough and the wind pushed it open again. It moved slowly, creaking painfully, and when it opened, freezing cold air rushed into the room from outside. Mrs. Sveilis quietly crept over and shut the door.

There was a long pause during which none of them said a word. The events that had just taken place were too strange and their impressions too varied and consequential to be dismissed by casually tossing out a few words or clichés.
The wind was howling around street corners again and rattling the shutters. Their upstairs neighbours' children were fighting and bits of plaster were raining down. It seemed like all that had happened was something out of a dream or fairy tale. And yet they had no choice but to believe it: a basket full of bottles, a table piled high with unimagined delicacies with rectangular and round, silvery green and bright flower-patterned containers. The bottle with a pair of scissors stuck into the cork was still in the middle of the table. And there, off to the side... No, it wasn't a dream! These couldn't just be visions, and yet this reality seemed more incomprehensible and unbelievable than any dream or fairy tale.
With her hands holding her head, Made stood and looked around, thinking and not comprehending any of it. How many times had she stood gazing at store shelves holding countless containers just like these? And every time her mouth would start to water. Without intending to, she glanced across the table at Roberts, but he wasn't looking at any of it, not any of these wonderful things, each with its own aroma and colour, teasing and tempting, and holding the promise of as yet untasted flavours. In the past, however, he'd been ready to fight over a single toffee! Today hardly anything had been eaten. She looked over at her father; he too was looking off elsewhere. She made a point of biting into the cake she'd started eating earlier, but no longer liked the taste of it.

A kind of fury overtook her, and she didn't know what it was directed at or why. She dropped the piece of cake and began to clear the table. She wrapped everything back up into its packaging and took it all over to the cabinet. When everything was put away, she pulled the scissors out of the cork and grasped the bottle by its neck. "Shall I put this away too?" Her voice sounded sharp, almost threatening.

Her father waved her off and stepped away from the table. "All of it... I want all of it out of my sight. Who does he think he's doing, bringing who knows what into our house! He can take it all back, we don't need anything."

"Let him get the boys on the street drunk with his liquor." Roberts added as he turned towards the bed and began to undress.

Made put the bottle into the basket with the others, and gently placed it over by the wall. She was angry with the lot of them.

"Big men! Any other time you'd be licking your lips – now you don't need anything! God knows what you've got to be so high and mighty about."

Some buttons came off as Roberts tore open his coat. "You're the one who stuffed herself with food and drink until you were practically crawling on the floor! Now you're happy like never before."

Clenching her fists Made stopped a step away from him as she had been passing by. It looked as though she would have liked to scratch his eyes out with her nails, and for a moment she couldn't find the appropriate words to match her angry thoughts. "Arrogant beggar!" she finally blurted out.

One of Roberts's hands got caught in his sleeve. "You... you're the one who's the beggar! If you don't take anything, you're not a beggar... But anybody who crawls around, licking their lips, and catching whatever's thrown to them – they've got to be a beggar!" He tore off the rest of his clothes, threw himself into bed, turned towards the wall, and pulled the blanket up to his neck.

"Children! What kind of talk is that!" their mother interrupted, still trying to calm them down.

Sveilis didn't like that strong language either. But his heart was so heavy and his head so clouded that he didn't know what to say. Made also realised that this kind of argument was ugly, and would ruin the beautiful moment they all had experienced, undermining her vision of a bright future stretching out before of them all. Keeping her feelings under control, she wiped the table with the corner of her apron. She carefully avoided the pile of gold; in fact she even tried not to look at it. She took a few steps back, but then came forward again. The yellow metal pulled her closer with its mysterious force. "Are we leaving that here?" she said and was just about to gather the money up into her two hands, when Sveilis yelled, "Don't touch it! That's not ours! And what's not ours, we don't need. I don't want other people's property sticking to our fingers."

"Crazy! You're completely crazy!" Made flounced towards her bed, and hissed, "We've been waiting for this our whole lives: nobody has ever tried to help us, nobody! And now, when somebody does – it's other people's property!"

For a moment Sveilis didn't know what to say because of his continuing confusion. He couldn't take that money – he absolutely couldn't! He knew that much for certain. He didn't want to look at it, although his eyes kept being drawn to that patch of yellow.

"That money wasn't earned honestly," he muttered to himself, more in sadness than in anger.

Made laughed scornfully. "So the only honest money is the kind you earn with a needle and scissors? Or at the laundry tub?" She grew even angrier than before. "Didn't you hear? He didn't steal it; he hasn't murdered or robbed anyone! The lady of the manor gave it to him for loyal service..."

Nobody knew what to say. The room was silent for a long time. Everybody quickly undressed and climbed into bed. Roberts shifted in his bed. "We're not beggars," he grumbled.

Sveilis went to put out the light, barefoot in his dirty, patched, coarse flax shirt and percale underpants. He walked on his tiptoes, as if he didn't want anyone to hear him, as if someone were hiding in a corner of the room and watching him carefully. He was pointedly looking sideways at the window and the darkness outside, lest someone might think he was actually looking at the money.

He bent over and blew out the candle as hard as he could. He instantly relaxed and his heart grew lighter. The darkness had extinguished that repulsive yellow glow emanating from the end of the table, which had strangely distorted their facial expressions, and darkness had also expunged those unbearable and incomprehensible things they'd previously witnessed and experienced. Here in the dark he could finally be alone with himself, his thoughts and his feelings, and the person he had become over many, long, difficult years. Like a wheel that had broken free of its wagon, he could now slide back into his old familiar groove and move forward at his own speed.

Now he continued the walk to his bed with his feet flat on the ground and his calloused soles stuck to the cold, damp, dirty floor, but for some reason this evening it wasn't at all unpleasant.

Sveilis sat down on the edge of his bed, clasped his hands together, and began to pray. He said his prayers more loudly than he usually did to emphasise that nothing had changed – that everything was the same as it always had been and couldn't possibly be otherwise. Curled up right against the wall, his wife was quietly whispering the same words and sighing peacefully. Made and Roberts were each lying quietly in their beds. It was no different from any other night.

In bed, Sveilis pulled his covers up to his neck. At first the sheets seemed unpleasantly cold. But after a few moments a welcome warmth began to spread from his chest down to his legs. When he touched his toes together, he felt how freezing cold they were, but gradually they too warmed up, just like every other night!

Sveilis sank his hands deep underneath the warm blanket, stretched a bit, got into an even more comfortable position, and let out a long sigh. It felt like the day had never happened – no tedious work, no difficulties, no worries and no poverty, only the warmth of sleepiness and the delight that came with it.

The orange glow of a distant, flickering streetlight barely shone through the fogged-up glass panes in the door. The glazing bars within the frame were occasionally visible but only as indistinct grey shadows. The darkness thickened the further you went into the room. Then the clock began to strike. A stiff rod moved the rusty steel hammer, lifting it with a clunk that jarred and then releasing it. No one counted the number of times it struck: ignorance of time and unawareness of the surroundings belonged to this intangible and motionless darkness. For now darkness was king. The unsteady chimes were dispersed around the room and their efforts were in vain. Then there was another sound: surely the buzz of a bee's wings, but that too gradually ebbed away. It sank down somewhere in the farthest corner of the room, and then there was silence again.

For a long time it was quiet, but then the clock struck again. And again the bees searched and could not find each other as they buzzed around the room only to fall silent in the darkness once more. The wind howled outside, which only intensified the darkness and silence in the room.

Someone would scrunch a pillow filled with hay, and someone else would sigh at length as they struggle with their tiredness, and yet someone else would yawn sleepily. The Sveilises were catching up on their sleep.

But darkness did gradually disperse. It was of course exactly what would be expected, as everything was as it had always been, and yet it was as if something significant was incubating somewhere. As if an inaudible and imperceptible breath was pushing back the soft wall of darkness. Something flickered and then its presence disappeared. But then this would be repeated. As the back window became visible, supposing it wasn't just a trick of the eyes, or maybe eyes accustomed to that space which were only seeing what they had seen in that spot so many times before – impressions collected in visual memory rather than anything actually there to be perceived. But no – it was now definitely possible to discern the cross bars of the window frame and the glass panes, which gradually became brighter, while the cross bars appeared darker in comparison. Now the drops of condensation were lighting up. The oil can on the windowsill began to shine.

Roberts lay there for a long time with his face turned towards the window, and it took him a little while to realise what was causing that spectral light: it was the moon sidling over the skyline.

First it shot out a single ray of pale light, which felt its way up along the side of the window, poking at the drops of condensation, which began to slide down the glass as if fleeing a predator. The playful ray of light chased after them, then it gave up and started toying with the oil can; it tried to reach a bit further, but hesitated, being afraid of the dark. But there was nothing to fear anymore now that two other rays – one long, one short – chased after the first one. The top pane sparkled to life first, then the one next to it, and then gradually the lower ones too were aglow. The end of his parents' bed emerged from the darkness, and then the outline of Made's pillow. Roberts watched it all just as if he were witnessing a miracle.

The lamp stood darkly in the centre of the table – it seemed confused or ashamed by this intrusion. The beam of moonlight extended diagonally across the table. But now another tributary was already starting along the other side. The lamp continued to stand right in the middle of the cold, ever-flowing, relentlessly growing light, and could not grasp whether it was its friend or foe. Roberts watched only for a short duration while the lamp's brass fittings took on a pale gleam. He didn't want to look; he fought against it, but it was as if some powerful force was turning his gaze to the far end of the table.

The moon hadn't reached that far yet. Its pale white beam kept gradually moving further and further up the table, and it was clear that soon it would get there too... There... Did he need to know where? Did he even need to look? He clenched his teeth and forced his eyes to close. What did he care? He wasn't some kind of beggar!

The beam of pale light kept moving slowly. Nothing was clear yet, but bit by bit a brighter spot did begin to set itself apart at the end of the table. The higher the moon rose, the more the darkness fell away from that spot. Now the two pools of light merged, and it was impossible to say which one of them had won. But that particular spot started to glow, to sparkle, and one after another those yellow discs set themselves apart. Ultimately they produced a vibrant inflorescence.

Made, who had been dozing for a bit, opened her eyes and could see the stove, the pans and the iron in the corner. There was the bundle of dirty laundry, with a sleeve hanging from it like an unnerving disembodied arm. Made felt dizzy and felt disheartened.

The pile of gold was shining on the table... No, that wasn't money! It was no more than a little mound of hot embers that had been chucked away and then reignited by a gust of wind! Were these the embers spoken of in legends, which turn into gold in the hands of the wise but into ash if taken by the ignorant? It just burns through the pockets of these people's old torn coats. Shivers of both fear and uncontrollable desire ran through Made's body. She curled up and hugged her knees with her arms, suddenly feeling the cold under her thin blanket. She shivered and clenched her teeth to stop them chattering.

How could she be so cold so close to that mound of embers! The brighter they burned, the colder she felt. Was there perhaps a calm beneath its intoxicating warmth. More moonlight had now flooded across the table, and enveloped all of the tailor's tools thrown together in their pile, and it filled the entire room with a pale glow which now for some reason seemed mysterious. Made observed it with wide, crazed eyes as if she had been hypnotised, and all of her earlier dreams – which now seemed unbelievable and thus impossible – went around in her head again and again like a disorientated flock of birds. She couldn't keep up with her own reckless fantasies, and felt their awful side-effects. She was dizzy, but she couldn't look away. Off she went high above the ground to some unknown, far-off place, driven by a fantastical whirlwind of bright yellow light.

Sveilis coughed comfortably, turned his head, and stayed in that position.

Oh no, he had never given it a thought. He had no need of that dirty money whose provenance was unknown! He didn't know a thing about it, and besides how much money did he actually need? Had he ever gone to sleep without supper? If a person works and is at peace with what he earns, that means he's not a beggar, that means he has enough. He'd never wanted Augusts's money... Maybe a few roubles for the holidays or for buying firewood in the winter, or for when he couldn't get customers to pay up. But that fat wallet on the table and handfuls of gold – no. he didn't want that!

When Sveilis came back to his senses, he could barely stop himself from screaming out loud. Damn it! Why had he been staring at that table so long! He tried to pull himself together and turn away, but no matter how tightly he shut his eyes, he couldn't stop them from seeing those yellow discs at the end of the table. No matter how hard he pressed his pillow over his ears, he couldn't stop them from hearing the jingling of soft metal. The jingle and glow of the gold poked at his senses like a dull needle. Lying in the warm bed he slept in every night had suddenly become unbearable. He wanted to twist around, bend all his joints and shift his blanket about, but he had to stay still so he wouldn't wake the others, because if they did, they would know that he was awake and thinking about that damned gold... He held his breath and listened.

No, he didn't hear a thing. But the fact that he couldn't hear anything was precisely what made him suspicious. Roberts would often breathe heavily at night and his wife would smack her lips. But he didn't hear a thing. Sveilis began to breathe deeply and evenly. If anyone was awake, he wanted to make sure they thought he was asleep.

Although he wanted to sleep, he simply couldn't doze off. The jingle of the gold didn't let up, and its bright glow never diminished. That unpleasant sensation was joined by another strange feeling he'd never experienced before: he tried to reach for his scattered thoughts, but couldn't catch a single one. An entire handful of gold was now his to spend! How much could be there? It could be more than he earns in a year, even two. He'd been counting on Juškans's ten roubles – and now he had handfuls of them!

In spite of his tightly closed eyes, he felt that a red flame was close by and a burning shudder ripped through his body. Now his forehead was damp, and he couldn't stand it. He lacked nothing! He had to sleep, so he could get up tomorrow morning and get to work.

Quietly, ever so quietly, he slid his feet out from under the blanket and hung them off the side of the bed. Then he pulled off the blanket and sat up. For a short while he sat and listened, and then he tiptoed over to the table. There was enough light to see everything clearly. Sveilis took a wool rag from the far end of the table and threw it over the pile of money. And it seemed to him that the room immediately became darker. As he tried to walk back quietly he bumped into a chair. In bed, he started to listen carefully: his wife stirred. She moved her hand up and felt around for the piece of cake she'd started eating earlier and had stuck somewhere behind her pillow without Sveilis noticing. She sighed and fell silent. This was followed by the sound of Made turning towards the wall; her clothes were rustling and she was pulling at her blanket. Roberts too began to breathe loudly like he always did.

Sveilis was lying stretched out on his back, his eyes shut

tight. But his thoughts kept scattering in every direction like a startled flock of birds.

At daybreak he was the first to get up. He got dressed, walked up to the table, slid the pile of money into his palm, and dropped it into his trouser pocket.

PART TWO

A mountain of things had been driven up to the front doors of the building owned by Lodziņš, the director of Unity Savings and Loans. Two porters wearing blue shirts and blue patent leather caps waited outside, another two entered. The heavy sprung doors kept swinging behind them for a few seconds. Through the thick, blue-tinted window panes the yellow arch of the doorman's cap was visible.

The doorman emerged, along with the two porters, shrugging his shoulders. "Maybe in the basement, or from the courtyard into one of the apartments? It's only my second week here; I don't know them all that well yet," he said.

"No," the older porter said, looking again at the crumpled sheet of paper in his hand. "Moon Street 15, at the Lodziņš building, apartment number nine – for Mr. Sveilis."

"Number nine..." the doorman scratched his head. "It'll be that young man with the blond whiskers then. He had visitors here yesterday; seemed like they were from the country." He walked over to the brightly-coloured cement slabs lining the edge of the pavement and stared at the mound of personal effects. He didn't step down onto the road: it was covered by a thin layer of black, melting snow and he was wearing light-coloured, freshly shined boots. "You can't bring in rubbish like that through the front door. Bring it into the courtyard."

He walked over to the gates, but they were locked. A boy and a girl on their way to school came through the smaller door with their bags on their backs and, as they walked off, they kept turning back to look at that pile of miscellaneous stuff. The doorman hurried back to his doors.

The porters leaned back against the pile as they waited, except for the one who sat down on the carriage shaft. But just as he did, the iron gates creaked open and revealed a strong, bearded caretaker.

"Well, come on then, drag it all in here!" he called, and helped with one side of it. "Number nine? For Mr. Sveilis? Right, yesterday he had those relatives here from the country. Looks like he's here to stay." He closed the gate again and then glanced back and said, "What a mess! Where are you planning on putting that junk?"

The porter standing closer to him shrugged his shoulders. "We're just going to move it all upstairs – it's none of our business!"

One of them disappeared upstairs for a while and then came out again. At the same time a window opened on the third floor. Made leaned out of it. "Hey you down there!" she called out. "Well, bring it up then, bring it up!" She closed the window and disappeared.

Mr. and Mrs. Sveilis came down to help the porters. He was in his best suit – a well-worn but clean long coat – with rubber boots and his collarless shirt. She was in a grey suit with old-fashioned sleeves ruffled at the shoulders, and her hair combed flat over her head. He was looking at everything with mistrust and suspicion. She was, as ever, somewhat befuddled and smiling in a forced, unnatural way.

"Careful, be careful!" Mr. Sveilis warned the workman untying the different bundles from the mound. They had got to his sewing machine and he jumped up to help the man untie it.

The caretaker, who had been watching everything from a distance, approached and reassured him, "Don't worry about a thing, old man: they know what they're doing. This isn't their first time."

"Sure, sure..." Mrs. Sveilis nodded her head, and still smiling, she stepped back.

By now, Made had come downstairs too. She was wearing the same old worn brown wool dress, but had jauntily thrown on a white scarf laced with pink ribbons. On her feet she had brand new patent leather shoes, with large black rosettes made of ribbon, held together by yellow metal hoops. She was standing up straighter, and was more animated in her movements than she had been before. She appeared to be more self-confident, but there was something in the way she moved which seemed a little forced, which may have arisen from some hidden insecurity and anxiety she kept to herself.

"Take it on up!" she urged, motioning kindly but with a certain air, to the porter closest to her.

"We'll unload it all first," one of the men on the mound called back.

"Don't worry yourself, miss," the caretaker interjected again. "It's not their first time."

Made felt flattered and laughed.

"Yes, yes - I can see that... Then take it all on up. I'll unlock the flat. My brother's not at home, but I've got the key."

She was twirling a small, shiny key around her index finger and was tapping her foot to the beat of some dance. Just then she noticed that a woman was looking in their direction, smirking from across the courtyard as she leant out of a second-floor window in the far wing of the building. She snapped back and walked towards the gate, swinging the key as she went. She walked through the smaller gate and tiptoed across the wet pavement to the front door. She gathered up her skirt so that her new shoes with their bright white soles could be easily seen, and stood there staring straight into the eyes of anyone passing by, as if to say, I'm the sister of the rich Augusts Sveilis. I live in this brand new, fancy building on the third floor. Number nine. It's written on the name board right next to the front door.

When she got past the front door, the doorman lifted his hat and greeted her. She returned his greeting with a smile, but then felt anxious: what if he takes me into the lift? I wouldn't know what to do! She didn't know, she truly had no idea how to operate it... With a skip in her step she trotted up the stairs as if she loved to run and jump like that all day long.

The long red-cloth runner seemed to go on forever up the smooth wooden steps, which gently creaked under her hard heels. The walls were decorated with brightly-coloured garlands of flowers - painted individually. There were colourful images in the curves of the windows through which the gentle twilight flowed into the narrow stairwell. Up in dimly lit corners there were greenish glass shades for electric lights. Made just couldn't get – or rather she wasn't physically capable of getting – used to living in this new world. Every object she encountered looked like something she'd only ever seen in pictures, or like something from her dreams.

A slender woman in mourning clothes, her silk dress rustling, was coming down the stairs towards her. Made stood up even straighter. The lady walked past without even acknowledging her. But Made took note of everything she saw: a plump, black boa around her neck, slender black gloves on her hands, one of which held the long train of her skirt, the other a purse covered with glittering silvery beads dangling from a long string. She also had transparent stockings with black stripes down the back, and a blue, lace petticoat. Looking down from the floor above, and then from the door of her own apartment, Made observed with envy as this apparition of wealth and good taste swaggered her way out of the building.

She unlocked the door while reading what was written on the large metal name plate: Augusts Sveile, Jr. This was the third time that day she'd read it. She didn't really know what the "Jr." meant, but was too shy to ask her brother. In fact, there were many things she wanted, but was too afraid to do or ask about them.

Downstairs the doorman jumped up from behind the blue window panes and pulled the door open. He greeted the man by putting his hand up to his cap and hurried over to the lift.

"Please, Mr. Sveilis."

Augusts Sveile Jr. unbuttoned his kid gloves and made an unintentional squeaking sound with his half-length galoshes as he walked towards the lift. The doorman adopted a deferential posture as he stood waiting for him. But then he remembered.

"Ah, Mr. Sveilis... They brought your...furniture."

"Furniture – for me? Then maybe –"

"Yes, yes, probably from the country. They brought it into the courtyard."

Sveilis thought for a moment and then turned, took three steps, and walked past the stairs out into the courtyard.

His father, who had clambered up to the top of the mound, was handing down his sewing machine, while two porters at the bottom were standing up on tiptoe and reaching up towards it.

"Slowly, slowly!" he warned. The caretaker was still standing in the same spot, hands in his pockets and a cigar between his teeth, watching with his lips half-open, smirking at him.

"Don't you worry, old man. They know what they're doing."

"Are you going to have your own tailor up there too?" the third porter said sarcastically as he folded up the binding rope.

On both sides of the courtyard, people – mostly women – could be seen standing at every window. Some of their faces seemed cross, others indifferent, but most seemed to be finding amusement in the events that unfolded below them. Sveilis winced: two shabby beds, eaten through by woodworm, had already been lifted down and placed on the ground, others identical to them were up on the mound. Boards to be used for the bed frames... Old, scratched tables, the tips of their legs crumbling away, along with their worn-down crosspieces. A couple of old-fashioned chairs made by a country carpenter, a couple of reed chairs with their material torn in a few places and sticking straight up into the air. A brown cabinet without a lock and mould across the back... A sheaf of twigs tied together to make a broom – and on the far side of the mound, a cast iron kettle hanging from the hook of the lifter used for the burner rings... An impressive collection of all kinds of cheap, useless rubbish!

His mother appeared from the other side of the mound carrying a large basket which held a pile of wool blankets and twists of flax, as well as empty spools and others that had been on the spinning wheel but still had some thread on them, half-knitted socks, and hundreds of other tiny, worthless pieces of tat.

Sveilis Jr. scowled. "What are you doing with all that..." he called out to his mother, before turning towards his father.

"Get down right now! You're going to fall and break your neck!"

The caretaker yanked the cigar out of his mouth with one hand and lifted his cap with the other.

"I've been telling your old man the same thing. It's not their first time doing this."

The porters looked back and lifted their caps. The sewing machine was on the ground. Old Sveilis clambered down from the mound.

"I didn't..." He brushed off the scuffed-up edges of his good suit. "It's just my sewing machine...I didn't want them to break it..."

"That bloody machine!" Sveilis growled angrily. "Why the hell did you bring all this rubbish! Where are we going to put all this junk?" He motioned towards the caretaker. "There's got to be some empty space in the basement, or in the attic, right? Show them where it is so they can take it all and pile it up down there."

The caretaker rushed off. Sveilis's mother stopped next to him with her basket.

"But son...where are we going to ... find a place to sleep..."

Sveilis ignored her and was more worried about the windows full of curious onlookers.

"Later, later. We'll figure it out later. For now, let's just have them take this rubbish and put it away somewhere." He turned back to his father. "Why the devil did you bring all this garbage! Didn't I say: only the things you can't live without. Just the absolute essentials. But look at you - a whole mountain! A whole mountain of rubbish. You've made us a laughing stock in front of all these people."

His father fidgeted uncomfortably on the wet snow-covered asphalt.

"When you live somewhere, you end up needing it all in the end."

"Come on! Go upstairs and they'll bring everything inside." Sveilis turned towards the porters. "Wait for just a moment and you'll be shown where to put everything."

He couldn't stand it any longer. Already ashamed because of the nosy onlookers, he spun round and hurried up the steps. As he walked, he thought about and understood what all of those people must be thinking: about his parents and their tacky, uneducated way of life. It was almost unbearable. They hadn't even the slightest idea of what's acceptable and what isn't. Worst of all, when people laughed at them, it turned him into a figure of fun as well.

He opened the door to the flat in a fury, and Made happened to be standing right in front of the door. She looked warily at her brother and immediately understood that he was incandescent. This in turn made her anxious.

"You don't have any idea do you?" Sveilis screamed at her. "Why did you bring all kinds of rubbish... and all kinds of rags... There's no room for any of that here! Straight on the bonfire and don't spare the flames!"

"Do you think I had any say in it, brother? Do you think anybody listens to me?" Made rushed over to the window then turned around again. "I told them: we don't need any of this! He has six rooms, all furnished with fancy things. Nobody needs your old furniture, and it wouldn't look right anyway."

"Utter idiocy!" Sveilis tore off his coat. Made hurried over to help him and then hung it up. "All the windows around the courtyard are full of people, all of them laughing. And why wouldn't they? All that junk and clutter. This isn't Bieriņmuiža or Kuzņecovs... Where's Roberts?"

Made shrugged. "He left this morning... drank half a cup of coffee, and then left. No sign of him since then. He'll just be kicking around somewhere. If only he would go to that school..."

"He starts on Monday... He probably went to the office to register."

Their mother came in with her basket and walked through the kitchen towards the back room. Sveilis followed her reluctantly.

"Why on earth did you drag along all that clutter!" He stood in the open door and frowned at his mother who was stooped over her basket.

"Oh, son, how can you say that! We can't do a thing without this stuff. We need to be able to mend socks, at least."

Sveilis let out a mocking laugh.

"Yes...if you want to wear mended socks and cheap country shoes – but we can buy new clothes!"

Made laughed too, joining in with her brother.

"I keep telling her. But does she ever listen to me?" she turned and yelled at her mother, "Why do you keep messing about with those things. It's only making everything dusty. Leave it there, there'll be time to put it away later."

"And where are we going to put the maid, if you're going to be in here?" Sveilis started up again. "We'll have to put the maid in there – he motioned with his thumb over his shoulder towards another room."

Still a little confused, and still trying to please her son, their mother objected and waved her arms, "We don't need any kind of maid here! There's only a few of us. What I suggest is that Made can learn a little about keeping house and I'll clean the rooms, while your father can carry up the firewood – and Roberts can also help here and there, or just work on his studies... Why on earth would we need a maid!"

Sveilis shook his head. "It won't work! Maybe you could live like that, but it doesn't work for me. How could I... What would I...When my mother is cleaning rooms and my father is carrying around firewood!" He dismissed the idea with a wave of his hand and turned away sharply. For now, Made didn't say anything: on this point she wasn't sure who to agree or disagree with.

"Son!" their mother said accusingly. "There's no shame in work. We're not a family of lords and nobles. We've spent our whole lives working extremely hard."

"Lords, nobles!" Sveilis strode over to the window again. "When I have money in my pocket, those lords and nobles are happy to polish my boots. But you still think I'm not their equal..." He pulled out his silver cigarette case and lit a cigarette. "Six rooms, a kitchen, a room for the maid, and a bathroom...We'll need a maid and a cook."

Their mother waved her arms, and asked, "What is it about these rooms that makes it impossible to sweep them every morning?"

"Have you even looked at them?"

"I'll get to it!" their mother responded as she turned away. "Our shoes are a bit muddy."

The cook came in with a basket over one arm, full to the brim with all kinds of root vegetables and heads of lettuce, as well as plucked birds and other food from the market. Out of breath, she threw down the basket and began to take off her coat. She behaved with quite obvious contempt towards the Sveilises.

"Please, we need sugar and potato flour." she said to Sveilis.

Sveilis reached into his waistcoat pocket, pulled out two roubles and handed them to her. The cook tossed them carelessly onto the table.

"Lonija, you'll need to sleep here in the kitchen for a few nights," Sveilis said, fussing with his cigar. "Just a few nights, until we're settled in." He stopped, blushed a bit, and went off into one the other rooms: the two porters were visible through the kitchen door carrying the large, treadle sewing machine.

Roberts came home around lunch time. He had been to the administrative office of the business school to register and take care of the last few formalities. He had also walked all over the centre and outskirts of town, reading street sign after street sign at every corner, looking into the windows of shops selling firearms, books, and stationery. He brought in a small package but was trying to keep it hidden behind his back.

He had his own room – just off the front door with its own entrance from the hallway. It was a small, pretty room with a nickel-plated metal bed, an armchair, a small table, a book case and two Viennese chairs. His books were as usual thrown in a disorganised pile on a chair. After taking off his coat, he began to move them to the book case.

The previous night he had slept very badly on that beautiful bed with its elastic spring mattress. The constant noise bothered him – the clip-clopping of hooves and the clattering of trams – as did the glare of the streetlights, which came in through the window over his head and almost perfectly illuminated the lovely colour of the ceiling. But what bothered him most of all was the unfamiliarity of it all, and the complicated thoughts that accompanied all of these new sensations.

Just like his father, he hadn't wanted to come. He wasn't a beggar and didn't need anybody else's charity. But conversations with Made, and to some extent also his mother, had gradually worn down his opposition. As well as the handful of gold coins in his father's pocket. He had a hundred repulsive feelings and a thousand repugnant thoughts, arguments, and conclusions. But each kopeck – for a long time merely tolerated, now accepted and easily spent – spoke its own unique language – without words, without meaning – but, slowly and surely, remarkably persuasive. Without even noticing, he'd already begun arguing against his own negative feelings and thoughts. Gradually, the weight of the gold was luring him over to its side. But for the moment, unease continued to eat away at him. He still couldn't speak calmly to his brother, who seemed to be trying to buy them off with his newly found money. He didn't show it, of course, but Roberts sensed it all the same. He seemed to always be distracted, hardly listening to what any of them were saying, and when he did bother to glance at what they were doing, it was always with a look of complete indifference. What they thought and felt had nothing to do with him. He had money: he was in charge, and they, the rest of them, were his servants and inferiors!

Colour suddenly rushed into Roberts's cheeks and he stopped what he was doing. And how was it that Augusts had come to have all that money! He'd heard so many strange rumours around town, riddled with jealousy, a maelstrom of confabulations, lies, and accidental distortions. And yet, some measure of truth can often be found in amongst such stories, even if it is just the tiniest detail. it might not be possible to truly grab hold of that truth, but a sense of it remained nonetheless. He also felt a strange nausea and he couldn't tell whether it was caused by shame or disgust towards his brother, himself and all the rest of them. Where did that money come from! It stuck to his fingers, staining them, and they couldn't be rinsed clean.

Roberts got up, closed his eyes, and shuddered. It's better not to see anything! And yet he looked again. The books were neatly arranged on the brown shelf. Next to them, a small bronze alarm clock, artistically designed, stood ticking away. The white curtain with small, embroidered ruffles lining its edge hung ready to be drawn across the window. He looked at the nickel-plated bed with its spring mattress, and smelt the subtly sour smell of fresh paint...

Shivers ran up and down his body generating both pleasure and disgust. Augusts had given him seventy-five roubles. He'd paid sixty for six months of tuition this morning and still had fifteen left over in his pocket. Fifteen roubles! For the first time in his life he had money like that in his own pocket!

He pulled himself away, as if from a shameful embrace, and began to unwrap the package. He had bought an inkwell: two round dishes with gold-plated covers shaped like tiny towers that sank beautifully into a smooth marble board. He'd thought and dreamt of having one just like this since he was ten years old. And now it was on his table! Now he could have everything that he'd always wanted so badly – especially, because his family's resources could never have promised anything of this kind. The lids dropped with a tiny, resonant ping as their golden tops came in contact with the smooth, shiny crystal.

Sveilis opened the door from the hallway. "Oh, you are home after all!" he said in a slightly slurred, blustery voice. "We're going to take a look at all the rooms. You should come too!"

Roberts walked out and everyone was waiting for him in

the hallway. Made, who always deferred to their brother's will, was looking proud for some reason and standing by the other door. Their mother was timidly clutching her hands together as usual, while their father was diligently cleaning his boots on a hemp mat and shaking them off on the pristine linoleum floor.

"What are you doing?" Made yelled at him. "Can't you use a brush?"

Sveilis walked ahead of them with exaggerated insouciance and almost a hint of contempt for the beautiful rooms and fancy furnishings. Roberts remained a few paces behind the rest of them. He'd already seen most of it through the open doors.

The parquet floor creaked beneath the hard heels of Sveilis's fashionable boots, his mother's old shoes, and the wet soles of his father's boots. The footsteps of these five people echoed through the large rooms, which were not yet fully furnished. As they processed through the flat, their conversations merged into a single wall of sound.

They started with the dining room next to the kitchen. In the middle there stood a round table standing on a single carved leg, covered by a white cloth. It was surrounded by twelve low chairs in the modern style, and above it was hanging a yellow brass lamp lit by electricity and decorated with three green tulips. By the window, a large tropical plant in a majolica pot, decorated with yellow flowers, had broad fronds which almost reached the centre of the room. On one wall there was an oak clock, its pendulum glinting as it swung back and forth behind its thick pane of glass. On the others there were paintings of fruit and flowers, of plucked and tied birds and a moose shot by hunters, all rendered in thick layers of oil paint and hanging in narrow oak frames. But the main attraction here was the sideboard: golden brown and enormous, it took up nearly one entire wall. Divided into three parts, with all manner of carved ornamentation, and adorned with a colourful floral design on glass, it stood there as an imposing mystery no one felt permitted to approach.

Sveilis discerned their awe and laughed boastfully. He slapped his hand down on the unpainted oak board, and exclaimed, "Six hundred and fifty... A special order. You can't get these ready-made. You have to select a drawing and have it made. They brought it the day before yesterday..." He opened one of its doors, then another. It was full of metal, crystal, porcelain and majolica dishes, and all manner of wondrous things – enough to make your head spin. Old Mrs. Sveilis sighed, and old Mr. Sveilis searched for a handkerchief but couldn't find the pocket of his long coat.

Next they came to the sitting room – a giant room with shiny red wallpaper, a rose-coloured fireplace with an impressive medallion in the centre and huge notched cornices. Half of a wall was occupied by a grand piano, while the rest of the room was filled with so much red plush upholstered furniture that there were only narrow gaps for moving around. An immense picture hung in a gold frame over the four-seater sofa, depicting in brilliant reds and yellows a sunset in a village in some far-off land. But best of all was the gargantuan ceiling lamp made from slightly reddish, frosted glass, which looked like a giant frozen orchid with branches bending in all directions with lamps attached.

Sveilis glanced around and laughed with indulgence. He pressed a button somewhere by the door with a loud click and instantly the red orchids lit up and the room which had been illuminated by the autumn twilight overflowed with an indescribably gentle, rosy glow.

His mother was standing with a helpless, sorrowful grin. Made gasped and her eyes snapped shut instinctively. His father was bewildered and tried to shield his eyes with his hand. Roberts looked on stunned and appeared to almost glow himself. With his hands in his trouser pockets, Sveilis fell back onto the sofa laughing and throwing his head back onto the soft cushion, as he stretched his crossed legs across the rug before him.

"We still need a few more bits here and there," he declared nonchalantly but not without glancing at his relatives one by one as if he were trying to gauge their reactions.

His father waved it all off with a dismissive motion of his hand. "What else could you possibly need! There's already..." He didn't know what else to say, so he shrugged his shoulders and in his bewilderment he absent-mindedly took another look around the room.

"There's plenty here, son, plenty," his mother murmured.

Made had already been trying to demonstrate that she understood better than the rest of them how to appreciate her brother's wealth and the beauty of his apartment. She now spent all her time trying to treat the ornateness of her surroundings as something obvious and necessary, but she was not yet able to do it with absolute conviction. Her cheeks burnt, her eyes sparkled and her fingers twitched nervously. She leant over the bouquet of fresh flowers in the Venetian vase on the table, and commented, "They don't smell like much..."

Sveilis smiled and said, "They've lost their scent already; I got them the day before yesterday. We'll have to have new ones fetched."

"Son..." his mother muttered.

They walked on, looking at the office and the bedrooms: comfort and luxury everywhere – soft chairs, patterned blankets – gold and glamour. Made's room was between Sveilis's and Roberts's. She lingered there when the others left for lunch. She wasn't hungry and couldn't calm herself down. She burnt as if it were the hottest day of summer, but didn't feel fatigued. She would sit down and get straight back up again. She could spend only a moment on each object. An incomprehensible, insatiable sense of restlessness was driving her from one place to another. Her fingers twitched without reason and her gaze would drift around without finding a single place where it could finally come to rest. She felt as if she had embarked on a straight and unending path without darkness or impediments, and if she started to run as fast as the wind without effort, she would only have to lift her arms like the wings of a bird to suddenly take off in full flight. The air itself seemed to carry her and anything was now possible. But she didn't run. In her heart something quivered and wouldn't allow her to believe that now everything would be attainable. The immeasurably long and trouble-free road stretched off into the distance like a white silk ribbon, and the horizon was a strip of gold. No matter which direction she turned in, the sun always smiled back at her. Her heart was pounding like a drum, and her flesh ablaze with expectations. This uncontrollable happiness made her want to scream with joy.

They called for her from the dining room and she went to lunch.

The entire table was covered with plates and dishes filled with food. The silver – or rather silver-plated metal – glittered, the crystal clinked and the bouquet brought in from the sitting room sat fragrantly in the middle of the table. Cold hors d'oeuvres and spirits were served first.

"A vodka for me and father, what do you think?" Sveilis placed his fork on the edge of his plate and reached over to fill his father's glass. Then he reached for the green bottle and tried to pour some into Roberts's glass. "Would you like some of this?"

Roberts blushed and bent down over his plate.

"N-no... I don't drink."

His mother nodded as she nibbled timidly at a bone. "He doesn't drink. And doesn't need to."

Sveilis smirked and said, "He'll learn. And the later he learns, the more he'll end up drinking." He put down the green bottle and reached for the red wine. "But at least you can join the women. Please!" Smiling gallantly, he nodded towards the ladies and raised his glass. Made smiled back at him and toasted buoyantly, but their mother's hands shook and she started coughing violently after taking a sip. The fork with the smooth metal handle slipped from their father's hand

and fell on the ground. Roberts was bent over his plate and still grimacing because of the foul-tasting drink. The maid was watching through the kitchen door, while Made became angry at her parents' and younger brother's awkwardness and foolishness. She threw her knife down on the plate, grabbed her glass and drank all of its contents in a single motion. When she had finished she handed it to her brother, "Could you please pour me some more?"

They had soup. They had a quail roast with an unusual salad, which combined both fresh and preserved ingredients, and drank beer. They ate thick and watery desserts, and fruit: local apples, giant green pears, oranges and grapes were piled onto four glass plates stacked on different levels. The bunches of white and red grapes that didn't completely fit in the space between two of the plates spilled over the sides. Their colour shined as if through a light, sugary fog. The sweet-sour aroma of fruit and wine wafted across the room, intoxicating and warming these simple, small-town folk who had been pulled out of their grey poverty. Gradually their movements became slower and more focused, and their eyes seemed to glow more brightly.

Towards the end, everyone began to eat less and drink more. They ate and felt as if they had never eaten so much in their lives. An overfilled stomach brings a strange kind of fatigue that overtakes the whole body. The tastiest things no longer seemed as tasty. Previously, they had felt the need to choose carefully, to sample things and only eat them if they liked them, otherwise to put them down and look for something else. But now they could eat and drink even if they didn't want to at all. Oddly it felt as though they were working or fulfilling some responsible task! And yet most of all it was a welcome relief to realise that there would be no work and no responsibilities, and they could just sit there in no hurry and carefully choose what they wanted, while they enjoyed the sweet and sour smells that drifted into their nostrils, the cool liquid flowing across the tongue and the pleasant warmth of their bodies.

Sveilis got up and turned on the light, and immediately the violet-flowered porcelain service with strips of gold around the edges glowed with an enchanting brightness. Every single one of its cups was made in the same style. The angled and semi-circular serving trays whose bottoms and slightly bent handles were fashioned from a white engraved metal, but the edges were made of crystal. The vases with gold wrapped around their middles, the green-tinted long-stemmed glasses, the knives with smooth, cold, white handles... They had finished eating, but no one wanted to get up and leave. It was enough to stay seated, slightly dizzy and wonder whether this was all just a dream that would disappear when they awoke.

A poor tailor's family was having a waking dream filled with things they had never even imagined. They felt a little scared, perhaps triggered by a sense of guilt. Did they deserve all of this? Wasn't this a sin against some unknown, incomprehensible and invisible force? Would there be sooner or later a terrible price to pay for all this? Might a ghostly hand reach through the dark hollow of the open door and extinguish this wondrous glow, dashing all of this astonishing luxury to pieces and wiping it away, forcing them to wake up around their old pinewood table with a bowl of cottage cheese and a half-eaten pretzel? They would gradually grow accustomed to their surroundings and forget about such misgivings. The aromas tickled their nostrils and their bodies felt agreeably warm. In the glow of the electric lights, a blood-red drink glinted in the half-empty glasses. Their old worries and fears and dark imaginings were alleviated by the comfort, gentle warmth and constant and inescapable temptation to placate their appetites. Their old awareness of humility before sin retreated and all that remained was laziness and fatigue, which spread from an overfilled stomach across the rest of the body, bringing with them a new kind of hunger – to eat more and drink more, to eat and drink without ever tiring for the rest of their lives.

Behind it all remained the mystery of how and by what

means this luxury and pleasure had been brought about. Unseen and rarely considered was the gold that made this cornucopia possible. It clinked as two glasses came into contact, it gleamed in the redness of the wine, it glinted in the misty juiciness of the sagging bunches of grapes, and it wafted through the air, tickling palates, warming hearts and intoxicating heads. It was everywhere – it gripped the human body and soul in a thousand different ways, wrapping itself around every feeling, every nerve and every fibre with its yellow arachnoid tendrils.

The grovel before it, as before a god.

"Where oh where can I get these beautiful clothes..."

"Mr Tilaks – my sister..."

"The day before yesterday already..."

My wife – Mr Sveilis..."

The ends of Sveilis's moustache were sagging a bit. His soft, moist lips were hanging open languidly. Leaning far back into his chair, he gazed across his people with a smile.

Everyone had finished eating except his mother who was still finishing her dessert.

"Eat!" Sveilis pushed the plate of fruit closer to her.

She waved it away as she held her knife. "No, no! I can hardly stand up as it is."

Made nudged Roberts in his side, and said, "Finish your glass."

Roberts was drinking his third glass of wine. It no longer tasted disgustingly sour, as it had at first. Later he burped and a pleasant flavour seemed to waft through all his senses. Gulping awkwardly, Roberts drank on, and when he'd finished he looked over at his brother and almost smiled at him.

Sveilis glanced at the clock and rose to his feet. He stretched as if he'd just stepped out of a warm bath and said, "Tomorrow we'll need to go shopping," he nodded towards Made. She nodded back smiling. "What about you," Sveilis turned towards his brother, "did you have enough money?" When Roberts responded in the affirmative, Sveilis pulled his fat wallet from his pocket. "You'll need books." He put twenty roubles down in front of his brother.

Roberts blushed. He wanted to say – and he should have said – that he'd already set money aside for books, but something restrained him for just a moment, and then Sveilis had already turned towards his father and mother.

"Maybe you both need something too?" He put ten roubles down in front of each of them.

His father coughed dryly. "What could we possibly need..." But even so he gently reached for the red piece of paper with the tips of his fingers and carefully examined it as if he were calculating what he could get for it.

His mother didn't want to take hers. "We have plenty...Save it for yourself, you need it more. We'll surely survive. What could we possibly need?"

Stuffing his wallet back into his pocket, Sveilis dismissed their objections with a wave of his hand.

"I've got four thousand in credit at Lodziņš's bank, at the Seventh Credit Union... And that's just the start. I've had that hotel for a while, and it works. The rooms are too small; I'll have to tear down one of the walls. But by and by, twenty-five roubles profit per day. It's a fine living! And that's nothing – I'll get fifty for it yet – enough to get settled in... I've got credit at Lodziņš's bank, I'm a member of the Seventh Credit Union, I'm a member of the Twelfth, I applied at the Fifteenth – they'll take me. All the money I need. Next spring I'm going to start building a house. The purchase of the building plot is almost complete."

As if pushed by some inner force, he nimbly spun around, tapping his heels against the parquet floor, snapping his fingers along with the rhythm of his steps and whistling as he walked around the room.

Made looked at him, captivated, his father wrinkled his brow and stared at the floor, Roberts bit his lips and his mother shook her head. She knew nothing about these credits, but intuited enough to know that they were serious business.

"Lord, oh lord..." she babbled. "With you, Augusts, dear, it's always more, more, more. When you have twenty-five roubles – what more do you need? Isn't that enough?"

Sveilis chuckled haughtily. "The two of you think that you can make all this happen for just twenty-five roubles?" He moved his arm in a circular motion around the room. "Rubbish! I don't need to be miserly and starve myself. I've got credit."

"Lord, oh lord..." his mother couldn't stop shaking her head, which prompted Made turned to her in a rage: "What do you know about any of this! He can do what he likes, if he's got the money! The two of you have spent your whole lives miserable and pitiful. You think it has to be the same for everybody else too."

Sveilis was laughing loudly. He turned off the lights and nodded at Made. "Get dressed – let's go."

Hiding them behind his back, Roberts took both of the red banknotes back to his room. He put them on the table first, then in the drawer, but after a moment's consideration, pulled them out again to give it all some more thought. His mind was hazy; his thoughts made no sense. But he had to find a way of protecting his riches. That amount of money, that astonishing amount of money was something he'd never had before. When he'd only had ten kopecks, there were a hundred different things he needed, but now it was awfully hard to figure out what to buy and what not to. The money was practically burning a hole in his pocket and so he put it back down on the table, stepped back, still staring at it, and then finally picked it up again. He arranged the two banknotes neatly – corner to corner, side to side, folded them over twice, but the shiny pieces of paper were getting wrinkled. He unfolded them again and after separating and smoothing them both out, he looked at each one separately and then carefully placed them behind the cover of his Russian geography book...

In the tiny maid's room, behind the carefully closed kitchen door, their heads placed together, old Mr and Mrs Sveilis whispered secretively to each other for a long time. Then old Mrs Sveilis pulled out a basket full of spools of spun yarn from underneath the bed and picked one out. Meanwhile, Old Mr Sveilis was carefully folding the two crisp red banknotes until they were quite small, so that Old Mrs. Sveilis could wind them into one of the spools of yarn.

Sveilis rode around town with his sister. Made felt ashamed sitting there in her old coat and hat, and wearing last year's fashions next to her smartly dressed brother. She worried that people would think she was his maid. A light rain began to fall, but she didn't allow the top to be raised over the carriage. She wanted to see the city and wanted the city to see her. She spoke resonantly, laughed often, leaning over and looking into her brother's eyes as she laughed, and trying in every way she could to show that she was this wealthy person's sister.

Sveilis felt a bit self-conscious around this shabby, old-fashioned, and fairly unattractive woman. But he didn't show it – he just sat and affably received greetings from his acquaintances with his trademark smirk. He wasn't a wicked man; he never forgot the people he'd come from.

They began to feel relaxed around each other. Made was beaming as she looked at both sides of the street. Sveilis didn't have the energy to show and explain everything to her, but he, too, was enjoying the ride. His sister's naive joy amused him greatly.

The cab driver turned into one of the city centre's narrow, lively streets. The flour hauler's horse had slipped and fallen at the corner. While it was being lifted up, both those who'd been traveling by foot and by carriage were being held up in a queue along both sides of the street. The Sveilises had to stop as well.

A young student navigating the mess had ended up right next to the Sveilises' carriage and was supporting himself on one of its front wheels. He jumped down and opened his coat, which had a brown fur collar. He noticed Sveilis and lifted his black cap, which had a small metal star on one side. Then he noticed the lady, leaned in to look closer, flashed a quick smile, lifting his cap again, and then moved his hand dramatically in a semi-circular motion all the way down to his knees. He lifted it again and walked off with a thick, gnarled walking stick shoved under his arm.

Made had nodded back so quickly and forcefully that her hat had slid down over her eyes. She blushed fiercely. She shot a furtive glance at her brother, but he wasn't paying attention and was just looking angrily at the driver tending to the injured horse. What a young and attractive man! And so exceptionally polite and friendly. How he'd leaned down and looked straight into her eyes! She felt the warmth rush to her cheeks. And isn't that him standing over there, ten steps behind them on the other side of the road, looking at her? Made could feel his gaze on her back, her neck, her ears. She couldn't stop herself – she turned around and looked. But no, he was gone. She leant in closer to her brother.

"Who was that?" she asked, sensing that she was blushing even more.

"Who?" Sveilis couldn't remember and looked in vain for the person she was talking about. Then he remembered. "Oh – him! That's young Mr. Lodziņš's student. A solid fellow..." Remembering something, he flashed a telling smile for just an instant. His lips opened and his eyes narrowed.

There was so much to see – the glamorous people and the elaborate shop window displays – that Made soon forgot all about the student. They started going into shops. Made didn't even want to get out of the cab, but the driver stopped at the hat shop. It was so comfortable sitting in the carriage, which carried them so easily across the cobblestone street with its gentle rocking motion. She reluctantly got up and went inside.

At first Made was completely overwhelmed by the rush of activity inside the hat shop. If it hadn't been for her brother, she would have spent all day in there struggling to reach the counter. She couldn't keep track of the shop clerk and all the hats she was trying on. And what an amazing selection they had! Simple designs, with a round base, wide brim, and a velvet ribbon tied around; narrow ones, others pushed upwards, some with ostrich feathers on the side and down along the brim;. small black, blue, and red velvet forms surrounded by crushed ribbons; brightly coloured pieces of cloth wrapped around the head several times in the Eastern style; completely unique, fantastic styles! If only she could wear them on the street, she would be able to truly evaluate each of them. But in the shop they were all mixed together in one huge mess. How were these other ladies able to select them so confidently, try them on, examine them in the mirror, and request others? They seemed to understand their own bodies, and they knew whether an article of clothing should accentuate something here or hide something there, or if it just needed to be modified. Made didn't know anything. She didn't know if an item of clothing needed to be matched with her face or whether she could use a hat to create that desired harmony. For the first time in her life she sensed how uneducated and inexperienced she was. She felt ashamed standing next to these self-confident ladies, who would cast quick sneering looks in her direction. Her brother stood next to her and cleared his throat. Made let herself get more and more muddled. She could feel the tears welling up in her eyes. She wanted to throw the brown paper box down onto the floor and run out of the shop. But the experienced salesclerk understood the situation and managed to gain Made's trust. She decided to wear her new hat out of the shop and her brother had the old one sent back home.

 The golden discs dropped one after the other down onto the carved marble plate at the cashier's window spinning and jingling as they went. How elegantly he threw down those coins! Made felt a surge of heartfelt gratitude towards her brother and straightened her back as she stood there in her new hat. Wasn't everyone here equally a gentleman or a lady who just happened to have money in their pocket? And her brother certainly did! Maybe some of those haughty ladies were taking so long to pick out a hat because they couldn't actually afford one. She and her brother could pay without needing to haggling over the price. A handful of silver coins spilled from the cashier's window. He haughtily collected them with nimble fingers and dropped them into his waistcoat pocket without even counting them. He had no need: ten, twenty kopecks weren't even money to him! She walked out of the store feeling slightly faint but she was steady on her legs and held her head high.

Once more there was the sound of horses' hooves on cobbles, and the soft seats in the carriage gently rocked as it moved along. All around them were teeming crowds of pedestrians and their carriage in the centre of this human tide split it down the middle causing waves of people to spill onto the pavement on both sides. Other pedestrians had to back up against walls to free a path for them. How red their cheeks were!

Their next stop was a shop selling ready-made suits. The diversity and dazzling beauty caused another wave of dizziness to wash over Made like a searing heat. The velvet sat heavy and serious, the silk swished by, and other light, translucent fabrics seemed to float through the air. There were some fabrics which needed to be lifted with both hands, and others which seemed so delicate that she dared not touch them, let alone breathe on them. Their colours ranged from fiery ones that stung the eyes to the mildest and most nuanced shades, which you could stare at for hours. Heavy, thickly flowered ruffles and others as fine as spider webs. Gold and silver tassels, red and yellow glass beads, green and crystal-clear jewels... And in the midst of this frenzy, women forgetting their propriety – their hands greedy, their staring eyes covetous and their speech animated. But Made had her own intentions: she had quickly come to her senses, steadied herself and made a selection. It felt like a dream when she looked at the mirror's reflection. She didn't want to leave; she didn't want to wake up in the poverty and misery she'd known in the past.

The fresh banknotes newly retrieved from the bank crunched, the gold jingled on the carved marble slab, and the siblings drove on to the shop selling coats and jackets. They purchased a huge assortment of things from the shop selling linens and sundries. Three or four pairs of boots and two pairs of shoes at the shoe shop. At the jeweller's they selected an enamel watch decorated with sapphires, a long gold medallion hanging from a braided chain, a bracelet, a pendant, two rings and a purse. At the luxury goods shop, they purchased an immense photo album bound in grey leather with gold edges, two postcard albums, and a few dozen trinkets made of porcelain, majolica, bronze and precious stones. At the perfume shop, they had the shopkeeper pack up some tooth elixir, several containers of various skin care creams, and a bottle of Japanese lilac essence. They drove all around the centre of town.

And everywhere there was the sound of crunching banknotes and jingling gold. The crowds in the shops and the noise on the street began to merge into a single ceaseless, undifferentiated drone. Only the jingle of gold could cut through it all. It could be heard everywhere. Could it be a gold piece, tiny yet commanding, that was chiming along with the clock in the church tower, sending its blustery rattle high up into the air? And wasn't it even gold's yellow spark that shot up from horseshoes as they struck the mud-covered cobblestones? It was in everything and everything belonged to it.

Tired and indescribably happy, Made leaned onto her brother's shoulder. The street with its damp, grey buildings and black stream of humanity no longer interested her. She had become accustomed to how their carriage effortlessly split the oncoming stream and the waves it generated on both sides would wash up onto the pavement and press up close to the buildings. The people who walked alongside them had to wade through mud that clung to their boots and shoes, while the Sveilises rode on in their comfortable carriage. She had already accustomed herself to her new status.

After waiting until her brother had finished lighting his cigarette, she took his hand and held it lovingly.

Sveilis laughed. He enjoyed his sister's shy appreciation. It was worth more than all the money he had spent on her that day.

"Don't worry," he said to her light-heartedly. "I've got two thousand on my current account. And credit...What I've spent on you today is a trifle." Her brother's carefree attitude was beginning to have an influence on Made. After all, she'd seen with her own eyes how much money he had in his pockets. She let out a weary laugh.

"Where oh where will I go with all these beautiful clothes..."

"Well, you can go out and live a little! Later on you may not want to eat lunch at home. If you need anything else, just ask...But what about Roberts ... that boy is always scowling ... does he need anything? Have I done anything to offend him?"

"Him, that boy!" Made said sarcastically. "All he deserves is a spanking, nothing else. He's sniffing at all of this like he's too good for it. If it's not good enough for him, he can go back. He must have a need for something. He won't run off anywhere, I'm sure he'll calm down and come to his senses..."

Sveilis tapped the driver on the shoulder with the top of his walking stick. The carriage stopped by a set of wide double doors. Above them written on frosted glass, it said: "Hotel Baltika". This same inscription was written in gold letters on a black sign stretched from the door across four windows.

Sveilis jumped down effortlessly and gave his hand to Made with a smile.

"Come down; let's go take a look at this tavern of mine."

"You, wait here; I don't have any small change!" Sveilis called out to the driver over his shoulder. Made listened with wonder at how imperious and commanding his voice sounded. There was something in the arrangement of his words and the way he stressed them and clipped them that reminded her of the way German landowners spoke. A commoner would always respect someone who liked to talk with that pronunciation.

The courteous doorman, adorned with epaulettes made of glittering cords, was already holding the door open for them when they approached. Sveilis let his sister go first up the slatted iron steps, then followed, his head held high almost running with stiff, hurried steps. Holding the door open with one hand, the doorman lifted his hat with the other.

Made didn't know which way to turn. Across from her was a white staircase with a red carpet running down the middle. Past the staircase there were double doors on the left with an inscription above in frosted glass that read "buffet" in Russian. A board was hanging on the right side intended for guest registration.

Sveilis had already spoken with the doorman, so he turned, placed his arm around his sister's shoulders, and guided her along. With his other hand he opened the doors to the buffet.

"Here we are; please go in."

They were met by a gust of warm air in a bluish haze of tobacco smoke and the light aromas of the kitchen. There was also the strong smell of alcohol accompanied by the clinking of glasses, the knocking of billiard balls, the friendly chatter of conversations and the din of laughter which flowed over them in an instant. All this echoed in their ears, and enveloped them completely.

Made stood there blinking, not seeing anything in the brightness of the electric lights. A waiter with white cord epaulettes rushed past them with a much used, crumpled rag over his shoulder. He greeted them with a bow and took Sveilis's coat, hung up his hat and walking stick, neatly put away his galoshes and lightly brushed off the chalk on the elbows of Sveilis's jacket.

Made also began to take off her coat and the waiter, watching her with one eye, and rougher in his movements, prepared to help her. But Sveilis didn't permit this kind of tactlessness.

"We're not staying long..." He pulled the coat back onto her shoulder. "My sister is only here for a moment," he said to the man, emphasising the word 'sister'. The waiter stepped back with a bow and immediately looked back with contrition.

The waiter walked in front, clearing the way for the gentleman. But Sveilis stopped at the end of the buffet, on the right side, situated in an alcove. He reached over the dish of lampreys, the large pink ham, and the plate of steaming Thüringer sausages, to greet a stout, broad-shouldered, buffet attendant with a dark complexion, whose hair was cut right down to his scalp. He then turned to introduce her.

"Mr Tilaks – my sister..." Mr. Tilaks extended his hand towards Made and clutched her fingers, and bowed so low that the fabric of his jacket bunched into folds. As he bent towards her, he didn't release her hand from his. Although he was smiling, there was a hint of irony in his movements, which Made didn't notice. She had been distracted by the pockmarked man who was pushing past Tilaks to get towards them.

"Hello, Miss Made!" He took her hand – her fingers still white from the earlier handshake – and clenched it even more tightly as he shook it. "So you too? You've also decided to join us?"

Made couldn't believe her eyes and suddenly sincere, spontaneous joy overtook her.

"Mr. Juškans, what are you doing here?"

Juškans lifted his head and laughed, flashing his prominent white teeth.

"I'm training to be a buffet attendant. It's only my second week and they're keeping me very busy! That's how it is, miss: an innkeeper learning how to be an innkeeper..." His chuckling faded and he let his small, kind eyes wander in the direction of the overflowing buffet. "A little tavern is one thing, but this is something completely different." He stepped back suddenly when a guest requested more drink.

Made looked around. Her brother was walking through the thick crush of people along the buffet saying hello to everybody. Everyone knew him, and he drank and exchanged a few words with all of them, argued with some and clinked glasses with others. Some clapped him on the shoulder and looked into his eyes as they laughed, with others he held their hand in his and put his other hand on their shoulder. Some were young and others older, but the great majority were middle-aged. All of them were smartly dressed – in furs, modern coats and karakul collars, most were wearing round hats, but some wore plush hats or sportsman's caps sagging down over their eyes. Made watched as one of them tossed back a shot of liquor, another bit into a steaming, dripping sausage, and yet another was carefully examining the buffet with a small fork in one hand and a plate in the other. All were red-faced with bright eyes, and all were talking over one another – it was impossible to make sense of any of it.

Juškans leaned over towards Made again.

"Yes, it's my second week working hard in here. I'm still getting used to it! It's not like back there at the tavern: some days a few people came in and other days nobody at all, but it's always full in here. You haven't seen anything yet. If you come here around nine or ten, you can't even turn around. The space is too small. Yes... Mr. Tilaks is leaving on the first and after him it's my turn... Mr. Tilaks is opening his own café restaurant... And what about you, Miss Made? Did you arrive yesterday?"

"The day before yesterday."

"Oh yes, your distinguished brother did tell me that..." He pulled away and began to laugh heartily at a joke Sveilis had just told, which practically everyone behind the buffet, including Mr. Tilaks on the other side, were also laughing at. Then he slumped onto his elbow on the corner of the buffet table. "We don't get too many guests at the hotel. But at the buffet..."

"And what about your wife?" Made asked.

"She came to the city too, of course! It took us two days of searching before we found an apartment. We didn't want one that was too far away, you see, otherwise I'd have ended up having to walk home late at night..."

"She should come and visit us sometime..." Made hadn't meant to say that at all. She wanted to bite her own tongue for being so careless. A buffet attendant's wife – quite a guest!

But Juškans, beaming like the sun itself, bent over the corner of the buffet.

"Thank you so much for the invitation. Why not – she'd love to come. Why not..."

"Turn around, new buffet attendant, turn around!" Tilaks, pouring six glasses, rapped on the buffet with the corkscrew. Three thirsty guests stood impatiently in a line on the other side.

The waiter from earlier approached and said, "Miss Sveilis, please follow me." He brought her to a small table covered with a fresh tablecloth at the back of the large room. He stooped over obsequiously until Made had sat down. "What would Madam like me to bring her?"

Made didn't know what to say. What should she have him bring? What's appropriate in this situation? Dismayed she looked over at the alcove where part of the crowd was standing at the end of buffet with the ham, the dish of lampreys, and the artificial palm.

"Forgive me," she nodded blushing, "I'll just sit here until my brother returns..."

When the waiter left, she examined the buffet room more carefully. It was only about half full, and yet there was someone sitting at every table. Some ate quickly, some calmly sipped their beer and some – as if passing the time of day – were reading newspapers attached to long rods. At the corner of one table there were three youths sitting with a young woman wearing a wide, red hat. Around the long table, two families were seated with their acquaintances: two handsomely attired women – one somewhat rotund, the other skinny, two portly older men – one with a small beard, the other with a moustache – and finally two young, attractive men. Those sitting alone were quiet and occasionally glanced at the larger groups who were speaking, joking, and laughing loudly while they ate and drank. When Made had come and sat down, about ten pairs of eyes had overtly turned towards her. One pair belonged to the young woman in the red hat, who continued to study her. The fat lady at the long table had just lifted her soup spoon when she craned her neck to examine this newcomer from head to toe with a disapproving stare. Behind her head the steam from her soup billowed up from the white bowl. One of the young men on the other side of the table leaned over to the skinny woman and whispered something with a smirk on his face.

A hot burst of anger rushed to Made's head. Why were these people staring at her like that! Didn't she have the right to feel at home there? Didn't everything they were eating and drinking belong to her brother? Her eyes were aflame. How dare they sit there talking about her!

When Sveilis decided to see how she was getting on, he came towards her, smiling at everyone he passed, saying hello or nodding. He would extend his hand to the ones he knew, exchanging a few words with them, and just smile and nod at those he didn't know. There were far more people he knew than the ones he didn't.

He stopped at the group with the young lady in red, and bowed performatively. Made observed something strange in her brother's movements and his faint smile, hints of which could only be seen in the corners of his mouth and his eyelids, but she didn't understand what it was. All the men along the table were bowing towards him and the women rose to their feet, dignified and respectful. The fat, bearded man also rose and shook her brother's hand; he kept trying to pull him over to their table, constantly grinning and never taking his eyes off of Sveilis. He extended his other hand in the direction of the thin woman.

"My wife – Mr Sveilis..."

Bowing and smiling politely, Sveilis took the woman's hand. As she was shaking his hand, she rose about a hand's width up from her chair, but then immediately slumped back down and bent over her soup bowl again. Sveilis extended his hand to the other fat man and this same ceremony repeated itself.

Sveilis passed a smiling gaze across the entire company.

"Have you just arrived in Riga?"

"Yes – yes – yes..." three or four voices answered simultaneously. Their beaming faces did not turn away from Sveilis, but continued to look him directly in the eyes.

"Yes," the bearded man declared and rose to his feet obligingly, "I had business here – at the insurance company, you know..."

"Oh yes." Sveilis responded. "Didn't your house burn down, over at the seaside?" He clasped his hands on his back underneath his jacket so it was easy to see his slightly round stomach covered in a brightly patterned waistcoat with a gold watch chain threaded through his button hole stretching from one underarm to the other.

"Yes!" someone else piped up. "There were two of them."

"What are you babbling on about," the woman interrupted without lifting her gaze from her bowl. "It wasn't two; three were burnt down."

The bearded man shot a long, annoyed look in her direction, before dismissing her with a wave of his hand.

"Oh yes, but there's nothing to add to the claim for that old shack. Only about three hundred..."

Everyone laughed except the ladies. Sveilis laughed loudest of all out of politeness.

"How many of those summer houses do you have all together?"

"Five or so..." The man put his hands together just like Sveilis did. "Two burnt down, three still standing."

"You sold one of them last year," one of the younger ones added.

"Yes, I did sell that one. Just a bloody shack made of splinters – it wasn't bringing anything in anymore. I got a good price for it too. Four thousand five hundred..."

Sveilis laughed again.

"It seems like you have a fire over there every summer! But you got compensation, I suppose?"

"From the insurance? Ye-e-es." The bearded man nodded as if he were surprised by the question. "What do I have to show: my premium is paid – they can just count it all out on the table." It was clear he wanted to show that all these money matters were of no real concern to him. He stretched and leaned back. "I ended up having to waste half a day there. We had a board meeting at the savings bank today too, but then I had to run for my train. A man's not just a beast of burden after all... So, I said, let's go have a bite to eat at the Baltika..."

The moustachioed man had been listening carefully this whole time, and was waiting for an opportune moment. Now he skilfully inserted himself into the conversation.

"And I've got a meeting with the excise board... I've got a tavern and warehouse. But in the new year I'd like to have an inn. Beer on its own isn't enough."

"I'll tell you what!" The bearded man slapped Sveilis casually on the shoulder. "Your herring is fantastic!"

"Ye-e-es!" two or three voices echoed in agreement. And one or two heads nodded as well.

Sveilis smiled as he looked at the plates covered with the heads of fried white herring and other remnants and at the half-empty carafe of spirits.

"Yes, I have them brought in fresh every day."

"Who do you get them from?" the moustachioed man began to ask, but the bearded man interrupted him.

"But please sit down, Mr. Sveilis!" he said as he tried to pull him down onto the empty chair. Sveilis would not acquiesce.

"Excuse me, my sister is over there... One shot of spirits though, that I will have." Without saying a word, he took the small glass filled with a green liquid, swiftly threw it back, and ate the leftover half of a herring.

Made instinctively straightened her back when both of the women at the other table simultaneously looked over at her. A-ha, so you heard! Of course, his sister! She took off the yellow kid glove she'd squeezed onto her left hand, but when she caught sight of how red and chapped it was from too much washing and manual labour, she scratched one of her knuckles and quickly pulled the glove back on again. Then she placed her right hand with her purse across the corner of the table. Its silver and black sequins glinted in the electric light. The metal strap crunched ever so softly as it responded to the grip of clean leather. A-ha! Made proudly threw back her head and slowly closed her eyes. Her new coat was open. The ruffles of her blouse pressed up around its collar, the long golden medallion sinking into them. Too bad she couldn't take off her gloves to give her rings a chance to shimmer. The bracelet – yes, she could slide that out from her sleeve.

Sveilis walked over with a smile on his face and sat down. The waiter rushed over with a food and wine menu.

"Well, what will we have?" Sveilis asked as he casually twiddled the menu in his hands.

Made shrugged disdainfully, partly because she wasn't at all hungry, and partly mimicking the gestures of the other women she'd observed.

"We have fresh pig's feet in aspic... roast goose... Would sir like a warm or cold dish?" The waiter leant down obligingly over the menu.

Sveilis tossed the menu down onto the table.

"No, you know what; are there any herring in the kitchen? Yes? Have them fry them up for us." He leaned over the table towards Made. "They're not bad. You'll see." He turned back to the waiter. "Tell them to make it quick. Fairly salty. And don't spare the butter... Wait! First bring me one glass of homemade beer and for my sister..." He tapped his fingers on the table as he thought. "Does the buffet have any – well..." He tapped his fingers some more. "Malaga – yes, dark Malaga?"

"I'll look – I think we have some..."

"I think I'd rather drink...I'm thirsty..." Made said in a lofty tone, but then became embarrassed and almost blushed again.

"Yes? Well in that case first bring my sister a glass of tea – with red wine. And a glass of homemade beer for me."

When the waiter had walked away, Made leaned over closer to her brother.

"Who are they?"

"Them over there?" Sveilis's voice no longer had a hint of the friendliness he'd expressed a few moments earlier. Now his look was one of complete indifference, and he took no care in what he was saying, almost mocking the group. "They're from the seaside. That one with the beard is Sietiņsons, a timber merchant and summer cottage owner. The other one – Berķis – owns a tavern or something... Both of them are real sons of bitches... But good customers. They always come here."

Both of the ladies at the table were whispering to each other and looked over.

The group with the young lady in the red hat had also been whispering for a long time and kept casting surreptitious glances their way. One of the young men got up and approached their table, while the others looked on after him. His gait was solid and he wasn't swaying or staggering, but a more observant bystander would have immediately understood that he was drunk – as a professional reveller, he managed to keep up appearances. He was a fairly young man with a kind, likeable face and a completely bald head.

He walked over and extended his hand towards Sveilis, while also trying to bow courteously towards Made. He barely kept his footing and almost fell onto their table. The young lady in red and her companions were barely able to restrain their guffaws. Made didn't know what was going on, but Sveilis's face took on a dignified gravity.

"Please don't let me impose, Mr. Sveilis..." Standing by their table, he was now also bowing towards Sveilis. "Would it please you to sit with us? Both you and the young lady? The greater the company, the more it is merry!"

"Forgive me," Sveilis answered coolly and in a clipped tone, "my sister and I would just like to have a quick bite to eat here."

The affectionate youth seemed not to have heard them. He put his hand on his heart and somewhat intrusively leaned over towards Made. "Please, please!"

"My sister and I will stay and eat here," Sveilis declared in a voice that was firm and louder so that everyone around could hear him.

The young man snapped back and retreated. The woman in red looked at Made from head to toe with a provocative smile on her face.

Made was perturbed by all of these odd smirks and stares. She felt like she was in another world, one in which she was a stranger and where she possibly didn't belong. But why shouldn't she come here? Didn't these rooms and everything in them belong to her brother? But why did he keep saying: my sister, my sister. As if the whole world needed to know... Let them know! It was nice that he did, but he said it almost as if no one would believe him - as if someone would argue with him about it. Made was mystified.

"You see over there - that one..." Sveilis leaned in closer and nodded in the direction of the young lady in the red hat. "She's supposed to be or have been an actress or something." He laughed unpleasantly. "I don't know what she's starred in, or when! She's here almost every night. Around here they call her Little Flame. And she looks like one too, don't you think?"

Made studied the bizarre woman carefully.

"Here every night? Why would she do that?"

Sveilis grimaced slightly and bit at his lip.

"She drinks and has fun... You don't really know much about city life, do you? Crazy things happen here sometimes..." He reached across the table and nudged Made in her side. "Look, look," he whispered excitedly. All of the hardness that had been in his face a moment ago was gone now.

The young lady with the red hat slowly got up from her table. And only when she was standing and had turned against the light was it possible to view her large, full figure and beautiful pale face. Her black dress gently swished as she moved, her dark hair flowed out from one side of her hat and over her ear, coiling around the precious stone in her earring. Her ample bosom accentuated by her corset pushed out her black blouse decorated with sequins, the gleam of her pale skin visible through thick black lace and her low neck line. Her arm – bare up to the elbow – was holding up her skirt indiscreetly but her face had a serious and respectable look. While she was passing Sveilis, she gave him a haughty nod, her lips produced a suppressed smile and her eyelids narrowed mischievously. She didn't look in either direction as she walked around the table, moving both grandly and gracefully towards the doors to the street. Her silk clothes swished and her narrow heels clicked across the floor, while guests and waiters, men and women followed her with their eyes. The two ladies at the long table brought their heads together to whisper, smirk and also observe their husbands' behaviour. Both men had stopped looking at Little Flame; Berķis was lining up the herring heads on his plate and Sietiņsons coughed and adopted a stern expression on his red face as he struck a match and lit his already smoking cigar.

 Made was also captivated by the way this beautiful woman walked out of the room. Her body and gait clearly revealed what she herself was lacking. She was stung by jealousy or something resembling it. She looked back at her brother. As always in such moments which she always found difficult to define, his soft lips were open, his white though noticeably decaying teeth visible behind them and the ends of his long, light-coloured moustaches sagging. When his eyes squinted, they formed a web of tiny wrinkles on each side of them. There was a strange glow across his face – maybe it came from some hidden smile, restrained laughter or secret delight... Maybe it was all of that together, and yet something else was there. All men nowadays seemed to have this look in given situations. In some of them this was almost attractive – delight seemed to radiate from their faces and across their entire bodies. But on her brother...no... She couldn't yet understand it, but she knew she didn't want him to look that way. She poked his arm casually, gestured with her eyes and gave a slight nod towards a young man in uniform who was sitting at another table close-by drinking tea and reading the newspaper.

Sveilis awoke from his dream – it seemed to Made that he was just about to rub his eyes as if he had to force his gaze away from the door.

"Him? I don't know." He shrugged his shoulders. "I can't keep track of them all ... Just some kind of clerk. Must be from the State Bank or Treasury."

Made stared at the clerk from the State Bank or Treasury. A nice-looking man – short, black hair, a black moustache and a sincere look in his eyes. His uniform looked so pretty with its green stripes! As she looked at him, he pulled his coat up higher and extended his leg so that the buttons on his new boots shined in the lamp light.

"And that bald one over there," Sveilis nodded off to the side in the direction from which Little Flame had come. "He used to have two houses – inherited them from his father and aunt. He sold them and has squandered it all. All day long he just drifts from one tavern to another. There are rumours that some old widow is supporting him." Sveilis shifted in his seat. "Spends all day long in restaurants, treating musicians – that's his specialty. He spends his last kopeck on liquor and women. That Little Flame..." He caught himself, forgetting for an instant who he was speaking with. He hurriedly moved the conversation on to something else. "Fricis, that's what they call him..."

Made had never heard the language of the taverns before, nor had she ever paid close attention to the voice of a professional carouser – the voice that her brother was beginning to adopt. She gazed over with wide eyes at the young, slightly heavyset man with the flax white hair and yellow fluff over his upper lip. He came out from the buffet, looked around and saw them, hunched his shoulders, and walked over.

"Yesterday that student didn't pay again..." he started telling

Sveilis, still a fair distance away. Made pretended not to notice him.

"Which student?"

"You know the one..." The young man scratched his side. "I forget his name... They call him Rodolfs."

Sveilis furrowed his brow in a lordly manner.

"So, you're saying it's young Lodziņš? Mr. Lodziņš?"

"Yes, Mr. Lodziņš. He was playing last night until half past eleven, but didn't pay up."

"He wasn't alone then?"

"No, but the others did pay when they left. He just kept saying: I'm not paying tonight as I need the money for other things."

Sveilis nodded. "This fellow... Well, what did he end up owing us?"

The young man pulled out a crumpled and stained sheet of paper from his waistcoat pocket. He unfolded it and pushed it close up to his eyes.

"For four hours – it was four roubles. And thirty for the carafe, three pickles – that's nine kopecks, and six bottles of beer – that's seventy-two – altogether it was five roubles eleven... oh, yes! And then he broke a glass," he took a gnawed segment of pencil and hastily scribbled, "that's ten kopecks extra... So then it's five roubles twenty-one... I don't have any money, he said, I'm not paying. Send the bill to my old man, I'm his heir..."

Sveilis shrugged his shoulders.

"What a fellow... To his old man! Well, there'll be another scandal there then..." He thought about it for a moment, then pulled out his wallet. He handed the young man two three-rouble coins. "Pay at the buffet." He saw that the man was reaching around in his pockets looking for change. "No need, no need."

He thanked him, glanced at Made whose gaze he had avoided the entire time and returned to the buffet, navigating his way through the tables with some difficulty.

"Isn't that Andrejs Skrastiņš?" Made asked.

"What?" Sveilis was watching Little Flame as she walked back and had barely heard Made. "Yes. Skrastiņš. I brought them with me. A high-quality restaurant can't make it anymore without music. I really need to have this wall removed to enlarge the space...But in the end I needed a ladies' orchestra. And then I didn't know what to do with these musicians. I put the old one at Lodziņš's Savings and Loans as a security guard, and the young one over there by the billiard table. But he's completely good for nothing. Sluggish as a bear."

Made was listening with glee. Andrejs Skrastiņš... Back then – back there...he'd believed all kinds of nonsense, acted so high and mighty, sneered at everything she did and then just left her. Ha! Go ahead – stand by your billiard table, add up each game, bring everyone carafes and pickles, wipe spilt drinks off the tables and know who you are. You're a servant. Never forget that! And that's what you deserve, nothing more!

She was so carried away by her thoughts that she didn't even notice the waiter carrying a bottle in a bucket wrapped in white cloth high over his head over to Little Flame's table. She didn't notice that everyone was looking over there again – some with hidden jealousy and others with affected irony. Little Flame became livelier, more animated and more talkative. She was resting her breasts on top her arms on the edge of the table, putting her head close to Fricis's and whispering something to him secretively, but then she leaned back and turned towards her other admirers, laughing so loudly that her earrings rattled as she shook. Then she refilled her glass. Fricis just watched and used his left hand to toy with his whiskers. There was an innocence to his gaze, his thin, blond whiskers and the bashful way he fiddled with them, which contrasted with the clear signs of debauchery and corruption engraved on his face that had aged before its time.

A new guest approached the Sveilises' table: a red-faced man with a thick, extremely well-groomed beard with tiny wavelets combed into it, narrow kind eyes, and a drooping sportsman's cap that he had pulled down nearly all the way over them. Mr. Paeglītis... He squeezed Made's hand perfunctorily and sat down heavily between sister and brother. Made indignantly pulled her legs and dress in closer to herself. She no longer had full view of the smoke-filled room, which had continued to gradually fill with more and more guests. The end of the buffet was no longer visible at all behind the constantly mutating group of drinkers standing around it. With every passing minute the noise became louder and more disorderly.

"Well, well, how's it going with that cheese?" Sveilis asked with inoffensive irony, then motioned with his finger. "Pauls – two glasses!"

Paeglītis supported his head on his hand, having almost completely turned his back to Made, whilst looking over indifferently at Little Flame's companions.

"Can't complain..." He spoke in a small, sweet voice. "I sold the whole lot today for thirty roubles."

"Oh really?" Sveilis seemed surprised, but his voice betrayed how little he cared about Paeglītis's cheese and his thirty roubles. "So you made fifteen roubles in profit?"

Paeglītis muttered something, rolled his shoulders back, and looked at Made. She was looking over his shoulder, trying to act like she wasn't listening.

"You need a bigger operation..." Sveilis spoke, searching for the right words. "There's only so much you can do at that Daugava Market... or any market for that matter..." He shrugged his shoulders, but sustained his air of condescending amusement.

"That's not necessarily true..." Paeglītis's tone showed that he didn't think much of Sveilis's practical knowledge. "Business is a sure thing at the market. It's not too often that there's...well –" He couldn't remember the proper word and tapped his fingers on the table. "A crisis – so to speak... As long as there are people in the city, they need to eat. And as long as they need to eat, we've got business." He coughed and looked back at Made, but she pretended to not hear or be listening.

"A bigger operation would be great – sure... But when you've got no credit... They won't give me a loan based on the house. It's impossible to get a loan for a completely secure bond... You can't get fifteen hundred for that..." He shrugged his shoulders and grimaced in disgust.

"I was talking to Lodziņš." Sveilis spoke slowly, then noticed the waiter near them again. "Pauls!" He beckoned.

"And?" Paeglītis began to listen more closely.

"Well, he's neither here nor there. But Bramberģis, he's against it."

"Against it!" Paeglītis became more animated. "Against a completely secure bond! But that's not the case. Bramberģis wouldn't be against it. But Sausums!"

"Oh, because of that same auditor?"

"Of course! He was so ambitious, and obviously it's not far to go from auditor to director. And I'm supposedly responsible too. I'm the one responsible for getting Tilaks elected. I too was lobbying on his behalf. And that's why he's whispering all this nonsense in Bramberģis's ear."

"Could be, could be. How do you think they accomplish that?"

Paeglītis was deep in thought and didn't hear him. He only caught what he was saying when Sveilis asked again.

"What? They don't do it themselves; their wives do – or their sisters' daughters or something like that." Just then something occurred to him. His narrow little eyes squinted even more. He leaned even closer to Sveilis. "Do you know the joke about Mrs. Sausums?"

"Yes... no..." Sveilis knew it, but wanted to hear it again. He leaned in towards Paeglītis, his whole face radiating restrained glee.

"The one where he's thrown her out into the corridor without her dress on." He was moving around this way and that and making all kinds of mysterious gestures. But there was no need to understand them. This joke had been told dozens of times and was known to everybody. Looking into each other's eyes, they both began to sway holding back their laughter and smacking their lips affectionately with delight.

Sveilis stopped first: Made began to listen more closely. He leaned back, coughed, and began speaking in a raised voice.

"A schemer – a terrible schemer. I only just learnt that he'd also lobbied against me. Incredibly amicable to your face, but behind your back... If Lodziņš hadn't been firmly on my side..."

"Well," Paeglītis dismissed him with a wave of his hand, "you're safe. You had so much cash from the start. Deposits in all the banks on current accounts... People trust you. But a person who has his own respectable store and a completely secure bond – he can't get a damn thing!"

Sveilis listened carefully, and his face took on an expression of unmistakable delight. He was wealthy and had won the trust of the bank, while this man was burdened by his needs and unable to get what Sveilis took for granted.

Someone else approached, interrupting Paeglītis's complaints. A respectable, grey-haired gentleman with a short, well-trimmed beard, gold spectacles, and an incredibly stiff expression. His body and movements signalled that he had an inflexible and uncompromising character. Sveilis swiftly rose to his feet and stepped in his direction.

"Mr. Lodziņš... My sister."

Made also scrambled to her feet. She understood right away who this Mr. Lodziņš was.

"Charmed, charmed." Lodziņš squeezed Made's hand and tried to smile, but it stopped half-way and faded. The trimmed bristles of his beard looked sharp and stubby. "So, we're neighbours now," he said as he sat down. Made smiled and nodded in reply. "My wife sent up some flowers for your..." For a moment he stared intently at the edge of the table. "I hear you'll be running your brother's household. Well, keep a good handle on him. Otherwise these old boys tend to run riot."

Made didn't really understand. She tried with all her might to force herself to think, but couldn't find any words. She felt ashamed and angry with herself. She nodded again, but her eyes were filled with tears.

Sveilis and Paeglītis laughed obligingly, Sveilis especially loudly.

"Glass of beer? Or maybe a vodka?" Sveilis asked as he stood leaning across the table.

Lodziņš, who was still staring at the edge of the table, shook his head.

"I've had enough for today. I'll have some tea." He beckoned. "Pauls! A cup of tea! With cream!"

"With cream!" Sveilis repeated his words and nodded at the waiter.

"Cheers, Sveilis! Cheers, gentlemen!" Sietiņsons bellowed as he turned around to look at them, his chest resting on the back of the chair, raising his glass. The women on his table had already stood up. They looked irritated as they tugged at the boas around their necks.

"Cheers, cheers!" Sveilis lifted his beer glass just a little bit. Then added in a whisper, "He's in a mood again."

"How do things stand with my business matter, Mr. Lodziņš?" Paeglītis leaned in towards Lodziņš, who was frowning as he stared at the edge of the table. He shrugged his shoulders.

"I don't have any objections, but my two colleagues aren't willing to go along with it."

In an instant, Paeglītis had become animated and began to fidget.

"I know, I know, it's Mr. Bramberģis!"

"It's both of them. Strauss too." Lodziņš lifted his finger haughtily: "Where's that house of yours – is it close to where he lives? Yes – then he knows the circumstances. Two and a half thousand still on the mortgage... For a little old wooden house... It's not ideal."

Paeglītis had turned dark red.

"I promise you, Mr. Lodziņš: that place has a future. If they clean up that bit of land jutting out into the Daugava, so that ships can stop, then coal storage sheds could be built there, and that would increase its value greatly. Just this year alone the prices for lots there have risen – ten roubles a fathom. I could sell it – I'm being promised ten thousand – but I don't want to: in five, six years, I'll get twenty. That place has a future! Next year the new bridge will be ready..."

"We-e-ell," Lodziņš said in a low voice, "what good is it to you?" Paeglītis was unrecognisable, he had become so red and agitated.

"That place has a future! Just the other week there was an article in Dzimtenes Vēstnesis about it. Did you not see it? You can't get fifteen hundred for a property like that! It's a joke! You don't hear about things like that happening with the Germans. But we don't know how to defend each other. A Latvian would rather push another Latvian down than help him up. It's just endless jealousy and intrigues with us...That place has a future!"

"My dear Mr. Paeglītis," Lodziņš's voice sounded as shrill as a spoon striking the edge of a glass, "My dear Mr. Paeglītis, we can't loan money based on what will be. We can only look at what is. Think about it: an old wooden cottage with twenty-five hundred still owed on the mortgage..."

"But that's exactly the problem!" Paeglītis interrupted him. "A Latvian doesn't want to look towards the future – a Latvian doesn't want to take a risk and doesn't know how to gauge the value of something. That's the reason why our industry and businesses can't develop. When someone spends a kopeck today, they expect it back tomorrow."

"My dear Mr. Paeglītis," Lodziņš's voice had become even sterner. "We have to think about every single kopeck. It's not our own money that we're dealing with: it belongs to the people. It has been scraped together by simple folk, and we're just the administrators. We're accountable for every single kopeck."

Paeglītis was clenching his beer glass with both hands. "Oh please, spare me your words, Mr. Lodziņš. I've seen your accounts. When you want to do something, you can do it, but when you don't, it's just endless excuses."

Lodziņš looked offended and coughed dryly. "We'll put it before the board and let them decide."

"The board, the board!" Paeglītis angrily waved him off. "Has the board ever decided anything other than what's put in front of them? Is it any secret what that board is! It's Bramberģis's and Sausums's colluding, nothing more. Don't try and blow smoke in my eyes."

Sveilis sensed that the argument was getting too heated. "Pauls, two more! Come on, Made, drink up your wine!"

Sietiņsons's company dramatically bid their farewells around the table. At first it wasn't clear what was going on in all the confusion: hands were extended, goodbyes said, regrets expressed and laughter echoed around the room. Sveilis and Lodziņš had moved closer together and were quietly speaking to each other as they looked back at the people who were leaving.

"...yes, brought along all the way to the seashore. Wined and dined for two days... But no idea how they ran into Mrs. Berķis. Just as she opened the door, that lively young girl was right there. What's her business there? The lady isn't at home; sir has gone off to the station. And she, who is she? She's the maid. From the countryside. Well, Mrs. Berķis isn't dumb, she sees what's going on right away. And so all summer long the whole seashore is laughing about that maid from the country..."

"So crafty though, who would've thought it!" Sveilis wondered loudly.

Made didn't hear and wasn't listening. Her attention was occupied by something else, a pair that had just entered – a man and woman. The man was about fifty and had clearly enjoyed his life so far: he had a slender frame, a short, cropped moustache and a painfully deep furrow across his forehead. The woman was young with false teeth, slightly sunken eyes, an attractive face and awkward movements. All the men standing nearby stared at her and she looked right back at them without a hint of shyness. Her escort didn't seem nearly as interesting to her as he did to everyone else, but she was soon occupied with other matters. The waiter brought her the roast suckling pig with cabbage and she began to eat it greedily. She would eat, nudge her escort and then swiftly throw back the contents of her small, grooved glass. Her escort seemed completely oblivious and didn't pay the slightest bit of attention to the looks, whispers and gestures coming from those around them.

Made looked at them both, but saw an entirely different world. The restaurant continued to fill with newcomers. There was no longer a single unoccupied table in sight. The noise grew louder and the blue smoke grew thicker. The room thundered like a giant, bubbling kettle. Money continued to jingle at the buffet. Invisible fumes of alcohol circulated round the heads of those who were seated and tickled their noses, befuddling those unaccustomed to breathing them in.

Maybe it was through this haze of alcohol that Made saw a completely new world. There was no work, no want, no worry here – only never-ending freedom and pleasure. Where was all this gold raining down from, the gold that constantly jingled on the buffet and in the waiters' pockets? There must have been someone somewhere doing something to earn it so that they could pay for these glittering earrings and all that swishing silk, which so gently caressed the supple, electrifying bodies of the women she was watching. Somewhere, in some other, distant, and forgotten world... but not here in this world of only freedom, desire and delight.

How fiery were the men's stares! Little Flame's head had almost completely collapsed onto her breasts, which were still resting on her arms. Fricis had placed his left hand on the back of her chair, almost embracing her, his mouth right up to her ear. The other two didn't take their eyes off of her either. They spoke quietly, but the whole time something barely hidden under the surface flickered in their eyes and every few moments their faces would contort strangely as they held back their laughter.

Those twisted faces were repulsive, the sudden yells seemed disgusting. Made turned away and looked again at the slender escort and his young lady. They weren't looking at each other. She had a withdrawn and unpleasant expression on her face as she ate, and he made sure her glass was never empty, even for an instant. He'd lean over and speak to her, then call the waiter over. New items kept appearing on their little table. When there was no more room, the waiter took away the excess. But the empty space would soon fill up again. The young lady leaned back in her chair and crossed one leg over the other. Her eyes had glazed over. She looked around, but didn't notice anyone in particular. Her escort least of all. But he kept rushing to fill her glass as soon as it was empty and beckoning the waiter. There seemed to be no end to this cycle of summoning the waiter, and then feeding this woman and pouring drinks down her neck.

A group of young men hunkered down around the table which had become free after the earlier group left. Some were in uniform, some in civilian clothes. Some were bold and some reserved, but all of their faces showed signs of too much high living too early in life. Premature fatigue, and behind that an insolence and unquenchable desire... At first, their heads pressed together, they whispered to each other and smiled maliciously. Gradually they grew rowdier and more bad-mannered. Turning towards the woman, their hands stuck in their pockets and their legs extended in her direction, they would cough and jostle each other. They would punch each other in the ribs, while winking and gossiping with each other.

Her slender companion seemed not to see or hear them. His pale face remained as indifferent and calm as ever. From time to time the woman would look over at the boys, but she didn't seem to detect their winking and smirking. Her glassy eyes remained just as slow and lifeless as before. Only her cheeks seemed to get rosier and the blue around her eyes became less noticeable – her entire face seemed younger and fresher. Though her smile stayed just the same, frozen as if she'd pulled a mask over her face.

She drank unhurriedly but almost without stopping, one glass after another. Her body began to sway from one side to the other. She tried to find the back of her chair or the edge of the table with her elbow to support herself. But she missed – her elbow slid past and her body collapsed sideways. Her grey blouse crumpled into tiny creases along her hunched sides, and her corset crackled as it bent. Then, just below her neck, her top button snapped open and the triangle of pale flesh grew larger until the edge of a white lace shirt appeared at its lower point. It was obvious that she was drunk. But in her stupor, she must have thought that it was still possible to put on a show and hide it somehow. She pretended that she'd intended to bend over like that by pulling up her sleeves, lowering her eyes, biting her lower lip and attempting to tie her boot laces. The white laces flickered in between clumsy, grasping fingers. Above, the white of her shapely slender legs shimmered through a patterned strip of her sheer black stockings. Then with a purposeful motion she sat up again, placing her arms in an arc behind her head as she leaned back in her chair, crossed one leg over the other and looked provocatively at the group of youths. Her glassy eyes were suddenly aflame. Sparse, white teeth shone in between her moist half-open lips. Then she got up with surprising steadiness and strode out of the building.

Made turned her gaze towards the long table and recoiled. It was as if a firework had suddenly hit all of them. Frozen smiles... expressionless eyes... tottering bodies whose movements were unpredictable. One of them had his glass half raised, while another had his mouth hanging open, and Made thought she could see moisture beginning to trickle from a corner of his mouth down across his chin.

It felt like a burning hot hand had moved across Made's body. It was so repulsive that it made her want to jump up and spit in all of their stupid faces. She wanted to push away that hot, shameless hand; she wanted to bite it. But at the same time a strange kind of pleasure seemed to come with it... to lean back, to trust it... to let it caress her, to let it burn like hot water being poured over her!

Wrenching herself away from her very self, she got up. She couldn't see or sense anything anymore through the thick haze of tobacco smoke and alcohol fumes. She couldn't hear anything over the racket of the teeming mass of people in this overfilled room. Her head was nothing but noise, fog and dizziness. An unfamiliar heaviness seemed to press down on her body, and her senses felt like they were strangely enflamed.

"Do you want to leave already?" She heard her brother's voice as if from a distance. Through the smoke she could see the kind faces of those sitting near her.

All three men came to see her out. More due to inertia than seeing or sensing her way, she navigated the narrow, winding path between the tables. She saw, but didn't fully comprehend that pressing past them just past the door were the table of revellers from the seashore who'd now returned.

"Back again?" Sveilis clapped his hands and laughed loudly.

"We missed the train! We missed the train!" Sietiņsons and Berķis yelled back, together with all the younger members of their party. Berķis pushed out in front and continued on his own. "We left the ladies at the station to wait for the next one..." He pulled out his watch. "Two and a half hours! What's the point in waiting around there? So we said, let's go back. Makes more sense to have another glass and talk a bit of sense."

"Well, let the ladies go," Paeglītis said seriously. "All of you can take the night train later. As it is, you won't get anything else done today."

"Now that's what I call a sensible thing to say!" Sietiņsons yelled as he took Sveilis by the arm. There was such warmth and overwhelming enthusiasm in his voice, his face and every one of his movements.

"I ended up having to waste half the day at the insurance company. We had a board meeting at the savings bank today... And yet a man shouldn't be just a beast of burden ..."

One after the other they took each other by the arm, jostled and slapped each other on the back, and then walked back into the room talking and laughing.

The long table was now surrounded by youths, and there was no longer enough room for all of them at Sveilis's table. One of Little Flame's companions suggested putting both tables together so that everybody could sit around a single table. Everybody was delighted and agreed. Those who didn't know each other yet quickly introduced themselves, while they waited for the waiters to put both tables together and cover them with tablecloths.

Sveilis, as the man of the house, sat down at the end of the table with Fricis on his right corner and Little Flame on his left. When he stretched his legs, they hit Little Flame's. When he reached for the matches, his hand brushed against the silk of her sleeve. When he leaned forward, he felt her breath on his face while the softness of her hair caressed his forehead – and he could feel her warmth and the strong aroma of Reseda perfume.

"Pauls!" Sveilis yelled, looking rosy and animated. "Bring us another half bottle – no, bring a whole bottle of Curaçao! Or do you gentlemen want Chartreuse instead? No? Well then – one bottle of Curaçao! And do you have any apple cake? You do?"

"It's too early!" Berķis said as he coughed and wiped his sweaty face with his handkerchief. "I want to drink more liquor. Over here! One carafe – a small carafe – of that dry wine with a little mixer – you know the one, right? And caviar! You have caviar – red caviar? I don't want the black stuff. Yes? Good!"

"I'll join you on the liquor," Lodziņš said as he carefully tucked his napkin into the opening of his waistcoat. "And what do you have over there?"

The waiter leaned down obligingly.

"Fresh pork ribs – perhaps the gentleman would like some?"

"Ribs?" Lodziņš became livelier – to the point where he was almost smiling. "But are they really fresh? Yes? Then bring me some – that's fine for now. And also give me the menu. What do you have for lunch today?"

"Roast goose... Veal cutlet with peas... Beef stroganoff... Ham with asparagus... Fried salmon... Fried pike..."

"Uh huh. Give me the menu."

"Over here! Ten glasses of beer – God damn it!" yelled one of the younger men from the seaside as he slammed his fist on the table.

Blue tobacco smoke and alcohol fumes mingled from floor to ceiling. Hunched, red-faced, animated men sat around tables covered with white tablecloths and spilt their drinks. Someone was calling out for food or drink almost all the time. The knocking of billiard balls and raucous shouts from the players could be heard through the crush of people crowding around the buffet. And the constant jingle of money on the marble table and in the waiters' pockets competed with the money accidentally dropped on the floor where it rolled aimlessly.

Made hadn't quite come back to her senses when the driver stopped at the Lodziņš building. She sat and stared blankly at its windows, as if she had returned from another world. But when the usual doorman appeared, she used all her strength to pull herself together and put on an air of distinction as she climbed down from the carriage.

Walking up the steps, her legs felt heavy, her whole body was tingling as if it had fallen asleep and was refusing to obey her, as if it wasn't really hers. But her head was clear. So, at least she wasn't drunk and dizzy. Tiny shivers ran through her as she thought – what if she was like that woman in grey back at the hotel.

The higher she climbed, the emptier and clearer her head

became. As if it were tearing itself away from her torso, it felt like it wanted to lift itself up into the air. It was devoid of all thoughts: she no longer had any sense of time or place, and she didn't know if she still had far to climb or where she had to stop. Then she found herself at her apartment door. She stood there for a moment before pressing the bell, and it felt to her as if she had to wait a long, long time before her mother opened the door.

Her mother opened it and immediately shoved it closed again. If Made hadn't grabbed the handle, she would've locked it too.

"Let me in!" Made wanted to call out angrily – but there was no anger in her voice which sounded weak as it echoed through the winding stairwell.

In spite of the unfamiliar voice and the equally unfamiliar clothing, her mother eventually understood that it was her daughter. She opened the door and began to make excuses for the misunderstanding. She let her daughter in and followed from behind, clasping her hands in astonishment and shaking her head.

"Oh, my child! Why have you done this?" She felt that she wasn't permitted to enter her daughter's room, so she stood in the doorway.

Made walked over and looked in the mirror, but it was obscured by a bluish haze and showed nothing. Even if it had showed something, it would have been so alien, so incomprehensible, that there was no point in even looking, let alone thinking about it.

"Oh, my child, my child!" her mother kept say and shaking her head in sorrow.

Standing exhausted in the middle of the room, Made turned towards the door and looked at her. Her mother... yes, it must have been her mother. But why was she standing there and shaking her head so sorrowfully? What was she saying? Was any of this her business? She wasn't from that world which Made had just passed into. Her mother reminded

Made of something old, long forgotten and repulsive. But Made didn't feel angry now, and she turned away with only a hint of revulsion on her face.

"Oh, my child..." her mother sighed, as tears started to run down her face, and she turned around to slowly walk away.

Made locked the door as though she were afraid of something unknown. She stiffly removed her hat and took off her fancy clothes. And with every article of clothing she removed, her body felt lighter and her head felt heavier.

It was only when she was finally standing by her bed in her old, worn underclothes and felt the coolness of the room on her bare, bony hands, that she suddenly remembered everything. In haunting detail, she recalled all of the experiences of this afternoon. It all spun around in her brain like a confusion of restless birds, as she couldn't clearly pick out any particular moment and she also wasn't able to comprehend what had happened as a whole. The haze enveloped her head, her eyes were dazzled by the glow of the electric lights reflecting off her earrings, the chatter of drunken men droned in her ears and cutting through it all was the unforgettable sound of that metallic jingle... Pulled down by her own weight, she fell head first onto her soft bed and lay there half-unconscious. She moved her legs into a more comfortable position and turned face down, after which she didn't move again.

It was only in bed that she realised she had a terrible headache. It was similar to the old pain she would get when she was washing her second or third tub of laundry. And yet it wasn't the same. Back then, she'd been kept awake by the waves of stabbing pain and she'd seen visions of the most recent episodes she'd been forced to endure as part of her dismal, poverty-stricken life. Her entire life appeared to be submerged in darkness: no joy in her past, no hope in her future. She would have been overcome by so much despair that it would have made her want to die – in fact she had wanted to die so very much... to fall asleep and never feel that pain again, to never again be forced to watch how the grey light illuminated their fogged-up window every morning. But now her impressions of this first afternoon shimmered in an incomprehensible jumble. It wasn't possible to understand it, nor did she want to. It just kept growing and spreading inside her head, choking her brain and splashing up against the inside of her skull with a continuous humming sound. But there was no despair, no wish to die and no blinding pain. It was like a distant golden glow rising up through a rustling pine forest, fresh from a recent shower of rain – beyond the numbness there appeared to be a pleasant sensation.

At some stage she fell into a deep sleep. How long she slept, she didn't know. But when she awoke, her headache was gone. It was cooler but she didn't feel like covering herself. She didn't want to move but only to think and think again. In her first moment of awareness an unfinished thought was already flitting around deep within her consciousness. She had within her as many old thoughts as new ones she'd just acquired. She had as many expectations of enjoyments to come and as she had memories of enjoyments already experienced. Her headache seemed to have further defined the nature of her senses and sharpened them. A wave of elation had been gently flowing through since the moment she awoke and it was growing stronger in the absence of any release.

With this ever-amplifying joy coursing through her, Made turned and opened her eyes. As she did, a warm calm wave of light flowed into them. In the ceiling decorations there were giant flowers she had never seen before blossoming quietly, and silvery stems head been woven into garlands. Blushing vines bent at the corners and stretched from the ceiling across the wall – probably as far as the wallpaper or the wall-hanging, which touched her bare elbow softly.

Made laughed to herself quietly. All of that afternoon's experiences lit up in her memory like a flock of white birds flapping their wings as they passed over a high wall. She would now have to live in that alien, bright, noisy, repellent yet enticing world whose gravitational pull made her feel like a moth staring into lamplight.

She rolled over onto her side. Something as gentle and soft as a large snowflake dropped down onto her cheek and partially covered her eye. Made was caught off guard and for a moment she looked out in a cloud of incomprehension. And when she sighed, she felt the breeze on her ears.

Then it came back to her and she understood. She couldn't lie there any longer. She sat up barely restraining herself from shouting for joy.

Yes, the sleeve of the blouse thrown onto the end of the bed had slid down onto her face. The ruffles of her delicate, brand-new blouse had collapsed onto the pillow and were glistening as they shivered slightly, as if someone were moving them on purpose. Or perhaps they were cold too and yearned for a warm body to embrace?

Made chuckled quietly. She lifted the beautiful piece of clothing. It was puffy, but light as a feather. Right there at the end of the bed was her skirt, and her rose-coloured petticoat, rustling musically, with a triple pleat along its bottom edge. Made got dressed slowly and she handled each piece of clothing lovingly, running her hand over every pleat. Her chapped fingers scratched and caught on the silk fabric, and she had to be careful to avoid damaging it.

It was difficult to be careful. Her both innate and instilled female passion for expensive possessions burnt brightly within her. She wanted to keep looking, to press it up to her cheek and kiss it. She was afraid to put it on and wrinkle it, but her desire didn't relent. Her trembling fingers couldn't find the small loops and buttons amongst the pleats and ruffles. A warm breeze billowed through the clothing and hit her in the face.

The table and chair groaned under the weight of the packages containing her purchases. Much as she tried, Made couldn't resist and began opening them. The strings binding the packages snapped open – the thicker ones cut painfully into her finger and she had to use her teeth. The grey and yellow crumpled papers collected in a pile on the floor. The table and chair and wherever there was free space was soon covered in colourful clothing, shoes and accessories, as well as various shining trinkets. The more items appeared, the more she wanted. One could never have too much opulence and glitter; one could never have enough... With feverish, burning eyes and her face twisted into a crazed grin, Made snatched each package, unwrapped it, bundled it back up, and then grabbed for the next one.

She unwrapped the package with socks and fell back onto her bed. She tore off the harsh, red-striped socks her mother had knitted and threw them across the room. She hated the rough, colourless wool and the old-fashioned stripes. The store-bought socks were soft and embraced her foot so gently and it was like being caressed by a soft hand, like a warm breath blowing directly onto her foot. And then there were the white shoes decorated with pearls! They were so narrow and light and with such fine heels, and so beautiful that they should have been placed on display rather than worn. They pinched. They felt narrow on her feet, which had swelled in those battered old shoes of hers. But she would get used to them. She had to get used to them! Made walked with tiny, timid steps. How oddly her heels clicked and slid across the parquet floor – she had to steady herself so she wouldn't fall. Her foot slipped forward into the narrow front of her shoe – her whole body felt like it was lifted up and stooped forward. But she had to get used to it! She had to! Lifted up by the pure joy of it all, Made moved around the room as she tried out her new shoes.

It was night. Everyone was asleep. It might have been nearly dawn. But what did she care! She saw the hat thrown down on the chair – she grabbed it and tried it on. It was too big: her head and her whole body sagged to one side. But she had to get used to it! Made walked up to the gold-rimmed oval mirror.

She stood and stared. She stared and couldn't believe what she saw, it took her breath away. Was that really her? Her gaunt face with its flushed cheeks and radiant eyes stared back at her from underneath the giant hat decorated with ostrich feathers. Was that her face? Was she really strangely beautiful? She smiled, intoxicated with delight, and only then did she recognise herself by the darkened front tooth appearing from behind her lips. But even that black tooth no longer seemed as ugly and repulsive as it had been before. All of the surrounding splendour cast a radiance over that too. It seemed to disappear, to hide and not to be the first thing that caught a person's eye. Once again she felt like she was at the start of a smooth, straight, endless path. She only had to lift and wave her arms, and she would fly up into the air with the gracefulness and spontaneity of a bird, leaving everyone looking on from below with their heads spinning. And in that moment she actually did lift up her arms and begin to move them up and down. The ruffles of her blouse billowed at the seams and the mirror seemed to light up with a rose-tinted fog. Made laughed but caught herself: it wasn't proper to fool around like that. She turned towards the table and noticed her jewellery. The medallion... the bracelet... the watch decorated with blue stones... The purse tossed on the corner of the table with its shimmering black sequins... She walked over, put it all on, walked back and stood adoring her own reflection for a long time.

She looked at herself from every direction. Gradually she grew used to her appearance and then was able to look a bit more critically. And then she understood that her jacket had not been the best possible selection. Her slender body required a somewhat heavier and darker coloured material... Her strenuous life had caused her breasts to sag too soon and so the area of her blouse intended to highlight her bosom instead showed an unattractive hollow... She grew more serious and began to undress. Slowly, she took off each piece of clothing one after another, and carefully put them down.

Suddenly, the bell rang. Quickly and unevenly, as if someone had pressed it in jest as they walked by. Could it have been for a different apartment? Made listened. No – she could hear someone rummaging around and, it seemed, talking outside the front door. She thought she recognised this voice and went to open the door.

She kept the chain on and opened the door only a crack through which she immediately saw Augusts. He was fumbling around with an electric torch, but every few moments his finger would slip off the button. Then he would fidget and mutter in the darkness and tut-tut angrily.

"What's going on, why won't anyone let me in!" he tried to yell while slurring his words. A spray of saliva stinking of alcohol covered Made's face. "How long am I supposed to stand around out here!"

This wasn't the kind, smiling brother she knew, but a completely unfamiliar person who was incredibly drunk. Made quickly threw open the door and helped her brother in.

"I didn't hear at first," she explained as she made sure he didn't trample her white shoes.

"Dammit! What are you all sleeping for..." He wasn't angry anymore. He was laughing like a drunk and sagging over onto Made with all his weight. "Damn... help me get over there. Support me a bit..." He seemed to be caught between laughing and singing.

"Not so loud." Made shushed him as she shoved him along, pushing him from behind. She was worried that one of the other members of the household would wake up and see her brother in this state. "Everyone's asleep..."

"Asleep? What are they all asleep for? Isn't it morning already? Why aren't they waking up? Can't they be awake at the same time as me for even a single hour?"

He reached with a slackened fist for the door of the salon, but Made quickly pulled him on and pushed him into his bedroom. She could hear him in the dark falling down with a heavy thud. Made quietly and carefully reopened the door and then found the button for the electric light by the door.

Sveilis had fallen back onto the chair at the end of the bed. Made looked at her brother with increasing disgust.

No, this wasn't her wealthy, kind brother anymore, but a complete stranger. Fallen down on the chair with his hat, coat and galoshes still on. His coat had flapped open and underneath it his clothes were hanging out sloppily. One of his boots heaved over onto one of his trouser legs, his galoshes dirty from trampling through the dirty street. His hat had slipped down over his eyes, his moustache was wet and was drooping down unattractively – his entire face was pale and delirious. His body slumped, as if he had no spine or muscle. He sagged sideways and his hands groped feebly around the edge of the chair as if searching for support.

A sudden feeling of pity overwhelmed Made's disgust. Poor thing! They tricked him and got him drunk without him realising it. He's been a bit slow in matters like these since the very beginning. Those bastards! They did this to her brother!

"I'll help you undress..."

"You..." Sveilis lifted his bloodshot eyes. "Help me? I... don't need any help... Fine then, go ahead... I want to sleep..." He extended his leg towards her and tried to start humming some melody.

Made pulled off his galoshes and untied his boot laces, which wasn't so easy to do. The drunk couldn't sit still for even an instant. And when Made tried to calm him down, he started to stagger on purpose and drag his feet along the floor. He laughed stupidly.

Though exhausted, Made tended to his needs. She took off his coat and jacket, pulled off his undershirt. The thought of taking the rest of it off disgusted her – and it probably wouldn't be possible anyway.

"Go ahead and get in bed – go on now!" She took him by the arm and led him over to the bed, then added accusingly, "Why on earth do you have to drink so much. You'll be making a fine impression!"

Sveilis laughed as he hiccupped. "Those fellows from the seaside... Sons of bitches, God damn them! Champagne... Bénédictine with coffee – an ocean of it. Just get in and swim around..." Somehow he'd ended up at the foot of the bed and it was all Made could do to shift him. "Both of them were just on fire for that Little Flame... almost started fighting. And her too... drunk as a pig. Practically had to roll her up to her room..."

He fell into bed face first, and his body started to shake. Made got scared: what if he suffocates or dies! With a great deal of difficulty, she managed to turn him onto his side. His face was white, his eyes closed. Maybe he was asleep? She leaned down and looked. Hot stinking breath coming from his half-open mouth hit her nose. She jumped back in disgust.

But now he opened his eyes too. He had the sleepy, half-closed eyes of a drunk. At first he didn't notice anything, but then his eyes seemed to light up. Made felt how this man's gaze slid over her socks, her short pink petticoat with its triangular pleats along the bottom, her low-cut bodice and bare neck... It was as if someone were moving a red-hot iron across her body, she felt a stifling heat on her flesh, and dark red flooded across her face.

Suddenly his entire body lurched. The drunk's trembling hand reached up sloppily, his hot fingers gripping her bare arm tightly above the elbow. His other hand slid over her and shamelessly groped at her silk skirt. His eyes flickered and his face twisted into an ugly smile, and then came the husky, drunken laughter... It was like boiling water poured onto Made's head. For a moment she stood frozen, unable to react. But then suddenly it dawned on her. Her brother! She wrenched herself away, slapped back his extended hand and ran out of the room.

She ran to her room like a hunted animal, and turned the key. She listened. No, nobody was coming after her: the house was quiet. She only heard the caretakers down below on the street sweeping the pavements and talking in sleepy voices. Made took a deep breath – so deep that it penetrated the pit of her stomach and her narrow-buttoned bodice began to press painfully against her. She couldn't slow her breathing.

Her breasts convulsed and she could hear her own sobbing and stifled moans. The sound of her unspeakable shame, revulsion and anger. Her quivering fingers manoeuvred to tear free each little button from its loop, she tore the fragile batiste fabric, mercilessly crumpling the narrow, delicate ruffles and crinkling silk. Made tossed away her underclothes and fell into bed. She pulled the blanket over her head and pushed the corner of her pillow into her mouth. But she couldn't calm down and she couldn't forget. The blood hammered through her ears, her breath burnt her face and her entire body was stung by the disgrace. Through her tightly shut eyelids she could still see his groping drunken hands. She couldn't get away from them or forget them. And that was her brother... Her brother! She whimpered as if she were being stretched on the rack. She turned over onto her back.

The repulsive experience simmered in her mind for a long time. She gradually began to calm down and her earlier memories began to come forward again, but the feelings of elation did not return. Every time they bubbled up, a sharp, black edge seemed to slice into the upsurge of positive feelings. The soft bed seemed too hot and uncomfortable. The twilight in the room too lonely and unsettling. For the first time it occurred to her that for her entire life she'd slept every night in the same room as her father and mother, that every night she'd awoken to the sound of their breathing and felt their closeness while asleep. How many winter mornings had there been when her mother would rise first and Made – half awake and half in sleep's warm embrace – would feel her mother quietly pulling up her covers and carefully tucking her in. Now, sorrow covered her. It was as if something sweet, which she had not appreciated or even noticed until now, had been lost forever. She wanted to cry.

Gradually it passed. When dawn came and a new day started, the noise in the street grew louder. The building was also waking and all different sounds could be heard both near and far away. Her head had cooled and she began to think more calmly. As repulsive as the night's events had been, it was just one unexpected though endurable blow against her overall feeling of joy. The repulsion had abated but her lack of understanding had not. A lump of mud seemed to have fallen into a clear stream. Nevertheless, things had become a little bit clearer... People do crazy things when they're drunk! Being drunk is just like being asleep. How many people every day wake up – after a night of drinking – and can't remember any of the things they did the night before? And so Made's thoughts leaned in that direction. Avoiding calculations, and barely realising it herself, she was searching for excuses. She was all by herself in this quiet room, yet somehow still felt constricted. She had her own feelings and will, but it was as if an unseen force guided and moved them. She was sleeping in a soft, warm bed, and although she didn't look, she was comforted by the fact that she was surrounded by colourful, gently rustling, lightly scented clothing, her beautiful jewellery glittering on the table. A brightly-coloured world, which she had only ever seen in her dreams, now surrounded her, and behind her lay a past filled with grinding poverty which sank like a black cloud on the horizon. The sunny glow returned. Made opened her eyes. The pretty flowers along the ceiling were blooming again, their long, silvery stems seemed to gently glimmer. Her awareness of this new, beautiful life expanded again, overtook and filled everything.

She could hear her father's dry cough through three sets of walls. There was the sound of clanking dishes in the kitchen and someone knocked into something nearby and muttered. Roberts turned over onto his other side and it wasn't clear whether he was asleep or awake. It must have been around the time when they would've usually woken up in the past. The ingrained routine opened all their eyes and turned their bodies from one side to the other. Made gazed at the ceiling decoration, but saw something else: a grey morning in that chilly, steam-filled room reeking of soap, the floor still moist from yesterday's footsteps. A wooden tub standing in a puddle of soapy water next to the stove with a washboard slanted against it and strangers' clothing, which had been washed at dawn and freshly wrung to dry. Her mother kneeling in front of the stove with kindling... Time to get up, time to get up, but how she had wished she didn't have to... Made shivered as she relived her sorrowful memories. Let them sink – let those dark clouds, those bitter memories sink completely behind the horizon! It wasn't like that anymore. She didn't have to get up, she could just lie there with her eyes open, lounge around and listen to the morning's hustle and bustle. The flowers on the ceiling shined brighter. The stream of sensations brought by her new life rinsed away all the grit and grime of the past.

Made's head was still a little hazy, but it was fine when she got up. She walked out into the hallway and listened. Roberts must have been getting dressed. But from the far end, from Augusts's bedroom, she could hear the snores of someone deep in sleep. Disgusting. But Made used all her will to shove aside those negative feelings and opened the door to the kitchen.

The maid was pulling the rings off the white stove and replacing them with a glittering aluminium saucepan. The metal clanked.

"Quiet, Lonija, be quieter!" Made warned. "The master is still sleeping."

Lonija gave her a crooked, half-ironic, half-spiteful glance.

"Let him sleep then – my goodness!"

Made blushed. The lack of respect was evident in the maid's voice, but it was more directed at her than her brother. Her anger welled up. Who was actually in charge here after all: her or this servant girl? She needed to know!

"What do you mean – let him sleep!" she snapped sharply and took a heavy step in her direction. "What kind of language is that? How dare you talk about the master like that?"

Both women stared at each other. Then the maid turned away and put the lid on the saucepan.

A-ha! Made's heart laughed. She stood down! Now she

knows! She took another step towards her, lifted the lid and looked in.

"There's too little water – add some more," she said imperiously. It was her first time seeing a pot like this and she honestly didn't know if there was too much or too little water in it. But that wasn't the point. "And when the master is sleeping in the morning, you must be quiet, very quiet, in the kitchen – so that nobody can hear you even if they're right behind this door. He's a light sleeper and wakes easily." She raised her voice. "He has so much work that sometimes he only comes home after midnight, you know?"

She watched the girl closely. No – she didn't know. Sullen, Lonija turned on the water faucet, added a good quart of water to a cup and threw it into the saucepan. Now it was full up to the rim. That's fine! As long as she knows who gives the orders and who follows them around here.

She could see her mother through the gap in the back door.

"Mum, you keep an eye on things around here in the mornings," Made said firmly. "I might not wake up this early every morning." She paused for a brief moment. "In the evenings I often read for a long time," she lied, "and then I can't manage to get up so early. You go to bed earlier…" As she spoke, Made didn't take her eyes off the maid's face. Look! The maid smirked and pursed her lips. Made began darting around the kitchen in a fury, lifting and examining dishes. "This bucket needs to be at the far end of the stove – sitting here, it's right in the way. And this rug needs to be wiped down with a wet rag every day, otherwise the dirt will pile up on it."

"It already gets wiped down," Lonija muttered. "After breakfast when I make the coffee."

"You need to do it in the evening, in the evening." Made cut her off mid-sentence. "When it sits overnight it hardens and then it's harder to clean off." She brushed the tip of her shoe across the linoleum floor. "A whole layer! That needs to be cleaned off. If there's no other way, then scrape it off with a knife. Everything in the kitchen has to be shiny, otherwise it doesn't look right. Mum, you keep an eye on her..." She started to pull out the drawers from the white kitchen cabinet, which had inscriptions on them. She shrugged her shoulders and gestured. "What's this: there's enough potato flour here for half a year, but the salt is almost gone. You need to keep more salt here."

"We'll get more... we'll get more delivered today..." The maid spoke through tears of anger.

"We will get more! And look over here: the rice is poured into the large box, and the sugar into the small one... How does that make sense?"

Lonija forced a laugh.

"Oh, miss! What am I supposed to do? There's writing on every box that says what it's meant for."

"Writing or no writing..." Made turned towards the wall. "Mum, you keep an eye on her." And then she turned towards the maid again. "Do you have to go to the market today?"

"Why wouldn't I be? There's only enough cooking butter for today! And we need fish for dinner."

"Then, mum, go with her... You go with her today, mum. I won't have time. I still need to organise the room. Augusts will give you money."

She heard a strange noise from the direction of the hallway. Made hurried over. Was it Augusts? No, his door was shut, though she no longer heard any snoring. Then it must have been Roberts... She opened his door.

He was stooped over the wash basin with his shoes on and braces across his back. Water was spreading across the floor all the way to his bed. Shards of broken white pottery were scattered amongst it.

"What happened here?" asked Made.

Roberts lifted his red, unhappy face. "It broke... It fell over and broke... I was opening the door and that... that jug fell over and broke..." He was nervously making a pile of the broken pottery.

Made became angry again and shouted, "You need to be

more careful! What were you stomping around for? Leave it alone. Lonija will clean it up." She turned back towards the kitchen where Lonija was tending to the coffee, and her mother was standing in the doorway rubbing her nose with the corner of her apron. "Get the floor mop, Lonija," Made said coolly. "Over there... the young master," she especially emphasised these words as she looked the maid firmly in the eyes, "The young master spilled some water on the floor. Go and wipe it up."

Without saying a word, the maid grabbed the mop from the floor and slammed the door behind her. Made turned towards her mother.

"Why are you sniffling around here so much. Watch that girl – she's used to acting like she runs this place."

Her mother looked extremely sad, and muttered, "Everything's so fancy, what do I know about any of it, daughter? I can't make any sense of it..." Made could hear the tears in her voice. She could sense that there was something heavier, more serious weighing on her heart. She kept squeezing the apron in her hands. "My goodness, daughter, I don't know... us, here! What are we..."

"What?" Made's eyes widened.

"I don't know, what are we doing here...?" Her mother shrugged and looked around the kitchen. "Everything's so lovely and fine here that I'm scared to touch it, scared I'll smudge it or knock it over."

Made sneered, as if she'd already lived there for years and was used to it. "You're talking like a child. What's so frightfully fancy and fragile about this place."

All this time, old Mr. Sveilis had been looking apathetically out of the window in the back room and he now came over to the door. He was wearing his boots and a long coat and a rather worn-looking shirt front without a collar, but with a large button through its front hole. His hair was combed down smoothly, his sparse beard was nicely groomed and he was wearing his spectacles. But his face showed the same confusion, boredom and worry as his wife's. "What are we supposed to do here, daughter? I was wide awake at four in the morning. Couldn't get back to sleep again. All kinds of thoughts swirling around my head. None of this is any good. Such riches! I don't know, I don't understand..."

"What do you know!" Made snapped.

Her mother looked over angrily at him too, and said, "Don't talk nonsense!" She took another step closer. "You don't know a thing about these kinds of money matters."

Her father shrugged helplessly. "But what am I supposed to do here? I'm not used to being without work. I'm up at four... But really... maybe you could see if there's a small room over at that restaurant... Your mum and I could help out over there."

"I'd be quick about learning how to do the cooking..." Her mother smiled shyly. It was clear they'd already discussed this.

Made dismissed them with a wave of her hand.

"He won't want that. It just won't look right. He has waiters and cooks over at the restaurant. Juškans and Andrejs Skrastiņš... He has fancy guests there." She thought about it for a moment. "I know... the firewood, you could bring it up from the basement. And you, mum, can do the dusting in the rooms. Here's a flannel rag and little brush." She hurried after her mother through the open door. "But just be careful that you don't damage anything. You're in the habit of dropping things ... And do it quietly – very, very quietly: Augusts is sleeping. He came home late and he had a lot of work."

After seeing to them, Made went back to her room. There was so much to organise and move around. But the most important item was in its place. The bed was sitting there soft and fluffy with a blue embroidered Atlas blanket across the foot of it and three chunky pillows with depressions still visible in them from last night's sleep. The maid will come to sweep the floors; she'll also make the bed. A small soft sofa, a couple of low, padded stools, a graceful writing desk with its feet bent outwards, and another one with six polished legs and a round, engraved bronze top. A lovely shelf, a mirror, a picture in an ornately carved gold frame of a moonlit bay with a charming couple in a boat and a Turkish mosque and palm trees on the shore... Soft red curtains on the windows... Made didn't know where to start, where to stop, where to sit. Last night's unpleasant experience was now almost completely forgotten. The sense of a beautiful life she hadn't dared hope for, an unbelievable, dazzling awareness of luxury and ease flowed through her once more and carried her along.

Made moved and rearranged all of her things a dozen times. But the more she rearranged them, the less satisfied she was. She didn't have any experience or real knowledge. But she'll soon find her footing - she had promised herself that she would learn. She paused, left everything as it was, walked over to the door, closed her eyes and then suddenly opened them again. She opened them and fluttered her eyelids: through a gap between the buildings across the street the sun was casting three or four rays of light through the window and flooding her entire room with a ripple of light. The reflection on the frame seemed to make the moon's paleness blaze against the dark sky in the picture. The ornate photo album sitting on the round table with its back to the window looked an imposing dark brown from this side, only its edges and slender cylindrical supports glowed like coals in a fiery stove. On top of the shelf, two white porcelain dogs sparkled in between several small, yellow Majolica vases and fierce-looking bronze statuettes and below a brilliant black lacquer jewellery box with a silver flower on its lid sat like a stone sunken in a golden river. The shimmering stream of dust particles reached across the bed and sank lower and lower and lower before completely inundating the white pillows and the soft, blue Atlas blanket embroidered with hearts... Made couldn't remain still. She wanted to dive and sink into the soft blueness of the Atlas blanket, letting the stream of light flow over her, letting it pour into her heart so that it never runs dry!

All of this belonged to her, she was the owner and ruler here! Made laughed silently - but wanted to exclaim her indescribable joy and sing it. And all of this came from him – this sweet, good, rich man! He was great and noble; he was amazing. The last remnants of the unpleasant feelings hidden in the depths of her awareness seemed to evaporate and disappear.

Her mother was coughing somewhere nearby. Made spun around and hurried out into the salon. She grabbed her mother by the hand and pulled her towards her, even though she was holding the flannel cloth, the brush and the Venetian vase she had lifted to clean.

"Made... my child... leave me be! Don't break anything... my goodness!" Her mother struggled without success and wasn't sure whether to laugh or be angry. She laughed as Made dragged her into her room.

"Come and have a look! Just look... Don't you think it's pretty?"

Made trotted over and switched around one of the bronze statues with a yellow vase. She stood the album up a little straighter, and then spun round to smile at her mother, "Isn't it pretty?"

Shaking her head again, her mother smiled nervously and self-consciously, and uttered, "It like a manor house, and it's not meant for the likes of us... Oh, why did he have to go and do this... I hope that it'll turn out alright in the end..."

Made's face darkened. "You and your eternal worrying! Who do you think those lords are? Whoever has money is a lord. You're impossible..."

She heard a noise and followed her mother out into the hallway. Yes... Augusts was coughing, spitting things up and banging around. She stood there for a moment. Now the door was opening too, slowly at first but then bursting completely open, and then creaking mournfully as he slowly closed it. Sveilis walked along the corridor, coughing and rummaging around in his coat pocket for something as he went.

In an instant Made decided how she would behave. A drunk doesn't remember anything that happened during a bender and she too will pretend to have forgotten. She'll act like nothing had ever happened – nothing at all. She didn't see and she doesn't know...

"Good morning!" she greeted him warmly and practically curtsied in front of him like a schoolgirl.

But when she heard the way he growled back his greeting, she only had to glance at him to know that he remembered everything... He was ashamed and was angry at himself and at her... He didn't lift his eyes off the floor, continued coughing and kept digging around with both hands into his coat pockets.

"Isn't there... a cup of coffee?" he asked in a strangely stiff voice which also sounded angry. Made saw and understood that this was his way of getting rid of her. He remembered everything and was uncomfortable with her standing there looking at him. She hurried off towards the kitchen.

"Lonija! Lonija!" she was already calling from a distance. "Bring the coffee! The master is awake."

And when the "master" and the others were sitting around the dining table, she was the only one in the kitchen: was it better to stay there or to go and join them? He remembered everything, and it would be awkward for him. But if she didn't go, it would look suspicious and maybe even worse for him. She summoned up her courage and walked into the dining room – her heart pounding but her steps light and carefree.

She sat down easily in her usual place. He wasn't looking, but still saw her. Augusts bent down over his coffee cup and didn't lift his eyes, but blushed. Made blushed too and had difficulty pouring the coffee from the porcelain pot into the cups. She spooned in the sugar and stirred the coffee with much clinking and splashing over the sides as she did. Even though they knew nothing, the others sensed that something was wrong. Quietly, as if fearful of what might happen, the Sveilis family joylessly drank the genuine mocha coffee with thick, fresh cream for the first time in their lives. But they didn't enjoy it... A Japanese woman standing in a strange pose in between two white bushes in bloom had been painted on their saucers, but this morning she didn't amuse any of them.

Made gradually calmed down. She stole a glance at her brother. There were two deep lines across his brow, and his face looked old and cross. His eyes were burning with shame, and he accidentally lifted them up. There's more to this, she thought. There was something else behind this tiredness and crossness. Something... Made didn't really understand it, but could sense it. Her memories of last night's events came to her again, and from there her thoughts drifted to Little Flame and to that other woman she'd seen at the hotel. She resisted it, she didn't want it, but a kind of stifling darkness seemed to be emanating from her brother. She didn't want to, but she carried on looking at him.

He dipped his silver spoon into his coffee and tried to lift it to his lips. He stooped down low, but still couldn't manage it, as his hand was shaking. The spoon clinked as it hit the edge of the cup and brown liquid drenched the Japanese woman and the white table cloth. Sveilis angrily grabbed the entire cup and drank a large gulp. He then put the cup back down, and his entire face twisted in a grimace of disgust. He might even have shuddered. He grabbed the carafe, filled his glass with water and drank it. This time he definitely shuddered.

"Lonija!" he called. No, this wasn't the kind Sveilis from yesterday. His voice now sounded hoarse, unfamiliar and angry. "Lonija!" He allowed his hand to fall heavily onto the table, and it looked almost as if he was hitting it with his fist. "How many times have I told you that there needs to be fresh water in the carafe every morning! This is dishwater, not the slightest bit fresh..."

Lonija carried the carafe off in a huff. The Sveilis family sat around the table in silence. Roberts had been trying to speak but just couldn't get the words out. After his third attempt he pulled out his handkerchief, wiped his face and blew his nose. Finally, he summoned up his courage.

"I... broke a jug..." he muttered and looked with desperation at his brother.

Sveilis was slowly pouring himself a second glass of water. He drank it and looked back crossly.

"Which jug?"

"A jug of water," Made hurriedly intervened. "It fell off the wash basin and broke. It was an accident..."

Sveilis dismissed it all with a lethargic wave of his hand.

"An accident... Tell Lonija to buy a new one." He propped his head up sullenly on his hands and closed his eyes. It was clear just how bad he felt. A much-relieved Roberts blew his nose and got up. His father coughed, pulled at his beard and adjusted his glasses.

"Your mother and I were wondering...," he began, quickly stopped and blinked as he nodded towards his wife. "What are we going to do around here without any work... Can't we help with something at that restaurant?"

His wife kept nodding in agreement with every word, and said, "We're not used to it... I got up at four this morning."

"I'm just not tired," his father continued. "My whole life I've been used to getting up like that. Just can't fall asleep again."

"It's hard to sleep when you're not tired," his wife added.

"And living without working... That's why your mother and I were talking. We don't have anything to do around here. Over there at that restaurant, we could help out with this or that."

When Sveilis opened his eyes, he looked so furious that his parents stopped speaking immediately.

"The two of you can't help out with anything over there. Help out..." And without any clear reason he became angrier. "What do you want? Do you not have enough to eat and drink?" He shoved the coffee pot, which hit the sugar bowl with a loud clang. "There's more here - and if you're missing anything else, tell Lonija, that's what she's here for! Is your room not warm enough? Damn it!" He slammed his fist onto the table. "Tell me - what else do you need? What - else - do - you - need?" He looked at his father and mother with madness in his eyes. Avoiding Made, he shoved his hand into his pocket and pulled out his wallet. He snatched out two five-rouble coins and threw them down onto the table. "There you go – and if you need more, if it's not enough, just tell me!"

His mother waved around her arms excitedly. "We don't need it, son, we don't need anything! That's not what we're talking about. We have it so good here; my goodness, if only it could always be like this... But we were thinking... money doesn't grow on trees for anybody and look at us all, so many people without work. But if you don't want that... my goodness!" Tears filled her eyes. Wringing the corner of her apron in her hands, she left the table. Old Mr. Sveilis coughed as he followed her.

Sveilis sat there for another moment, staring morosely at the tablecloth. Then suddenly he lurched to his feet, as if someone had pushed him or terribly offended him. He moved with long strides, knocking his boots loudly against the parquet floor as he went, so it wouldn't be obvious that his feet were unsteady and shaking. He slammed the door and started violently coughing and spitting in the hallway.

Made breathed a sigh of relief. All that time she'd forced herself not to look at him. She remembered, and again turned a deep red colour. Not just her face – her ears and neck too. She felt the searing heat of inextinguishable shame. She was ashamed because of her parents, because of Lonija – but especially because of her own memories. Like the brown flowers on the cushion of her chair, this terrible event was stitched into her memory. It seemed like it would never fade away.

Two yellow discs were lying next to each other on the white table cloth. Two small orange spots! Their brightness overshadowed the white of the porcelain, the grey of the silver and the glint of the crystal. There wasn't anything else, aside from those two golden discs... Tenderly caressing them, Made placed them in her hand. Immediately everything became easier when her hot palm felt the cool heaviness of the gold. She closed her hand and opened it again. She looked with both eyes, then shut one. She extended her finger and slid them across her palm. She lingered over the coins, toying with them.

She was stopped by a sudden realisation: they didn't take the money! Her brother gave it to them, but they didn't take it. The way she saw it, giving it to her parents is practically the same as giving it to her. It was true after all: what did they need that much money for? They had plenty to eat and drink, a warm room... But she had so much more to buy!

She closed her eyes for a second then went back to her room.

Gentle warmth, brightness and fragrance; luxury and ease, she felt good again, so good! Her dear, dear brother! Where does his money rain down from? With his full pockets, he can grab it by the fistful. The rich, they have everything, they can do anything! Made's small, drooping breasts suddenly lifted up. She had slaved away for far too long, and now she had to live. Now she can live! Last night's events... He was drunk... people don't know what they're doing when they are in that state. She would forget it all...

There were two small flower pots on the desk. In one of them were white asters in bloom, wrapped with white tissue paper, and in the other violet asters wrapped with light-brown paper. Made felt as if this was the first time she was seeing these asters. She had looked at them, but hadn't seen them. She remembered: these were a gift from Mrs. Lodziņš. She walked up and examined them more closely. Ordinary clay pots and frail, scrawny flowers. But they practically had an entire forest of fresh, fragrant, expensive ones in the salon! Her lips formed into a smile. They didn't need this gift from the Lodziņšes; they were rich enough themselves.

She dropped both gold pieces onto the broadcloth covering the desk and walked back out into the hallway.

"Lonija!" she called out loudly, as if she needed to be heard two floors down. "Take these flower pots and put them on the kitchen windowsill."

And then she stood in front of the mirror again. Daylight didn't have that excessive, deceptive brightness electric lights had. Set against the black background of night everything appeared brighter and more beautiful. Now everything looked duller and greyer. Her face was grey and her body less attractive. Her shoulders were ungainly, her breasts barely noticeable, her waist not narrowing gracefully, and her hips without that fantastic, seductive roundness. The indentations in her neck and at the small of her back were too deep. There were two prominent lines across her brow, her nose was large and pointed, her teeth were too spread-out and her eyes lacked that lively youthful sparkle. She took it all in and contemplated. Only her ears were small and attractive, closely hugging her head. Her brilliant, ash-brown hair was unkempt and disorderly, twisted into braids that hung heavily over her ears, her forehead and even down to her shoulders. She started to comb her hair and get ready; she got dressed and left so she could go out and buy more things.

Returning home around lunchtime, she heard a half recognisable voice through the door as she walked up the penultimate flight of stairs. Her mother's voice could be heard easily but after the door closed all she could hear was a muffled drone coming from inside. By the time she got into the hallway, her mother and the stranger had already gone into the next room. She definitely knew this woman's voice. Intrigued, Made quickly changed and went into the dining room.

Oh – Mrs. Juškans! She'd brought a cake and a bottle of red wine. The cake was sitting on the dining room table, and Mrs. Juškans herself was still breathing heavily from the climb up the stairs. Disorientated and a little flushed, she didn't really know how to behave here, so she smiled bashfully, talked incessantly and sat down in the chair red-faced and sweaty. Her narrow eyes darted around like mice. Catching sight of Made, she immediately lurched to her feet again and began to smile even more cloyingly.

"Good morning, good morning!" she said as she squeezed

Made's hand for a long time with her hot, wet palm. "I thought that I should come over and see how you are all getting settled in here. Yesterday morning, I said to my husband: on your way to work, stop in at the bakery on the corner, and order a cake... I can't show up empty-handed. And a bottle of wine. This is what he found..." She nudged the bottle next to the cake.

Made looked over. A small, simple sponge cake. A little bit was missing from one edge – she must have tried some herself. And the wine – she took the bottle and examined it. Madeira, for a rouble. She turned in a dignified fashion towards the kitchen door.

"Lonija! Take this cake... and this bottle, and put them on the table in the kitchen."

Mrs. Juškans was too naive and out of breath to pick up on the sting in Made's voice. She stared jealously at Made's new, beautiful suit. Her saccharine smile grew wider. Now she turned her eyes over to Made's mother and shook her head in amazement.

"I can't recognise her anymore, can't recognise her at all! What a lady..." She reached over with two fingers towards Made's dress. "Is it silk?"

"No, a silk mixture," Made snapped absent-mindedly. "This is just for wearing around the house." Then she turned angrily towards her mother. She disliked how she was standing around looking uncomfortable and smiling obsequiously, apparently flattered by such an important guest. And what a guest! Her husband works for Made's brother as a buffet attendant! Now they had switched roles. She threw back her head proudly, "Mum, take our guest into the salon. I'll come too in a moment. I have a few matters to attend to."

She didn't really need to do anything at all. Barely restraining her glee, she hurried into her room. She wanted to laugh, to sing at the top of her lungs. She danced around and then walked over to the mirror, smiling as she looked at her reflection and caressed her silky dress with both hands. She found the medallion and put it on. But then she hesitated: Mrs.

Juškans would notice and think that she had dressed up just because of her. What does she care about Mrs. Juškans! Whether someone like her existed in this world or not wouldn't make any difference to Made. She put down the medallion and tried out several haughty expressions in the mirror before walking back out again.

Mrs. Juškans was sitting in a low, soft chair in the salon. For what seemed like the hundredth time, she was looking around with astonishment, jealousy and delight at everything in the room. Clasping her hands together on her stomach, she shook her head constantly, though barely perceptibly. Made's mother had stuck a vase filled with fresh flowers under Mrs. Juškans's nose and was visibly cheered by her old acquaintance's surprise.

"Smell them, Mrs. Juškans, smell them."

"Yes, do smell them, Mrs. Juškans." Made repeated. She rubbed the back of the sofa and lifted up an edge of the machine-embroidered tablecloth before putting it down again.

Mrs. Juškans smelled the flowers and was out of breath again.

"It's like summer in the country..." She hunched her shoulders and looked around again. "It's practically like visiting a lord's manor house."

Made felt real joy in hearing the jealousy so clearly audible in Mrs. Juškans's voice. She tried to look on at the scene as if from outside her own body, and her lips curled into a smile.

"Oh, you know how it is, Mrs. Juškans! These days whoever has money can live like a lord. It's not like the old days anymore."

She gave her guest a tour of the other rooms, and her mother walking behind them. As Mrs. Juškans's astonishment increased, so did Made's mother's self-respect and pride in her son. Seeing how Made had already grown accustomed to this new way of being, and how confidently she walked around this luxurious apartment, she too felt a little surer of herself. Now she was no longer afraid to touch the smaller valuable items;

she picked them up, examined them and showed them to their guest. She sat down in the soft chairs, patting them down with her hand, and she stretched out her legs across the flower-patterned rug. Gradually she became more self-confident and put on more airs towards their guest. She didn't yet know how to behave or how to speak: she mostly just watched Made and listened to how she acted. She stopped constantly referring to her as "Mrs". If she interjected something as she listened, then she would be more restrained, cooler and less direct: oh, come now, my dear... And just like Made, she pressed her lips into a cool, thin smile and nodded in the same haughty manner. Who was Mrs. Juškans anyway? As she listened to her exclamations of amazement and flattery, old Mrs. Sveilis began to understand her guest's inferiority and her own superiority.

They stayed in Made's room for quite a while. Mrs. Juškans was overwhelmed by its beauty and luxury, which encouraged Made to show her more examples of it. She showed her treasures and described what else needed to be purchased and put in order. Not all of it was meant seriously, but it was fine to boast a bit for the sake of creating the right impression. Made would tell their guest whatever came to her mind in that moment. And wasn't it true that at this very moment nothing was actually impossible? Didn't her brother have pockets filled with money? Right here on the broadcloth covering the desk, two five-rouble pieces were glimmering at them. Dreams and reality flowed together. Her tongue moved of its own accord – involuntarily, easily and quickly. And her mother smiled a restrained smile and confirmed each of her words with a nod.

Later on they shared lunch with their guest. Both of them hurried to attend to her and see to her every need. There were two reasons for this exceptional attention: one was so that their guest would see how polite and refined they were in this wealthy life, and the other was that she would have a chance to be amazed by their fine china. The table was completely covered with dishes and all the doors were left open on the sideboard, so that even items that didn't have a spot on the table were visible and could be admired. Their guest ate and drank, and was clearly stunned by all of these wonders.

After Mrs. Juškans had left – in fact for the rest of the day and well into the evening, the mother and daughter remained in a state of ecstasy.

Only in comparison to another's inferiority does a person come to realise their own significance and importance. Another person's unstated, though clearly evident, jealousy had made them experience even greater joy in their wealth and abundance.

After some large snowstorms, February began to thaw and the streets were smooth again. The driver turned onto Moon Street, with a graceful turn and without slowing down at the corner. The spirited grey horse snorted, nodded its head and gave the sleigh bells a good shake. The sleigh's runners gently swished over the soft, slippery snow.

With his hands stuffed deep into his coat pockets, an unwrapped bundle of books snug under his arm, Roberts was slumped in the corner of a cab, travelling home from school. The karakul collar of his coat folded up partway, his hat hanging slightly over one ear, a twist of hair which had been purposely curled was sticking out sideways from underneath its green brim.

Roberts didn't take the carriage home every day; when he'd been stuck in a chair all day, he liked the chance to take the long walk home. But tonight was the Charity Association ball so he had to be nicely dressed. He'd stayed at school later than usual, and then he had stayed on for his music lesson. So now it was already growing dark.

The driver hadn't come to a complete stop at the front door of Number Fifteen when Roberts jumped out, tossed twenty kopecks over to him, grabbed his violin case up from under the blanket and ran towards the door.

On the street, old Mr. Sveilis was walking towards him past the Lodziņš building. He was wearing Augusts's old overcoat, a large rabbit fur hat, galoshes and holding a black steel cane with a polished nickel-plated handle. Moving with tiny steps and in no hurry, he was carefully examining every individual who walked or rode by, and so he walked straight past the door. Every day after lunch he would go for a long walk, enjoying his new-found leisure.

After almost colliding with Roberts, he stopped with surprise and examined the slender young man, smiling slightly. Roberts just looked at him.

"Is Augusts at home?" he asked as he brushed by, but didn't wait for the answer.

In the flat, he tore off his coat and threw it down, quickly washed his hands and hurried into the dining room. His mother, hearing his approach, immediately brought him the lunch she had been keeping for him in the kitchen. When she removed the covers from the plates, the room filled with warm, aromatic steam.

Roberts poured one ladle of meatballs in gravy onto his dish, swallowed a spoonful of it and scowled. His mother, who was standing opposite him, looked over with concern.

"Don't you like it?"

"I-I don't like it..." Roberts muttered back. "It's so salty!"

"I don't know," his mother shrugged. "We all ate it, and it was fine. Lonija, did you maybe add some more?" Lonija appeared in the doorway. "Did you add any salt to that soup?"

Lonija looked back with an impish smile. "For the young gentleman? None at all. I'd be more likely to pour in sugar for him."

His mother laughed, but then stopped when Roberts turned and scowled at the maid. "She knows how to chit-chat, but she doesn't know how to cook."

He shoved the dish away and reached for the roast. His mother hurried over to help him.

"Roberts, dear, take this one, it's more tender..."

She stood around for a while but when Roberts, lost in his thoughts, didn't say anything and was seemingly half-satisfied with his roast, she quietly went back into the kitchen and sat down in her usual spot.

Her favourite place was across from the large, white enamel stove. The embers from the birch firewood took a while to go out, and a calming warmth flowed from them. Old Mrs. Sveilis shifted in her chair, trying to get comfortable. She pulled her large, soft shawl tighter over her shoulders and clasped her hands cosily as she sat in her comfortable knitted coat. She stretched out her legs, supporting her feet on the red, floral cushioned stool and closed her eyes.

She could sit across from the stove like that for hours. Softly, softly, so quietly that others might not even hear it, the embers crackled, dimmed and went out. But even so, a gentle warmth continued to come from the stove. An oddly pure and calming warmth flowed from this polished white stove. There were well-scrubbed pots and pans hanging from yellow hooks, coloured metal boxes and cans on the shelves, and in between there was the transparent glimmer of crystal. The door to the dining room was slightly ajar. There was always a mixture of the smells of roast meat and boiled fruit in the kitchen – sweet and rich, it gently tickled the nose and nerves.

Old Mrs. Sveilis would sit there for hours with half-closed eyes. The shiny white and warmth of the stove, the glitter of the dishes, and the sweet smells all mingled together – the pleasant warmth flowed through her body. She thought about the recent past and remembered the crumbling, smoking brick stove with rings that had been mended by the blacksmith, and the cast iron pot for boiling water. It was so wonderful, so indescribably wonderful to remember it while feeling her warm knitted jacket on her back, the soft wool shawl around her shoulders, and the warm felt boots on her feet. Even the rheumatism in her legs didn't feel as bad. She dozed off easily – waking up and then dozing off again and not even knowing herself when she was asleep and when she was awake.

Her entire life had been transformed into endless dozing!

Made had her elbows on the windowsill in her bedroom,

and she was looking out onto the street. As night fell, she could no longer discern the pedestrians down below, but she didn't feel like moving away from the window. Though she couldn't make out the individual figures, the bustle on the street below continued to hold her attention. The quiet, lonely winter days had grown so dull – so very dull. There was an unfinished bit of knitting sitting in a box, a copy of A Guide to German open on the table, and a dog-eared copy of Instructional Notes in the Russian Language – all of it had grown boring and loathsome.

She wasn't used to life without the need or willingness to work. Work just for the sake of passing the time seemed incomprehensible and therefore unbearable. She needed to study... With every person she met in these circles, her sense of her own lack of education grew deeper. At the very least, she needed to learn languages. But she couldn't – she was too old and such a stranger to it. She hated to look at those guides and notes. Better to just look out the window and pass the time that way.

Strange feelings arose from the lack of work. Strange thoughts emerged from the boredom. She had gradually grown accustomed to this easy life and seemed to have relaxed as a result. A human being grows accustomed to everything with time, and in the end everything becomes dull. Only the desire for more luxury and even more gold kept growing stronger. Something was constantly being sewn or made for her now. She always had to go for a fitting or look at something new. Her wardrobe could no longer be closed. But she still didn't have enough. The more she had, the more she wanted. Like a drunk who is thirstier with every drink. There was only one boundary for that kind of desire – self-destruction...

Her perception of life was turned on its head. She no longer noticed what she'd gained, only what she was lacking, what she desired. Anything she acquired would immediately lose its value. Only what she sought out held any meaning. And so dissatisfaction gradually grew out of her delight. She was dissatisfied with everything and with herself.

And this aching desire increasingly governed her feelings. It was the same desire she'd once felt on some quiet, lonely Sunday nights when she could hear the distant sound of music drifting over from the city gardens, and her chest would tighten and tears would fill her eyes. A longing for a wider and faster world. But back then those feelings were mixed with deep sorrow and fatigue born of hopelessness. Now there was an awareness hidden behind this longing, the knowledge that an even more impetuous wave of ardent passion was coming to lift her up and sweep her along. She didn't understand or know it yet, but a strange desire or inclination was growing within her with each day and taking her ever closer to this invisible force.

Depressed by work and poverty since childhood, she awoke to a belated but genuinely carefree youth. Her body which had grown slack from lack of work slowly regained its vitality: her blood – long suppressed – began rushing faster, her dulled instincts came back to life. Her hands became whiter and softer, her entire body more flexible. After a long night of sweet, dream-filled sleep, every morning she would stand in front of the mirror for a long time just looking at herself. She would take a long time getting dressed and would do it with great attention to detail, listening for any sound coming from the hallway. As she lazily slouched and dozed on the sofa, she would also listen; as she walked along the street, she would carefully observe the people coming the other way. He should have been coming... He had to come!

Oh, she already knew who... Him – Rodolfs Lodziņš, the young, handsome student with the colourful hat and the striped ribbon running diagonally across his shirt front. An hour ago he'd left his house, hailed a cab on the other side of the street, got aboard and looked up as he was buttoning up his coat. He looked right at her, and she saw it! Since then she had stood at the window and waited. But he didn't return. Now it was getting dark, she couldn't recognise anyone anymore. But he would come; he had to come!

She turned away from the window. Swinging back her arms, she lifted herself up onto her toes, and stretched with happiness. He'd been here three or four times now. He'd come to see her brother, but Made sensed other motivations. Why did she always happen to run into him? Why did he always linger for a moment just with her? Why did he always come straight away when she'd invited him to her room? So friendly and polite, always smiling as he sat on the sofa, talking, joking and laughing! Made remembered every one of his words. She could see each of his expressions, every smile. A refined, beautiful and kind man!

And why did he forget his cigarette case here? Like a hidden treasure, like a sacred object, she took down the silver case with the engraved monogram on its cover and gold-plating inside from the spot on the shelf where she'd so carefully placed it. The spring clicked slightly and the top flipped open; inside were three hand-rolled cigarettes. Made slid them around with her finger and laughed a quiet, happy laugh. He'd rolled those, they'd been in his fingers! She put one in her mouth and turned towards the mirror. She laughed out loud at her funny appearance, took the cigarette out of her mouth, carefully wiped off the moisture, and put it back. She closed the case and stared at it for a long time. His dad had given it to him when he finished Realschule – she knew it all! They were already close friends; they had a personal connection. He's sure to come! She pressed the cool, smooth metal case up to her cheek and carefully put it back again.

There was still plenty of time, but nevertheless she started to get dressed. She couldn't think about the ball tonight without getting nervous. It was her first time in such high society! She couldn't wait and yet she was weighed down with fear. Please let it all go well! Her heart was beating quickly. Her lips stretched into a smile, but her throat closed up as if clenched by soft fingers.

She got undressed and spent a long time washing. Fragrant glycerine soap and warm sweet-smelling water – she'd poured in a fair amount of perfume. She spent even more time brushing her hair. She parted it in the middle, fluffed it up into crimped curls and on the back of her neck she plaited it tightly together. The heavy, ash-brown fullness of her hair seemed to overshadow her face, neck and shoulders – everything nearby that was left bare. Accentuated by her hair, her face no longer seemed so gaunt, nor did the hollow in her neck seem so pronounced. The small, ugly, blue veins seemed to retreat deeper and disappeared underneath her skin. No, she was not yet old and unattractive.

She put on her dark brown silk outfit, but tried in vain to click the buttons closed along her back. She opened the door to the hallway. "Roberts," she called impatiently, "come here!"

But he was in no hurry at all, having his own business to attend to. It was some time before the lanky youth appear and he was flushed, nervous and wearing the coat of a dress uniform buttoned all the way up.

Made giggled when she saw him. "All dressed up are we! Practically an officer! Isn't it choking you?" She stuck her finger behind his tightly buttoned collar.

Roberts pulled away angrily. "What are you scratching me for! You should cut those nails."

Made looked down and saw that indeed, her nails were a little too long. She dug out the small scissors and turned her back to Roberts.

"Button me up!"

She cut her nails as she listened to Roberts clicking shut each button. He was clumsy, didn't really know how to tell apart the three rows of buttons. He'd mix them up and mutter crossly, then tear them open again. But all this just made her laugh.

"Clumsy... oh so very clumsy!" she teased. "What are you going to do when you get married and need to help your wife get dressed?"

Roberts jumped away angrily. "Don't step on my feet!" Bending down he used his fingers to carefully brush off the grey spot on his patent leather boots.

Made laughed, and said, "Wash, wash your hands, otherwise you'll smudge my dress... Is your bride going to be at the ball?"

"Is your bridegroom?" Roberts shot back.

"Mine will be, he'll definitely be there." Something more than just a joke echoed in Made's laughter. True, unfeigned ecstasy. "But have you learned to dance yet? How many classes do you have per week?"

She turned her head to the side, looked away, and bit her lower lip to keep from laughing out loud. Roberts was bright red. He had thought that nobody else knew his secret. But Made had heard how in the evenings, throwing his boots off to the side, he'd hummed a dance melody, and quietly practiced. And she would sometimes stick her head through the door, and see him standing in the middle of the room sweaty and out of breath. Oh, she knew it all!

"What are you blabbering about..." He muttered and clicked the last button shut with such force that she yelped. He hissed angrily. "You smell like a perfume shop. I can barely breathe around here."

She smiled as she looked at the mirror, first turning one side towards it, then the other, as she examined her outfit.

Roberts was rummaging around by the shelf.

"Leave those books alone!" she called out, worried about her cigarette case. If he sees it, then it'll start all over again... But he wasn't listening, rummaging around the bottom he pulled out a stack of books and threw them down angrily onto the table.

"Pulp novels." he yelled crossly. "Why do you hold on to this garbage? No educated person would actually put them up on their shelf? I'm taking them off to the kitchen straight away. What if somebody sees them? The shame of it."

Made felt ashamed. She didn't really understand, but if everyone felt that way about those books...

There were a lot of books on that shelf – all of them in lovely gold covers. Amidst the works by Latvian authors there were also a few trashy translations – just because they were so beautifully bound. All of them were nicely arranged by size, their golden spines facing out. Most of their pages were uncut and had never been turned, except for the poems of Poruks – she had read those. Her favourite poems were marked by folded down page corners: "Close your dear eyes and smile", "Sweet Lisa of Tharandt"...

Roberts leant down to pick something up – Rodolfs Lodziņš's cigarette case was in his hand. Made didn't know what to do.

"Oh," he said slowly as he examined the silver case. "What's this?" He opened it. "Oh, cigarettes! Have you started smoking?"

Made lunged at him. "Why are you rummaging around in my stuff? Give it to me!"

But her alarm made Roberts suspicious. He lifted the case up higher and refused to give it back to her. He batted her away with his other hand as he looked mischievously at his sister. Then he began to study the monogram. He spelled it out and laughed loudly.

"Oh, I see how it is! Hiding it away like a treasure... So it's him!" He bent over laughing.

"What are you laughing about – like some kind of a buffoon!" Made screamed at him. "Give it back!" Finally, she managed to tear it away from him and threw it down onto the table. "There's nothing to laugh about, nothing at all. He was here and forgot it. I'm looking after it until he comes back..."

But Roberts wasn't laughing anymore. He had turned away and was looking out of the dark window, tapping the windowpane with his fingers.

"You're so dumb... you're completely dumb." he became quiet and then said through his teeth. "Young Lodziņš... that student... he's so arrogant... He's just playing around with you, nothing more. And here you are thinking who knows what. It's just plain stupid!"

She was flushed and breathless with worry, biting her lips and probing her brother with a piercing stare.

"Why are you talking nonsense? How do you know?"

Roberts shrugged his shoulders dismissively. "There are things you don't know..." He tapped the stack of pulp novels crossly with his finger. "You've got garbage like this on your shelf, but you don't even know how to speak your own mother tongue correctly. And he's... a man of letters, the sole heir..." He dismissed her with a wave of his hand and a mocking laugh. "It's stupid!"

Without taking her eyes off of him, her cheeks red, her hands clenched into fists, Made leaned close to him. "You're the one who's dumb. You're just a boy! What do you know? You're still at school..." But then she noticed that her voice was shaking and her eyes were filling with tears. She turned away and tried to keep speaking casually. She raised her voice. "You're talking all kinds of nonsense... I can't bear to listen to it. Your imagination! What's it to me... What do I care..."

But Roberts wasn't listening. He walked out with the stack of novels under his arm.

At around half past eight, the entire Sveilis family were walking down the front steps. Augusts and Made were first, behind them was Roberts; old Mr. Sveilis was three steps back and his wife brought up the rear.

Sveilis had been saying during the day that he would order a motor car. But his mother was anxious; there was no way she was riding in some wicked contraption like that. His old man grumbled too that there was no need to be so fancy. So that's how they left it.

They were divided into two sleighs. Sveilis sat in the first one with Made, their father and mother in the other. None of them invited Roberts to sit with them and he hesitated for a moment. There was more room with the old folks, as his siblings' coats barely left any room on the seat next to them, but his father was sitting stooped over in his old coat and his mother, with a black scarf around her head, was leaning completely over to one side and holding onto the armrest with her hand. He was ashamed of these two uncultured old people. But then, he thought it better to sit at the back of the second sleigh.

The sleigh bells began to jingle. The runners whooshed across the damp snow packed down by other drivers that had passed over it. But Roberts wanted them to go even faster. He couldn't calm down and wanted to get there as quickly as possible. His impatience and pent-up excitement made his nerves tingle.

Affected by a mellow melancholy, Made closed her eyes and relaxed in her warm coat, while her thick white scarf decorated with pink ribbons softly caressed her cheeks. Expectations of the evening to come and the possibilities it offered also warmed her heart, but what had happened earlier in the evening still left a bitter taste. Those ugly feelings mingled together and she would have liked that journey to last forever – if only she could sit there and never get up with her eyes closed as she listened to runners scraping the icy road and the sleigh bells jingling!

And yet it was over too soon and time to get out, and Roberts was already on the pavement shaking the snow off his trouser legs. Augusts, hopping down gracefully, having unbuttoned the tightly fastened blanket and extended his hand to help Made climb down, as if she were some fine lady! Made felt simultaneously pleased and ashamed.

"It's fine, it's fine!" She laughed, batting him away.

"Now, now..." Sveilis grumbled as he let her pass and cleared a path through the crowd pushing towards the door.

The front room of the building was filled with people. Every hallway and every staircase was teeming with crowds. Putting her hand in her husband's coat pocket, old Mrs. Sveilis squeezed inside with those walking in front. Her head was swimming because of the overwhelming crowd and their chatter, and her eyes were dazzled by the brightness of the electric lights.

In the cloak room, Sveilis helped everyone again. After removing his coat, he pulled out a small brush, arranging his hair and grooming his moustache in the mirror over the shoulder of a short plump lady. Made looked on and couldn't suppress her delight. What an attractive and dignified man! Slender with a straight back, but respectably rotund. His light hair was parted in the middle from his forehead all the way to the back of his neck – shiny, oiled, smooth and combed evenly. A bit patchy towards the back, but he'd combed it over and covered up the slight baldness so it was barely noticeable. His blonde moustache was a little curved, both ends pointing up and quivering ever so slightly. His face was pale, rosy and round, his lips were soft. He had a long black coat with a collar lined with shiny silk, a snow-white waistcoat and cravat, a high, turned down collar – modern cuffs with gold chain cufflinks sliding out of his sleeves. A chunky gold chain crossed his chest from one side to the other, and his fingers were full of rings. An honorary pin from the Cyclists' Association on the right side of his silk collar... An attractive and refined man!

Made's heart soared with happiness and pride. She walked up to her brother from behind and tucked a bit of his white cravat underneath his collar. When he turned around, she fixed the front. There wasn't actually anything to fix, but she wanted everyone to see that he was her brother.

Nearby old Mr. Sveilis was standing around in the crowd bashfully blinking his eyes. His wife was clinging to him and fighting with all her strength to keep the streaming crowd from separating her from her husband. They both did their best to keep from being separated from their children. Roberts already had his foot on the first step of the stairs. He was tugging at his shirt collar impatiently. Everyone began walking up.

Made struggled to squeeze through the open ballroom doors filled with people. There were already dancing couples twirling around in the centre of the room, and a human wall formed from onlookers standing along the sides. When her eyes had adjusted to the blinding light of the ballroom, Made began to look around. She was so startled by the sea of fancy ladies that she and her dress could not compete with. She had never even dreamt of such dresses and jewellery. Refined and steady movements, soft smiles and appropriate expressions; bare arms, necks, chests and shoulders. Her tiny décolleté covered in ruffles remained unnoticed here... But there was no time for regrets. Inviting music, spinning pairs of dancers, the scent of dozens of perfumes mixing with the steam rising off of hot bodies, the glitter of gold and precious stones – all of it drew her in, pulled her along and transfixed her. The intoxicating quality of the ball enticed even those who weren't dancing, frayed their nerves and dizzied their minds.

Sveilis whispered something into her ear from behind. She didn't hear what he said, but when she looked back, there was no sign of her brothers or her father, only her mother was standing in the crowd nearby, not taking her eyes off Made. Her mouth was forced into a kind of happy grin, but her eyes looked confused, even despairing. Her worn, old-fashioned, black jacket didn't fit in with the glittering throng of guests around her.

Made grabbed her mother angrily by the arm.

"Get over here, why are you milling around there getting in everybody's way!" She pulled her over to the wall and when a lady nearby was invited to dance, Made sat her mother down on the empty chair. "And don't wander off anywhere."

But her own eyes were already looking elsewhere. Her earlier daze had now passed. She wasn't watching the fancy ladies and comparing herself to them anymore. What were they to her! Who cares if they exist or not! She was looking for only person...

She squeezed through the crowd again and out in front of the crowd and at the edge of the dance floor close to the front doors stood Rodolfs Lodziņš in the company of Bebrītis, his good friend and fellow member of a fraternity. They were both wearing tailcoats and light-coloured waistcoats crossed diagonally by a striped ribbon with a silver pin shaped like a gosling attached to it. They both had colourful handkerchiefs in their waistcoat pockets and were wearing white gloves and shiny boots with wide, upturned toes and thick soles. Their clothes were identical, but their appearance was completely different: Lodziņš was slight, young, his cheeks smooth with blue kind eyes and thin parted hair combed flat; Bebrītis was thick-set and dark-skinned with dark eyes, a thick black moustache and short thick hair that stuck up in the air. Lodziņš was light and straight as a reed, Bebrītis had hunched his shoulders, and was stocky and heavy.

They had just finished dancing and sat their ladies back down again. Bebrītis moved the cap he'd been squeezing with his left hand over to his right one. Lodziņš had stuffed his cap into his coat pocket so that half of it was hanging out visibly.

"It's hot..." Lodziņš complained. "And crowded... it's like the Midsummer's market..."

"There are at least a hundred other fellows standing around here." Bebrītis smirked and looked on at the groups of more senior high school and business school students walking by. Then suddenly he grabbed his friend by the elbow. "Look! Is that one over there staring at you?"

"Which one?" said Lodziņš looking into the crowd but unable to see where his friend was pointing.

"The brunette... with the black belt." Bebrītis gestured with the drooping end of his cap. "She's definitely staring at you. Do you know her? Of course you do! Your taste is getting worse."

Lodziņš could see her now and he scowled.

"That's her... the one I told you about... Shush!" He grabbed his friend's arm, and the crowd momentarily hid Made. "Let this cup pass from me... What a crazy girl..." Both of them slowly moved along the edge of the crowd. But suddenly the crowd parted in front of them and they found themselves little more than a step away from Made's smiling, flushed face.

"Your cross to bear..." Bebrītis managed to whisper to his friend.

Biting his lower lip, Lodziņš took a half-step in Made's direction and bowed deeply as he greeted her. Holding her gloved hand in his he pulled her over towards his friend. "My friend, Bebrītis – Miss Sveilis." He held both of their hands together as if he were blessing their union.

Like a schoolboy, Bebrītis clicked his heels together and bowed deeply, very deeply as he squeezed the young lady's hand. "Charmed – absolutely charmed."

But Made saw only Lodziņš. "Have you been here long, Mr. Lodziņš?"

"Oh, we've been toiling away for a good long while ..."

"...for the good of the nation." Bebrītis added and began to fan his face with his cap. "Oh, miss, you've already missed a great deal – a great deal!"

Bebrītis made a very tragic-looking face. He didn't take his impertinent eyes off Made, failing to notice the winking smiles and gestures being made to him by his friend. He noticed only when Lodziņš muttered something and melted back into the crowd. Bebrītis clicked his heels together again and bowed deeply in front of Made. He was fairly certain that Made wasn't familiar with any modern dances.

"May I have this dance, miss?"

At first Made didn't even notice. She was looking over trying to see where Rodolfs Lodziņš had spun off with that young lady she didn't know dressed in blue. But then she snapped back.

"Thank you very much..." Realising that she'd probably said the wrong thing, she hurriedly stuck her hand into Bebrītis's outstretched hand. So that's what Lodziņš is really like!

They began to turn. It was a new sensation for Made, her expensive shoes on the hard, slick parquet floor. But after two or three awkward movements, it was starting to go well. There wasn't time for her to concentrate. She kept searching for Lodziņš and his blue lady. Bebrītis, standing tall with an exaggeratedly dignified posture and a barely perceptible smirk under his black moustache, tried to look straight into the eyes of everyone dancing nearby who he knew, just to make sure that all of them could see that he was only dancing with this unattractive girl as a joke, but he noticed Made's searching eyes.

"An attractive man – that Lodziņš," he said almost without smirking at all.

"But who's he dancing with?"

"Miss Ziepēns, the school director."

Now Lodziņš and his partner were directly across from them. Made managed to see that the school director wasn't exactly young and not all that attractive. Her heart immediately grew lighter. But she was speaking nonstop and looking her partner straight in the eyes. Made became worried again.

"She must be well educated?" she whispered into Bebrītis's ear.

He could barely stifle his laughter.

"Absolutely! What do you think: she's a school director..."

They had just arrived at the spot where they had started and Bebrītis had had enough of this joke. He was just about to leave his partner with the others standing along the edge. But five steps away Lodziņš was dancing with his blue lady. It was all Made could think about. Not letting the pair out of her sight, she kept turning her partner, moving in their direction.

Roberts felt uncomfortable in his new, tight dress uniform. He felt shy around these impeccably dressed, well-mannered people and couldn't squeeze his way through the crowd. He was staring keenly through the constantly moving, shifting gaps, in one direction, then the other. And then he finally saw her.

She was standing in between two laurel trees next to the stage filled with musicians. The trees were sickly and wasting away, so much so that they were leaning in towards each other, their tops meeting above her head. Her round, slightly too round, face looked especially rosy and vibrant in this green frame. She was wearing a white wool dress, simple shoes and socks knitted for her by her mother. Her brown braid with its fire red ribbon was hanging casually across her shoulder.

She and her friend must have just finished dancing. Now

they were about to part. They held onto each other with one hand and covered their mouths with the other – their heads together and laughing. And when her friend finally tore herself away and ran off, she threw back her braid with a single motion and kept laughing on her own. Her white teeth glistened and the sizeable gap between her wide front teeth was clearly visible.

Roberts elbowed his way through the crowd in her direction, awkwardly shoving into ladies and stepping on the polished boots of other men. But he didn't see any of it. He didn't hear their caustic comments and didn't notice their angry stares; flushed and excited he squeezed towards the stage.

She appeared not to see him. She wasn't laughing anymore but turned her head away seemingly to carefully study something in the far corner of the room. Her lips, though, were pinched together in a mischievous expression and her long dark trembling eyebrows betrayed her mood.

"Oh, Mr. Sveilis!" she pretended to be very surprised.

"Why, hello, hello, Miss Milda!" he responded excitedly and awkwardly, and he blushed as he crushed her soft warm hand in his. She had to rip it away by force.

"Don't squeeze it like that; it hurts." Pulling away her hand, she lightly slapped his fingers and began to adjust the rose, which had shifted in the crush of people.

"Can I help," he offered.

"Mr. Sveilis!" She lurched sideways. "How would that look! The director is just over there."

He hadn't seriously intended to help. Everything was good, so good that he wouldn't have wanted anything to be otherwise. He laughed with delight.

"Alone?" he asked and shot a coy look in both directions.

She shook her head vigorously. "No, of course not! My mum is here from the country."

That wasn't at all what he'd wanted to hear... Behind her there were two empty chairs. He gestured towards them.

"Should we sit down?"

"But I want to dance," she objected, and still looked back.

Roberts wasn't listening. He pushed the chairs farther back, right up to the stage.

They both sat down. Above their heads the musicians were stamping their feet, clattering their chairs, and playing their instruments. The laurel trees were obscuring the lights, two steps away from them there was a sparse line of people standing around – compared to the brilliant bright ballroom they were sitting almost in moonlight.

"Why didn't you come back yesterday?" Roberts spoke with a tinge of feigned reproach in his voice.

"To the skating rink? I was there."

"You're lying!" he almost shouted as the disappointment and pain from the previous day flashed across his face. "I was there until eleven, but you never came."

"Oh, then you must have been at the park. But we were by the new polytechnic school. There was too much of a crowd at the park, I don't like it there at all. And then, Mr. Lausks was going with Miss Zvaigzne to the Russian theatre and we tagged along. After the theatre, I came straight home. It's much better there. The company is of a higher calibre – students from the Nicholas High School..."

Something in particular jumped out at Roberts from her story. He leaned back a bit and his smile seemed to cool slightly.

"Who else was there with you?"

"Berta Vīksna... you don't know her, she's from Tailova. And Vilks... from the drama course, he's sort of an escort of hers..." She laughed giddily. Then came a suspicious pause. "And Freimanis..."

Roberts sat straight up. Above his head someone was energetically dragging a bow over slack strings. The sound of that name felt like a sharp shard of glass slicing straight into Roberts's heart.

"Oh, Freimanis..."

Milda must have understood from the tone of his voice,

or some other sign. She threw back her head, then with half-closed, laughing eyes looked at him and wrapped her hands around his knee.

"He's from the Nicholas High School. Berta's cousin. Just a little kid... in his second year..."

A weight rolled off Roberts's chest. In his second year, and Milda Caune was sixteen. There was nothing to worry about. Just a little kid – she'd said so herself. Of course, he's a kid. His shoulder brushed against Milda and everything felt good again, so good! Just the two of them and nobody could see them, hidden there.

"I waited at the park... I stayed there all evening." He laughed.

"I didn't know: we'd never agreed where to meet." She also grew silent and for a moment sat quietly and happily.

"By the polytechnic school..." Roberts began again, looking for the right words. "That's where we first saw and met each other..."

Milda nodded quietly.

"I saw you in the tram... You were sitting with a pretty young lady and I got on at the corner of Mill Street..."

"Was she very pale? That must have been Miss Zvaigzne; she's the one I'm living with."

"Yes, it was there at the skating rink..." Roberts interrupted her. "You'd fallen and hit your knee..." He gently put his hand on her knee.

"And you helped me take off my skates and walk over to the shack..." She put her hand on top of his. Now he was warm both outside and in. The warmth climbed up to his chest and spread across his entire body. He dared not move, almost holding his breath, he just sat there beaming. Milda became even more animated and talkative. "Why didn't you come yesterday – we had such fun celebrating my birthday. Mum had brought some tarts... and three brand new shirts. Vilks brought a bottle of wine and Berta brought an apple cake. We all had a drop or two," she laughed heartily. "Two pairs of socks from Mrs. Zvaigzne and a copy of Rainis's Distant Moods... And I received your card. Thank you so much for that!" She squeezed the bottom of Roberts's hand. "Such a beautiful drawing! Is it your own? It is? Where did you learn to draw like that? Why didn't you come last night?"

"I didn't know anyone..." he answered shyly, staring at the floor, "you had so many guests."

"Nonsense! The more, the merrier. We had so much fun. Freimanis knocked over a glass. He stained the whole of Miss Zvaigzne's tablecloth."

She stopped and looked at Roberts. He turned his hand over, grabbed hers and began to squeeze it, pulling it over towards him.

"Excuse me..." He muttered, completely muddled. "I just wanted... I'll..."

At first she was surprised and resisted, but then quickly understood and relented.

A small ring glittered in his other hand. Nervous and clumsy he pushed it onto her ring finger. It was too big. But, as it turned out, just the right size for her middle finger. Having put it on, he leaned back and took a breath.

"That's just... for your birthday..."

Milda was surprised. The small, notched gold ring with a green stone practically glowed on her pale finger. Her first ring! She'd wanted one for so long. Blushing with joy, she couldn't take her eyes off of it for a second.

"No - but how thoughtful you are! I hadn't expected this at all. Thank you so, so much..." Roberts felt how hot and nervous her hand felt squeezing his. "But was it expensive?"

He laughed, even happier than her. "Oh, it didn't cost much: six roubles! Just a trifle. My brother has plenty of money."

Milda became more serious.

"Oh, I see... that rich Sveilis, he's your brother... I didn't know... why didn't you tell me?"

Roberts beamed. For the first time he felt how nice it was to be a rich man's brother.

Two students in tailcoats with white gloves stopped in front of them. One leaned down and looked through the gap under the laurel trees. Roberts was stung by Rodolfs Lodziņš's mocking stare.

"Oh, excuse me…" Lodziņš bowed and moved off to the side with his friend.

Milda was squeezing Roberts's hand even tighter.

"How rude!" she grimaced. Then she got up and straightened out her dress. She looked at the ring, then, smiling playfully, she looked over at Roberts, and said, "You probably don't dance?"

Blushing, he jumped to his feet and bowing clumsily, he said, "Let's give it a try!"

They passed into the vortex of dancers. It all went about as well as could have been expected. In the crush and noise he lost track of the rhythm and then mixed up his steps. But as the other dancers spun around them, they were spun around too. Somehow they managed to make their way around the ballroom – until some tall, unfamiliar, grinning young man practically tore his partner away from him and spun her back into the whirl.

Roberts didn't get a chance to be angry. Tired and unspeakably happy, he wiped his sweat and looked off into the crowd. He couldn't see anyone, not even her. The electric, intoxicating joy he was feeling had completely overtaken him.

Rodolfs Lodziņš slapped him on the shoulder.

"Well, young man? Are you toiling away for the good of the nation?"

He didn't have the strength to be annoyed by Lodziņš's usual, somewhat offensive and mocking familiarity. He smiled back.

"We have to, there's no other choice…"

"You've found yourself a cute little filly. Probably some farmer's daughter from the country, a high school student – right?" He took Roberts by the arm in a friendly fashion. "Let's go outside for a bit to cool down. If you stay here like this, even your coat buttons will be soaked through by tomorrow morning. You'll get rheumatism. It's clear that you still lack discipline."

He started walking towards the back of the ballroom. Behind the Sigulda decorations, tables were set on a raised platform with parents and those not dancing seated around them. They were completely full. But Lodziņš knew where to go.

At the corner table, Augusts Sveilis Jr. was sitting at one end. On the far end, hunched in a corner, but with a cosy smile on his face, was Augusts Sveilis Sr. who was currently drinking out of a large glass, filled to the brim and foaming over. Sitting at the same table were Tilaks, Sietiņsons, Strauss who was the third director of the Unity Savings and Loans, Paeglītis, and the journalist Kārlis Roblapainis. They were drinking rowanberry liqueur and eating hors d'oeuvres with black caviar. Kārlis Roblapainis was the only one with a half-bottle of Sinalco in front of him – he'd said he didn't drink alcohol. You could tell instantly that the conversation wasn't going well. Sveilis was speaking with Tilaks, Strauss with Sietiņsons – each pair had their heads together and were murmuring quietly. Old Mr. Sveilis was drinking from the large glass by himself and peering over its edge with cheerful eyes at his son. Kārlis Roblapainis's fingers were twisting around his half-empty glass while he looked over at one pair, then the other. He wanted to participate in the conversations, but nobody was paying any attention to him.

Old Mr. Sveilis winked merrily over the edge of his glass at Roberts.

"Do you want a drink too? Here – have a drink..."

Roberts took a sip from the foaming glass. The tart, sweet and also slightly bitter drink was very tasty and cooled him down nicely. He sat down next to his father.

"Look how much you've danced!" His father gestured at his damp forehead and, since he was a bit tipsy, continued to blabber on. "Sit down, rest for a bit. And have a bite to eat...

Are you hungry? Have a bite – there's plenty of everything. I wonder where your mother is – someone should take some over to her too..." Taking the glass from his son's hand, he took another long and eager swallow.

"Greetings, countrymen!" Lodziņš greeted them and swept his cap across the table farcically. But nobody was interested in his jokes. Each one of them quickly turned their head back towards their partner in conversation. Only Kārlis Roblapainis gladly received this new, interesting arrival.

"Hello, hello!" Rising up partway he shook Lodziņš's hand so affectionately that both his and Lodziņš's cufflinks made a clapping noise as they rattled around inside their sleeves. "Don't you dance?"

"Of course, of course, Mr. Kārlis Roblapainis. But those who dance also need to rest. Work and rest always go hand in hand. You wrote as much just a little while ago in that paper of yours."

"Ha, ha, ha!" Kārlis Roblapainis laughed loudly and stood up straight. "Yes, yes, yes... You're very witty... truly very witty!" He took Lodziņš by his arm and dragged him towards the ballroom. He wanted to watch the dancers.

With the fifth wheel now gone from their table, the rest of them became livelier and raised their voices.

"Yes, I'll say it too: it is and remains an outrage!" Paeglītis had been listening this entire time to what Sveilis and Tilaks were saying and now he almost shouted. His sweet, tiny voice sounded unusually harsh. The waves combed into his full beard appeared to tremble, his face a dark red. "I'd get a loan for five thousand from absolutely any German bank without a single word. But these places refuse to give fifteen hundred... That's absurd! A debt of twenty-five hundred on the mortgage – paid off. I rebuilt the lavatories last autumn... In just the past year alone, land prices have risen by ten roubles... But a Latvian doesn't want to take a risk!"

"I'm not saying that I need it right away," interrupted Sietiņsons as he pulled away from Strauss. "I don't even want it right away! I've got some from the insurance... I've also rented out those three summer houses... I've got enough for a start. But when early May comes around..."

"But don't you have that bank of your own over there," Strauss said stroking his smooth, cleft chin. "Borrow from that one. It's easier that way."

Sietiņsons arched his shoulders up high and replied, "What are you saying, Mr. Strauss. Where do I have a bond for ten thousand? I just brought it over from Riga last summer – there I get only six and a half percent: we don't skin you alive like they do in Riga. And in exchange for collateral I've got another sixty-two hundred there. And I just can't do more than that: at the last shareholders' meeting some of them were starting to grumble. We've also got some reds there..."

"They'll back an outsider, sure they will... but a Latvian won't back a Latvian..." Paeglītis who appeared offended to the very depths of his being turned his back on Tilaks as if he were the guilty one.

"Excuse me, Mr. Sietiņsons." Strauss said, making excuses. "I can't do anything all by myself. I did what I could, and I can't do more. Mr. Lodziņš wouldn't be against it, but Bramberģis... There's a crisis now, he says, we can't expand our operations that way. Right here in Riga we have our old membership and we have to see to their needs first. Deposits have shrunk at every bank... we can't spend our very last kopeck; we have to continue to keep a certain amount for the payment of closed accounts."

Paeglītis laughed bitterly and dismissed him with a wave of his hand. "A Latvian doesn't know how to take a risk... Latvians are swine!"

Sietiņsons swung his hand, knocking over an empty glass. "Tell me, isn't this madness! Where is this going to get us? If it keeps up, all Latvian property owners will be wiped out in a few years. Well, why do you need to keep that amount on hand? Isn't that clearly a loss? Account deposits... Let them wait if there's no cash on hand. Why does it say on the deposit slip that you have to give six months' notice before closing your account?"

"Again..." Strauss shook his head in disagreement, "that's only in exceptional circumstances. The practice has been – always and everywhere – that deposits are paid out immediately. I can tell you that if a bank began to ask for six months' notice for payment of deposits from closed accounts, then the result would be widespread distrust. That's how you end up bankrupt. You can't play around with things like that."

"Rubbish, total rubbish!" Sietiņsons became even more agitated. "Nobody would go bankrupt. We've already experimented with this at our bank. Anybody who has more than five hundred in his account – it's a six month notice period and not a minute less." His voice started to become threatening. "But if such large sums held by the bank are simply not being utilised and not accruing interest, they won't be thanking you at the shareholders' meeting; they most certainly won't."

"All irregularities have to be brought up at the shareholders' meeting," Paeglītis added.

"And also at the auditors'!" Sveilis observed. "Pūslis and Zaķītis are friends of Bramberģis, but Tilaks should insist."

Tilaks had a hard time speaking: he sat stretching his neck and moving his mouth for a few seconds before he was able to get a single word out.

"Zaķītis is the director... the director of the board of auditors. I'd say... but he'd say..."

"He'd say... but then you'd say what you need to. He's not the only expert."

"Excuse me, gentlemen!" Paeglītis tried to shout over the others and tugged at Sveilis's sleeve. "When that spit of land in the Daugava is cleaned up and ships begin to dock there, then they'll make sure that sheds are built there..."

"I have to finish that summer house by the beginning of the season," Sietiņsons interrupted him. "If I can't rent it out next season, it's a clear loss of two thousand for me. I have to pay the interest anyway; I have to pay the insurance..."

Strauss spread out his arms dramatically. "Speaking for myself, I'm on your side, Mr. Sietiņsons. I've done all manner of things. But Bramberģis is against it. He says: we have our old membership right here in Riga..."

Sietiņsons interrupted him with a laugh laced with sarcasm and bitterness, "Yes, yes! That's what you're like here, you wealthy socialites! Six-storey dwellers! You don't care a bit about those of us living on the outskirts. But when the City Council elections come along, then you'll know very well where the outskirts are! Then the words 'nation' and 'people' will be constantly on your lips."

"Reactionaries and blood-suckers, they've got all of our monetary institutions in their clutches," cried the deeply indignant Paeglītis, who grabbed the whole of his large bushy beard in a single motion.

Strauss nervously glanced to one side, then the other. He leaned forward and spoke more softly.

"Bramberģis says, 'There's a crisis right now, and we have to be very careful.' We can't get involved with just anybody who has a cottage in Pārdaugava and a mortgage. We have to guard against those swindlers who are not used to making money but only taking it."

"Dammit!" Sveilis slammed his fist on the table and jumped up from his chair. "Where are these swindlers? Let him show me just one..."

Strauss dismissed him with a wave of his hand. "That's what I say. But what can I do all by myself? I've got almost no influence as it is. He's the director, chief clerk and has the board on his side. He says we have to support our nation's business and industry, and we can't get involved with swindlers, bar-room agitators, or innkeepers... Waiter, another half carafe of Ryabinovka!"

"Now, now...," said Sveilis, red and agitated, in a voice profoundly choked by anger. "Isn't an innkeeper also just another son of his native land?"

"If our financial institutions support anyone," Paeglītis

interrupted him with genuine pathos, "then, I think, it should be precisely those small-time entrepreneurs and merchants who don't yet have as much credit or six-story buildings. They have their whole future ahead of them, and they're the ones our culture can rely upon. The millionaires, they don't know their people anymore."

"That's what I always say too!" agreed Sietiņsons and he moved his whole body to prove it. "Support those on the outskirts if you want to achieve anything. There's still fresh, unspoiled energy out there..."

"And what about my land..." Sveilis pushed his glass away and leaned forcefully over the table. "Honestly," he pressed his palm against his chest dramatically. "If I'd offered it to the Seventh Credit Union or the Twelfth... oh right, the Twelfth doesn't need it anymore... Yes... to the Seventh or any of the others... they would've received it happily, extremely happily and thankfully! Just imagine, my property is on the corner in the busiest location, right in the centre! I wouldn't give it away for anything, I'd build there myself... But Lodziņš was the one who suggested it; they need to build a new building and the right lot is hard to find." He shrugged his shoulders and spread his arms. "I agreed... very happily... if I can help the financial institution with which I have connections... Did I need the profit? Honestly, just those tiny additional fees. I submitted an estimate..." He turned away as if those sitting at the table had offended him terribly.

The rest of them just sat there stunned with guilty looks on their faces. Sveilis's offence was too apparent and his distress too deep and honest. For a moment each of them just looked down at the table in front of them. Only Strauss was pouring the contents of the pale red narrow-necked bottle into their glasses and accompanying each splash with a word or two.

"I'll tell you, gentlemen... For me as a leading person in a financial institution..." He lifted up a bottle he glanced around at the others drinking near them and then, leaning in closer to his companions, he continued more quietly. "I shouldn't really say anything, but we are all close acquaintances with the same views... and when I feel that someone has acted wrongly, I just can't stay quiet... that's something I simply can't do. I was elected at the shareholders' meeting, but who cares? Let them sack me tomorrow. Otherwise what the point of me being there? I don't just want to sit there as a yes-man! Cheers, gentlemen!"

He eagerly swallowed a gulp of the bitter red liquid and with his glass still held up in his hand he listened for a moment. But his face showed that the bitter drink had done little to diminish his inner bitterness.

"That's not how this works." Tilaks began again as he stared at the table and pressed his fat thumb onto its edge with every word he spoke. "Isn't it a joke: all of us are members and auditors and directors – and who knows what else... and yet none of us can do any good at all. It's a clique over there, it's Bramberģis with his relatives, and it's only them that get to use the bank to their advantage..."

"Bramberģis!" Sveilis almost screamed. It was astonishing how much hatred could be thrust into a single three-syllable name. "Who is Bramberģis anyway? Couldn't Mr. Strauss be the director-clerk? Or you, Tilaks, couldn't you carry out the duties of the director just as well as Mr. Strauss? Wouldn't even I know how to go through the books and deliver a report at the shareholders' meeting?"

Tilaks inadvertently grinned with delight, but then put his hand on top of Sveilis's in an attempt to calm him down. What was the sense of yelling out loud what had long been clear to all of them? Others sitting near them would be bound to hear.

Paeglītis leaned back in his chair. "We'll show them that they can't survive without Pārdaugava..."

Sietiņsons signalled his agreement by nodding and gesturing. "And without Jūrmala... without the outskirts. The outskirts have got a future. And if our financial institutions, if our banks..."

Strauss nodded in agreement, while trying to calm his too agitated and loud-mouthed companions.

"Quieter, gentlemen, please! There are many ears around us. Actually, matters like this shouldn't be discussed here... Waiter!" He motioned with a slender, ringed finger. "Menus for all of us... and then bring us... two..." he counted everyone at the table again. "No, bring all three!" He slumped back into his chair, his hand placed diagonally across his mouth, he whispered something into the waiter's ear, and understanding what he had said the waiter nodded his head. Strauss wanted to surprise his friends. But they already understood from his expression and became merrier, livelier.

"Finish it off, dad!" Sietiņsons stretched across the table and poured the last into old Mr. Sveilis's glass. He looked over: the big one still had some in it. He nodded his head happily.

"Maybe... it's too much..."

But nobody was listening to him anymore. Coughing and gazing at the gentlemen around him, he took the glass and threw it back. He grimaced, but kept drinking anyway. He pushed the large glass over towards Roberts.

"Try this one, it's good."

Roberts drank for the fourth time. He began to notice that the tart, sweet drink was not at all as innocent as it seemed at first. It was going to his head. All his joints seemed to become a bit lighter and suppler. An easy, warm feeling flowed through him. The music sounded swift and inviting as it drifted over from the far end of the ballroom. His feet seemed to be moving all on their own. He wanted to smile, talk and spin along...

The gentlemen lit new cigars. A cloud of smoke swirled around the back of the Sigulda decorations supported by a lattice and small sticks. Pressing their heads together, concealed by a cloud, the offended members discussed the fate of the Unity Savings and Loans. The inviting music echoed from the far end of the ballroom where those both known and unknown to them squeezed by looking for their acquaintances. None of it made any difference to them, no difference at all. They were living in their own world and nothing existed outside of it...

Roberts stood up and walked back to the ballroom.

It was much brighter there because of the decorations. For a moment he stood blinking his eyes at the chandelier with its hundreds of lights. He couldn't tell anyone apart or see anything in the packed crowd. But he thought that as soon as he looked, he'd find his girl right away and walk up to her, and that was all he needed! But he couldn't see her. His eyes adjusted and he looked around carefully but still couldn't find her.

His smile first seemed to freeze and then it disappeared altogether. Slowly a deep line appeared across his brow. His right hand behind his back, drawn into a fist: the fingers of his left hand absent-mindedly twisting a smooth metal button.

He had spotted her. She had returned with her dancing partner behind the two laurel trees, where just a little while ago they had both been sitting. It was the same partner who had practically torn her away from him.

Roberts felt his cheeks and ears burning. It felt as if cold, stiff fingers were grasping his throat.

A-ha! So that's how it is! She must think he's desperate and is playing with him. His first thought was to go back to that table and sit there drinking until he was flat-out drunk and forget all about her for tonight. Who cares if she's amusing herself with her partner! But then it occurred to him: she might think that he was doing that out of jealousy or envy. Of course not; what did he care? Let her have her fun.

He squeezed through the crowd and stood right at the front. He crossed his arms over his chest, stuck out one leg in a confident fashion, tilted his head back a little, and looked out at the dancers. He looked long and hard at every single pretty girl, purposefully avoiding the slightly older unmarried women and ladies. He didn't want anyone to think he was simply looking out of boredom. No, he was interested: those young girls were of interest to him. He looked intently at each of the prettier ones and smiled. He made an effort to smile merrily while appearing both satisfied and comfortable. There's more to the world than just Milda! He, the brother of rich Sveilis, could have two on each arm. He didn't even need to look over there, towards the far end of the room. And he didn't look. But still, when the crowd flowed together and only the tops of the two laurel trees were visible above the throng, his throat would tighten again. His arms were crossed so that his joints began to ache and his palms were completely drenched with sweat. His cheeks and ears burned and his frozen grin was beginning to make the muscles of his mouth twitch.

The dance ended. The couples began to promenade around the ballroom. They flowed past him in an endless stream. The gentle patter of patent leather boots, the rustle of silk dresses. The glow of both genuine and artificial smiles, the gleam of both real and fake teeth, chivalrous speech, laughter. It all flowed together into one huge, dizzying puzzle. Roberts was straining to hold back his misery.

It's not her fault. I was the one who walked away, he tried to comfort himself. I'm sure she'll come over. But nothing helped. The pain of that moment was just too much. His thoughts felt as if they were bound by a steel hoop, his feelings felt as flat as a stone at the bottom of a pond.

Made passed by on young Lodziņš's arm, radiant with joy. She leaned over and tugged him by the elbow.

"What are you standing around for? Go find yourself a young lady!"

Lodziņš agreed and then leaned in closer to Made to tell her something about Roberts. Tears of anger filled Roberts's eyes.

No, he won't forgive her for this! He'll think of something dreadful and will have his revenge: something she won't forget. He'll show her that nobody humiliates him. He'll show all the Mildas...

Just then he jumped up as if someone had pushed him. His mouth hung open and he could barely prevent himself from screaming out. She had come up right behind to him!

She was standing right there, a little shorter than him, her head tilted, looking straight into his eyes. Her lovely face looked so happy and kind!

"What are you standing around here for?" She gave him a good shake. "Let's have a turn around the ballroom."

He had been so angry that he couldn't start laughing right away. She had offended and hurt him, and she needed to understand that. He tried to keep his face serious, indifferent even, just to stop himself from smiling and giving in!

"No, I'll just stay here..." he muttered. He wanted to add: you already have someone to go with. But he heard that his voice didn't sound indifferent or sarcastic at all and so he thought better of saying it. He tried to gently free his elbow.

But she, chattering loudly and fearlessly, wound her arm around his.

"You have to come!" She yanked him into the line of the procession, and there was no stopping her now. They had to be careful not to shove those in front of them, and to avoid those behind them from stepping on their heels. "Where did you disappear to? I was looking around the whole time and couldn't find you." She leaned over and looked into his eyes.

He couldn't help it, he had to be kind too.

"Over there," he motioned with his head towards the back, "my brother is sitting with some other gentlemen." And then he caught himself. "But listen, you must be thirsty?"

"No, not at all!" she said, tossing her head so that her brown braid hit his shoulder.

"Well, what about food... Something to eat? Yes, yes, definitely." He didn't let her get a word in. "Let's go there, and then..."

"Do you have any money?" she asked half-jokingly.

"Me?" he answered loudly and patted his trouser pocket with his free hand. "My brother has more money than either of us could ever spend."

She shook her head and became more serious. He liked the way she shook her head and also her seriousness. He understood that his worth had increased in her eyes, and his earlier heaviness disappeared. He had a strong desire to laugh.

Milda's companion from earlier had come up to the laurel trees and was standing right next to them. He was picking at some invisible fluff on his upper lip and – it seemed to Roberts – was looking on jealously at them. Roberts was secretly watching Milda, and she didn't look in that direction once. His heart became even lighter, and again he wanted to laugh. He clasped her warm hand tighter in his own.

At the end of the ballroom he pulled Milda behind the Sigulda decorations. He nudged her in the side.

"That's my brother – on this end, the one with the long, blonde moustache."

They looked over at his brother's back as they passed by. Rodolfs Lodziņš and Bebrītis were also now sitting at the table. Made was also there, taking off her gloves and putting them back on again. But they had no business with any of them.

It was impossible to move around in the buffet room. The streaming crowd pushed them apart and then close together again. They held on tightly to each other's hands and didn't let go. Every moment they'd look over at each other and smile, but you couldn't hear a word over the monstrous din. Holding onto each other and laughing, they squeezed their way over to the end of the buffet. Waiters with empty glass trays pressed through and a boy was dragging a new beer keg over to behind the buffet. They were being pushed and shoved the whole time, but they didn't care. They drank three bottles of lemonade and ate cakes.

The movement in the ballroom was growing quicker. Dizzy from drink and dancing the couples didn't want to stop even when the music fell silent. They were no longer changing partners by walking over to one person, then another. Everyone had found their other half and stayed with them. Complete strangers were melting together in the heat of the ball. Couples danced, and when they were done dancing they'd walk hand in hand around the ballroom, and then when they had walked enough they would sit down close together, only the proximity of other people and ingrained modesty prevented them from sitting together on the same chair or one seated on the other's lap, allowing the warmth of their bodies to unite, allowing their intoxication to grow... The slight waft of perfume had been completely erased by the steam rising from hidden, sweaty flesh. The electric lights seemed to be obscured by a heavy grey veil. But underneath it, eyes shone with fevered brightness and cheeks beamed and blushed. Not just those of the dancers: older ladies too, who hadn't moved a single time during the entire evening, had become intoxicated by watching the swirling festivities. Their eyes were clearer, a natural pink – late in its season though it may have been – filtered through the artificial paleness of their faces, and their hands held up iridescent fans in vain.

Only Lodziņš and Bebrītis had asked Made to dance. But that was plenty for her, and she could have gone without Bebrītis. She hated his black-moustached face which he would press too close to hers, his intrusive, shameless eyes and his mocking grin. She couldn't count the number of times she'd been angry at Lodziņš for abandoning her in the hands of this swarthy man, while he spun around with that school director dressed in blue. But then he'd come over again and all would be forgotten. She would flow along in this hot whirlpool with only one thought: if only this night would never end...

But now those two were walking over to the corner table behind the Sigulda decorations all too often. Taking off her gloves to cool down her hands, Made followed them. From just past the edge of the crowd she heard a strange noise. The clatter mixed with loud talking, and everyone turned around and looked in one direction. Made stopped in her tracks and looked over there too.

Old Mr. Sveilis was completely drunk. He was supporting himself on the edge of the table and was trying to stand up – he clambered up and fell back heavily. His hands slid off the table, pulling off the tablecloth and everything on it. His knife and fork were on the ground, and the large glass lay broken on its side on the table. The entire table was covered with brown liquid. Everyone who had been seated had stood up to protect themselves. It was only dripping onto the jacket and trousers of Old Mr. Sveilis. His spectacles had come loose from one ear and were hanging from the other by their arm, sliding crookedly across his nose. One of his eyes behind glass, the other blinking nakedly. His face was pale as a corpse.

Some of the gentlemen turned away crossly, others tried to help. Less because of the old man, but more for young Sveilis's sake as such a scandal could be very unpleasant. Those sitting nearby laughed with genuine delight. Both students joined in the merriment.

"Things sure are going well for you, old man, aren't they?" Lodziņš clapped the old man warmly on the shoulder.

"Absolutely!" Bebrītis laughed and handed him his glass across the table. "Here, throw back some more, let's see what happens."

Made angrily shoved away his hand.

"You should be ashamed of yourself! What a good joke, getting an old man drunk!" She burned with shame and anger and hurried over to her father. "What are you fooling around here for? Have you turned into some kind of pig? Straight home right away!"

Just then two waiters rushed up; they fixed Old Mr. Sveilis's spectacles, wiped off his drenched trousers with a napkin, and then each one took him by an arm, and led him towards the exit. Sveilis's closest acquaintances pretended not to see and only stole a few hidden glances. The more refined strangers stared harshly and with derision. But the great majority were just delighted by the unexpected scandal. Fancy getting so drunk at a fine, respectable event like this! A few pompous ladies shrugged their shoulders and wrinkled their noses and said something about the authorities and the newspapers.

Kārlis Roblapainis hurried over to the embarrassed company and put his hand comfortingly on Sveilis's shoulder.

"Don't worry, it isn't so grave. Nobody has been injured, have they? No! The newspapers have no business with trivialities like these."

"Old swine!" Sveilis growled angrily, moving his chair further away from the table.

"How could he get that drunk so fast?" Sietiņsons, also looking rather uncomfortable, shrugged and looked at each person seated at the table as if he were about to ask them a question.

Kārlis Roblapainis put his hand on his shoulder and comforted him.

"He's an old man who probably just isn't used to it. A bit tactless, of course, but sometimes things like this happen."

Strauss wanted to bring the dismal situation to an end. He dismissed it all with a wave of his hand and sat back down again. He gestured to one of the waiters who was hurrying over at that moment with a clean tablecloth.

"A round of coffees and a half bottle of Bénédictine... but make sure it's good and cold!"

That helped. Everyone sat down. Kārlis Roblapainis moved towards the chair where Old Mr. Sveilis had been sitting.

Made was rushing around the ballroom, looking for her mother. She walked around the entire room twice. Finally, she saw her. Hidden by some decorations, her mother was sitting alone looking bored and tired, covering her mouth with her hand as she yawned.

"What are you doing?" Made hissed crossly. "Can't you keep a better eye on Father. He's as drunk as a pig..."

"You mean... Father... what?" The old lady jumped to her feet with a start. "Oh, my goodness! But he doesn't even drink."

"Doesn't drink! When there wasn't anything to drink, he didn't drink. But give him a bottle - and he drinks so much that he ends up completely senseless! What are you looking at - come on, take him home."

Shaking her head anxiously and mumbling something under her breath, old Mrs. Sveilis followed Made through the crush of people and down the steps.

It wasn't easy getting the drunk old man into the sleigh. The more he moved, the dizzier he became. He slumped over hiccupping onto the arms of those helping him. As soon as they had got him seated he almost fell over the backrest. Old Mrs. Sveilis had to sit down next to him and poke him hard in the side, swinging her arm around him to sit him up straight.

"You old rascal! Have you completely lost your wits?"

Old Mr. Sveilis didn't have a care in the world. He grasped at the sleigh blanket with fingers so stiff they seemed almost frozen and looked around with lifeless eyes.

Rodolfs Lodziņš was waiting for Made at the door of the ballroom. He seemed to have realised that their jokes had gone too far. Either way, it made no sense to get on the wrong side of that rich simpleton Sveilis. He walked confidently towards Made.

"Did you see off your dad? That's for the best. They should've known, really – an old man and not used to drinking – that he couldn't handle that much. It's fine if you just stick to spirits or beer... but when you start mixing them... Anyway, it's not the end of the world. It can happen to anyone..."

And, taking her by her arm again and walking around with her, he began to tell a lengthy tale pulled from the lives of drunks inhabiting the finer echelons of society.

But this experience had considerably upset Made. The elation she'd felt earlier at the ball was now lost. She no longer liked Lodziņš or his tales. She started getting ready to go home and asked her companion to look for Roberts. But Lodziņš returned from the buffet and attempted to explain to her with all kinds of ambiguous phrases, gestures and winks that her brother couldn't be disturbed right now and had important duties to attend to. Her wealthy brother also had no thoughts of leaving yet. He had once again become extremely animated. His entire company were now drinking with great enthusiasm, gesturing and growing redder in the face, not at all embarrassed, instead loudly discussing the problems at the Unity Savings and Loans. With every new bottle of Bénédictine, the problems at the financial institution appeared greater, and the outrage of those who felt they'd suffered injustice also grew proportionately. Even if you couldn't hear what they were saying, but only see them from a distance, it was clear that they were grossly offended.

Director Strauss was among those who felt that he had suffered.

"I can't do anything!" he declared as he rose to his feet and pressed his hand to his chest. "Bramberģis is against everything and the board is always on his side. I've said for a long time that the membership of the board has to be changed: otherwise nothing will change."

Sveilis slammed his fist on the table. "We'll change it! I'll see to that."

"Everyone one of us must work for it," Paeglītis added. "We have to follow the example of the common workers: they're nothing on their own, but nobody dares to touch their party or organisations."

"I've heard that I assessed too low of a value for your home and land...," said Strauss as he moved closer to Paeglītis, still pressing his hand to his chest. "With God as my witness, I don't remember what really happened, but it wasn't like that... It never would've occurred to me to do that. It's just that the price of land keeps increasing there with every year and when that piece of land jutting out into the Daugava gets cleaned up... Going home already?" He turned towards the new arrivals – Made and young Lodziņš – and pulled his watch from his pocket. "Not me yet... we still have –"

Sveilis gestured to them to and said, "You two can go. We need to take care of a few more things here."

"Do you know what," Strauss leaned over towards them a bit too affectionately and said, "My motor car should be pulled up outside. Have yourselves driven home. I'll be here for a while."

And so their plans had been made for them and they both

left. Rodolfs Lodziņš wanted to stay longer, and he expected to return. He would take the girl home and then come back; there was still time. Anyway, going with her wasn't a completely negative prospect. His head was spinning from all the drinking and dancing, which made everything seem more attractive. It's true – she was no great beauty, but still, she is the sister of a wealthy, useful person. And his male ego was gratified by the fact that, without a second thought, she stuck to him like glue. That kind of boldness aroused his male instincts. This girl is up for anything... Crazy girl! He took her by the arm and they walked out to Strauss's motor car.

The motor car's engine sputtered. Its fat, springy tires squealed as they turned. Sitting above these soft, supple wheels felt like being gently rocked in someone's arms.

Ah! It was so lovely to stretch out on the soft, comfortable seat! It was only by sitting still that they could feel just how exhausting the ball had been. Now that crowd and noise were all behind them. The deceitful electric lights, the thick air of the perfumed interior, the heat – it was as if none of it had ever existed. The motor car sputtered down the empty, half-lit streets and a crisp early morning breeze cooled their cheeks.

But they didn't feel cold. Wrapped in her warm coat, slumped against the back rest, her feet on the seat in front of her, hands buried deep in her hand-warmer, Made sat dreaming with her eyes wide open. It was quiet all around, the stars twinkled above – yes, everything seemed light and distant – just out of reach – like in a dream. It was enough to know that he was right there next to her... Made had never experienced such a beautiful night before. The bitterness had gone – its dregs lying at the base of her memory had been quietly rinsed away – and a profound sense of peace engulfed all her senses. She wanted to dissolve into this happiness, to live forever in this feeling of being divided from her constituent atoms and carried away on warm and gentle waves.

What, here already? Already?! The greying yellow Lodziņš building with its six rows of black windows suddenly appeared out of the pale night. It was such an unwelcome sight that a cold shiver ran down her back. Made pulled her hand out of her hand-warmer and tugged Lodziņš by the sleeve.

"Listen, let's drive around some more..."

"Yes... yes?" Lodziņš sat up with a start from his corner and blinked his eyes. He'd fallen sound asleep from being rocked by the motor car. He only came to a moment later. "If you like... it's all the same to me..." He leaned over to give the driver instructions.

Again they were driving down the quiet, empty streets, away from the centre, towards the outskirts. They turned off of the wide, straight street onto a narrower side street. A light tingling travelled up and down her nerves, there was a tickle at the back of her throat. They drove past a factory with brown walls and dusty openings for windows wrapped with wire. They drove down a dark, narrow gap in between small brick and wooden houses, past bent gates and broken fences, past taverns closed for the night with the only light streaming from tired lanterns hanging above their doors. A young man sat underneath one of the lanterns, his hands hugging his forehead as he crouched low over a book. A window shined brightly on the corner and Made looked through to see the interior of a poor worker's room where a mother sat hunched on the bedside rocking a cradle.

The motor car couldn't speed down the narrow, winding streets. This gave her a chance to carefully examine everything she saw. As she turned her head slightly to look from afar at the scenes of poverty and misery, it was as if a distant but recognisable panorama taken from her own past were sliding by. And it was so indescribably satisfying to look out at this glow of cold memories from her warm coat, sitting on a soft springy seat, next to a handsome, refined and wealthy man. Made turned her head. His hands shoved into his sleeves, Lodziņš was slumped over in the corner, but dignified nonetheless. Each time they approached a streetlight, his colourful cap would emerge from the darkness like a rainbow and shine so beautifully in the yellow glow. Her earlier ecstasy coursed through her again, her blood also seemed to be running hotter.

But now the spectre of the Lodziņš building stretched out before them again. They couldn't keep going forever. Again, Made felt like something precious and irretrievable were sliding from her fingers and sinking back down the side of a steep mountain slope into the dark crevasse below. She was sad and afraid – she held on with both hands and refused to let go...

"I'll be afraid by myself... on those dark steps..." she stuttered getting out of the motor car. She was glad it was so dark, so no one could see how she blushed from her own shamelessness.

"Afraid?" her companion had fallen asleep again. He shook himself off and clambered out of the motor car. He must not have fully realised what he was doing or saying. "There's nothing to be afraid of. I've got a revolver in my pocket..." Not altogether stable on his own feet, he groped around in his pockets, and looked around for an attacker, but there wasn't even a night watchman anywhere near them. Then he came to his senses. "It won't be too dark. I've got an electric torch."

He also had a key to the outside door. As he was unlocking it he remembered that he'd wanted to go back to the ball. He lurched away from the door, only to see Strauss's motor car disappearing around the corner.

"Swine!" Lodziņš shook the key in that direction. "Absolute pig! Didn't I tell him to wait!"

He was sure that he'd told him to wait, but Made could only laugh.

"Let him go, let him go. What were you going to do there anyway? It's just about to end."

Cursing, Lodziņš unlocked the door and led the young lady up the stairs. Made pressed closer to him at his door.

"I'm afraid to go up alone..."

She herself didn't even understand what had happened to her. She sensed that she was behaving improperly, but none of that mattered now. Just as long as he doesn't go back to the ball... to that woman in the blue dress. Just to be sure that he stays home too.

Lonija was half-dressed and screamed as she opened the door, noticing the man. Even when Made was in her room, looking for the light, she heard the woman making a racket in the hallway while Lodziņš whispered something and laughed. But she didn't care about that. All that mattered was that she knew he was home. Let that woman in the blue dress try to find him!

Taking off her coat, scarf, and galoshes, she fell back onto the corner of the sofa. It really was wonderful to be home.

Looking back, muttering and gesturing, Lodziņš opened the door. He entered, but then caught himself. He tore off his cap and gloves.

"Excuse me, miss. I only... I'll go right away."

Tossing back her head, her hands clasped behind it, she yawned inwardly with half-open eyes and smiled.

"It's fine, it's fine. Stay a moment."

A-ha! He understood. No ceremony was necessary here. He unbuttoned his coat – he didn't even fold down the brown fur collar. He sat down heavily on the round tabouret making its springs creak: he leaned back against the desk and yawned loudly.

"A person gets sleepy riding around in a motor car!"

But Made didn't say anything, she just stared intently at him.

Damn it... that seductive way she's looking at me! And sitting like that! After all, she's not that old, not that bad looking. He grew livelier.

"So, how did you like the ball?" But she stayed silent. She just kept looking at him with narrow eyes and smiling. Oh! So she wasn't thinking about things like that anymore. He leaned closer.

"Pretty silk... and it suits you..." he first touched it with two fingers, then put his entire hand on her knee and slowly began to stroke it. At first she didn't say anything at all, she didn't move, just looked at him smiling. But then Lodziņš's expression changed and his hand became bolder and slid further up her leg – she let out a loud laugh and shifted to a different position.

Lodziņš pulled back. Confused, he bit his lower lip. God only knows what this girl wants. Made knew she wasn't behaving as she should. By giving in too easily she would lower herself – in his eyes, too. She didn't know what he took her for. But if she holds back, he might get bored... She kept smiling the same drowsy smile, but her brain was working very quickly. With all her strength she tried to force herself to speak, but she couldn't figure out what she had in common with this pretty, spoiled, educated young man. How she could attract him and hold his interest. She considered all of her trivial knowledge, before shrinking back at the thought of her own poverty. She didn't even know how to speak her mother tongue correctly! What else did she have? Wealth? But he had no shortage of that himself. Tossing her head back, she gazed at the mirror on the opposite wall. In these new clothes she didn't look old and unattractive at all. Had he come here in vain. As if listening to him talk, she stretched out even further. Her sleeves slipped over her bare elbows, her breasts pushed out – she knew, she sensed, she saw in Lodziņš's eyes what kind of impression it left. She didn't have anything else besides this half-withered body of hers wrapped in expensive clothing, but it had its value, its power of attraction. At least she had that! She hated it, she felt cold, as if rough hands had stripped her naked in front of a large crowd of people. Lodziņš's fingers slid over her naked flesh caressing and burning it – all of her joints tingled deliciously and her head was spinning.

She leaned over and took something down from the shelf.
"Isn't this your cigarette case?" she said showing it to him.
"Yes!" Lodziņš perked up. "I thought I'd lost it somewhere. You know, I've got this bad habit... I always forget something. My gloves... Three pairs of galoshes every winter, at least.

Dad is always angry at me. One time I left my walking stick in this... well, in this place... and they sent it over in the morning and left it with the doorman... they'd figured out the address from the monogram or something. Total swines! It could have turned into a real scandal back at home: it was a good thing I was able to lie my way out of it..." He laughed, but then stopped abruptly and stared intently at Made. Well, he didn't have to worry about this one... she didn't understand anything anyway. He reached over. "Give it here then."

But Made didn't. As soon as Lodziņš's hand touched it, she lifted hers up higher.

"Too slow!"

He tried to grab it, but she managed to avoid him. At first Lodziņš started to get angry, but then he realised she was teasing him on purpose. So he decided to play along. He pretended to be more drunk than he really was, and leaned in until he was right up next to her - with one hand he'd grab at the cigarette case, and with the other he'd touch her knee as if by accident. His face was red and he was becoming more aggressive. They were both quiet, except for the sound of heavy breathing. Made tried to push him back, but she didn't take her eyes off Lodziņš's face. Hot breath stinking of alcohol and tobacco seared her neck and cheeks. A brazen hand touched one, then another part of her body...

A dangerous game. Made felt that she was beginning to forget herself and everything else. She felt like she was back in that vortex again - except this time it was stronger, and even more intoxicating than at the ball. But she didn't care now.

Lodziņš had moved onto the sofa and pushed her into the corner. He had one arm around her shoulder and was grasping for the cigarette case with his other hand. Nobody was laughing anymore: both of their flushed faces were adorned with strange frozen smiles. Not joking or teasing anymore - their hands gripped, as if they were actually trying to see who was stronger. Their hands came together with a thud and then their fingers and joints pulled apart again with a crack.

It seemed to both of them that they weren't fighting over the cigarette case, but something else, something more important.

Made started to give in. Not from fatigue or because she was submitting to a superior force. From the outset she had felt that this man couldn't overpower her. Her hands and all her joints were firm, forged by work, accustomed to difficulty from childhood. Lodziņš's soft, pampered hand held her so softly and weakly around her shoulders that she was afraid to press it firmly against the back of the sofa. When his frail, child-like fingers grasped her hand, it was easy for her to pull it away. But she lost: she noticed what seemed like pain flash across his face each time she'd move faster or resist more intensely. It felt almost like shame to her – so for her sake and his, she gave in.

He ripped away the cigarette case and sat panting heavily for a moment. Then he noticed her looking at him with a mocking smile and turned down the brown collar of his coat.

"It's hot! Do they always overheat it like this in here?"

Made laughed loudly.

"Not always – only sometimes."

He heard something else in the tone of her voice – something provocative, encouraging. He became calmer and more confident. Biting his lower lip, he considered it all for a moment. Then he pushed himself closer to her and with awkward fingers began to grope at the middle part of her dress.

"Don't say a thing," he said slurring his words as tiny drops of saliva splashed onto her hand. "Me, no... I'm just..."

She could see how hard he was struggling to unhook her belt, but she let him. For the second time in her life she was in a man's embrace... and this time at least it wasn't her brother! She wasn't repelled – it was fascinating and exciting: she didn't want to move or speak.

Her belt was open. Lodziņš leaned back and took a breath. He stared at this woman – even the whites of his eyes were red.

Made sat, stretched out loosely. The earlier tidiness of her hair was now replaced by disarray; brown curls flowed across her ears and neck down to her shoulders. Flushed and tired, but she was not unattractive now. She didn't take her eyes off this man. She waited. And thought: any moment now he'll take me into his arms and squeeze me warmly and lovingly. He'll lean over and hold me even tighter. He'll kiss me firmly and affectionately. As she waited her entire body tingled.

She watched his hand twitch nervously once and then again. Then it lifted up. She shut her eyes and sank back into sweet anticipation. But then she instinctively jerked away, as if she'd been splashed with ice-cold water. He was just the same – just like her brother. Her shivers of anticipation had felt like thousands of sequins gently shaking, and now they all fell away. She came back to her senses in a cold room, dizzy from alcohol and other things, in a weak man's embrace. She jumped to her feet.

She just barely restrained herself from slapping him or, as was the small-town custom, cursing at him. All the rosiness had drained from her face. Pale and cold, and standing up straight, she looked down at her surprised, clumsy companion.

He was sitting in an awkward pose, his hand stretched out, but now slightly slumped down on the sofa. Staring at the floor, he looked as confused and helpless as a boy who'd just been scolded by his mother.

Made was ashamed and a little sorry for him. So she restrained herself from saying what was on the tip of her tongue.

"It's time to go to sleep... I'm getting tired." She forced a yawn, and once again felt that she shouldn't have done that, that she spoke out of turn. He'll get angry and leave... But she couldn't figure out how to fix what had been done and what to say.

Lodziņš muttered a good night and moved towards the door. He looked utterly dejected as he shuffled outside. At the top of the stairs he stood for a moment in the dark. Then he went back over to the locked door and spat on it.

Due to its upcoming expansion, the Baltika restaurant was to be closed for a month. Sveilis's choice to do so received many objections from old businessmen and other experts. The one who playfully scolded him most was Gailis: a lemonade, ink and canned goods manufacturer. He was one of the few people left standing from the days of Krišjānis Kalniņš, whose struggle in the Latvian Association he had joined. But these days he was motivated by more ambiguous and mundane considerations, and had abandoned such cultural circles for the company of people more closely associated with the smaller, newly founded banks.

"You're clearly not an expert," he said for the hundredth time as he slapped Sveilis on the shoulder. "Why on earth are you investing huge sums into that refurbishment – and now of all times? The summer is almost here. Winter, the quietest time of the year – that's the time to do something like this. That was the time for an extension! You'd have had that capital for three months practically without interest. Please remember that I tried to warn you!" The bare back of his neck was dewy with sweat and his red cheeks shined through his white beard; he looked genuinely upset, as if the loss was his own.

Sveilis nodded, smiling in agreement.

"You're right," for the hundredth time he gave the same answer. "But what do you expect from an uneducated man! I never went to school –"

"Scho-o-o-l..." Gailis lingered on the word. "Just don't move too quickly. Before you start something, come and ask the old experts. That'll be the best school for you."

Sveilis smiled as he listened to the old man's caution. Truth be told, he didn't mind it. He wasn't much of an expert, of course not. But he didn't want to be one. He didn't need to twist every kopeck around in his fingers ten times. He had plenty of money! He had credit at the Unity Savings and Loans as well as two other credit unions – as much as he needed! The hotel was already returning fifty percent profit for him and when it is expanded, and he hires a ladies' orchestra... and when on the first of May he opens his wine shop... he'd better order another bottle of Rüdesheimer!

Taking a sip and looking at his wine glass against the light, Gailis abruptly propped his elbows upon the table and shook both his fists.

"The main problem is that we won't have a centre anymore. We'll be scattered like in the desert. They have the Hotel Paleja, they have Punga – we have no place to meet. The opposition doesn't have its own centre. And without that nothing will happen. Mark my words."

"Our faction is completely secure," Sveilis tried to object. Now he was becoming more serious.

"Secure!" Gailis shot back. "Ask any expert and then talk. What do you think it was like at the Twelfth Credit Union three years ago? Back then these random types had ended up there – just boys really, nothing more. Grambahs laughed and said that on election night he would put up a bottle of champagne for every opposition vote, as there wouldn't be more than a dozen. And guess what happened! They only just won it, just by twenty-seven votes. Hear that! They held on with twen-ty-sev-en votes. They were just boys, but they showed us what campaigning can do."

Sveilis scratched his ear.

"Tilaks is taking care of it... Paeglītis... Strauss..."

"Let me tell you something," Gailis interrupted him. "Tilaks's restaurant is just not suitable for us. Our party has more people from the outskirts and they won't go into the centre of town. Sure, one or two will show up, but what good is that. Five or six aren't enough for us – or a few dozen, we need a hundred. If we can't get organised, right up to the last man, then there's no sense raising the issue, nothing will come of it."

For a moment he let the wine flicker against the light and then took a large gulp, eagerly, angrily.

Sveilis, deep in thought, struggled for a long time to light a cigarette.

"If Brambergis's faction get the upper hand for a second time, then I don't know... I won't have credit there anymore...

and the entire refurbishment and wine shop... all of that requires a massive investment. But," he shook his head and straightened his back, "that can't happen! Whatever happens, we've got to get those people out of there! Cheers!"

Gailis clinked his glass but didn't drink. He just kept holding his glass as he always had – tightly gripped in his hand – so that no one would notice his hand shaking from age and forty years of drinking.

"I hope so too," he sighed heavily. "It's a good thing those newspapers are on our side."

"Yes," Sveilis agreed happily, "on the side of progress. Yes, this time it has to work. To your health!"

On this occasion Gailis did drink. "Yes...," he said as he pushed away Sveilis's cigarettes. "Thank you, but they're too light for me." He beckoned someone, "Žanis! Bring me a couple of Imperials. But that Tilaks is just not clever enough. You have to know how to handle these kinds of things. Of course, truth is on our side, but you also have to prove it and convince others. You might be right ten times over, but if there's no one to vote for you, then it's over. The main thing is: we can't fall asleep on the job..."

Pressing their heads closer together, both opposition members of the Unity Savings and Loans began to quietly discuss the secrets of campaigning.

The governor had annulled the results of the first meeting, at which Bramberģis's faction won the vote. The second was scheduled for April 25th. The whole city was abuzz. Fifteen hundred members, split into two factions who hated each other, and would do whatever they could to destroy the other side. If you had listened Bramberģis's party, you would have had to agree that there couldn't be a more honest or ideal group of leaders for a credit institution than themselves. But if you had talked to the other side, it would have only taken five minutes to convince you that nobody had ever come across such a large group of cutthroats as the Unity clique, and that the bank would face inescapable bankruptcy if it weren't removed. But if members of both sides happened to be together then it was impossible to understand or be convinced of anything. The only things you would see would be agitated faces, threatening gestures, and loud arguments which gradually developed into cursing and usually much more than that. Friends became implacable enemies as a direct result of the anticipated meeting. Five complaints had already been submitted to the courts due to verbal insults made in public places, and one for a physical offence.

It wasn't only the members of Unity and their close associates who were upset. All of the traditional Latvian taverns were full of people, and you hardly ever heard anyone talking about any subject other than the meeting set to take place on April 25th. Either inspired by hope or fear – everyone drank without constraints. During theatre and concert intermissions, on trams and on the municipal railway, everyone was discussing and arguing over this fateful meeting. The nervousness was also palpable at all the Latvian banks and among their employees and customers. Leading up to the anticipated fight all manner of calculations and worries flowed back and forth. Numerous questions were raised and predictions made. The least of which was that a wager of a hundred bottles of champagne had been made on the outcome of the fight on April 25th.

In the final week before the decisive battle the final reserves were mobilised. The opposition dispatched three motor cars for this task; the ruling faction, it was said, had dispatched six. The more active faction members didn't rest from morning to night. They walked around the most popular restaurants and campaigned tirelessly, without losing their fervour. Catching sight of someone they knew crossing the street, they would stop them and try to change their mind. And if nothing else worked, they'd drag them into the nearest tavern. Beer and spirits, or champagne in more delicate cases, flowed freely, without measure and without caring about the cost. All manner of promises would be whispered into the ear of the intoxicated person. A thousand roubles credit, a six-storey house for just one vote! Fortunately, Latvian idealism had blossomed to an unbelievable extent because of the elation stemming from a new awareness of truth and justice, the fight for the nation's welfare and for honest bookkeeping at the nation's credit institutions. As well of course as the expulsion of useless and harmful elements from Unity...

The newspapers compiled, analysed and highlighted all that was discussed at meetings, on the street and in the taverns. They were contributing to this great cultural struggle. The conservative papers defended Brambergis's party; the more centrist papers tried to take a neutral stance and speak objectively about the matter at hand and were against factional divisions; the progressive papers – out of principle along with other reasons – helped the opposition. All of them published long treatises on the history of Latvian credit in general and the history of Unity in particular. Some listed the great accomplishments of the current bank directors and described the correctness of their actions, others brought to light even the tiniest oversights and mistakes with irrepressible glee. Poorly written prose or even more poorly stitched together verses described in a veiled manner the families and private lives of either the men currently in charge of the bank or those seeking to replace them. Sharp personal attacks also appeared and anger-filled reviews featuring threats of settling accounts elsewhere. Buckets of swill were emptied out on the opponents' heads in front of the readers while also shamelessly putting their own undergarments on display... The chronicles of thefts, fights and suicides were reserved for the bottom of the newspapers' third page and remained there. Half of the columns every day were taken up by matters connected with the Unity meeting on April 25th. The closer the historic day approached, the more feverish the activity became. Long articles served no purpose anymore. Now short, biting comments were being written and printed as calls to action and proclamations. The members of each faction themselves didn't know what else there was to say, they'd written it all out over and over again, and were exhausted. Next came the critiques and endorsements from the editorial boards themselves. Everyone who cares about the truth and the welfare of the nation absolutely has to take a stand on this important moral issue. Gradually, even those who had no business with Unity, its factions or their battles were systematically hypnotised and influenced. The entire nation was waiting with bated breath for the outcome of this fight. The power of gold held all of them in a state of tireless anticipation and consternation.

The meeting was set to begin at nine. But it was before seven when the corridors and stairs of the building began to fill. A few people lingered downstairs at the restaurant, but most squeezed their way straight up to the hall. When an assistant police inspector, two district commanders and six policemen appeared, they tried with great difficulty to drive the throng away from the locked doors and get them to stand in two straight lines. But when they managed to get the first ones to take their places in line, the others followed suit. By the time the doors were opened, the arrangement was firmly in place and newcomers wordlessly took their place at the end of the line. The great majority were seasoned professionals - members of five or six credit institutions, of which two or three ended up in this kind of tussle every year.

Government officials were sitting by the door of the hall carefully checking the membership booklets and documents of everyone entering. The hall continued to fill up slowly, terribly slowly. The lines moved forward a step at a time every minute. And became longer with every moment. The members arrived in motor cars, in private or rented carriages, some with one, others with two horses. Overheated and out of breath, they hurried into the building in ones, twos and groups, discarding their outdoor clothes and getting in line - hot and sweaty as they wiped their faces and straightened their cravats. Sometimes the lines would grow so much that their ends would stretch out the door and onto the pavement.

A cool April wind was blowing down the street, but that concerned no one. These fat, rheumatic citizens who couldn't stand the slightest opening of a door or window in a train compartment, were standing on the pavement sweating and running their palms again and again across their bald heads or the patchy remnants of their hair, which the wind was drying and tossing about. Dandies in their fashionable silk-lined jackets, for whom five minutes was too long to wait at a theatre's box office, were now waiting patiently for the big event. Out of breath innkeepers and country landowners, who would find it difficult in other circumstances to propel themselves into a carriage, were moving effortlessly up step by step. Worn out teachers, clerks used to sitting down all day, starving students, three or four editors and journalists, a few writers, and an actor – the vast majority of them Latvians, but also an occasional German master craftsman or merchant. Citizens – no! They were soldiers loyal to their oath, who weren't afraid of any difficulty or obstacle. A group inspired by the same idea, a crowd carried away by the same enthusiasm, where the narrow and personal was forgotten and all that remained was their shared and overarching values.

From the first to the last, they were all convinced that this was a fight for an important and noble cause. If someone recognised an opponent, he stared at him provocatively. But the great majority were strangers to each other; they were seeing each other for the first time and didn't know how to tell friend from foe. And they didn't linger on this. It would all get sorted out upstairs. If only we'd been able to get up to the hall sooner, was the thought on everyone's mind. Representatives from the opposition and the ruling faction trotted up and down the gap along the middle of the stairs pressing a manifesto into everyone's hand. But those didn't hold much weight anymore. At the first meeting that was the case, but now everyone knew which side they were on. Some carefully read and studied them, others glanced at them quickly and shoved them into their pocket, and still others, giving them a look, laughed derisively, crumpled them up, and threw them on the floor. Whenever this happened one hundred pairs of eyes brimming with curiosity would turn towards the source of the disturbance. A solemn hush would pass over the narrow room. A church vestibule was never so silent.

Two long lines of people stretched from the outer doors through the narrow entryway, up along the four flights of the staircase to the small space in front of the doors leading into the hall. The scrupulous soldiers of the Unity Savings and Loans marched upward in single file quietly and ominously. Only when one of the organisers from the opposition or the ruling faction would dart up or down the stairs to count their members would the lines quiver a little. Friendly, comforting smiles – the wink of an eye, a determined nod, a quick handshake, a whispered word said so hastily to be rendered incomprehensible to others... and from somewhere off to the side a sarcastic smirk or a quiet, stinging comment.

As could be expected, Unity's ruling faction were more self-assured than the opposition. They were more established and better organised. A certain group of debtors who were the protégés of the current board had to look out for their protectors. Victory or abandonment was for many a question of life or death. The opposition's interests weren't yet as coordinated or well-defined. There were those debtors who clearly knew their goal, who had tried or used up all other sources of credit and now were laying all their hopes and efforts on what happened at Unity. But there were also those who had been moved by wounded vanity, and even a few who had been inspired and dragged along by gold fever. The opposition had more reason to doubt their success. But the ruling faction couldn't be entirely sure either.

The narrow gap at the doors leading into the hall pressed the two lines together into a single tightly-packed cortège. Slowly, but not retreating or relenting by even half an inch, this cortège slid forward towards the narrow gap. Those who were closer could already see the half-empty hall where the first arrivals were anxiously walking around alone, in pairs, or in groups talking amongst themselves. Officials from the leadership of the governing body, sitting behind a long table by the doors, were carefully examining the membership booklets and documents of every new arrival and distributing ballot papers. The assistant police inspector was on the other side of the doors, while the two district commanders were on the inside attempting to hold back and split this stream of humanity. But there was little they could do. Individually they couldn't move, turn around or stop someone. As if drilled in by a screwdriver, a steady force drove this mass onward slowly but ineluctably. A shortness of breath. No desire to talk. Slowly and ominously the stream moved towards the doors of the hall. From the final flight of the stairs, every eye was turned in that direction. Impatience and anxiety building with every step. But still they waited and continued to move little by little.

Now an inexplicable commotion could be heard coming from both sides of the doors. It wasn't possible to distinguish individual words or phrases. But it mixed together into a frenzied uproar and flowed down all the way to the bottom of the stairs. And immediately both lines swayed along the loops of the staircase – outstretched necks with every face turned upward. Anxious questions were intoned, but no one could say anything for certain. It was however clear that something significant had happened.

From the outset, those closest to the doors had been able to see three men leaning over the long table, carefully monitoring that everything was in order – Strauss and Bramberģis on one side, and Lodziņš on the other. Sveilis Jr. could be seen at the other end of the table – with his silk-lined lapels, the pin from the Cyclists' Association and the gold chain threaded through a button hole stretching across his chest. He looked unusually flushed and kept pulling his handkerchief out to wipe his face, but was standing straight with his chest out. He was trying to look self-assured and indifferent. Now he began to move too; he came closer, leaned over, looked and listened for a moment, and when he turned around again towards the crowd standing in between the doors, his face shone with genuine, heartfelt delight.

First one, then another, then a third squeezed out from the tightly-packed mass of people by the doors and went back down. Agitated, grumbling loudly, with painfully furrowed brows, deeply offended by the astonishing, boundless injustice of it all... Quickly a fresh piece of news began to spread: the sixty new members accepted following the first meeting would not be allowed to vote. A heavy blow to Brambergis's faction and a gain for the opposition. Some were agitated and felt angry in solidarity with those who were leaving. Others called out merrily to people standing near them who shared their views and exchanged glances, winks and smiles with those standing further away. The throng was gripped even more tightly by a fever of uncertainty, impatience and disquiet.

At around eleven the hall was full. All the seats had long been taken, the latecomers crowded together along both sides at the back – they sat on the windowsills, the orchestra barrier, on the steps of the stage. The hall had never been so full of people during any theatre performance or other event. Those seated in the balconies looked down with surprise at the swirling mass of people. But they were soon obscured by smoke rising from cigars and cigarettes. The great majority of the guests were here for the first time. They carefully examined the curtains, lamps and ceiling frescos, the people seated in the balconies, and the decorations. But their necks soon grew tired. Their heads turned down again and bald scalps dewy with sweat reflected the dispersed light moving through the smoke – dozens, entire rows of bald heads. Gradually the conversations began to die down, and a fever of agitation and impatience once again overtook the crowd.

Those who were standing next to someone they'd come with or about whose views they didn't have a single doubt, spent their time secretly counting, watching their friends and enemies, and trying to determine the outcome. Those who were alone just watched intently as the leaders of both factions ran around animatedly at the front, and the officials overseeing it all took their seats at the table.

But as soon as the chair of the meeting began to speak, it began to get noisy again. The meeting hall was boiling over like a giant cauldron, beginning with a soft murmur and culminating in loud shouting. Agitated members rose to their feet, gesturing and trying to shout over their neighbours. Those who had been outshouted tried to rebuke but also convert those who had outshouted them, and so for a long time nothing coming out of this uncontrolled racket could be distinguished or understood. But after about ten minutes, everyone calmed down a bit, separated and in the end only two names could be heard. "Raibums!" yelled the crowd standing in front of the ruling faction with dozens of different voices echoing their call. "Zīle!" Sveilis yelled even louder as he stood facing the hall – sweaty and as red as a beetroot – and the opposition repeated it from every corner of the room. And so for a time these two names were like stones flung by two powerful hands; they would hit each other and fall to the ground with a loud crack, only to hit each other again and shoot loudly up towards the ceiling. The opposition had the advantage in this fight, as their candidate's name was so short. They could yell it out twice in the time it took the ruling faction to yell out theirs only once. But from the perspective of phonetics, the ruling faction had the advantage. When ten men at a time would yell out the first syllable "Rai...", the windows of the hall and even the floor would shake and everyone could feel the vibration through the soles of their boots, while the opposition's "Zī...," sounded small and meek as it buzzed by somewhere over the crowd.

A bell jingled, but it seemed almost as if it were ashamed, clearly aware of its own ineffectiveness. A torrent of dark waves suppressed and overpowered its small silvery drops.

The election of a new chair of the meeting would decide this evening's fight: the faction that would win here would take all. Hence the inability of Unity's members to calm down. Every one of them understood that nothing was going to be achieved by yelling, that each one of them had a ballot in their hand on which they only had to write their candidate's name, and each one of them already knew for whom they'd be voting. But this stream of heated, stirred-up feelings overpowered reasoned thought and cool heads. The desired result seemed closer, more secure and more within reach when one yelled out a name and heard a hundred others yelling it as well.

They calmed down and began writing. Those who were more confident reached for the ballots of their less convinced acquaintances, checked them or just wrote in the name with their own hand. Others didn't have anything to write with – those who did immediately broke their pencils into three pieces and passed them out. Now nothing was too dear for anyone – they would give the shirts off their own backs. The leaders squeezed through the lines of chairs and made sure that everyone was writing, and collected the completed ballots. There was a fear that some wouldn't write anything or even submit them at all out of sheer negligence or laziness. The most sharp-eyed men from both factions formed a wall around the table where the officials were assembling the completed ballots – they counted along with them, watched each other, and if one of their own couldn't squeeze through to the table, they would reach back and take the precious item from them.

Counting the ballots took some time. The relatively steady buzz in the hall did not quieten down. The smoke and heat increased incessantly. Those who were fatter, and those who were out of breath or had weak hearts, went downstairs to the buffet to get something to drink and refresh themselves. But there weren't too many of these. While the identity of the new chair wasn't yet known, neither was the outcome of the entire meeting. Uncertainty held everyone in a vice. They were being rocked by shifting waves of hope and doubt. A single word spoken by a stranger standing nearby could exalt or depress.

There were conversations, but all of them were forced and artificial; voices sounded affected and all eyes were looking over at the crowd standing around the table. People wanted to smile at members of their own faction squeezing through with a stack of ballots and trip up their opponents for doing the same thing.

Using his elbows and shoulders to great effect, Sveilis made his way out of the crowd. He leaned back against the lectern and wiped his sweat with agitation. For now, it seemed like Raibums's pile was larger.

Zvanītājs – the master tailor – bowed deeply and squeezed his hand warmly.

"Well, how does it look in there?" he smiled sympathetically, looking Sveilis in the eyes as if the outcome of the election only interested Sveilis and not himself.

Sveilis shrugged his shoulders. "Still no way of knowing. They campaigned... campaigned hard...," he couldn't finish his sentence, as his heart was too full. So he just waved his hand to express his helplessness.

"Yes," Zvanītājs agreed warmly, "a visitor this morning who knows them well said that they've spent twenty thousand..."

Sveilis didn't have a good opinion of the master tailor. He turned partly away from him.

"Not twenty, but I have heard ten."

The master tailor stood uncomfortably. "I...don't know, but he said it was twenty..."

Writing something down in his notebook, Kārlis Roblapainis squeezed through the crowd. He stopped by, and smiling, he poked Sveilis's sleeve with his pencil. "Well, Mr. Sveilis, how does it look?"

Sveilis shrugged his shoulders. "Too early to say..."

"Y-yes..." Kārlis Roblapainis grinned as he nodded his head, writing down something else quickly in his notebook. "Definitely too early to say, but it does seem that the majority is on the side of the board..." he continued, still smiling complacently, and looked Sveilis straight in the eyes. With a nimble motion of his fingers he popped a rubber band around his notebook and placed it back in his inside pocket.

Sveilis bristled... "Perhaps. That clique didn't spare any expense. And how many of those here were forced to vote against their own conscience? How many of them had a loan or are guarantors for a loan? Their hands are tied, and they have to follow orders."

"But you, Mr. Sveilis, if I'm not mistaken, you also have... old connections..." Kārlis Roblapainis communicated the rest of what he wanted to say through gestures.

"Me? Yes, but I'm not only looking after my own interests," Sveilis responded. "I've got connections there, it's true, but I can also see that everything has gone badly wrong. If a person gets a loan, but someone else with even more collateral, doesn't, then I just can't... I'll tell you... I... for my... overall interests..." So agitated was he that he couldn't finish what he was saying. All he could do was wave his hands about.

"That's the main thing," Kārlis Roblapainis agreed. "A community institution must defend community interests."

"You say that now," Sveilis said ruefully, "but why didn't you print that in your paper. Is it the responsibility of a newspaper to defend the common interest or only that of a specific clique?"

"Forgive me, Mr. Sveilis," Kārlis Roblapainis felt offended by such suspicions. "We've always endeavoured to take a non-partisan position towards our credit institutions. We can't know which side is right and which isn't. Those things have to be decided by yourselves."

"But we know who's right, don't we?" Sveilis slammed his fist against his chest. "But you don't print it! We submitted all the evidence to you... with all the facts... and you don't print it."

"I think that we gave both sides of the story."

"Both sides..." Sveilis became even angrier. "But that's the problem. You let thieves and cheats say what they want, but when you're given... all the facts... all the evidence... you don't print it!"

Kārlis Roblapainis was becoming a little nervous, so when somebody joined them, he he started to move away: "Maybe... I don't know. Those things are under our editor's jurisdiction."

"Oh, so this gentleman is from the editorial board?" interjected the lawyer Blics, who had just come up and heard the last few sentences. "Then tell your editor that he can't expect people's approval if he carries on behaving in this way. Our principled efforts require no advertisements; we only ask for non-par-ti-san-ship. Nothing more! But what do you do! I submitted an article with all the facts and evidence – and it was pulled to pieces! Everything that was most important... everything that had meaning... was deleted."

Kārlis Roblapainis quickly found a gap between two chairs just as old Lodziņš, looking cross and staring at the ground, was coming through it the other way.

Sveilis, laughing bitterly, shook his fist after him. "The press! And when the other side gets twenty thousand for campaigning, there's nobody to hold them to account. It'll come straight out of the bank's coffers in the end!"

"What? How dare you?" Beitans the engineer had stood there for a moment listening and now suddenly turned towards Sveilis. His tall, slender form bent menacingly, his grey beard shaking, his eyes angrily drilling into Sveilis. "Do you want to accuse someone here of dishonesty? Are you trying to call someone a thief?"

Sveilis jumped back a bit. But his anger was considerable and he straightened his back again. "Did I call you that? What do you want?"

"No? There are witnesses here!" Beitans moved even closer. "I want a clear answer from you: who was it that stole that twenty thousand from the bank?"

Sveilis glared back with twice the hatred. He tried to bare his teeth sneering as mockingly as possible. "Well, if you want to see thieves..."

Blics, who was a legal expert, wanted to protect a member of his faction from making any ill-considered statements, so he placed his hand on Sveilis's shoulder, and then turned around with cold contempt towards the engineer. "Nobody was mentioned by name here. What are you intruding for?"

"Oh, not mentioned by name, huh? Oh, I'm intruding!"

"Yes. Why the intrusion?"

Agitated and out of breath, Berķis pushed back from the table. Sietiņsons was behind him.

"Good, that's okay!" Berķis could barely talk. He just smiled and said, "We have more votes!"

"Really?" Sveilis and Blics exclaimed at the same time.

"No, we don't have more...," Sietiņsons turned away in resignation. "There's no way of knowing yet."

"But listen to me, we definitely have more!" Berķis was trying to convince the unbelievers with his head, his gestures and his entire body. His fists and his elbows were pressed to his sides, and his brow furrowed as if from great pain. "I was standing there watching the whole time. At first they did have more, but towards the end, whatever came in, was for us. Three or four slips at a time..."

Sietiņsons dismissed him with a wave and turned in the other direction. He hadn't had a drop yet this evening and was in an extremely pessimistic mood...

Gradually everyone grew calmer and sat back down again. Fifteen minutes of waiting seemed like an eternity. In the heat and smoke of the overcrowded room, some had turned quite pale, but held onto the backrests of the chairs in front of them, refusing to abandon the battlefield. The nervousness reached its peak, and their overstimulated nerves now felt numb. They were no longer aware of anyone else - either friend or foe. They all sat still watching one thing only - the table in front of them and the crowd surrounding it.

Gradually the result of the vote became known. It was absolutely wonderful! Nobody was walking around announcing it, but occasionally someone would lean over to his neighbour and whisper a question in his ear, and almost everyone appeared to sense the outcome. A known leader from one of the parties might leave the table with either a beaming or a darkened expression, and he could either go and sit down heavily in the front row or walk over and light a cigarette leaning against the orchestra barrier self-assuredly – these were all actions pointed to the likely result. Practically hypnotised, as if they were waiting and praying for salvation, the Unity competitors stared at their leaders' eyes. The ones who detected an inner spark of delight, their faces stretched involuntarily into a smile – they wanted to laugh out loud, exclaim, run over, hug them and press them close to their chests. Just as the leaders up front fought back these inclinations and attempted to appear indifferent and respectful, so too did the others only exchange glances and smiles, confirming their suspicions of victory to each other. But those who noticed their leader's pursed lips and drooping gaze, seemed to fall back exhausted into their seats. Still they too waited for their suspicions to be confirmed from the platform. Some couldn't, just couldn't imagine that all of their long and carefully laid plans and calculations were about to collapse; while others couldn't believe that the dreams they'd secretly nurtured would be fulfilled.

When it was announced that the opposition candidate Zīle had been elected with a twenty-three-vote majority, the room instantly fell completely silent, only to be followed shortly afterwards by a thunderous rumbling. They were clapping their hands so fiercely that it didn't sound as if they were striking one hand against the other, but instead were using clackers constructed from some inanimate material just for this occasion. They stamped their feet without mercy against the parquet floor, they threw back their heads with wide grins howling at the top of their lungs. And, when they had calmed down, they tried to spot a nearby acquaintance or faction member and whisper to them happily over the downturned heads of their sullen opponents.

Dr. Zīle, a slender man with a thick black moustache, was distinguished by his solemnity. He climbed the steps up to the lectern to more thunderous applause. Zīle read off ten previously memorised points about the unwelcome qualities to be found in Latvian credit institutions. Institutions whose work had been so significant in raising the nation's level of culture and prosperity. He spoke of the narrow-minded spirit of cliques, of self-interest and egotism, and about the contemptible internal divisions that were an affront to the name "Unity". He asked all upstanding members to rid the bank of undesirable elements, to discuss everything without hatred or passion, and to elect only the most honourable of honourable individuals to all offices. Zīle's speech was altogether appropriate, but it was clear where his sympathies lay and in which direction he leaned. The opposition's majority was still rather small – the winners couldn't feel completely secure yet, and the losers still had a small glimmer of hope. The battle was only beginning.

It went on. The schedule was on paper, but nobody followed it. At first, the behaviour of the board during the previous invalidated meeting was criticised the most. Opposition speakers had been arbitrarily interrupted, objections were disregarded, the statutes were ignored in a dozen different ways and illegal campaigning had been encouraged. More ballots were counted than there were voters. And afterwards, a cleaning woman had found thirty ballots with names of opposition candidates written on them, hidden under the tablecloth. Thirty or forty full members were barred from entering the meeting hall. It wasn't clear where the boundary lay between truth and lies; it was hard to say how much of this was painful truth and how much was intentional or accidental fabrication. But it was clear that every speaker was convinced of his own truth. Excited and trembling voices, red faces, hands wringing, shoulders shrugging, heads shaking – all of it seemed illuminating and convincing. All of these outer signs pointed to inner conviction and truthfulness. The opposition accompanied their speakers with loud applause and hurrahs. But the ruling faction did exactly the same for their speakers. Both sides interfered with speakers representing the other side by yelling, jumping to their feet, and making all kinds of noise. Others tried to hush the speaker – and at times there was such a racket that there was real fear it would all come down to blows. The chair rang his little bell in vain, he pounded the lectern and tried to shout over the savage din to no effect.

When seven men from the opposition had said their piece and three from the leadership and board had made their excuses, Zīle, as an experienced bank and board room politician, brought the opening debates to a close. Three to seven – it was clear which side managed to make more accusations and which ended up looking worse. "It's no coincidence," Zīle said as he closed the debate, "that the government itself has acknowledged that the behaviour of those chairing the previous meeting was incorrect and therefore repealed all of its decisions..." This addendum came at just the right time and place and made a considerable impression. The delighted opposition applauded and hollered again, those agreeing with the board sat in glum silence.

The announcement by Zaķītis, the chairman of the board of auditors, was accompanied right from the start by jeers and laughter from the opposition; the more he spoke, the louder they jeered and laughed. The angry hissing from those agreeing with the board was drowned out by the overwhelming sound of ridicule. The speaker managed to restrain himself again and again, he paused at length waiting for the noise to die down so he could at least hear his own words again. But finally he'd had enough. He dropped his hands and stood up straight. "Do you want to hear what I have to say or not?" he yelled, glaring at the jeering, laughing faces.

"Don't talk rubbish!" someone yelled in response from the back of the hall and a wave of laughter accompanied this call. "Tst! Tst!" the defenders of the board hissed in response, but that only fired up the laughter even more.

"You're at a bank meeting, not a tavern!" the auditor tried to yell over the racket. And then he really had had enough, too. "Utter louts!"

His words were like explosive material thrown onto a fire. "Get him out of there! How dare he? Get him out!" the incensed crowd roared. It seemed like they were just about to rush the stage and attack the thoughtless offender. He demonstratively stepped away from the lectern, took his stack of audit papers, threw them down heavily, and then sat down. Zīle rang the little bell over and over again until finally everyone calmed down.

Prompted by Sveilis and other acquaintances, Tilaks rushed up to the lectern. Always incredibly assured and sharp-tongued behind the buffet, here he seemed completely confused and unhappy. He spoke very quietly, choking on his own words, and forgetting what he was going to say. It was hard to understand him.

"...I don't agree... not at all... but what can I do, by myself... Zaķītis and Pūslis... with the board on their side..." He was more annoyed than anyone else by his befuddlement, and became ever more animated, started to wave his hands around with increasing energy. For a long time, he was only able to stutter along until finally the crowd began to respond with cat-calls: "A clique! Swindlers, nothing else."

The angry screams of the offended and applause from the opposition at just the right moment interrupted his speech. Shaking his fists and nodding towards the hall, Tilaks jumped away from the lectern. He looked around and went over to stand next to Sveilis.

"You should've said more," Sveilis whispered in his ear. "You should have really given it to them."

Pūslis - the master painter - was already standing at the lectern. Appealing for quiet, he hit his left hand against the lectern, while casting withering glances at the loudest troublemakers among the opposition. He had a loud, piercing voice and fairly fluid speech. The troublemakers gradually quietened down.

Pūslis was amazed, truly amazed at the member of the board of auditors who participated in all of the committee meetings and yet couldn't bring himself to object to any of the audit board's decisions. It was probably because, along with the other two members, he had found nothing amiss. He was surprised by the members who didn't wish to listen to the nonpartisan report from the chairman of the board of auditors, but instead blindly agreed with two or three troublemakers and schemers. Here he was interrupted by Strauss's calls: "Who are they?" And he was immediately backed up by five or six calls: "Don't just insult them! Make him call them by name!" Pūslis angrily pounded his hand on the lectern and continued to speak with a raised voice. The current leadership had acted selflessly, had made sacrifices for the greater good. In the name of the board of auditors he proposed that the most heartfelt gratitude be expressed to them. And the troublemakers and schemers should be thrown out.

He didn't get any further. He pounded his hands and stamped his foot in vain. The noise slowly grew louder and eventually drove him from the lectern. In the front, on the left side of the meeting hall, Paeglītis had gathered together a proven group of opposition fighters – and when all of them put their hands and voices to work, there was no argument or fine speaking ability that could stand in their way. Calling out something inaudibly, Pūslis darted through a gap in the crowd and out of the meeting hall, slamming the door with a loud bang behind him.

Without much success or protest, three or four others also spoke. Then the lawyer Blics walked up to the lectern looking incredibly solemn and holding the annual review in his hands. Following the accepted rules of rhetoric, he first made a few introductory comments, then divided his topic into theses and supporting points, and only then did he begin to examine each of them separately. He began with the simplest and least important points and moved gradually towards the more serious ones. He didn't have an especially good voice, nor was he gifted with any particular talent at speaking. But following the stuttering and agitated yelling of those before him, he sounded good. The troublemakers had also grown tired and so didn't interrupt him. It was as if Blics were descending down staircase of a hundred steps – ever lower, ever deeper into the disastrous business practices of Unity's current leadership. He began with small, simple oversights and mistakes, with inaccurate statements made by board members which had been overheard but could not be confirmed, with the loss of a few kopecks here or there, all of which were only significant as evidence of how system was operating. He moved on to partisan denials of credit, without mentioning them by name, he rebuked Sietiņsons and noted Paeglītis's unrecognised fifteen hundred rouble bond. He finished by pointing out the astonishing trust and availability of credit to those who sided with the clique, their close acquaintances and all manner of doubtful businesses, while noting that at the same time the clique recklessly ignored the interests of the majority and defiled the notion of working for the public good by bringing Latvian credit institutions into disrepute and in effect compromising the entire Latvian nation.

Following thunderous applause and shouts of agreement, any attempts to defend or support the old leadership became impossible. Those defending it were no longer met with jeers or other means of driving them from the stage; however their words were met with sombre faces even though the atmosphere was calmer. It was clear in which direction the balance of power was shifting. Bramberģis, though, would still attempt to save himself and his faction.

The appearance of this silver-haired, respectable gentleman left a very positive impression on his opponents. His speech sounded just as respectable as he looked. He doesn't need that bank himself. Everyone who knows him knows that he, thank God, is completely secure financially. But he had been there when Unity was born, had worked with it from the very beginning, and had seen how from its humble beginnings it had grown into one of the most powerful and respectable Latvian credit institutions. Of course, he is only human, and has made a mistake or two like everyone else has. But that was never done wilfully, or as the result of some evil intent. And it's painful, very painful, that this is exactly the brush he's being tarred with. It might even be that it isn't happening intentionally – he doesn't dare consider even his opponents to be such depraved people – but in that case it's definitely down to a misunderstanding. He doesn't need to make excuses, but he does have a responsibility to clear up any misunderstandings... At the same time, he acknowledges after having glanced at the annual report now and again that tiny mistakes have been made and doesn't deny the loss of a few roubles, which may have occurred due to an oversight or an employee's carelessness. He carefully explains the reasons for the various denied and approved requests for credit and refutes the accusation that personal interests or partisanship were involved in decision-making. And then for an instant he fell silent, as if he were reconsidering his words. Those in attendance sat quietly and waited. It seemed like something else important was going to be said. He wished to reiterate that he hadn't come to make excuses, to beg that he be left in his position of director-clerk. His conscience is clear and his hands are clean – and his old age is secure, thank goodness. He felt he was probably standing up there for the last time and so couldn't keep quiet about everything that seemed so blatantly clear. Unity had been established and had been lifted up through the joint action of the Latvian nation. The people's pennies have been entrusted to Unity for safekeeping. Not one, not a single one of them can be allowed to go missing! The members can depose the current leadership and vote with their conscience. But they should make sure that an institution working for the public good does not become the home of speculators, those looking for easy profits, and barroom agitators. A position on the board is a position of trust, therefore, those holding such a position must be known and proven men.

 Brambergis's speech made such a powerful impression that

those agreeing with him forgot to applaud and the opposition forgot to make noise. Now there truly was no way of knowing how it would turn out. Sveilis fidgeted uncomfortably, craning his neck and looking around. Is there really no one who can contradict him, tear him to shreds, come up with evidence? Even he felt a little ashamed after Brambergis's speech. But he didn't show it. He coughed provocatively, and tried to look as if he were smirking sarcastically. He burned with anger, knowing it was impossible for him to say anything, for him to go and tear Brambergis to pieces...

Now came Gailis's turn. He began by speaking of a distant past. He spoke of how he had come to this city from the countryside with nothing but a walking stick in his hand and a sack of bread tossed over his back. He spoke of many things and almost made himself cry, but he never got to the point, nor did he refute Brambergis's words. Sveilis could barely sit still.

But then Padegs, a high school teacher, came to the lectern. A slender, dignified figure with short-cropped black hair and a beard. He had a modern high collar, a long black coat and a university pin attached to it. He passed a probing glance across the hall from the left wall to the right, and then began to speak. He spoke in a steady, solemn voice, intelligently and skilfully, expressively and beautifully.

He doesn't belong to any faction here, not to the ruling one, not to the opposition, not to those doing the attacking, not to those defending themselves. He can speak as a neutral person and even the most elementary logic states that only a neutral evaluation is of importance when completely understandable passion and agitation was in evidence on both sides. Based on his own perspective, examining the situation from an independent critical viewpoint, he cannot completely condemn either side. He is most of all opposed to the notion that Unity should be treated as an object to be fought over or to be inherited by one or another selfish faction so that it can become that faction's source of power. Latvian credit institutions are the collective property of the nation – there he completely agrees with the honourable Mr. Bramberģis. The value of a credit institution can only be judged based on the degree to which it works for the greater good, for the national good. Surely the most influential men have gathered from both sides to compete for seats on Unity's board. However, which of these two groups is most able to advance that greater good and the national good? Undoubtedly, there are truly honourable men on the current board, their hands remain unsullied. They've done their best according to their abilities to work for the good of the bank. But they're the children of a different time, a time when the only accepted wisdom was to save, to set aside every kopeck and to carefully put away those savings. The current period – one characterised by capitalism and a manufacturing boom – demands much more courage, more risks and greater ability to analyse the financial situation. In these times there's no way of getting ahead or surviving unavoidable competition with savings alone. These times demand constant, well-planned and wide-ranging transactions – these pots filled with the nation's money must be given to businessmen so that they can in time return them to the nation along with their fruits.

God had blessed the older generation with money. This is why they're satisfied with things as they are and cannot understand those individuals who, like new shoots, are still breaking through and reaching up towards the sunshine. But it's exactly these individuals who must be supported, as the future of the nation depends on them. It's true: the gold piled up in Latvian credit institutions belongs to the people. The small, hard-working toilers have brought it there, grain-by-grain. But the keys to this wealth should be given to those who understand how to circulate it and make it grow. The older generation has done what it needed to do – and they deserve much gratitude for that! But the time has now come for them to step aside, to make space for a new generation whose hands are shaking from their overabundance of energy, whose entire future is still before them. And if the older generation doesn't wish to do this voluntarily, then – no matter how unfortunate it may be! – they will be forced. Just as streams break up the ice and carry it away every spring, so too the young, progressive forces in Unity will wash away the old slag so that new life can bloom and blossom!

Tempestuous applause and shouts of agreement accompanied the orator from across the entire meeting hall. Sveilis kept gazing at him as if he were his own brother. Padegs quickly walked off the platform without looking to either the left or the right and sat down in the back row, where he pulled out a Russian newspaper and immediately immersed himself in his reading. Gailis rose to his feet, his face beaming with joy, and looked in Padegs's direction as he clapped so forcefully that his white beard flapped around. Bramberģis rose to his feet, but after a moment's thought, waved his arm and sat back down again. Nothing more could be done to change the outcome.

With a majority of about 150 votes, the old leadership of Unity was deposed. Strauss and Lodziņš remained directors, but Tilaks took Bramberģis's place. The auditors included Sveilis, Blics and Padegs. Members of the opposition also ended up on the portion of the board eligible for re-election. A complete victory. The opposition cheered.

The Unity contenders poured down in a black stream towards the buffet. Loud conversations and laughter flowed across the halls. It was time to relax after the recent unpleasantness and nervous agitation. Gailis grabbed Sveilis by the arm and tried to get down the stairs with him.

"I'm... I'm an old expert..." he spoke completely out of breath, stopping on every step, "but even I didn't see this coming. How strange that I didn't see it coming..."

"What did I tell you!" Sveilis laughed out loud.

Happy people crowded around the buffet. They sat down at the small tables, waving and gesturing as they spoke and laughed. The waiters rushed around out of breath, bottles and glasses clinked, and corks popped. All manner of drinks – bubbling and still, cold and hot – were poured into glasses, sloshed around, spilt onto black suit jackets and decorated the white table cloths with yellow and red spots. But now nobody cared about any of that.

It was difficult to find a familiar face in this teeming mass of humanity. Sveilis would catch sight of an acquaintance and then they would immediately vanish again into the noisy maelstrom. But Sveilis did see Blics the lawyer. And when he lost sight of him, he still knew where he was standing – surrounded by happy, thankful victors – and he pushed in that direction.

"Excuse me...," he freed himself from the dawdling, overly friendly Gailis. "Just a moment..."

Smiling, as he pushed acquaintances and strangers alike gently out of his way, he moved in Blics's direction. He bumped into Lodziņš, leaning awkwardly against the back of a chair, his hands shoved into his trouser pockets. Lodziņš was standing alone, his brow furrowed and seemed to be thinking about some difficult subject.

"Well!" Sveilis slapped him across the back in a familiar fashion and winked at him with smiling eyes. "What are you standing around here for? Let's go... the others are over there..."

Anger, distress and perhaps something else could be seen in the former director's eyes. But he knew how to control himself. He just shifted back a little.

"Yes, but I need to rest... from that great battle..." He looked deeply into the eyes of his former protégé. But he could see only unfeigned, undisguisable, almost childlike joy. "I really don't know if it was necessary to make such a significant change. Maybe... but Bramberġis wasn't that bad. I just hope those new ones make the right decisions..."

Sveilis laughed out loud. "Bad – who's saying that? Oh, you think it's because, up there... But it's a well-known fact: a meeting is just a meeting! Is that any reason for us not to be friends, to meet, to have a drink together? Come, Mr. Lodziņš!" He tried to take him by the arm, but Lodziņš managed to evade him.

"Fine, let's go, let's go...," said Mr. Lodziņš, "I don't want to say anything bad about my new colleagues. But... experience! Experience in running a credit institution is the most important thing. Experience, non-partisanship and the good of the bank. The good of the bank most of all..."

Sveilis laughed. "We'll take all that into account. We've already learned all of that from Mr. Bramberģis." He felt that he too was one of those whose hands now held Unity's gold – the greatest and smartest of them all. And in realising his own power, he felt no anger towards anyone else. Everyone seemed dear. He could have hugged and kissed the entire world. "We'll express our sincerest thanks to Mr. Bramberģis for his selfless work."

The unsuccessful candidate for auditor Sausums, a relation of Bramberģis's, came up and shook Sveilis's hand vigorously, and said with a smile, "Congratulations, congratulations! Tilaks's faction won fair and square this time." It was the smile of someone trying much too hard to look genuine, for his guarantee at Unity was to be extended and so he couldn't be on bad terms with the victors.

Tilaks's faction... Sveilis felt slightly offended. Why not Sveilis's faction? But that was just a trifle. This Sausums wasn't evil. "You're not angry with me?" he said.

Sausums grabbed his hand again. "Mr. Sveilis! What do you take me for!" He pretended to be utterly offended by this undeserving suspicion. "I'm not some nitwit, and this isn't my first election. Both factions couldn't... both of us couldn't be elected. This time I lost, next time..." He stopped himself just in time.

"Waiter!" he cried on seeing one rushing past them at the right moment. "Another half carafe!"

"Let's go!" Sveilis was about to take Lodziņš and Sausums each by the arm, but Beitans the engineer interrupted them. Smiling sorrowfully, somewhat comically yet simulating genuine warmth, he extended his hand to Sveilis.

"I wanted to congratulate you! The struggle is over, now we

can meet as friends again. Right?" He owed Unity interest for three terms and so he needed a friend.

Sveilis responded warmly. "Merci! Merci! Of course, as friends... Let's go, gentlemen!"

They all squeezed through to the table around which Blics, Strauss and Tilaks were sitting along with other victors from that evening. Three champagne bottles were already bathing in their ice buckets. First Sveilis walked around the table and whispered a kind word into each of their ears from behind them. When his glass was also filled, he looked around holding it in his hand: Sausums and Beitans had already gone. It must have been too difficult to sit at the same table as the victors. But what did Sveilis care?

"Waiter!" He sat down and loudly clinked his glass against the metal bucket. "Three more!"

"Padegs was outstanding!" Tilaks praised him. He was so comfortable that he slouched back into his chair and a thick, soft fold of flesh at the back over his neck sagged over his collar.

"What a speaker... what an orator!" In his enthusiasm Sveilis couldn't find a better word. Shrugging, he looked around to see whether everyone else was as amazed as he was.

Blics was more circumspect. He finished his glass and then turned it around pensively in his fingers.

"Yes, yes...beauty and enthusiasm. But very little evidence grounded in logic..." In the end the great victory blotted out all the rivalry of competition. Blics was also ready to forgive Padegs. "Y-yes... but sometimes at a large meeting such as this, more can be accomplished with poetry than with logic."

And then Sietiņsons and Berķis were dragging Padegs in through a side door, each taking him by an arm. However much he smiled in comic confusion, his protests were in vain. Those who were seated greeted the new arrivals with loud cheers.

"Sietiņsons and I were walking down the street..." a flushed and breathless Berķis started to tell the story, "and who did we suddenly see: Mr. Padegs! We said to each other, this really isn't right..."

"Have a seat, Mr. Padegs!" Having found a free chair, Strauss placed it at the end of the table next to Blics. "You surely won't object to sharing a glass with us."

"Don't be proud," Sveilis said as he pulled Padegs by the corner of his jacket over to the chair.

With a serious expression, Padegs fixed his crooked university pin. He opened his jacket with a single motion and sat down.

"One glass – but no more. I don't really drink."

"Now, now..." Sveilis protested, filling his glass. "Don't be proud."

"We're so glad you came." Strauss nodded warmly towards Padegs. "The result of the vote is largely thanks to you."

"Yes!" Sveilis rushed to agree again. "We're not much for speaking."

Blics coughed. Padegs had become very serious.

"You see, gentlemen...I've always said and it is my most deeply-held belief that Latvian experts and entrepreneurs, and also the intelligentsia, must stick together. Practical skill and industriousness are strengths, and intelligence is a strength. And where two such strengths are brought together into an honest corporation, cultural progress cannot be absent." He had to have a good relationship with the men at the bank because he'd found a piece of land he wished to purchase. Blics became anxious again for no clear reason, but he calmed down and smirked as he shifted in his seat.

"It's good that you've come to these realisations. In the past you didn't feel the same."

Padegs broadened his smile: "I think you're the person least entitled to accuse others of incessantly changing their views during their lives as the result of improving their social status."

"Accuse you? No, not at all. I'm merely expressing an observation. Besides, I believe that you have misunderstood my relationship with you. After all, we're now colleagues in the same line of work."

"Our money men and our intelligentsia must work together, must go hand in hand." Sietiņsons, still standing behind Padegs, interjected loudly and then immediately fell silent due to a surge of emotion. His eyes filled with tears.

"Sietiņsons and I are going..." Berķis started again, proud that he had brought Padegs back. But Sveilis interrupted him. Suddenly jumping to his feet, overcome by enthusiasm, he grabbed his pocketbook and threw it down onto the table with a crash.

"Dammit! Tonight we have to drink! Waiter, give me the bill, what does it come to..." Tearing open his wallet, he began shaking out the banknotes inside it onto the table.

"Careful, careful," said Tilaks, who knew Sveilis well, calming him down and hiding the banknotes under his hand. "We can have a drink, why not. But don't shout. Many members of Bramberģis's gang are still here."

"To the money men and the intelligentsia..." Sietiņsons sat down across from Padegs and tried to shout over everybody else.

Padegs smiled as he nodded his head...

The Unity victors were still drinking together at lunchtime the next day, spilling champagne on the tables and floor, and forming friendships left and right.

The Baltika restaurant was closed today. Sveilis was unveiling the newly expanded rooms and at the same time celebrating the opening of the wine shop. Hotel guests with rooms were brought food and tea directly from the kitchen. From early in the morning all the employees were occupied with preparing for the celebratory dinner.

Guests began to arrive around nine. Wearing his English fabric tailcoat for the first time, with a low-cut waistcoat, an artfully pleated shirt front, and a red rose in his button hole, a rosy-cheeked and very excited Sveilis Jr. greeted each guest personally and took them to their table. At first there was only a trickle; but at ten past nine they began to stream in. The doors decorated with myrtle branches and illuminated by an electric globe did nothing to diminish the clatter of horseshoes and rumble of motor cars outside.

At around half past nine, the last seat in the restaurant was filled. The electric lights were strung in two ellipses across the ceiling, each bulb set inside a pink, angular shade. The ladies' orchestra were sitting at the back of the room on a rather high stage, directed by a portly band leader. Behind the orchestra, the entire back wall was made of mirrored glass. At the end of each row of tables there was a well-pruned, half-shrivelled tropical tree, so that if you looked from one side there was a delightful green path of trees stretching across the room. Off to the sides in the corners of the former cloakrooms, there were partitions and portières as well as paintings of naked women on the ceiling and the open spaces along the wall.

The orchestra played at the beginning of the meal – those sitting closer together conversed in groups of two or three. They were served fine foods and even finer drinks: there were about ten ladies among the guests. The rules of tact and politeness were subsequently painstakingly observed. Only when the music stopped was it possible to hear that the merriment was increasing and with it the sound of conversations and laughter, the clanking of dishes and popping of corks.

Their hunger had been sated; their tongues had been enflamed by seasoned foods and could no longer respond to anything other than the spiciest sauces and the sweetest hors d'oeuvres. Their stomachs began to rebel against the slow but constant flow of food. Though their eyes were still drawn to the steaming bowls and trays overflowing with juicy, fragrant fruit, their hands now moved slowly and reluctantly towards them but only lingered over them. But drinking was still fine. The more they drank, the more they wanted to drink and the better it tasted. A little bite perfectly matched to each drink did not overburden their stomachs; it seemed to melt away and completely dissolve into the sip of sparkling fluid, further igniting the senses, making them even thirstier. The head of the restaurant at the Baltika had put his talents in the art of hospitality on full display.

The backs of the chairs began to creak from the heavy weight of the bodies leaning against them. A pleasant fatigue soon overtook this flesh, which had been treated to too much fancy food and drink. The effects of the alcohol continued to increase. Here and there a corner of a napkin tucked behind a moist collar would accidentally hang into a half-empty glass or a bowl piled too high with food. A button would pop open on a waistcoat revealing – slightly indecently – a glimpse of the snow-white shirt below. Tired eyes lit up as flushed faces leaned ever closer and more confidently towards the ladies. Glances shamelessly sought out the light, transparent ruffles covering bare necks, lifted breasts and delicate white elbows. Hands heavy with rings were placed confidently on the backs of the ladies' chairs so that soft silk blouses could warmly caress yearning flesh. Plump fingers that had not been crippled by work would repeatedly and accidentally become entangled in hair whose curls unravelled, only to be freed again with a shake. Other instincts began to awake in this flesh fatigued by food and drink.

Having walked from table to table for two hours, Sveilis finally became too tired himself and he sat down. This was also partly due to old Lodziņš clinking his glass so that the guests would stop talking and listen to him; he was about to get up to toast and drink.

The representatives from Unity spoke, as did the representatives from the newspapers, a member from the Cyclists' Association, Tilaks on behalf of his fellow members, and then some other friends. At the very end, accompanied by thunderous applause and shouts, even one of the ladies said five or six words. There weren't any especially serious speeches. In the back, by the mirrored wall, the young ladies of the orchestra – red ribbons crossing their chests diagonally – were standing around as paintings of naked women looked on from above; every detail suggested that this was an agreeable place for relaxation and celebration. But even so, the speakers still tried to express some serious thoughts by making amusing comments with light humour as well as warmly praising the hospitable owner of the Baltika. They spoke about the diligence which is characteristic of Latvians (a topic never left unmentioned at any meeting), their practical achievements through work, and the high level of Latvian culture. They praised Latvian shops and banks, which supported the lively cultural movement and which continued to lift Latvian civil society and the people as a whole to a higher level. Those speakers who were familiar with it, also spoke highly of the exemplary chefs and extensive menu offered at the Baltika. This too began as a joke, but evolved into a profoundly serious comment: well-run restaurants served an important function for unmarried Latvians and for those without family connections; they were a corner that became a little family and a link to the wider nation, and they also looked after their guests' health and physical strength without which any intellectual work would be inconceivable. After all, Latvian restaurants accustomed young people to community life; they are effectively preschools that prepare people for a life of work and engagement with the community. Hence no one can deny their cultural value. All of the speeches were followed by music. Songs of congratulation and "Brothers, today rejoice" were sung with musical accompaniment, followed by "Trimpula", "White flower on the lake", and "Blow, dear wind" in louder voices unaccompanied by music. Sveilis, swinging his glass with the rhythm, sang along with all of it. Red-faced and happy, he was constantly toasting and drinking along with everyone else, but he especially enjoyed doing so with the ladies. The waiters were now already climbing up onto the stage with two bottles sloshing in buckets. Some jovial older gentleman was reaching across the barrier and had begun pinching the young ladies in the orchestra. Then the ladies began to get up and say their farewells. But the gentlemen remained. The celebration continued...

Aina Zvaigzne, the cashier newly hired by Sveilis for his wine shop, left with the rest of the ladies. When everyone arrived earlier in the evening it had been quite warm, but as the night wore on a sharp wind began to blow. She was cold in her thin overcoat. She wrapped her boa around her neck and pinned it down with her chin, sticking her hands in her coat pockets she moved quickly, stepping forcefully.

She had to cross the street and turn, but couldn't get across. One motor car after another was turning away from the front doors of the Baltika, one carriage after another – the female guests were riding past her on their way home.

Aina Zvaigzne became very sad. She'd already felt sad at the meal, but now it became almost unbearable. She'd sat there alone, a stranger to everyone, and almost no one had spoken to her. She didn't much like the food or the drinks. The fine, lavishly attired ladies had sat there looking quite distinguished, carefully tended to and regaled, everything was bountiful, overflowing, ornate and shimmering. At the very least, she looked out of place there in her smooth wool dress. She noticed two of the waiters smirking and whispering as they looked over at her... No, there was nothing about that night to make her happy. Finally she got across the street, and began to walk faster.

Turning onto the side street, she ran into her roommate Lausks on the corner. Out of breath, knocking along with a fat, knotted wooden staff, he hurried towards her. He looked a little funny with his chin buried in his coat collar and his brow deeply furrowed. Aina Zvaigzne giggled unintentionally.

"Where are you off to in such a terrible hurry?" he asked as he examined Aina closely. "You don't know where?" There was a hint of accusation in his voice. But gradually his face cleared. "You never came. This is the third time I've come out looking for you."

That was an accusation too, but that strange kind of accusation that makes the guilty party feel loved and warms their heart. Aina grabbed onto Lausks's arm and turned it over.

"Your third time... I could've come earlier, but we hadn't agreed on it. I didn't think you would be home so early tonight."

"I wasn't going to be. But, since the boss left, I got sent home too. Was he there?"

"Blics? He was. Even gave a speech." She laughed. "Did you have a lot of work to do at home tonight?"

"Well, so-so...Four pages done – just another half page..."

Aina pressed closer to him. Her voice sounded noticeably warmer and gentler.

"And I couldn't be there to help you... While I was amusing myself at that grand dinner, you had to work..."

He chuckled and pulled her even closer to him.

"Aren't I used to it! But how was it? Fancy?"

With her free hand, Aina pulled the boa tighter around her neck.

"Fancy – of course. Swishing silk and glistening gold. Easy to eat and drink too much. Somebody surely will get blind drunk there tonight. And some of them, praising Sveilis, will end up twisting their tongues..." She suddenly laughed loudly. "Just think what cultural workers we all are!" She became serious just as quickly again. "It would've been better if I hadn't gone."

"Really?"

"Really. You think it's fun to sit there in a grey wool dress, while these distinguished ladies with up-turned noses are studying you, and waiters are whispering and smirking..."

Lausks shifted uncomfortably.

"But why did you wear that grey one then? You've got a new..."

"But it isn't even because of the clothes!" Aina's voice sounded confused. "I didn't need to go there to compare myself with the wives of bank directors and wealthy businessmen. Why did I even have to go there at all? Why did I have to go?"

"But sweetheart!" He shrugged his shoulders. "Because he invited you. Because he says that all of his employees have to be at the opening celebration! Sveilis isn't bad, compared with other Latvian shop owners. For example – that same very nationalistic Gailis ..."

"Not bad..." Aina interrupted him. "It's hard to say who's good and who's bad when it comes to the treatment of employees. You judge everything too quickly and too superficially. That nationalist Gailis is just a regular businessman: he works his employees as hard as he can and they have to grovel in response. And each side knows who they are and what they think about each other. I'm very suspicious of this new style of friendliness and benevolence coming from those in charge. It's just a new way of taking advantage of people... I shouldn't have listened to you; I should have stayed at home..."

Lausks, who looked a little startled, lit a cigarette and threw the burning match as far as he could before replying, "Excuse me, but I think you've come down with some kind of exploitation hypochondria. A businessman can be a decent person too and treat his employees well. Or shall we say that he can, at the very least, try to behave that way. And there's no need at all to always search for some kind of malicious intent behind these attempts. As capitalism becomes more refined, the relationship between owners and employees will also become more humane."

"Does that include Blics's relationship with you?"

"Blics has never treated me badly. Have I ever complained? Remember what you told me back then: don't leave your job; just stay the same teacher's assistant you've always been. No private school teacher will take advantage of his assistant as a lawyer would his clerk. But now I can safely say: I haven't lost a thing. My wages, well there is that, but, in principle, his treatment of me is entirely decent, wholly tolerable. Of course, Blics isn't just any kind of a businessman, but an intelligent professional."

Aina had freed herself from him and had stuck her hands in her pockets again.

"Those more humane relations...I'll tell you what they mean. They're an attempt to return to the old patriarchal traditions.

The business owners of old first sought to imprison their workers' souls so that their workers' physical labour would be available to them without a fight; back then, a worker was completely under their power and could be treated as these owners pleased. That was triple slavery, because a slave was unaware of his situation. He pushed his wheelbarrow and thought he was pushing it for himself – that's what he'd been told. He sat with his master's family at one table and thought that he was on the same level as the master's children – that's how he'd been trained to think... We know who benefits from that. We know exactly what it means."

Lausks lit another match, but again threw it far down the street, this time without lifting it to his extinguished cigarette.

"Why do you keep telling me all of this? Don't I understand everything the same way you do? Have I ever thought differently about our bosses than you have? Lately you keep talking to me as if I were always arguing with you. Sure, you can say what you want, but this is just how things are ... Even now I agree with you; I acknowledge that you're right. But you don't want to acknowledge that I'm also right about some things. Isn't decent treatment better for a worker than the harsh severity of a slave driver? Wasn't the older patriarchal relationship still better and more advantageous in the end for the workers than the current direct, merciless servitude and exploitation? I don't know, but it seems to me that anything that helps a worker conserve his strength, is valuable to him – and the same is true of an employer's simple kindness, benevolence – even if it is coming from outside one's family – a moment in a warm, cosy, quiet room..."

"Conserve his strength? No, it just ensures there's some in reserve, so the worker doesn't run out of it – so that there's enough to exploit. Back then there was a shortage of labour and there was no other way. But now the army of the unemployed only keeps growing in size with every passing year, there are ten new applicants ready to take the place of anyone who is let go or unable to keep going..." She hunched her shoulders, as if something unpleasant had touched her. "Our current masters have no need for that sort of kindness. Their shops can survive without it. Decency is just a game for them or even something more malign than that. It is concealing something!"

Lausks shook his head crossly: "Exploitation hypochondria – like I said..." He struck a match and lit his cigarette. "It's alright – clearly you've got to understand class relations and be conscious of your own interests, but if that's all you think about, then you'll come down with an exploitation and persecution mania. And that doesn't help your own interests either."

Aina wasn't listening to him. She was walking quickly and hadn't noticed that he was barely keeping up with her as she said, "To sit there and gather up the crumbs that fall off their tables... To watch them stuff themselves with food and drink... Damn it, I can't get over that kind of cowardice! You should've talked me out of it, but instead you encouraged me..."

Lausks listened peevishly. He took one angry drag on his cigarette after another, and then blew the smoke up into the air.

They walked in silence, each deep in their own thoughts. Aina seemed to have completely forgotten about her companion. With his head pulled into his coat collar, he was trying to keep up and study her closely at the same time. He wanted to talk but he couldn't make peace while he thought that she was angry with him. He wanted to prove he was right. On the other hand he didn't want to disturb her, while she was so deep in her thoughts. At times like these he was even a bit afraid of her.

There was a long way to go. Their legs began to get weary and their backs sweaty. The biting morning wind pierced through their clothes to their skin every time they crossed a street. Dark streets empty of people are always cold.

"There's going to be frost tomorrow." Lausks spoke.

"No there won't," Aina answered absentmindedly. "If it were calm, maybe. But not with this wind."

They kept walking, again in silence – all the way home. As always, the small gate in the fence was open. There was nothing to steal here, or guard. A narrow, dark passageway reached somewhere deep within. Along both sides there were small, uneven wooden shacks and the back walls of larger buildings stretched behind them, over them. All of it was immersed in the damp, rustling twilight. Their feet stepped confidently across the uneven, wet cobblestones; they'd walked it day and night, and they were used to it. They knew every higher or more slippery stone, every hollow filled with dishwater or rubbish.

The old wooden steps had been brushed clean; nobody else used them – there was a single apartment on the upper level of the shack. They could overhear some strange noises apart from the slight creaking sound that came from the stairs; it suggested whispering, restrained laughter and shuffling. They both could hear it more as they climbed. Half-way up the stairs they stopped and listened more carefully, and then began to climb more quickly. On the final step Lausks struck a match.

The wind blowing up the stairs immediately extinguished it. But that brief moment sufficed for them to see what was going on. Further along by a half-open door next to the window on the small stairwell, two teenagers jumped away from each other. The girl screamed, tripped in through the door and slammed it shut. The boy, in a business school jacket, tore down the stairs – almost taking Lausks with him. For an instant, both of them stood in awestruck silence, then Lausks struck a second match. They both looked at each other until the flame swiftly went out again. They went inside quietly – Aina first, Lausks behind her.

The little kitchen was dark and humid, filled with the smell of burning fat and a wood fire extinguished by water. A door opened on the right and Mrs. Zvaigzne pushed a lamp without a shade through the gap and then looked out to see who was there. She was in her nightshirt and her hair was dishevelled. Somewhere behind her they heard Mr. Zvaigzne coughing.

"Oh, it's you." she said in a voice angry about her interrupted sleep. "We thought it was Milda. She was with that guest just now..."

"Sveilis?" Lausks asked.

"Well, yeah, that schoolboy with the green fringed jacket. He's been slinking around here in the middle of the night..." She said crossly and moved the lamp to the edge of the table and closed the door. You could hear that behind it Mr. Zvaigzne was tossing and turning and muttering angrily.

"Good for nothings! The rod! That's what they deserve."

Aina took the lamp and went into her room with Lausks. While they changed, neither of them said anything, but both kept looking at the back door behind them, through which they could hear Milda pacing up and down. Fixing his hair, Lausks leaned over towards Aina.

"That girl really is starting to misbehave too much."

Aina shrugged. Her face was gloomily serious.

"How many times have I scolded her. Nothing helps. At first she would be ashamed and keep to herself, but now that boy is around here more and more. That's fine if it's during the day, but if they're doing things like this..."

"That boy isn't so much at fault. He's at least half-way decent. She's leading him on."

Aina was standing supporting herself against the table, her hands clasped.

"Decent! I can't stand the sight of him. These quiet and shy ones are the worst of all." She stood thinking for a moment longer, then went in to see Milda.

Her knees up on the chair, her hands covering her face, Milda was staring intently at an open book. Even from the back, her nervous posture, her complete stillness – all of it showed that she had expected Aina to come in, that she was ashamed, but at the same time was being obstinate and wasn't really sorry.

Aina was angry, but she restrained herself. From past experience she knew that at times like this, anger brought the least headway.

"Milda," she spoke calmly but firmly, "what kind of behaviour is that? What are you doing! Why is that boy starting to slink around here at night?"

The girl jumped nimbly onto the floor. She popped back up like a weasel that had been stepped on.

"He's not slinking around! He's coming for a visit." Her cheeks were aflame. Her eyes – filled with shame and anger – were avoiding Aina's.

In the face of such obstinacy Aina grew a bit redder too. "At night that's all it is: slinking around and nothing else. Tell me, how can you not be ashamed of getting involved with a pipsqueak like that...with such an ugly, stupid boy?"

Milda shifted and wanted to say something, but then caught herself. She just flashed an angry look and became an even darker shade of red.

"Think about it: you're still so young, you need to study, take your exams. You're already not doing so well – sitting the same class two years in a row. And when you start up with boys too... How long are your parents going to be able to pay for your schooling? You'll be expelled and then you'll have nothing. You won't be a teacher; you won't be able to work a different job. Think about it!"

Biting at her lower lip, Milda stared stubbornly at the floor. Her silence annoyed Aina more than if she'd argued back.

"You're still just a complete child. And not ashamed about skulking around and flirting with boys in the dark! You shouldn't even dream of doing anything like that. A child of country people – I don't understand what could have ruined you like this..." And just then Aina's voice became harsh and brittle. "Is he bringing you those filthy books?"

Milda bit her lip so hard that she almost drew blood. Her breasts heaved as she began to breathe harder. She only answered after a long while – and when it came, her response was short, strange, through her nose.

"I don't have any...filthy books."

"You don't? And that one about sexual relations?"

Milda's hands were continuously twisting and squeezing her black apron. But now her eyes lifted and looked Aina straight in the face. It was hard to tell whether this was more masterful play-acting or childish naivety.

"That's a scientific book... And why are you digging around in my books?"

"I'm not digging around. Mum found it underneath your pillow when she was making your bed. I know what kind of science you're reading it for." She came closer and took her hand in both of hers. "Milda, dear, listen to me. You're too young for things like that. That science won't go missing, it'll have its time. You don't even notice or understand how that boy is ruining you with his books. You're in a swamp and can't see your feet sinking deeper and deeper. And when you come to your senses, it'll already be too late. Don't listen to that boy – to any man. Nine out of ten of them are cowards and hypocrites."

"Lausks – so he's from that good one-tenth?"

There was so much provocative disrespect in that single statement that Aina pretended not to hear it.

"Your whole life is still in front of you – like spring with its grass and flowers. Don't try to speed up the blooming of those flowers, don't tear open a growing bud by force. For yourself, for the sake of your own life, not for anybody else, that's why you have to study. And if you've got time, if you want to read, ask me."

"Well, the books you give me aren't any better. That one about women and Socialism... there was a lot of that stuff in it too."

"There is a lot there, and much of it you haven't understood or internalised. You only have eyes for the things that are tempting and destructive. You're deeply ruined, that's clear already just from your eyes. You're stubborn and don't listen. If there's no other way, the school director and your parents will have to be notified."

Milda let out a long, half-hysterical laugh.

"Spying – denouncing, what more do you need! That is, after all, a very responsible person's job. Well, run on then, inform on me – inform on me to the director, write my mother a letter! That seems like the responsibility of every socialist..." She couldn't stop laughing until she started to cough and her eyes filled with tears.

Overtaken by profound pain, Aina watched the obstinate girl intently. But she was staring at the floor and nervously stroking her apron.

"You don't understand me – or are misunderstanding me on purpose. Do you think I wish you ill? You've lived with us for two years, and practically become a sister to me. I can't just look on indifferently as you purposely head for ruin. I can't let that happen. Not in our apartment! If you refuse to listen...He better not show himself around here again. You tell him that!"

"Oh, my goodness! Do you think you're the only ones with an apartment? Are you keeping me here for free? Everybody survives on what they bring me from the country. If you don't like it, I can leave. Just let me know."

Without wishing it to, Aina's head sank. What good would any more talking do? She didn't understand and didn't want to understand. She stood for a moment, shrugged her shoulders, and then turned around towards the door.

"Do what you want. We're not keeping you here by force."

"No..." The words mixed half with tears, half with laughter, hit her from the back like a clod of dirt. "That's just what you want – for me to leave. I'm an obstacle here for you: you can't flirt so much with Lausks..."

Aina almost tripped back into her room. It was as if she'd been smacked across the face, doused in boiling water. No one had ever offended her so deeply.

Lausks was already undressed and lying in bed – huddled over close to the wall, so she'd have room along the side. Cold and tired from being outside, now in a warm bed, hands clasped over his head, he stretched drowsily and yawned. He smiled as he looked over at Aina and pulled himself even closer to the wall.

"Come to bed."

"But you still need to write," she said to herself, her thoughts elsewhere.

"Eh!" he shot back crossly. "You and you're writing...There's always tomorrow."

She slowly started to undress. He kept blinking his eyes as he tried to keep from falling asleep and looked over in her direction from time to time.

Barefoot and wearing a shawl, her mother walked in.

"Well – did you give her a talking to?" she asked.

Aina's anger had faded, but there was something in this question and in her mother's voice that stirred it up all over again.

"You go talk to her yourself!" she snapped back harshly.

Her mother seemed offended.

"Oh, so now I'm supposed to go talk to her! What business is it of mine? Did I give her those rubbish books and tell her who knows what about some sort of free love? Try to help her now if she's already starting to run around with boys."

"Mum, don't talk about what you don't understand."

But her mother became even angrier. She came closer and leaned over where Aina was taking off her shoes. Her deep-set eyes shone behind her silver eyelashes.

"No matter how dim-witted I may be, I'll say and stick to this. You and all of your freedoms are sending her straight to ruin and perdition. What is she missing, what other kinds of freedoms does that slip of a girl need? Dressed, washed, fed – like the child of a lord! And yet she has no shame at all running around with boys. Comes over – quite a suitor, let me tell you. My goodness, I wanted to get a rod and let both of them have it!" She spat. "Back in our day, we wouldn't even have dreamt of it! I was a big girl already – my goodness, and I was ashamed to look at a boy. And now! Oh, just a whipping, a whipping! Doesn't matter what kind of branch you do it with, any is just fine..."

"Well, why didn't you make him leave? You were at home, you saw."

Her mother shrank back a bit.

"Didn't make him leave! If I'd made him leave, what good would that do us. She'd complain to her mother straight away and go somewhere else. It's not like we're all doing so well." She became fired up again. "Why should I have to make him leave? You do it! We're schooling her like you wanted – and look what's happened. Learning about who knows what from those little books. It's all from those."

"Don't talk about what you don't understand!" Aina said again even more forcefully. "If she'd remembered even a tenth of what I gave her to read, she wouldn't be running around with boys. Then she'd understand other more serious work. But you can't do anything at all with these spoiled country girls. No character, discipline, or any ambition at all. It's just the fault of her upbringing and parents."

"What are you talking about?" Her mother brushed her off. "Don't sin, I would say! What mother puts her own child on the road to ruin. Is that the reason anybody gets sent to school – to devote themselves to mischief?"

Aina once again felt hot inside.

"They're taught... educated! A school isn't a factory where everyone is made smart and decent. The slightest gust of wind will twist and bend those who haven't already been acquainted with thinking for themselves and shown how to behave since they were small."

"Of course it bends them," her mother latched on to one of the words she could understand better and attributed her own meaning to it. "Parents no longer teach their children anything. What do those fools know! As for you and all of your new clever ideas. No need for God anymore, no need for rules. Everybody can live free – fre-e-e! And this is what your freedom looks like!"

Aina's laughter didn't conceal her anger. "No, it's your unfreedom! If your old prayers are so holy and powerful, why aren't you able to control that new generation? Or destroy all of that new knowledge..."

Lausks stretched over to touch her hand and comfort her.

"Calm down, Aina. Is there any end to this argument with her?"

Her mother seemed to get angrier. She immediately tore into him.

"And you – what do you want? Who are you anyway? Oh, this one's a big talker too. Lying aro-u-u-nd like some kind of a lord..."

Lausks tried to smirk ironically, but instead his smile appeared sour and wilted.

"Leave him alone." Aina said crossly as she turned away. But that seemed to only rile her mother up even more.

"Leave him alone – this one! Never! I'll keep cursing him until he leaves... Lying around and sniggering... What are you laughing at, you coward! How much do you pay to be fed, washed, and picked up after? Pay! Making just twenty roubles in wages... Oh, if only that old man of mine were a little bit braver – I'd bury you here! Like a millstone around our necks."

Lausks wasn't trying to smirk anymore. He was agitated and pulled his blanket up to his chin.

"I'm not a millstone around anybody's neck. I've got no business with you. I'm living with my wife."

"My wi-i-ife, my wi-i-ife!" Aina's mother mocked him. Her incredible anger even took her breath away for an instant. "Keep on talking, you damn Turk! What kind of a wife is she to you? What kind of a husband are you to her? What priest married you? Just lying around... Shameful, shameful just looking at you!"

"Calm down, mother." Aina said glumly without turning around as she walked up to the window.

"I won't calm down, I won't!" her mother screamed back and gripped the two ends of her shawl with such force that it looked like she was trying to rip it in half. "I'm not calming down, while this sin sits right before our eyes." She clapped her hands together loudly. "Who would have ever thought about this earlier! This kind of immorality! Unmarried, never seen such a thing - not hiding at all, not ashamed..."

Aina turned back sharply from the window.

"Leave, now!"

Her daughter's fiery stare made Aina's mother flinch, but her heart was too full of emotion. She left, but stuck her head back through the door.

"How can you scold that girl? Look at how you're living! She's learning from you - yes, from your example. She's following in your footsteps. And if she's ruined, then God's punishment will come down on your heads! Mark my words. I'll be the first to accuse you..."

Then she stopped and slammed the door, frightened off by the step Aina took in her direction. Aina slumped heavily onto the sofa. Lausks sat up and spat.

"I can't stand it. With every day they get worse. It can't go on like this for much longer."

Aina sat in silence for a moment, holding her head in her hands. She got up and began to undress.

"Have to get through it, have to get through it," she said quietly and there was a mournful irony in her voice.

"Is this life?" He propped himself up on his elbow. "All day long this crazy hag is walking around complaining. And even when she doesn't say anything, she's shooting daggers with her eyes. I'm sick of it - I've had it up to here!"

"You should have thought of that beforehand. I told you how sweet your in-laws would be." She laughed without intending to. Lausks face looked extremely gloomy.

"You think this is funny... for me it's a burden weighing heavy on my shoulders - and getting heavier with each passing day... I should have thought of that, you say. I knew there would be difficulties, but not as bad as this. I don't understand how all of it doesn't hurt you."

"Me - it doesn't hurt me? Why would you think that?"

"I see it... I think. You get angry, but then make peace with it all over again. I haven't noticed you shed a single tear. Your mother – she's always crying."

Aina laughed loudly and bitterly.

"Oh, so that's what you want? A cry-baby! Then, my dear Pauls, you've really made a mistake." She turned off the lamp and laid down on the sofa.

"What, you're not getting into bed with me?" Lausks asked surprised.

"No, not tonight," she answered sharply.

"Not yesterday, not the day before that... I went to meet you three different times." There was genuine hurt in his voice.

"Leave me alone, my head hurts," she said shaking him off.

One could hear Lausks lay down heavily and then spend a long time adjusting his blanket. He lay there quietly for a moment. But then couldn't stand it and spoke up again.

"Well, why don't you want to? I don't understand what the big difficulty is. The two of us aren't going to knock down this wall just by butting heads. We're stubborn and imagine that we're fighting something. But stubbornness alone won't change the established order."

"There's no way forward without stubbornness. No struggle has ever happened without it. Stubbornness is the beginning of the struggle. Without a beginning, there's no continuation, and there can be no victory. If we try to protect our heads, we'll have to wait until we grow horns."

"You're making fun again..." he shifted angrily. "I've got no time for jokes at the moment."

"But you have for words and deeds. It seemed to me like tonight you were ready to hide under the bed."

Lausks pretended not to hear that. "I don't know why you don't want it. How many open-minded, conscientious people are there who have also got married and got on with their lives. Marriage doesn't mean that you have to give up your convictions. A simple formality which removes so many unnecessary difficulties."

"Then isn't it better for you to just give up your open-minded... convictions, and with that all of your unnecessary difficulties would fall away. All of them! And you'll be good and honourable among honourable citizens... That's the newest lesson after all: don't be hot or cold, but lukewarm, then you'll do well in the world."

"It's not being lukewarm at all!" he protested fiercely. "It's something completely different. I call it taking advantage of your circumstances, as a tactic or otherwise, but without that a person can't accomplish anything except to become an object of ridicule and derision."

"I would call it adjusting to your circumstances and a technique for waffling. That road leads straight to philistinism." She also shifted noticeably on the sofa. "After you give in once, you'll be made to give in a second and third time, and then everywhere... Well, let my mother be angry and complain! It's completely clear to me: she's an old person stuck in her own world who can't and won't understand. In the past I would get terribly upset, but gradually I got used to it. Now I only get upset in exceptional circumstances."

"That's why I say that you have a unique nature. But I can't be that way. Every day I get more anxious. I'm afraid of developing a heart problem or becoming a maniac... You're laughing again? Well, I don't care. But I'm telling you: I can't stand this kind of life any longer. At work, at home, on the street or in society – everywhere I have to pretend and lie. Are you married? Well, how can I say yes? But acquaintances still figure it out and snigger... To hell with it!"

He must have expressed his disagreement in the dark. Aina laughed uncontrollably. "Poor thing. Then there's nothing left for you except lawful matrimony followed by a divorce."

He pretended not to hear her again. "And nothing is achieved by doing that, nothing at all. We only create difficulties for ourselves... and others... I don't know... I don't want to say so, but I actually think your mother is right. If that Milda loses her way, then we are a bit at fault there." He paused to hear whether Aina would laugh. But she didn't. "Of course: a country girl, raised with few rules, spoilt from her earliest days. Then she watches what happens around here and copies it...

She sees us and wants to try it herself... Haven't you noticed her occasional mocking expression when she looks at us? It's really unpleasant. And if she loses her way because of us..."

"You're naive. You get more and more naive every day. My mother has convinced you and trained you. You're starting to talk like her and don't even notice it yourself. Soon you're going to start going to church with her..."

"Your mother hasn't taught me anything, but life has," he retorted bad-temperedly. "Your mother can say whatever she likes, as far as I'm concerned. It's just for our sakes... most of all your sake. I can't stand it when some little girl winks at you and then smirks behind your back."

"Don't worry about me. I don't care in the least what little girls think. I don't need to explain my life to anybody."

"Well, for my own sake then... You think it's easy for me to sit around and wait while you drop in at grand feasts. Do you think it's easy for me to walk that distance three different times to meet you..."

Stinging sarcasm interrupted him. "So, that's why! Oh, so you're afraid of the possibility that I'll fall for someone else and run away with him? That's something new."

"What kind of nonsense are you talking about!" But she wasn't listening.

"So that's the reason you want to tie me down with the fatal bonds of matrimony..." She wasn't joking anymore. From the corner where the sofa stood, the sound of heavy, laboured breathing could be heard. She wasn't crying, she was fighting with doubts that had long ago begun eating away at her and slowly growing until they'd swollen like an abscessed limb. She tried to drive them away, or at least to pay no attention to this dark, threatening cloud which was obscuring her happiness. Everything has its measure. She'd put up with it for too long as it was. "We're both weak – you're right: we're both stubborn, not fighters. But that was good too. However much energy a person has, let that at least be put to work. A person only knows themselves when they're working and without self-knowledge there is neither a person nor a decent life. But you don't understand. You didn't have any self-knowledge when mother and father were scolding and cursing; your heart didn't laugh with pride when the slaves to old traditions avoided the road – as a rule – and then looked back from a distance, shrugging their shoulders or laughing scornfully. You began to feel guilty and surrendered."

Lausks tried to sound dry and offended as he protested. "Who have I surrendered to then?"

"You'd better not argue," she interrupted him. "And don't talk. Everything you want to hide is clear from the sound of your voice. I've been hearing and understanding that for a long time already. But you don't understand it. I just have to say it for once... It's not just out of stubbornness that I don't want what mother and father want... and what you're beginning to want. If it really were taking advantage of your circumstances and a tactic as you say... But it isn't! You don't even notice how your own voice, your own eyes... how all of it gives you away. The cowardice of giving in, you're afraid! You don't understand how stubborn I am about this. I don't want you to humiliate yourself on purpose and allow them to say that they got the better of you and me – both of us. So that they can slap their chests with self-satisfaction and think and even brag that their old wisdom and power is still stronger than our new one."

"But you always say... Who cares what they think?"

"Not them, but you! Why do you have to feel ashamed of yourself or me? Why can't you admit to yourself that you began our relationship carelessly without examining it or knowing your own strength? If you had, you wouldn't despise yourself later for being a coward who ran away at the first sign of conflict and hid... I wanted you to see yourself as a man, even with the failings typical of men, but not as a boy who is afraid of his parents' threats, who blushes at ridicule from strangers..."

"Maybe so," he said dryly and deeply offended. "But I've

never presented myself to you as some kind of a hero. I'm a human being with human failings. But a boy..." He became angrier. "What strange things to say... Then you'll never find any adult, any husband."

"For your sake – and also for another reason," she continued. "And that other reason is something greater and more important... You say that we're partially to blame if some spoilt young girl loses her way. But if we give in and surrender, then we'll be ten times as guilty. If a person can both ruin and motivate by their example, then with our example of cowardice and giving in, we'll be plotting a bad course – one of retreat and desertion – for all those young, active people who could possibly follow in our footsteps. Don't you realise that this would be the worst kind of betrayal, the shabbiest action of all. Let the cowards and hags stay in their old tracks. But those who start walking along the path of new ideas shouldn't look back or move off to the side! Those who start and retreat, they're twice as pitiful and harmful as those who never even began, but are satisfied to stay in their well-worn, comfortable rut. It encourages the old crowd to mock and point fingers and try to scare off the weaker ones still wishing to walk this path or having actually started to do so. It sullies and slanders that higher ideal they wanted to serve. That alone gives cover to those who think, say and point fingers claiming that this path is too weak, that it can't hold up and can't lead others. Therefore it was no ideal at all, but rather a collection of phantoms and fantasies. They'll say that this path can't fulfil that role, but neither can it conceal that they were the ones who couldn't endure it – they were like a rotten, cracked clay bowl coming apart when a fermenting, bubbling liquid is poured into it..."

"Does a person exist for the sake of an idea, or an idea for the sake of a person?" Lausks interrupted. "You insult me by calling me a boy, a coward and who knows what else. But listen to me: that cowardice you accuse me of can also be detected in your own great energy and stubbornness. You don't think so? I'm telling you, cowardice is the reason why some people put aside what they've begun and then found not to be useful or suitable as originally thought. Pig-headedness and stubbornness aren't the same as being a man; often that's exactly where that boyish immaturity and lack of courage are hiding – the very thing you attribute to me. But I don't want – I don't want to walk around as if I were in chains! An idea exists for the sake of a person..."

"What are you talking about, there's no idea and no person!" Aina interrupted him loudly. "An idea doesn't exist for the sake of a person, nor does a person exist for the sake of an idea – the two of them have mutually grown together, the two exist and are sustained – and live – through each other... Like sap to a tree, like wings to a bird – that's what an idea is to a person. Like a beating heart, like blood circulation, like the air we breathe – that's what it should be for a person. If their heart or breathing stops, then that person perishes. But you are in chains..." She stopped, strangely out of breath. "And you don't see or understand that I'm only doing this for you and precisely for that reason... You are in chains!"

She turned over onto her stomach and pulled the blanket over her head. He understood that something odd and dangerous was happening to her. He propped himself up onto his elbow, listened and began to comfort her, talking as he grabbed at this or that topic, asking her to come over, but she didn't answer. He didn't hear a single sound coming from her. He wanted to go over, but stopped himself, and laid back angrily in bed, adjusting his blankets and huffing to express his irritation. She had annoyed him enough for one night... And hadn't he gone to meet her three different times? Why did he have to experience so many difficulties because of her, all the time and everywhere he went?

He turned towards the wall and hissed angrily.

She lay on the sofa and not a sound could be heard.

With blanket pulled up over her head and her face pushed into her pillow, Aina Zvaigzne was quietly crying. She didn't try to suppress her sobs, and they were so muted that she could barely hear them herself. The store of tears that had been filling up for so long was now finally overflowing. She only realised this when she felt bursts of heat streaking across her cheeks and forehead and sinking into her brain. Those weren't the kind of tears that purify and bring relief. Pain and bitterness, and boundless despondency weighed ever more heavily upon her.

Because of him and because of that other matter... Oh, tonight she realised something for the first time that she'd never wanted to say. She'd sensed it long ago, but she had purposefully avoided giving it any thought, and had tried to drive it away and forget it. But she no longer could and she was certain of it. She read her soul like an open book and its red letters stabbed at her conscious self like red-hot needles.

Most of all for herself! This whole time she'd avoided admitting and accepting that she'd been bitterly wrong. She was disappointed; in her first bloom of emotion she'd given herself to a person who was captivated only by her body, but for whom her soul wasn't worth more than the distant glow of a reflection in a drinking glass. Angry that she was associating with someone who in a moment of passion would say and seem ready to perform truly heroic deeds, but who was in fact cowardly with a weak character and a little masculine pride. All this time she'd been fooling herself, trying to convince herself that this would pass and that her initial infatuation would return. But every day, every event, and especially every argument with her mother showed ever more clearly that he was the same as everyone else and wanted to live that way too. A quiet, warm, humble little life, both for him and her. He wasn't interested in societal struggles, his soul didn't yearn to be joined in a single group with others who were overworked and exploited; he wasn't attracted to noble and courageous goals, and had no enthusiasm which took pride in his class. Step by step he was moving off to the side and pulling her along with him... She couldn't take it anymore. She'd been pulled too deep into the accelerating current of river heading for a cliff edge where the roar of the crashing waters was getting louder. She couldn't take it anymore! Outwardly she no longer had life or vitality. She was too accustomed to breathing clean, fresh air – she had to suffocate in the corner directed and ruled over by her mother... And on top of this, she was associated with this person! Like a crystal chalice filled with a sparkling drink she had given up her young body, and that was enough for him. He was ready to use her chalice as a common, everyday utensil, but he didn't understand the value of her soul, nor did he yearn to search for it, hold it to himself and value it like a priceless jewel. She felt sorry for herself and ashamed of her feminine weakness. Her emotions made her feel old and dizzy, and in her confusion she also felt like a helpless child lost and alone on a steep and slippery road. She was supposed to be the strong, conscientious and independent woman whom her comrades depended on more than on themselves... She felt defiled and shocked. And yet she couldn't hate the man who had grabbed her with his undeserving, dirty hands. You couldn't just tear yourself free of someone who had once been so close – not torn from your heart and tossed away... Where two human beings are united, even if only externally, the fires of their souls will still flow and melt together, becoming a tiny crystal which chimes in its own unique way as it heads into a storm of emotions which don't abate until death decides that it shall.

Aina turned onto her back and pushed the blanket down to her feet. She was burning like a flame. She had to simmer down. Lausks turned his head quietly and listened. Why won't she say something? He was sorry about the argument and was ready to join her and make peace, if only she would ask him to.

But she didn't need that anymore. She had already forgotten about him. She had much to talk over with her heart that night...

Roberts Sveilis ran down the steps and flew out onto the street as if he'd been slapped. "Hoo!" he exhaled and caught his breath, while he found his handkerchief so he could dry off his sweat. Terrible luck. When they'd gone outside, they'd listened, but didn't hear any noise coming up from downstairs. They weren't even there that long... five or six little kisses... Well, of course, it was a bit more drawn out that... But inside that old hag was probably listening behind the door and still didn't hear anything. She didn't see Milda sitting in his lap, or him tickling her... A giggle escaped from Roberts. One hell of a girl, nothing less! If those two hadn't come up and seen... He became serious again. There's never a single moment when they can meet safely. Everybody's always staring, as if it were some kind of a sin. What fellow doesn't have his own girl? And what about them – they're fine ones to talk! He had it in mind to give that Miss Zvaigzne a piece of his mind sooner or later ... He was going to tell her straight to her face to keep her nose out of other people's business. Why doesn't anybody ask her what she's doing living with Lausks?

Roberts liked the last of these thoughts quite a bit; he repeated it to himself several times and played it out in his mind in several different ways. But still he wasn't completely satisfied. He couldn't forget the way he had been interrupted so rudely but also his own cowardice. Why did I need to run away like a fool, like a child. They surprised us... Let them! What business is it of theirs? I should have lifted my hat and lit my cigarette, nothing else... Roberts pulled out a pack of "Zefirs" and lit one. But the cigarette – while he was preoccupied with such disagreeable thoughts – suddenly went out. He walked up to his apartment in silent fury.

Here he had to tiptoe again – to be careful and hide. Again it was as if he'd committed some kind of a sin... He pulled off his boots and threw them angrily under his bed. He took off his coat and trousers, got into bed with his socks still on, and lay there for a bit. He wasn't sleepy – for a while he had been having trouble getting to sleep ... He got up again and stretching lazily sat down at the table.

His school books were scattered around. The sight of

the brightly-coloured corner of a folder and the yellow dust cover of one his books offended him. He was sick of those ugly books, bored with the dry repetition and interminable sitting around... He yawned irritably and began to move things around...
The poems of Poruks and Virza... Eldgasts' "Starry Nights" and "Frazil"... Mirbeau's "The Diary of a Chambermaid"... The works of Przybyszewski and Maeterlinck in the small yellow volumes from the Russian general library. He didn't want to read any them or even look at them. All of it bored him. He unlocked the drawer and began digging around in it. Milda's sweet letters... The pale pink envelopes with a little gold flower on their adhesive edge, tied together into a single package with a violet ribbon. He'd taken that ribbon from her hair once... He could still remember that night... She'd had a piano lesson. He'd been waiting on the corner – freezing and his patience was wearing thin. Finally, she came out, saw him right away and rushed over giggling... the dark little gap between her front teeth looked so sweet, so very sweet... He was carrying her music case and playing around with it in various ways. She walked next to him, grasping at his hand, making little faces, and scolding him. They ended up laughing so much that they both went red in the face and were ashamed to look at each other... Mrs. Zvaigzne was the only one up and about as all her husband did these days was lie in bed coughing. There was no need to be afraid of him, but the old hag's rat-eyes flickered as she stared at them. For no reason at all she'd stick her head in through the door to slyly ask them something. That witch! They couldn't lock the door, of course. A couple of times they'd almost, almost been taken by surprise, but managed to move just in time – she to the end of table, he to its side. As if they were sitting having a serious discussion. But their legs would bump into each other under the table, then cross, before ending up in a silly playful tangle. On top of the table they'd pinch each other's arms, quietly messing about, whispering all kinds of nonsense. All

the while they were listening to what Mrs. Zvaigzne was doing as she moved around the kitchen. But as soon as he heard her walking down the stairs, he'd lean over, grab Milda around her chest and pull her over onto his lap. Doing their best to make as little noise as possible, not even breathing loudly, they would kiss and caress each other. Mr. Zvaigzne would cough incessantly, but none of it was any of his business. Once before they just barely managed to split up and sit apart again when Mrs. Zvaigzne stuck her head in through the door. The witch! Milda's plait was half undone and he had her violet ribbon in his hand. Blushing profusely, he managed to lean down and busy himself with his boot laces, though there was nothing to fix down there... Afterwards he didn't give her ribbon back but put it in the inner pocket of his coat next to his heart. Milda pulled a face and threatened to tell Mrs. Zvaigzne, but she didn't tell anyone or ask for it back later. She liked it, really... Such a little tease...

He had already started to feel better. The memory of the unpleasant experience from earlier was fading away, and an upwelling of good feelings washed away all the dregs... Roberts undid that ribbon which now kept her letters together and began to reread them covered as they were with clumsy, sloppily script. My darling Roberts! I didn't have time to come and meet you yesterday, because my mum came back from the country and I had to go with her to the centre of town to buy shawls to give to the housemaids for Easter. That's why I wasn't where we'd agreed. You probably were and are terribly angry with me. Don't be angry, I'll make it up to you when we next see each other. Come over to my house around five, as the old witch is going off to the woodyard to buy firewood, so we'll be able to talk... Dear Roberts! Come to the round field at the Esplanade at around three - you know which one... My dear friend! I'm going out to the country on Friday at six, come to the station... A few dozen sheets of pale pink paper like that, each with a gold flower on the corner and two or three lines scribbled across it diagonally. And each brought to life the memory of an entire experience – beautiful, unforgettable hours. Roberts kissed the violet ribbon, locked the letters back in the drawer, and carefully secured the key in his wallet. But then something occurred to him and he unlocked it again. He pulled out a small, carefully wrapped bundle hidden at the very back of the drawer: a small pinchbeck watch with a long, fine, chain which he intended to give to Milda on her birthday. Although it had taken him a long time to save up for it, he had still managed to buy this expensive gift well ahead of time. How good it was to have a wealthy brother! She'd wanted a watch for such a long time. He could already picture her surprise and joy. He giggled and his heart started to beat faster.

Such a sweet, sweet girl! He was only worried about one thing: that she would take a shine to someone else and leave him. They were all crazy after all, can't trust them... He picked up the small hand mirror: he wasn't all that handsome. A long, slender face with a thin nose – the characteristic Sveilis nose. If only his hair had been a little darker – it was mousy-blonde: a completely indistinct colour. When he considered his appearance from time to time, this was what he liked least of all about himself. Now he was starting to grow a moustache, and that too was very pale. Even worse, there were all those pimples. He'd always had a clean and smooth face, but now he was starting to get these strange blemishes. He had first noticed five or six on his temples, then later on, one after another as they spread across his brow. Once the tiny red spots had colonised his entire forehead, a few more started to sprout along his cheekbones! And it didn't help to squeeze them or wash them with medicinal soap; once they had appeared, they would stay there for several weeks until they were dry and would peel off on their own. New ones would appear and it seemed like the red spots were getting more numerous. The ones he had squeezed too hard would swell up and turn into small boils. Even the healthy skin in between the red pimples had lost its original, lustrous whiteness, and instead looked strangely greyish and greasy.

A little irritated again, Roberts pushed away the mirror, turned off the light, and got back into bed just as he was. The early-morning glow was already creeping in through the window, and the daily clamour was beginning to rise from the street below, but he wasn't tired yet. His eyes were sore and his head heavy and befuddled. He couldn't sleep. It was always like this after seeing Milda. Tiredness, scattered thoughts, a slowly subsiding, exhausting excitement followed later by laziness and apathy... Everybody was saying that lately he seemed run-down and was getting very thin. But the wiser heads among them knew that it came from growing too quickly and studying too hard. He hadn't thought about it himself – about whether he had become so ugly that Milda would take a liking to someone else. He had no other worries – no other worries at all.

And yet, didn't he have a wealthy brother? Couldn't he buy Milda a gold watch to give her on her birthday? Who could compete with that? Who could stand in the way of the power of gold? It wasn't for nothing that Milda was so in love with him, so much that she was ready to leave school and everything. For him! Sweet, sweet Milda...

He fell asleep with a smile on his face whispering her sweet name. He slept a strange shallow sleep; in fact he was only half asleep. His slumber was interrupted by the growing noise from the street. Hot confusing dreams mixed with scenes from his recent experiences and the growing brightness of the day. He would be half awake and then fall asleep again. He turned from one side to the other. He was sweating underneath the soft, warm blanket. Then he'd uncover himself and, feeling too cold, would wrap himself up again a moment later as he lay there partially awake, partially asleep.

He was in a deep, deep sleep when his mother came up, but sensed her felt slippers brushing along the linoleum floor, and was aware of sticking her head around the door.

"Son!" Her voice was as cautious and mild as ever, but her rebuke was clear. "Are you still sleeping? It's almost half past eight. Get up quickly now. You'll have to hurry."

Roberts stirred and fidgeted with annoyance. He didn't open his eyes – he didn't want to. Sleep came like water, it poured like a warm current across his eyelids, it flowed into his brain, and caressed his entire body. It was so warm and pleasant to sleep – to sleep for a long time without having to wake up and think. Instead all he had to do was sense the pleasant afterglow of his recent experiences and dreams... Stretched out on his back, smiling sweetly, he was fast asleep.

Half an hour later his mother opened the door again and waved her arms in dismay. At first she wanted to speak to him sternly, but once she had moved closer she instantly fell silent. Her little son was sleeping so sweetly; it would have been a shame to wake him. Nevertheless she had to, as he was already half an hour late. She stroked his face and pulled off the cover.

"Son, how can you still be sleeping! It's practically nine o'clock. You'll miss your classes again. The teacher will be angry."

Roberts stared at the ceiling with cold angry eyes. That old... he bit his tongue, just stopping short of thinking that word he and Milda called Mrs. Zvaigzne to each other when they cursed her. But he knew that she wouldn't stop now.

"My head hurts," he lied and glowered.

His mother was upset.

"Oh no, not your head! I thought as much...I've never seen you sleep like this before... Is it bad?"

A cool, rough hand caressed Roberts's forehead. This contact was so irksome to him after his delightful dreams, especially when he remembered Milda's soft, gentle little hand... He jerked away angrily and turned his face towards the wall.

"It hurts! There's no escaping you people..."

"It's from all that reading," his mother postulated. "How many times have I said it: don't stay up so late. But do you listen..." Worried, she trotted off to search for medicine and brew some herbal tea...

Roberts yawned and closed his eyes. So be it. If I miss it, I miss it – no problem! Russian – I know it already and we're just repeating the same things for the third time. In history class we don't learn anything except dates... and a bit about wars and kings – no problem if I don't know the name of a war or a king... German... and algebra... As soon as he remembered those classes, shivers ran down his back. He couldn't stand algebra – and his maths teacher couldn't stand him. Two unrelated, incompatible elements... He turned onto his side. Maths did not come to him naturally. And there's no sense in studying something you don't like. Wasted time and wasted effort. Like music: he had tried as hard as he could, but then dropped it. There was just no point! There were so many musicians now and not enough work, bread, or fame to share out among them all! Now he was taking drawing and painting classes. He had a talent for painting, he knew that for certain. Today after lunch he would go to his drawing class and work a bit harder there. When your intentions are good, you can do more in an hour than you sometimes do in a whole week. He calmed down again and fell back into a deep sleep...

He woke up and fell asleep again several times. When he finally got bored of lying around and got up, he'd already missed his drawing class, too. He had to hurry off elsewhere though. He'd made plans with Milda... And when he remembered that, his drowsiness quickly vanished. He fibbed to his mother: his headache had improved a bit, and now he needed to get some fresh air. He had a quick bite to eat and was off.

He needed to stop at three or four shops – leaving each one with a small parcel. He carried them in his left hand; with his right one, he smoothed his hair back underneath his hat and tugged at the feathery wisp above his upper lip as he walked. He looked at his reflection in the shop windows and mirrors attached outside, buttoning and tidying himself up so that he'd look as handsome as possible. He stopped at a restaurant in Daugavmala, had two shots of spirit and a bottle of beer and snacked on some tough, unappetising sausage. He didn't really like the sausage or the beer, but he had to drink to give himself courage – for some reason he always felt a little shy, a little afraid of that girl...

Milda was already there waiting for him, standing on the bridge leading to where a riverboat was moored. She was wearing a soft, blue hat sagging over the back of her head, and a knee-length blue overcoat with a bundle of books hidden underneath it. She'd just come from school, and looked a little worried and a little skittish. Her eyes glanced around timidly.

"I hope nobody we know sees us..." she said quietly to Roberts as they walked onto the riverboat.

But Roberts didn't care anymore. His courage made him feel safe. The alcohol he'd had was slightly disconcerting and disorienting him, but the feeling was not unpleasant. All of his muscles seemed full of fresh energy. He wanted to grab something and shake it – to prove his strength to Milda. But there was no reason to do so. There were almost no other people on the riverboat. The captain was seated grumpily behind his partition, where he was drinking tea from a sticky glass which he grasped tightly. He didn't lift his eyes to acknowledge them.

The two of them sat down in deep-set, wicker armchairs. This wasn't completely to Roberts's liking: he wanted to sit closer to her so he could push up against her and draw her closer to him. But there was nothing he could do. He purposely stretched out his rather long legs at an angle so she could put her little yellow boots with their fine heels on top. He opened up his parcels and treated her with cream cakes, filled bonbons and raisins. After looking around to make sure no one was watching them, he pushed his hand behind her back. They both laughed loudly when she, her boots resting on his leg, leaned back and pressed his hand against the fine, gently squeaking wicker-work.

The boat rocked gently, almost imperceptibly, as it travelled down the Daugava. The warm sun flickered against the waves, a fresh breeze blew off of the water and across the deck. But they weren't cold – or maybe they were and just didn't notice it. They didn't see the sun or the banks of the river, which had grown quite green during the previous week of warm weather – they didn't see any of it. They just looked at one another and felt each other's presence. Roberts prattled on, joked and laughed without stopping. The more Milda enthused about his jokes, the wittier and more self-confident he became. And why shouldn't he feel proud? The gifts he'd brought with him cost four roubles and he still had two five-rouble pieces in his wallet. And small silver change in his waistcoat pocket! His head was slightly more befuddled. He started talking and laughing so loudly that Milda had to quiet him down. What did they care! Wasn't he the brother of wealthy Sveilis?

They both got out and started walking along the sandy pine-covered hills. Yesterday they'd agreed to take a trip and see a bit of nature. Roberts had been talking about his painting and perception of the countryside. Milda had changed the conversation to flowers. But now all of that was forgotten. Now it was just the two of them in the world. Springtime had awakened the spring inside each of them, which shimmered with its own sun and heat, and everything around them was just a reflection and an echo. They were on the riverbank, but a different current, one that was faster and stronger than the Daugava, was carrying them along. They didn't ask or pay attention to where it was taking them! They surrendered to it and its speed made them giddy.

Roberts hurried ahead with Milda's books in his hand. He chose the steepest part of the hill on purpose and ran up it to the top. On reaching it, he looked down and laughed as she was following him up, stooped over and climbing slowly. He gave her his hand and didn't want to let her go. But she freed herself and started playing with a pinecone she'd picked up. Examining it carefully, and smiling strangely to herself, she climbed down the other side. He followed her slowly without taking his eyes off of her ruffle collar, which curved like a little white frame around her neck.

They happened to run into an ugly old woman gathering

sticks and pinecones, who was withered and wizened as the things she was carrying in her apron. She stopped and examined them carefully with unmistakable curiosity and suspicion. They felt intruded upon and, as they'd already agreed earlier, they both walked off in a different direction, passing by with their faces turned away from her. The old woman turned her head as they went and stared after them for a long time, squinting her eyes. Gradually a sneer appeared on her face revealing her yellow, crumbling teeth.

"Oh-oh, young lady! oh-oh, my dears!" she called after them shaking her head. They rushed to get further away and climbed up the side of a steep hill. But the sparse vegetation caused the sand to subside. Milda slid down several times. Her dress got covered in pine needles, sand poured into her little yellow boots. The old hag wasn't sneering anymore; she squinted her eyes even more, a ferocious glare shot out from her wrinkly sockets and cut into the two climbers.

"A spanking, you deserve a good spanking! I would take one of these fine switches to the pair of you."

This, and the other things she said with the frankness typical of people living outside the city, made them both turn bright red, so much so that they briefly couldn't bear looking at each other. Only on the other side of the hill did Roberts catch his breath, take off his hat and wipe the sweat from his brow. He hated how it felt when his palm touched those hot, swollen pimples.

"Hoo!" he spat. "Dammit, where did a witch like that come from."

"Shameless hag!" Milda said, slurring her words angrily and looking back as the stick-gatherer toddled off and disappeared behind the other hill.

For a moment it felt to both of them like the old woman was still there following them. Like an evil premonition, like a bad dream, like a fateful warning...

They walked out towards the bank of a heavily silted stream filled with logs and sat down in a sunny spot. Milda sat higher and supported her back against the steep slope of the hill, which was covered in pine needles and tiny pinecones. Roberts lay down a little lower. They sat quietly for a moment, then started to look at each other, smiling and flirting. They tossed the pinecones at each other. Milda aimed at the back of Roberts's cap, but only occasionally managed to hit it. He, on the other hand, threw very straight – sometimes at her forehead, sometimes at her neck, other times at her breasts. She could never tell where he was aiming so she kept ducking and dodging in every direction. It was so much fun. But when he'd become a little too bold in his throws, she pretended to get angry and he had to stop. But then she'd snap back, and look at him with those laughing, mischievous, playful eyes and a smirk on her face. Roberts was getting confused again. This girl was going to make him crazy... He unwrapped his packages.

She looked on hungrily at the immense assortment of sweets. She tried all of them, and lots more, laughing with a full mouth and bulging cheeks.

"You rascal, you'll overfeed me!"

"Me – a rascal?" He grabbed both of her hands. "Take it back. Say you're sorry!"

He didn't give up until she'd apologised and kissed his hand. Then he unwrapped a bottle of raspberry liqueur from the final package.

"Now let's have a drink," he said, looking at her seriously.

Milda was truly surprised and waved him off with both hands.

"You want to get me drunk? I won't have any!"

But he just laughed. He took a nice swig himself, then poured her a glass. She tried to protest. But he sat down next to her, putting his right hand around her head and pouring with his left. Half of it spilled onto her blue coat, her hat got wrinkled and fell to the ground. She got tired of fighting back and finally gave in. She drank it and had more to eat. And after that she didn't argue anymore. Roberts poured some more for himself and some more for her. At first they carried on joking around and laughing a bit, but gradually they became silent. Then the silence turned into seriousness and the seriousness seemed to transform into sorrow. They both seemed to be listening to something far away, drinking quickly and eagerly as if they were trying to keep from saying something. Another awkward moment. They sat as if they were angry at each other, not looking at each other, not touching each other, half turned away. And then their hands would accidentally meet – just briefly, very briefly, as if they were afraid of each other, as if they might get burnt or a spark of lightning might leap out if they touched each other.

Black water, filled with logs and rotting bark, slid by slowly, almost unnoticed, near their feet. On this bank, two bright yellow marsh marigold blossoms swayed. On the other side, reeds were pushing out of the water. A butterfly, its brown and white wings speckled with silvery dust, flitted over the water as its wings caught the sun. Roberts and Milda didn't see anything at all. They didn't even see each other, only felt it too strongly – the searing burn of each other's closeness. And that's why they drank. Some strange, unknown feeling drove them to intoxicate, to numb their brains where at that moment a crystal-clear thought was hiding and slowly dying... Gradually everything became wrapped up and sank into a hazy mist.

Milda took off her boots and shook out the sand. Roberts sat staring glumly into the water and suddenly realised that he'd had too much to drink. He knew he was sitting and staring into the water, but oddly couldn't feel any of his joints. He saw how Milda had taken off her boots and was leaning back against the bank smiling and gazing at him drowsily with half-closed eyes – with a distant look of bewilderment. But she couldn't remember why she was here and why she was looking at him like that.

A half-empty bottle thrown with clumsy hands sank in the water and then from that spot little bubbles rose to the surface – at first quickly, one after another, later more slowly. Kicked by accident, the packages of sweets rolled away. Roberts lay down just as he had earlier, resting his head on Milda's legs.

She let out a quiet laugh, rattling it around in her throat, and lazily turned her head first in one direction, then the other.

What if someone happens to come upon them...?

Roberts didn't care. An irresistible heaviness was pulling him down towards the ground. Just to sleep without waking – that was his only thought and feeling right now. His eyes were closed, but still he could see strange, tangled circles spinning around. It gradually passed and he began to feel lighter and clearer. And then he started to notice the mild warmth of her body against his face passing through the roughness of her tight, black stockings. But his senses were too dulled and unresponsive. He didn't feel much enjoyment or desire. It was as if he was tired... But she laughed and didn't let him fall asleep. Then he moved up higher, put his head in her lap and turned onto his back. He lay there with open eyes, as she moved her fingers distractedly through his hair and every now and again would accidentally tug at it painfully. He stretched his arms back and held her around her waist. He tried to push her face closer. She let him and her hair tickled his forehead. He tried to kiss her and whispered incoherent, silly, sweet words. She laughed, but slowly became quiet and leaned back. She was bored.

Roberts realised it. But a strange kind of laziness, a strange apathy pushed him down against the ground like a gentle weight. Milda was right here, but also somehow far away at the same time. He couldn't understand why she was here and couldn't summon up any particular desire inside himself. He tried grasping at her with his hands and could barely tell if he had touched her or not.

Just then he came around. Was somebody calling him or was something else waking him up? He opened his eyes. A pine tree was leaning over him at a slant, looking him in the eyes, and thoughtfully shaking its green-grey head. He was lying on the ground and the unpleasant sensation of the cold spring ground was pressing into his neck and back, his entire body.

"Time to get up. Let's go home." he heard a familiar voice say.

He got up with difficulty, almost staggering. The sun had gone down behind the trees, the wind had shifted and was now bringing a chill across the black, slimy stream. Milda had climbed a bit up the hill, her hat with its pin was pressed underneath her arm, as she stood turned away braiding her hair.

"Where are you off to?" Roberts shook himself off. "I almost froze... Why are you running away?"

Milda didn't turn around, she just laughed sarcastically.

"Well, what am I going to do, sit around and watch you sleep..."

He felt as if he'd been stung. Not just from her voice and stance. He sensed that he'd behaved badly, that she was disappointed, that he'd fallen in her eyes... He stood around digging through his pockets.

"Don't be silly! Come on, let's sit down."

But she didn't answer. Without turning around or looking back, she finished fixing her hair and threw the braid back across her shoulder, singing some dance melody as she trotted across the hill.

Dammit! For a moment he stood alone, his brow furrowed. Then he shook off his hat and put it back on, pulling it down to his ears, he shook off his coat and angrily began climbing up the hill. But Milda was already walking past the second one. Slender and dignified in her smooth, blue overcoat covered in pine needles, in her yellow boots and her white collar around her neck... He choked up from anger and regret. He wanted to ignore her and to just go down his own path back to the landing. But then she disappeared behind the second hill. He could hear her singing and steps – the tiny pinecones crunched under her yellow boots as she walked. He just couldn't! He followed after her.

"Where are you running off to?" he said accusingly after catching up with her. Tears could practically be heard in his voice.

She walked staring at the ground – fatigue was evident in her face and also an odd half-ironic, half-bitter smirk.

"I'm cold...and my head hurts..."

He felt like he was to blame for that too. But couldn't think of what to say. He stayed back.

"Wait!" he stopped her. "I'll brush off your overcoat."

She stopped and he began to brush off the sand and pine needles that clung to it, first with one, then with both hands. Gradually the movements of his hands became smoother and stronger. He was already moving over her shoulders and arms, then across both sides – downward from underneath her arms. He felt every fold of the soft blue fabric, sensed the smooth curves of her body and the gentle roundness of her muscles underneath it. And he forgot – he forgot that he needed to brush off the sand and pine needles. But he remembered something else... His passion, which had been smothered earlier, flared up again. His fingers began to shake nervously, his cheeks flushed.

Milda turned her head in surprise and looked over her shoulder.

"What's wrong with you?"

But then he held her, pinning her hands to her sides and pressing his own tightly against her breasts. He pulled her so close to him that he could hear some of her buttons crunching and all of it taking her breath away. He squeezed his entire body against hers – pressed her head down mercilessly with his forehead and pushed his lips onto her neck above the white ruffled collar... She struggled, gasping in vain for breath, her neck became pale white – but he didn't care. He pressed his mouth even more tightly to her neck – his lips parted and his teeth touched her warm flesh. It was as if he'd become drunk all over again. He lost his senses, will and control; there was no other way for him. Without leaning back or letting go, he tried to sit her down.

But then Milda regained her composure and twisted forcefully out of his embrace.

"You're crazy...The road is right here – somebody will see us."

Tossing her head back, she caught her breath. Her breasts rose and her hand instinctively stroked the place on her neck where his mouth had been. But she wasn't angry. After calming down, she tried to smile at him. But he was standing there looking cross, slightly turned away, his shaking hands hidden in his coat pockets. But when she went to pick up her books off the ground, he rushed over to gather them up and walked behind her to the boat dock...

They travelled back without saying practically a single word to each other. Milda was worried that the school director or Miss Zvaigzne find out. Roberts cursed Miss Zvaigzne impertinently, pointing out her relationship with Lausks, but then fell quiet and sank into his gloomy thoughts. He thought about the wasted day, about the drawing class he'd missed, his class promotion exams which he was having difficulties with... Everything that was unpleasant and bad was swirling around his head, and depression came over him like a black cloud. Fatigue, apathy – and behind it all, the sense of unsatisfied intentions and a day gone wrong... He was angry at himself and at the world.

Stepping off the riverboat, they found it difficult to take the ten steps that led to where they could take a cab. Milda's shoulders were hunched as she walked, dragging her feet along wearily. She looked pale and annoyed. Now neither of them cared at all if they did actually run into someone they knew. If they're seen, so be it... It was practically impossible to walk. They sat close together, feeling each other's warmth, but not thinking about anything at all. They had turned away from each other looking in their own direction, but they noticed very little. The only thing that mattered was getting home as soon as possible.

Letting Milda out on the corner, Roberts had the driver turn around and go as fast as he could. Tired, angry, upset with himself, Milda, and the whole world, Roberts slumped back heavily in the cab. He wanted to sleep more than anything else.

In the middle of August, because of a poor summer, a small crisis in industry, and rumours of war, all aspects of life had become cautious and weary. Buyers stayed away, sellers' current payments began to pinch, financial institutions carefully selected guarantors and discounted only very secure bills of exchange. Notices of account closures had tripled and were still increasing. The pile of gold coins had slumped and the stacks of bank notes had shrunk dangerously in number. The bank directors looked with concern over the backs of their employees. Those seeking extensions on bills of exchange, notified debtors and credit applicants rushed in and out anxiously. The same person would appear at the same bank five times during the course of one day. Merchants and businessmen were worried, as were their creditors; employees whispered to each other with concern. Wage payments would be delayed by a few days, the bosses would claim to have forgotten about it and twist each three-rouble piece crossly in their fingers.

It was also quiet – very quiet – at A. Sveilis Jr.'s wine shop. There was a dusty oak barrel on display in the shop window. A dust-covered clay Moor was standing on top of it holding a foaming glass in his hand. There were a few boxes filled with sawdust in the middle of the shop, the counter was piled high with bottles wrapped in colourful paper, which had just been unloaded. The air was hot and aromatic. Timma, the clerk, was sitting behind the barrel, his back resting against the shelf, and was lazily swatting at flies with a leather hand attached to the end of a thin handle. His long moustache, which stretched halfway across his cheeks, was drooping wearily. His bald spot, shiny from sweat, was hemmed in by grey hairs sticking straight up. The bottles had to be arranged on the shelves, but Timma didn't want to do it. For a moment he was alone in the shop – the girl who worked as the cashier wasn't behind the shiny cash register. But then Timma jumped to his feet, straightened his cravat, and tried to smile. He could see his boss standing outside the glass door. He stood there for a moment with the lawyer Blics, said goodbye to him, and came inside.

He only lifted his hat a little bit, returning the clerk's greeting. He tossed his walking stick down on the open space on the counter, pulled out his handkerchief and wiped his forehead. He was wearing a thin, white suit with black stripes, but it was hot and he was sweating. He sat down heavily on the chair by the cash register and yawned. His red, swollen eyes made him look exhausted.

"Well, how's it going?" he asked.

Timma, smiling sadly, shrugged his shoulders.

"It's quiet, very quiet..." He came out, took the large ledger from the cash register, and handed it to his boss. He leafed through it reluctantly, glancing at each page. He yawned again.

"Do you think we should advertise more?" Timma asked.

Sveilis brushed him aside. "There's no point; nobody will come anyway. It's the end of the season. It seems like only half the population is in town as it is. It's a crisis. There's no money – everybody's complaining. Today they're saying that Ficners went bankrupt. And Ķirsis also won't hold out for long, I know that for certain."

Timma grimaced sympathetically. "One less competitor."

Sveilis nodded his head. "It doesn't mean anything. In busier times, there's enough for everybody..." He yawned. "One thing... Just one shop isn't enough anymore. You can't get anywhere without branches. In the new year we'll open three or at least two branches."

"Really?" Timma looked surprised. "Will that pay off for you?"

"Absolutely. These are times when a small business can't survive anymore. Now you have to act boldly. If you put one rouble into circulation, it'll bring you back - well, ten, fifteen, twenty kopecks profit. But if you put out ten roubles - what do you get then?"

"Of course - of course..." Timma agreed warmly. "As long as you have that much capital to invest."

"Me?" His hand slid into his pocket as was his habit, but this time he didn't pull out his wallet. "Me, well, thank God, I'm lacking for nothing. You know, our bank just bought half of my property... of course, I don't make a lot off of it, I just recoup my own expenses. The Seventh Credit Union increased my credit to fifteen thousand..."

"Yes, yes, of course..." Timma moved closer. His eyes sparkled, but his face only showed profound submissiveness. He liked times like these quite a bit. When the boss was a little tipsy, he became rather talkative and would blurt out secrets like these, which a clerk would otherwise never learn. And clerks were always especially interested to learn the secrets of their bosses. "But aren't you building a house there on the other side - construction materials are expensive right now, workers."

"That doesn't mean anything - as long as you've got credit. It all pays itself off in the long run - as long as you can wait. And if the bank gives it to me, then it has to wait. Our bank, thank God, has plenty...I've planned it out like this: two or three branches off in the outskirts - one in Pārdaugava for certain. Advertisements too, of course. And for the holidays, prizes for regular customers, increased discounts, and so on. And even if we don't earn a profit on some brands, as long as they move, as long as they don't sit around in the store too long...you'll see, we'll make money!"

Timma didn't manage to respond or object to any of this. A little old lady came in and asked for a half bottle of Riga medicinal balsam. There weren't any half bottles - only whole bottles. The old woman didn't have enough money for a whole one. She looked sad and left.

Sveilis noticed that the cashier wasn't there. He looked through the gap in the doorway into the back room. Probably not there either.

"Where's Miss Zvaigzne then?" he asked.

"Just before you came in, she went over to the pharmacy." Timma rushed to excuse her. "Her father is ill... Oh, so you're thinking of opening one up in Pārdaugava?"

A new customer came in and interrupted their conversation again. A stout man who spoke German. Sveilis lifted his hat towards him respectfully. He required one bottle of Moselblümchen and half a bottle of Arak. Sveilis watched carefully as the clerk wrapped the bottles. But he soon got bored and turned away with a yawn. The customer hadn't quite left when Kārlis Roblapainis came in and greeted Sveilis loudly.

"How fateful that I should run into the boss himself today! I have important business." He pulled a piece of paper covered in writing from his folder. "So, will Mr. Sveilis turn down contributing to the Charity Association's autumn festival? The members have to support it. All the best Latvian firms have contributed. Pēters Viļumsons gave fifty roubles of his own money..."

Sveilis looked reluctantly at the paper listing the contributions.

"Viļumsons...The people who own those big stores can afford it...There are always contributions, every week I have to contribute. When was it that I had to give money for the monument for that musician? And then also for that sick actor... We're not millionaires, you know."

Kārlis Roblapainis seemed a little offended.

"Excuse me... but we, all the members, each of us give as much as we can. Each according to his abilities for the sake of noble goals. They don't have to be specifically monetary contributions. As you can see - others are giving their products and wares."

"Ten - pounds of candy - ah, forty-five..." Sveilis read. "One hundred bottles lemonade - ah, that must be from

Gailis? Right? Yes, from Gailis... Five pounds of smoked sausage... three pounds..." He handed the paper back to Kārlis Roblapainis and reached over to pick up his firm's catalogue. He leafed through it. "Well, what - Mr. Timma - could we...?"

Timma, leaning over the counter, looked at the catalogue. Kārlis Roblapainis pulled his ink pen from his pocket.

"After everything is arranged, we'll make sure to mention all the details in the papers," he nodded. "It's also a kind of advertisement for the store. You won't lose out."

"That's very true," Timma agreed.

"Well, what do you think, Mr. Timma? Some bottles of cognac...one of the liqueurs?"

"I think," Timma said as he looked through the pages of the catalogue, "it'd be better if we gave something that isn't purchased as much. Kakheti, Vorontsov, Muskateller - one of those, I think."

"Yes, that's about right. Well then: two bottles of cognac, ah, a rouble fifty, and one of each of these." He dragged his nail across the page. "A rouble - a rouble ten - a rouble twenty - a rouble..."

Kārlis Roblapainis put down the paper and pen onto the counter.

"Would you be so kind as to write it all down."

"You write it." Sveilis pushed it over to Timma. He avoided writing as much as possible. "Too many different spelling nowadays."

Kārlis Roblapainis agreed, "It's true. It's hard for a non-specialist to orient themselves. Every newspaper has its own orthography; practically every writer has their own."

"Yes, yes!" Sveilis agreed enthusiastically. "There's no clarity at all. Everybody writes however they wish. Whatever comes into their mind is correct. But that newest one, all the papers are full of that one... I don't know, I'm no specialist... but I still think it's just a lot of foolishness."

"Yes... I can't really accept it either..." Kārlis Roblapainis said wrinkling his brow.

Timma listened too as he wrote. He truly had no idea about all these different spellings. He only wrote Latvian as he heard it, mixing all the different orthographies up into quite a jumble. But his handwriting was neat. Carefully and with evident delight he wrote each round letter, now and then adding a fine, oval loop above or below them...

When Kārlis Roblapainis left, Sveilis got up and stretched as he walked over to the shelves.

"You know, I haven't slept at all for nearly two whole nights... I sold half of my lot to our bank... We laid the cornerstone...There was some jealous drinking..." He said drunkenly and then laughed again. "A hundred bottles of champagne alone! We could have bathed in it..." He took down a half jug of English bitter ale and sloshed it next to his ear. "I need to try a drop to see what it's like." He went back into the windowless backroom and sat down. He uncorked the jug, poured some into his glass, took a drink, listened and then roared. "Dammit... Mr. Timma, please have one too."

"Thank you, sir, I don't drink bitter."

"Well, what do you drink! Goddammit! Have something."

"If you insist..." Timma grabbed the foreign-made miniature bottle of peppermint liqueur and, quickly uncorking it, went into the back room.

"Well, how do you like the taste of it?" Sveilis grimaced. He poured himself another one and drank. He watched as Timma slowly dribbled the green, sticky, strong-smelling liquid into a tiny slender glass. He filled it half way and then slurped a bit off the top. Sveilis turned away in contempt. "You're no drinker."

"No," Timma confirmed. "A glass of Pfefferminz if anything, otherwise I don't drink."

"And the young lady?"

"Miss Zvaigzne? She doesn't drink anything stronger than tea..." Just as they were talking about her she walked into the front room.

"Has he been here yet?" Aina asked loudly as she took off her overcoat.

"No, not yet." Timma nodded towards the back room and added quietly: "The boss..."

Aina came over to the door, said hello, and hung up her coat.

"Forgive me, sir, I was out for a half hour... to get some medicine at the pharmacy. My father is ill."

For the first time Sveilis looked closely at his cashier. Hm... pretty face... tall, slender body with a waist that's not bound up too tight. Rosy cheeks, hair a little messed up by her hat. What was especially beautiful was her lovely slender slightly bent neck with its heavy, brown knot of hair. How could he have missed all of that until now? He became very friendly. Kindness radiated from his eyes, and his round lips lightly smacked as he spoke.

"It's nothing, it's nothing, Miss Zvaigzne. Everyone has business to attend to sometimes. I certainly don't ask for my employees to stand here as if they were tied down...What illness does your father have?"

"Consumption...It's an old affliction. He's long been infirm, but for two years now he's been in bed almost the whole time." She walked out and hid a few school books in the cashier's locker. Timma saw, but didn't say anything. They were friends.

"Really?" Sveilis said sympathetically. "And is your mother still alive? Yes? And you're the only provider? Really? And how do you manage, making only thirty roubles a month?"

"Well, I manage as best I can," she answered reticently. Her boss's sympathy felt to her like a rough hand stroking a swollen, infected spot. "We also have boarders..." But then, thinking of something else, she walked back to the door. She looked back at Timma and spoke quietly, slightly muddled, searching for the right words. "Excuse me, Mr. Sveilis...It pains me to have to denounce or complain about someone, but I must do it. I wanted to ask you to have a talk with your brother. He's been behaving rather... uncouthly."

"Oh, yes?" Sveilis looked surprised. "How so? In what way has he been uncouth?"

"We have a boarder, a young girl from the country... who attends high school here. He has become her friend, and is always visiting her..."

Sveilis giggled as if someone were tickling him.

"Oh, Roberts! That son of a bitch – who would have thought it! What a little devil. Well, why shouldn't he visit? There's nothing wrong with that."

"Actually there is something wrong with it, that's why I have been forced to say something to you. If he just came over, that would be nothing. But I know for certain that they also often meet outside of the house, traipse around parks and cafés, and go who knows where together. They miss classes and don't study. That girl struggled to make it into the next grade."

"That brother of mine is lazy too. What will I do with him! He left business school – prefers art school... Says he's got a great talent for painting..." He shrugged to suggest that he wasn't convinced. "What kind of talent could he have?"

But Aina didn't feel like laughing. She began to get upset. "Laziness is just the first step, but not the worst one. One has to be worried about a person losing their way altogether. I don't know your brother that well, but that girl of ours is rather ruined already. She is becoming more insolent by the day."

"Oh, yes?" Sveilis had become quite interested. He seemed increasingly warm and amused. "Ruined, you say? How do you mean?"

Aina blushed. She understood that this person wasn't thinking about the same things she was. She saw that he enjoyed the complexity of this piquant situation and her story about it. She sensed that he was hoping she would descend to divulging indecent details... She immediately became revolted by this smooth, white face with its long blonde moustache, revolted by its probing, bloodshot eyes, eager round lips and gentle lisping speech.

"Figure it out yourself," she answered rather sharply and turned away. "Your brother is no child anymore. He brings that girl indecent books and leads her on in all manner of ways. Of course, she's most to blame of all. Still, I implore you to be sure and rein in your brother. It's impossible to look on dispassionately as a young person intentionally ruins themselves in this way."

She stepped up onto the ladder and asked Timma to hand her the bottles, which had been unpacked onto the counter.

Smiling with a glass in his hand, Sveilis moved towards the gap in the door so he could see.

"You are a strong woman," he said, not taking his eyes off of her for a second. Truly what a nice shape she had standing up there, the tips of her boots resting on the narrow steps and her lifted arms bare from the elbows down! Sveilis lit a cigarette and repeated: "You are a strong woman, Miss Zvaigzne... Would you like Mr. Timma to pour you a drop of something?"

"No, thank you," she answered without stopping her work.

"Just a small glass."

"None for me. I don't drink."

"None at all? Are you a member of the Temperance Union?"

"No, I don't drink out of principle..."

Lausks rushed in through the front doors – sweaty, out of breath. He said hello to Timma.

"Well, where are those pills?" he asked. "I've got an hour free to take them over. The boss is out."

Aina quietly showed him the package containing the pills. Sveilis got up and looked on with interest from the back room. How was it that this slender, good-looking man with a carefully trimmed beard was so familiar with his cashier? He began to remember something he felt he'd heard earlier, but couldn't remember it precisely. He studied the newcomer. He stood in the door.

"Aren't you the one...who works with Mr. Blics the lawyer?"

Catching sight of Sveilis, for some reason Lausks was at a loss for words and in his confusion shot a timid look at Aina.

"Yes... I work for him... Started this spring..."

"A-ha..." Sveilis became increasingly interested in this

confused man. "Well then, tell me..." He put a cigarette in his holder. "Yes, do tell me – is Mr. Blics at home?"

"No. He just left to go to the Land Registry Office. He'll be back in an hour..."

"A-ha... I had... some business. You'll be going back, yes? then tell Mr. Blics... or," he took out his watch, "it's better if I stop by. In one hour, you said? Uh huh, I'll stop by then." He accompanied Lausks to the door with an aristocratic bearing. "An acquaintance of yours, Miss Zvaigzne?"

"Yes," she answered and looked with astonishment down at her boss. "He's one of our boarders."

"You have a lot of boarders," Sveilis said with surprise.

Lausks stepped outside and turned at the corner. He stopped, unable to shake his feeling of confusion. Why was that bourgeois fellow looking at him and Aina like that? Wasn't he just as good of a person as Sveilis, maybe even a better one. He couldn't stop thinking about it. And yet, amazingly, Sveilis disappeared from his thoughts, and it was towards Aina that there was a sort of lingering annoyance, anger or worry. He approached the window of the wine shop and tried to look in over the barrel. The sun was shining straight onto the window and it was impossible to see anything deep inside. There were the crates sitting in the middle of the room that had been rummaged through; wood shavings were scattered about. Timma was looking over the counter. But he couldn't see either Aina or Sveilis... Lausks walked off in a huff.

In the evening he found himself standing at the window again. This time he could see Aina behind the cash register. But he felt uneasy about going inside. It would look strange for him to keep coming in, they'd start asking questions about his and Aina's relationship... What kind of an answer could you give to such questions? He was so sick of skulking around. Every day the situation became more unbearable. Blics had also started to come out with ambiguous statements here and there. Soon the whole city would know. These sorts of things can't stay hidden forever. Whenever he thought about it, he felt angry at Aina's stubbornness. Why couldn't they just get married? She wouldn't have to avoid other men's attention; he wouldn't be tortured by jealousy. It would be easier and more enjoyable for both of them.

He couldn't wait around for the shop to close, so he went home. As he approached, Milda was on the corner saying goodbye to her escort, looking back as she walked in through the gate. Fuming, Lausks picked up his pace and caught up with the girl in the yard.

"Where have you two been running around?" he called out to her. He grabbed Milda by the shoulder from behind.

"Hey!" She freed herself angrily. "What are you grabbing me for, are you crazy!"

"Where have you been – the pair of you?" he repeated.

"What business is it of yours? Do I ask you where you two have been?"

Lausks was so overcome with anger that he waited at the bottom of the steps until Milda came in and walked past him. She didn't look back and began walking up – he was on her heels following her.

"I'm going to break you two up!" he threatened. "I'll throw him down these steps if he ever comes here again."

She laughed cuttingly.

"Just take care that Miss Zvaigzne doesn't throw you down them first! Quite the big man. Who are you anyway? A boarder like all the rest. But worse: you don't pay rent – you just live off the charity of others. How dare you judge anyone else!"

For a moment he was speechless. "Insolent girl!" he hissed. And his fingers itched to grab her by that braid and shake her.

But Milda wasn't listening or paying any attention to him. She walked in and slammed the door in his face so that he would feel the wind blow past his ears.

When Aina came home, she could tell straight away that Lausks was in a bad mood. But tonight she felt the opposite: her heart was elated. A working person sometimes feels that way in the evening. When they've thrown off the burden of work for the day, everything feels so affecting and pleasant. Everything around them seems somehow more attractive. There's no need to think about tomorrow, just to forget and let oneself enjoy the beauty of the moment. She grabbed Lausks and spun him around with her in the middle of the room, so that the pages he was working on flew out of his hands and onto the ground.

"Spin around with me, lawyer!" she laughed in his ear.

He tried to smile bitterly. "Don't play around! I have five pages to copy tonight."

"We'll copy them, I'll help."

Her mother was also happier than usual tonight. She wasn't immediately cross, as she was most days. She was more lively, animated; she started to talk about how she'd found a different shop where the kerosene tap is much larger – the bottle was an entire finger's width fuller! And about how Aina's father was doing better today: he'd got up, walked over to the table without needing to support himself and sat there for a good long while. Aina's father also interrupted, taking deep breaths and coughing, saying he would have sat there even longer if his feet hadn't got so cold. Aina listened to both of them and thought that their liveliness and good-humour must have some other source.

And so it did! Her mother couldn't keep from telling her. Blics had promised Lausks a place at the Savings and Loans... Fifty roubles a month... And even more later on! Her mother could barely contain her happiness. It'll be time for them to plan a wedding soon. Then they'll be able to live like normal people...

A little annoyed, Aina returned to her room and asked Lausks if this was true. He confirmed that Blics had promised him this – in a month or a month and a half. Telling her about it, he became happier too. But Aina sat in pensive silence. Lausks began to fidget nervously.

"Well, aren't you happy... that I'll earn more?"

Aina carefully examined each of her fingers one after another.

"Why not..." she answered slowly. "The more the better. But..."

"Well?" he furrowed his brow. Another 'but'?"

She was quiet for a moment, then turned directly towards him.

"You think that if there's money then that's it, that's enough, then there's no room for any other objections."

"What are you trying to get at?" Lausks was increasingly get angry. "What do you want now?"

"Always the same thing again and again: money. Everything else is just a means... Mother is walking around dancing, even father got up and walked across the room. Wherever there's gold, they're ready to fall on their knees."

"Don't ridicule your parents!" Lausks growled.

"If the truth is ridiculous, what else can I do! I'm amazed how similar you are to them. You hurried ahead to tell them before you even told me. Yeah, yeah, you can't deny it. You're starting to relate to them better than you can to me. You seem to be tearing yourself away from me. That too is the truth."

"Your truth is also a great falsehood." Lausks rasped to interrupt her. "Haven't they sat around and suffered enough in their poverty? Apparently you don't even think your father deserves to have it a bit easier in his final days - a more comfortable life as he stands at the edge of his grave... That's what I don't understand. It's not true - is it? - that I relied on your charity all the time I've been living here with you. Isn't it the case that you needed my support at least in part? Am I not a man and do I not have my own sense of pride?"

Aina stared long and hard, directly into his eyes, as if she wanted to understand him right down to the depths of his soul.

"Your pride is strange and you've become strange. In our relationship based on love do we need to ask and seek out who cares for whom? Two interwoven rings - which one supports the other? You take offense in a place where there isn't and can't be any offense. But where it actually exists, you feel nothing. A hidden pinprick hurts you, but you don't even notice a brazen slap across your face."

"And?" His lips were shaking and his eyes were moist. But that kind of sentimentality only hardened Aina further.

"If that's what this much extoled masculine pride is actually like, then it's not worth much. Don't you understand why my parents couldn't stand you until now, and why they're suddenly so sweet? Because up until now you were poor, but soon you'll have more money. You're just the same as you were up until now, right? But soon you won't be walking around in old worn-out boots and won't carry around your entire month's salary in your waistcoat pocket. Doesn't your pride turn away in disgust from the kind of goodwill that can be bought for money?"

In his agitation, Lausks was briefly at a loss for words. But the unjust accusation weighed heavily on his heart.

"I don't need a thing from them... But think about their situation – their lives, views, and feelings. They have their rights..."

"Oh, don't worry so much about their rights! Think about your own views and feelings, and tell me whether you've ever felt demeaned by their judgement. You think that they hate our relationship in itself? If you were a rich man, if you could've filled their pockets with gold, you wouldn't have ever heard a single unkind word. They'd have accepted you and treated you as their own son. They would have known to silence their inner moral voice and awareness of our sin. The poverty of their lives has also made them poor in spirit. Poverty in life, poverty in thoughts and feelings. Are you not ashamed to become just as poor as they are!"

"You think everything I do is bad. You think it's just because of them? I thought of you first and foremost: if I could make more money, you wouldn't need to go and work for other people. You wouldn't need to waste away in some wine cellar with its Sveilises and Timmas... and where all kinds of strange men can stare at you."

She became unintentionally jovial.

"Lausks, there's a natural born property owner speaking through you! You're blindly and stupidly jealous. You don't allow anyone else ownership over your property – they aren't even permitted to look at it. What you've bought, belongs only to you alone. Next you'll need to build a glass case to keep me in!" She became more serious on seeing that he was very hurt by what she had said. "Anyway, never mind...I'm only teasing. Go and work at your bank and earn your fifty roubles. We won't change our lives or our views for that reason alone. We won't sell out for fifty roubles. Right?"

He muttered something crossly. But Aina didn't wait for his answer. She felt the warmth of her earlier joy flow over her again.

"Work at that bank for a few months...a year maybe." she continued. "Until I've passed my exam. This autumn – for certain. The shop has been so quiet this summer that I have been able to spend a lot of the time studying. I've studied so much that I have no doubts about it. I just have to take the exam, and I'll pass!" She hit one fist against the other in a strangely dramatic way, so that Lausks couldn't help but laugh. "And then – to hell with all the wine shops and banks, all the Sveilises and Blicses. Let's open up a school – right here in the outskirts. Will you say yes? See what I thought of today? Will you say yes?"

She leaned over and put her arm around his neck. He was so surprised that he didn't know what to say and just blinked his eyes.

"In the outskirts... for the children of the workers! We can meet with fathers and brothers at the unions and elsewhere. We're united by work and common interests. But the young, growing generation of workers are roaming around the streets, sitting at a school mixed willy-nilly with the children of the petite bourgeois, where uniformed officials mould them according to the same general pattern. The children of the workers are crippled and ruined, made renegades to their own class from an early age. And the older generation of workers don't see or notice it. They allow the streets and their enemies to ruin their children and then wait for life to awaken them later. People whose futures and fates are dependent solely on combined, conscientious efforts leave their younger generation to the blind forces of life... That is short-sightedness and a crime – the worst sin of all. It is unforgivable."

She looked Lausks in the face in search of support, but detected something very different, something distant and immeasurable. He understood one thing. He definitely wanted to end this unpleasant conversation.

"The kind of school you describe – it's impossible...You can't run a school in whatever way you want. You have to follow specific rules."

"What worker doesn't have to follow specific rules? Factory walls are covered with boards listing punishments, street corners are pasted up and down with them... Every year rules upon new rules. But one thing is clear: you can fence off the Daugava, choke it off with dams and logs, and divide it up. But try to dam it off completely, to cut off its path to the sea... and it'll break through... it'll destroy everything in its path and wash it away..."

Lausks moved a little bit away and coughed. "School is meant to teach, not raise children. Every family must raise its own children."

"They should!" Aina shot back passionately. "But is that possible for working families? Where are these families? Father and mother at work from six till six, and their children on the street. Nothing but riffraff, rabble – that's all workers' children are today...Every morning on my way to work I see groups of children in our yard, and when I come back at night, they're still there. And every time it feels like I'm losing a piece of my heart... How they creep around rich men's houses to see if they can maybe find a half-eaten crust of bread! And how do they greet every less able or poorer passer-by? With such ridicule and villainy! And how they argue and fight amongst themselves! And they're the ones who are supposed to grow up into a conscientious, powerful and unified group of workers…"

"You won't change them." Lausks muttered. "That's the way they've always been and how they'll stay."

"They won't!" she interrupted him. "They can't! The working classes can't forever remain ignorant to the things which are most important in their life's struggle. The time will come when workers' children won't be wandering around the streets, as they won't learn anything by creeping around, arguing, betraying or anything else that happens on the street. At kindergartens – in large, well-lit rooms and on shady lawns in the fresh air, they'll play together in harmony and their sensible teacher – a sister to their older brothers and sisters – will tell them ancient tales of the nation of workers and all of its heroic deeds, and relate the truth of the distant future through beautiful stories. She'll teach them to hold everything low, indecent and servile in complete contempt, and instead to desire and long for openness, freedom and beauty in nature, life and humanity…"

Lausks heard only the music of her language. Gradually, it started to move him too. He enjoyed rocking back and forth in its waves thinking about nothing, just feeling gently and sweetly dizzy. He gazed at her flushed face and blazing eyes and moved closer to her again.

"Dreamer…" He shook his head and gently ran his hand across hers.

"And at school – they won't just exercise the memories of workers' children by weighing them down with all that unnecessary, useless ballast. They won't repeat to them day in and day out that everything is as it should be, that a human being is a worm and a mote of dust. They won't distract their attention from everything that must be seen and understood – and solved. A worker's child must always remain in active contact with their big brothers and sisters and with the life from which they come and to which they must return. Kindergartens and schools must fill the void left by the destruction of workers' families…" She put her hand on top of his and looked lovingly into his eyes. "Go ahead and join that bank... for a while. We'll need quite a lot of money to get things started. But start we will! We just need to create an example and then others will appear and wish to continue it. Let no other worker's daughter go down the road which Milda is now walking..." She leaned in closer to him. "Without intending it, perhaps we are a bit at fault after all if that girl loses her way. I've thought about this and suffered quite a lot! But we'll fix things, we'll atone for our sin. For every hour of indulgence and pleasure, we'll endure a year of hard, unending work. That itself is joy – isn't it, my love?"

Her gaze continued to become deeper and more loving. He felt hypnotised, his smile blooming along with Aina's. He wasn't thinking about anything, just rocking along in delight and babbling like a child.

"Yes, my love..."

He pressed up close to her.

"As far as I'm concerned... I'm willing to get married after all. Not because of those old people and their world. But if it helps our work. Work is the most important thing after all... it's the only thing. We have to use every means to help accomplish it..."

"Yes, yes..."

He didn't know what else to say. She was so beautiful in her passionate enthusiasm; her beauty had enslaved him. He didn't have his own thoughts or desires, but was carried along like an iron shaving to a magnet. He didn't hear or understand what she was talking about. Of what concern to him were these far-off and foreign things such as schools and kindergartens, workers' children or whether or not people should marry. None of it mattered! Just as long as she was there! He held her tightly in his hot arms.

Pressed against his chest, she looked up at his face. She interpreted his elation and enthusiasm very differently. She lingered in her distant thoughts and didn't even feel his eager hands slowly sliding down her body.

Paeglītis came out of the office red-faced, sweating, agitated and clutching his sportsman's cap tightly with his autumn coat hanging open. Lodziņš followed directly behind him but stayed on the other side of the counter.

"Please, don't take it personally," he tried to calm his agitated client, "but we can't do anything more for you here. We understand your situation, try to imagine ours. We can't loan you more than twenty-five hundred based on your bond."

"You can't..." Tears came to Paeglītis's eyes. "Say what you actually mean: you just don't want to. That's the thing. You can do it for everybody else, but not for me."

"We give you as much as we can. The old board didn't want to give you fifteen hundred while we gave you twenty-five hundred. A whole thousand roubles more. What more could you want?"

"Another thousand – that's all. I told you: I need it. Without thirty-five hundred I can't survive."

"But, my good man, think about it! Your cottage isn't insured for three thousand. Twenty-five hundred in mortgage debts! What were you thinking? Do you think that money grows on trees? Aren't we responsible to the auditors and shareholders?"

"I told you," Paeglītis said with eyes turned bloodshot from white-hot rage, "Latvians are pigs. Latvians don't know how to take risks."

Lodziņš felt offended. "Do what you wish then. We can't give you any more money against that bond. We're in times of financial crisis, and we need to limit our operations and protect ourselves from unsecured loans."

"From unsecured loans, of course!" Paeglītis turned even redder. "When I need it, suddenly you're in a crisis and need to limit your operations. But Tilaks gets twenty-five thousand... Sietiņsons gets ten..." Lodziņš became a bit confused.

"In Tilaks's case, yes..." he began to speak more quietly. "But in Sietiņsons's I was against it, but was outvoted. I'm not alone in here. Besides their portfolios are completely different."

"Oh really! What does Tilaks have?" Paeglītis raised his voice even more. "And maybe you should ask how much mortgage Sietiņsons has on splinter board shacks."

"And anyhow, we have to treat older members differently. Mr. Tilaks has done a lot for our bank."

"And what about what I've done? Nobody pays any attention to that! But who put in the most hours before the shareholders' meeting? Truly, it's no lie: all my running around, the delays and expenses cost my business at least five hundred roubles."

There were a few strangers in the bank at that moment. An old woman had come to withdraw fifty roubles, and a grey-haired old man was discounting a bill of exchange. Lodziņš didn't appreciate Paeglītis's loud voice one bit: the employees and the public strangers can listen in to their conversation. He looked away. He was bored and shrugged his shoulders. "As you now know, we can't offer you any more credit. Get a guarantor, then maybe... I'll try and talk to them again, but I don't have great hopes. Please do come back in."

Lodziņš went first with Paeglītis in tow – they both walked back into the directors' office.

Behind the counter, on the far end, his hands stuffed in his pockets and smoking a cigarette, stood Sveilis Jr. He had no reason to be there at this time; – in fact he had no right to stand there at all. But that's what he did almost every day: he left his coat in the directors' office, came into the cashiers' area and stood around for a while behind the counter. His hands stuffed into his pockets, smoking a cigarette and smiling gently, he looked at the clients who came and went from the other side, as they paid and received their money. They looked at him and assumed he was a director, which he greatly enjoyed.

He certainly did like standing around by the cashiers' counters, moving amongst the employees and looking through some of the books with a knowledgeable gaze. Or he would just lean back against the cage enclosing the cashiers' desks and watch how bank notes rustled through the cashiers' counters and how gold coins dropped jingling into a concave glass surface. Low shelves were piled full of bundles held together by rubber bands. Peculiar shallow wooden boxes holding rolls of gold coins looked as if they were filled with scruffy yellow rope ends. People would practically run in looking at their watches, and then stand there out of breath, apologising and pleading incessantly. The rustle of banknotes and the jingle of gold didn't stop from ten in the morning to three in the afternoon. It moved by the pile and the handful through the cashiers' windows.

Sveilis watched and completely lost himself in deep, profound thought. How strangely and wonderfully all this was organised! Did he or anyone else even need to work or worry here? The people brought their money in on their own and deposited it, receiving six percent interest. And those who borrowed and paid the bank eight percent, earned twelve percent themselves. One only had to receive it, pile it onto the shelf, arrange it by box, count it and record it – and just for that you received seventy-five roubles per month. But those who sat there on the far end behind the glass doors and decided who would get money and who wouldn't, they earned five thousand a year. And contributions could be made to charity for worthy aims in the amount of five hundred roubles every year. No one had it bad and no one had to do much. It was good for everyone, and everyone just kept on earning.

He felt agreeably intoxicated as the smell of paper money dirtied by all the hands that had touched it wafted into his nostrils. Sveilis couldn't decide or understand where it all came from and why this happened. But he felt that there couldn't be a better or more pleasant arrangement than that which existed at Savings and Loans. Where was the wise person who had thought it all up?

To his mild annoyance Sveilis was obliged to interrupt his delightful reverie because Blics, the lawyer, was standing behind the counter and greeting him warmly. "Hello, hello!" Blics squeezed his hand as he shook it rather firmly and forcefully. "Are you already studying for the director's job?"

Sveilis greeted this suggestion with glee and even blushed a little. How had this lawyer managed to catch on to his most secret and cherished ambition? He artfully demurred.

"Don't be silly... I am just curious about how it works."

Blics's smile faded while he exchanged a few words about something at the cashier's window, but he then returned and appeared to be even more favourably inclined to Sveilis. He opened the folder he had placed on the counter.

"You see, here's the thing..." He took out a small piece of paper covered in print and writing with a torn postage stamp near its edge.

"A small bill of exchange at the Seventh Credit Union... I'd completely forgotten about it... One hundred and fifty roubles."

"Right, right..." Sveilis muttered, not yet realising what he wanted and casually running his eyes over the familiar-looking formal notice.

"It's such a silly thing. Yesterday I had to make a large payment..." He looked intently and pointedly into Sveilis's eyes, but Sveilis didn't respond, simply pretending to stare at the paper and nodding his head. Then Blics quickly folded up the paper and put it back into the folder. Its button clicked shut crisply and categorically. "Listen, Augusts...Could you maybe help me out? Just for a few days?"

"For a few days?" Sveilis didn't understand.

"Let's say, for three... Friday I'll have another deposit, then I'll be able to give it back to you right away. If it's not too much trouble."

Sveilis knew how Blics paid back loans... Still, he didn't think for a second that he wouldn't give him the money. Wasn't it just last week that they'd toasted to brotherhood and he'd kissed this refined, educated person? Wasn't it thanks to Blics's help that he had become an auditor at Unity and was likely to become a director someday. Not saying a single word, he pulled out his wallet.

"Why not, why not. One hundred and fifty, was it?" He

threw down a hundred-rouble note onto the counter and handed the other one to the cashier. "Zandmans, would you be so kind as to change this into two fifties."

He placed the remaining fifty back into his wallet and closed it so Blics wouldn't see that aside from that, he only had two fivers. He smiled back with utter indifference when Blics, squeezing and shaking his hand, thanked him effusively.

Even redder than the first time, Paeglītis came out of the director's room. His coat was open, his tie had pulled out of his waistcoat, his sportsman's cap clenched remorselessly in his hand. Without looking at anyone, he headed straight for the door. Sveilis just barely managed to stop him.

"Wait up, I'll come with you!" He threw on his coat, and both he and Paeglītis walked out onto the street. "Well, what happened in there?" he asked and looked sympathetically into Paeglītis's eyes.

Paeglītis threw up his hands in resignation.

"They won't give a thousand roubles. They just won't give me a kopeck. Isn't that shameful! I can't manage without it... I absolutely have to open that shop in the new year. There's no more business at the market – more sellers than buyers... I absolutely have to have it!"

This whole thing was rather unpleasant for Sveilis.

"As far as I know, it really is impossible for them. I've got a new building; Strauss has a building... Then there's the financial crisis we're going through – depositors are withdrawing their money. Yesterday it was six thousand was withdrawn in a single day. And debtors are bad at paying up. All you can get is the interest – next Friday there are four more cases at the court of justice. It's just not possible to expand operations right now."

"Not possible!" Paeglītis laughed bitterly. "This is exactly what I've been saying: Latvians are pigs; Latvians don't know how to take risks!" Deeply offended and agitated, he took a few large steps so Sveilis couldn't keep up, but then waited again. "Tilaks gets twenty-five thousand, Sietiņsons gets ten... But when I just need one, then the financial crisis is so momentous that it's impossible... How much money did I lose leading up to those elections! Has anyone worked harder than me for the bank?"

"That's true, of course!" Sveilis pressed his hand to his chest. "Nobody is trying to deny your contributions. But what they're saying is: we can't pay any more on that bond. You need to find guarantors..."

He suddenly understood how badly he'd phrased that last statement, but by then it was too late. Paeglītis enthusiastically grabbed him by the arm.

"Listen, why don't you become my guarantor!"

Sveilis pressed his other hand to his chest.

"It would be my very fondest wish – you know me. But... think about it yourself: I've got a building of my own and quite a loan to pay back. I guaranteed five hundred for Bērzītis, thirteen hundred for Blics... I can't do anymore, no matter how much I'd like to. And they won't take me either, even though I'd like to – they can't accept me. We're in the middle of a crisis right now."

Paeglītis didn't say anything. But Sveilis felt his grip slackening around his arm, his hand gradually slid downward, and then finally fell away completely. His face clouded over again and his eyes stared off into the distance. Paeglītis's handsome beard had not been groomed since yesterday; its little curls had come undone and separated.

"When one doesn't want to, then it's impossible..." he muttered. "So all of my running around, taking time off while my business suffered... was for nothing. The old board wasn't so bad after all. At least, Brambergis was honest – the same rules applied for one and all. But now it's every man looking out for himself, while those with less influence, they get nothing... What an utterly crooked business!"

Sveilis took him by his arm.

"It's not like that... not at all. Think about it: how could they do it? If they say that they can't – then it's not possible..."

They'd arrived at the Baltika. He turned his confused friend in the direction of the door. "Please. Let me buy us a round of kidneys."

They each ate their portion of kidneys and, while they were eating, they drank a medium-sized carafe of spirits. Then they ordered a bottle of mulled wine, snacking on fried fish as they drank it. Later, they brought to the table a large jug bubbling with a mixture of one bottle of beer, one bottle of lemonade, a dash of wine and another dash of spirits, along with a few ice cubes bobbing along on the surface. Sveilis paid for all of it. He was ready to pay practically any amount to cheer up his angry friend. But he was still sitting crossly, his chin resting on his hand, his large unkempt beard extending like a broom almost all the way down to the jug. He drank, but he did so with evident anger, and seemed that he didn't even notice the taste. Sveilis was glad to see a drunken Fricis walk up and invite Paeglītis to a game of billiards.

Sveilis got bored sitting by himself. There were a few acquaintances at the restaurant, but he didn't feel like getting tied up with any of them. He had already begun to sense his mistake: he had too many acquaintances – and of too many varieties. On the one hand, it was good for business but on the other, it could sometimes create trouble. Like the time when he was drinking a liqueur with Mr. Padegs and old Skrastiņš suddenly appeared, already drunk, of course. A janitor at the bank, but unaware of his condition or basic manners. And then what – a pointless waste of money. Losses occurred with various acquaintances here and there. Acquaintances of that kind were no use to him at all.

And now that young man in the short coat and shiny tattered sleeves, he was sure that he had met him somewhere. He was eating ham and eggs and took a drink from his glass of lemonade after ever fifth or sixth bite. When the glass was empty, he filled it up half-way and lifted the bottle up against the light – to see if there was much left. He ate slowly with evident delight, took a drink, and looked over at Sveilis with incredibly kind eyes. Maybe a teacher or something... Lemonade! Sveilis turned away in disgust and puffed out his chest aristocratically. He beckoned to the waiter with his finger.

"Pauls! Why is the fan not operating? The air is bad in here." Taking out his cigarette case, he lit a cigarette and looked on as the electrically operated ventilator's blades began to turn with a hum in the hole in the wall. Then he looked over towards the doors. Wasn't that Roberts who was coming in at that very moment?

Yes, it was. His hat was pushed back with bravado, his coat open, his blue trousers tied with a ribbon around the soles of his boots. His face was decorated with red pimples, but his behaviour and all of his movements were sprightly, swaggering and provocative. He was with two other boys, one a bit thinner and taller than him, the other a bit shorter and fatter – both with the same type of hat and their trousers tied the same way. All three disappeared into the alcove where the buffet stood. That's artists for you – Sveilis thought to himself mockingly. But then he became curious about what they were doing over there. He leaned over and looked. Of course: Juškans was filling up three shot glasses, and Roberts was moving along the side of the buffet – a plate in his left hand and a fork in his right – picking out sandwiches. It was clear right away that he was in charge and that this wasn't his first time here. Sveilis warmed to this little gang. He waited until the boy had thrown back two or three shots, then walked over.

Roberts was caught off guard, but wasn't too upset. He introduced his brother to his companions and then they all threw back a fourth shot. Sveilis toasted and threw one back along with the boys. He was surprised how much liquor they could hold. But he wasn't to be outdone. He wanted to find out more... The short, fat one was already starting to boast; he pushed the plate of egg sandwiches down onto the floor and trying to move out of the way ended up stepping on them. Roberts laughed and slapped him on the shoulder, then he pulled his brother off to the side.

"Listen, Augusts – I need some money... do you have any?"

Sveilis didn't mind, but he liked teasing the boy.

"Again!" He shrugged. "The day before yesterday I gave you ten roubles..."

"I needed to buy paints..." Roberts muttered.

Sveilis took out his wallet reluctantly.

"Five roubles...Is that enough?"

Roberts bit at his lip as he took the five roubles.

"I'm not sure...I need to buy those galoshes too..."

Sveilis gave him five more and turned back towards the buffet.

"Juškans, another round! We want to have a drink with these students today."

"Ha, ha, ha!" the tall man laughed as he staggered. "Cheers, Mr. Sveilis!" He ended up pouring half of the glass onto his coat.

But there wasn't much time left. The doors would open from time to time and through them he'd see a smooth autumn hat. Then the doors busted wide open and a teenage girl came in, clearly angry, with flushed cheeks and a haughtily upturned little nose. She ran up to the tall boy and yanked him by the arm.

"Well, what are you standing around here boozing for! Are we supposed to just wait around outside until dark!"

"I'm sorry, Sašurka!" With a piece of roast pork stuck on his fork, the tall boy clicked together his heels comically and bowed. "We're just having our second one."

"God's honest truth!" Roberts agreed and also bowed.

"It's fine!" the girl shot back. "Are you coming or not? Otherwise we're going home."

"Maybe the young lady would also like a glass of wine?" Sveilis had already lifted his finger to beckon Juškans over.

"Thank you, I won't have any!" The girl was extremely angry. "Come right now or we're going home."

She turned around and hurried outside, clicking her heels forcefully against the floor as she moved. Juškans's teeth gleamed as he watched her walk away.

"What a...!" Half-laughing, half-angry, the tall boy muttered a rude word. The short, fat one just smirked.

They drank another one and ate a bit more. But they couldn't linger for too long. They said their farewells to Sveilis and Juškans, and went outside.

"Well –?" The short one nudged Roberts in the side. "How much did he give you?"

"Ten..." Roberts wrinkled his nose. "That bastard, he's getting stingy."

"How much? Ten?" the tall one asked. "That'll be enough for tonight. I'm still tired from last night. Three hours – honestly I didn't get more sleep than that."

"You'll sleep when you're dead," Roberts joked. "Well, where do we begin our tour?"

They all stopped in the corridor by the front doors.

"I think," the short one said pensively, "the girls will want to eat."

"And have a drink!" Roberts added.

"The girls will want..." The tall one threw out a pointless, vulgar word. Resting his arm against the wall, he tried to read the names of the arrivals on the board listing the guests' names.

The other two doubled over with laughter.

The doorman was bringing in a large metal-lined suitcase. A man and a woman, bundled up in winter clothing, followed him inside.

"Well, what about it, young sirs," the doorman addressed them half-jokingly, half-mockingly. "Will you let us by?"

The three of them looked over as the new arrivals trudged heavily up the steps. The short one nudged the tall one with his elbow and motioned up with his head.

"Those two are probably just here for the night."

"That...lady..." Roberts leaned up close to the tall one and whispered something into his ear, then leaned over close to the short one and whispered the same thing to him. They all looked at each other and the three of them had a good laugh. Then they went outside.

Standing there waiting for them was the girl with the upturned nose, a second one with a knitted scarf around her head, and Milda Caune. The three of them looked sullen and were standing quietly by the gate. Milda had turned her back towards them.

"Hello, my ladies!" Roberts grabbed Milda around the waist from the back and spun her around. Milda tried her best to tear herself away.

"Calm down, you rascal! How dare you grab me! All of you get plastered, while we just have to stand out here and freeze..."

"Idiots!" the one with the scarf hissed and shoved away the short one's hand.

"Come on, you harpies!" the tall one scolded them as he hiccupped and forcefully intertwined his girl's arm with his own. After that the other two also gave in to their escorts. "You think we were just drinking in there... We were drinking and squeezing out money..."

"We squeezed out ten roubles!" the short one yelled at full volume.

The three couples walked next to each other – the boys with their hands shoved into their coat pockets, their caps on their heads and the girls hanging off of their elbows That's how they walked down the street, laughing and chattering all the way. Some older or simpler people stopped on the pavement to stare in astonishment at that strange company. But if any of the group noticed them staring, then that gawker got to hear the sort of word that would make them jump like they'd been stung and spit in disgust before going on their way.

There were pedestrians and vehicles on the intersecting street and the three couples had to stop for a moment and wait. When they were able to move again, they were forced into two groups. The crowd in front of them parted to reveal a haggard old man in a long jacket with rounded corners and a worn old overcoat wandering along down the centre.

"Hey you, old goat beard!" The short one grabbed him by the elbow as he walked by. "What are you staggering around for, here in the middle of the street..."

But Roberts looked and turned quickly in the other direction. He walked around the corner, blushing, craning his neck strangely, and turning his head, looking off somewhere to the side... The old man climbed up onto the pavement and poked at the ground with his cane holding its nickel-plated handle. As he fidgeted, his small, sparse, wedge-shaped beard seemed to tremble; he coughed dryly and kept blinking his eyes and looking in the direction of the strange noisy group even after it had long since disappeared around the corner and down the side street.

The tall one turned off to the side, stepped up onto the pavement, and stopped at the entrance to the cinema. Leaning down, the couple read the playbill pasted onto the rough wall.

"What's it with you always wanting to go to those cinemas..." Roberts grumbled without looking at the playbill. "Let's go down to the Casino Theatre."

"Curse of – Life..." Milda read through the gap between the couple standing in front. "A great social drama... That's not of interest."

"Queen of the Snakes..." The girl with the upturned nose poked at the playbill with her finger and shivered as she looked back and laughed. "Oh, that's terrible! It slithers around your arms and neck..."

"Rubbish!" The tall one pulled her upright. "Hold on, don't fidget!" He leaned down even lower. "Under the Spell of the Belle – a great romantic criminal. Sveilis, have you seen this one? Where she pushes that soaked handkerchief up to his nose and makes him dizzy and then those crooks rob him..."

"Where they drive that motor car?" the short one interrupted him. "What nonsense. Then let's go see Batavia instead. Captives of the Prairie Bandits – damn it, what a film! Six Indians attacking him, but he's got three revolvers –"

"You and your revolvers!" The girl with the scarf shook him forcefully.

"The Shortsighted Cyclist," the tall one kept studying the playbills. "Well, that's garbage. I've seen that one five hundred times already... Wedding Night – only for adults." He pulled his girl closer to him. They both exchanged looks and smirked and then bent down lower. "Tango Fever..." They stood back up again. "Well, what do you say, ladies and gentlemen? Shall we?"

"It's utter rubbish, but we can watch it..." Roberts muttered.

The short one reached from the back, pinched Milda, and whistled a tango melody.

"Idiot!" Milda pulled away and hid angrily behind her escort.

"Here's my thinking," the short one said. "It's still too early for the cinema. First let's stop over here on the corner – I know a waiter there and they have a quiet room. The esteemed young ladies must be hungry. And what else could we do with those ten roubles? Then – to the cinema and later on down to the Casino Theatre. Anybody who disagrees stay seated. Agreed? Unanimously? Long live war and Poland! ... Allons, enfants!"

They took about ten steps in the direction from which they'd come and piled – with noise and shoving – into the restaurant.

All alone now, Sveilis helped himself to a couple of morsels from the buffet, and then walked into the billiard room, where Fricis was known for erratic performances, but tonight he was losing one game after another due to the quantity of drink he'd imbibed. Because of his unexpected success, Paeglītis had partially forgotten all the unpleasantness concerning his financial problems. Now and then he even let out a small laugh. It made Sveilis feel good too to see his friend recovering and gradually making peace with his situation. He looked on for a while and was delighted with Fricis's clumsiness.

He returned to the buffet room and found Tilaks and Sietiņsons already there. As soon as they'd arrived, they'd sat down in the corner at a small uncomfortable table and sunk deep into conversation. They weren't drinking or ordering anything. The waiter was standing around looking rather miserable just three steps away from them.

"I'm saying that it's unfair!" Sietiṇsons pounded his fist on the table with agitation. "Why should I have to pay? Have I seen that money?"

Tilaks was also upset. "Then please just understand: we can't do anything about it. The bank can't lose money. If the borrower can't pay, then the bank has to get it from the guarantor. A guarantor has to know what he's doing."

"And the lender doesn't have to know anything, eh..." Sietiṇsons's eyes sparked with anger and the perceived injustice. "Why would you lend to somebody if you can't get your money back? Why - do you - lend - to - them?"

Tilaks began to lose patience. "My dear man... We can't investigate everyone and find out everything about them. Sometimes someone has something to put up as collateral, but sometimes he doesn't. That's why guarantors are so important to us. A guarantor has to know first."

"What are you talking about?" Sveilis asked as he sat down.

Tilaks, still addressing Sietiṇsons, ignored Sveilis. "But you don't need to know, eh? During the summer I told you: hurry up - he's on the verge of insolvency. Back then there was still time to get something from him. But you didn't do anything. You hesitated - devil knows what you were waiting for then!"

"This man!" Tilaks said pounding his fist on the table. "Hasn't paid a single instalment of interest he owed. We haven't gone for anyone's throat..."

Conscious of Sietiṇsons's situation, he became more friendly again and added, "But maybe we could still get it out of him."

Sietiṇsons laughed bitterly. "From him? You won't get twenty roubles out of him, let alone two thousand! Our bank needed four hundred - we got that, but only with very great difficulty. He had two horses with carriages... furniture... inventory... all of it's been sold. And what hasn't been sold, has been impounded all the way down to the last spoon."

Tilaks sighed heavily and turned towards Sveilis. "See, that's how it all goes... Everyone screaming: Berķis, Berķis... He gets ten thousand! A few days ago it was the same with Sietiņsons, they're just like brothers. Well, he turned out to be quite a brother: now he has to cough up two thousand!"

Sveilis shook his head and tried to sigh sympathetically. Tears were almost welling up in Sietiņsons's eyes. "A brother... well, he was more than a brother to me. If my brother asked, I would never... But for him - right away. How much do you need?"

Sveilis also felt sorry for this good man. If only he could help him somehow. "Maybe we still can get it from him," he said optimistically. But that only upset and saddened Sietiņsons even more. He turned away from both of them and stared at the wall.

"If you'd only listened to me," Tilaks said, "When I said that you needed to act right away. You haven't gone for anyone's throat... But you think those two thousand don't matter to me?"

Sietiņsons had had enough. He jumped to his feet and grabbed his cap from the stand. "That Berķis is a crook... and all of you are crooks at that bank! If there are cutthroats anywhere, it's here!"

Tilaks fell back ominously into his chair. "Let's avoid the insults, please!"

"The way you lot behave, you deserve to be insulted?" Sietiņsons spat and gave Tilaks a withering look. "You're worse than the Jews who would take your very last kopeck. But you won't do this to me, no sir; you're not going to get away with this!" He pounded his fist against his chest. "I'm not some kind of a school teacher or student. I have thirty thousand in insurance on my summer homes. I won't pay - I promise you that much, I won't pay!"

"Oh, you'll pay, and soon!" Tilaks smiled darkly.

"Not even a few kopecks, I promise you! I'd rather pay those two thousand to a lawyer. I'm the guarantor and if I tell you to stop, you have to listen. But you decided not to, so pay it yourselves. I want to watch you deal with your own crooked business."

"No insults, please!" Tilaks yelled, slammed his fist on the table, and jumped to his feet. "Mr. Sveilis, are you hearing this?"

Sietiņsons moved back a little, but wasn't especially afraid. "Call over ten witnesses, for all I care. I'll prove that all of you are crooks. I'll prove how much champagne you poured out for votes in the elections! I don't want to stand with you cowards. Oh, you think that new banks can't be established! That you're the only ones smart enough! No sir, you're not." He was so furious that his voice got stuck in his throat. Shaking his fists, he rushed out of the building.

Sveilis moved a little closer and tugged at the edge of Tilaks's coat.

"Damn it... I hope he doesn't make trouble."

Tilaks, who kept shooting furious glances in the direction of the doors, stifled a laugh. "Him? What can he do! He's talking rubbish. Let him try, we'll have him locked up for swearing. And after that behaviour, we can call in his debt. Let him try it." Agitated, but growing calmer by the moment, he sat back heavily and beckoned with his finger. "Pauls, two Ryabinovkas... and bread with caviar." Sveilis calmed down, too. He was already fairly tipsy, and as a result everything seemed easier to resolve.

The doors flew open with a crash – a new group crowded in. Bebrītis in the front, with his coloured cap pushed towards the back of his head, and his sagging, wet moustache. Behind him was Lodziņš with glassy eyes, pale and wobbly on his feet and behind them were two young, moustachioed men, Ziemelis and Taube. Both were the sons of rich fathers and well-known for living it up. They didn't notice Sveilis or Tilaks and began to drink rowdily as they collapsed around the buffet.

Tilaks looked back and shrugged.

"They're here again." He leaned closer to Sveilis to whisper,

"That young Lodziņš...," but he didn't finish his sentence, just shook his head. "Be that as it may, it's still a bit too much. You know, his old man seemed completely lost at the bank yesterday and today. Doesn't want to talk, can't work. Sits a while and then gets up, then sits down again. You can see that he has a heavy heart...The whole group got fired up the day before yesterday, they all left for Dole Island and after that who knows where else. They weren't seen at home for two nights. Mrs. Lodziņš is very ill. Though Zīle did say over the telephone this morning that it isn't anything dangerous. But Lodziņš is worried – and how could anyone not be worried."

Sveilis shook his head. "But then he's a real carouser..."

Strauss came in with a folder under his arm, as if he'd come straight from the bank. Just then Lodziņš tottered over from the buffet. His shirt front was stained and wrinkled, poking out through the opening in his waistcoat, and the end of his cravat was hanging out from his coat pocket. His eyes were bloodshot and glassy, his face pale and weak, and his boredom and disgust were evident. He sat down heavily. As he sat down, his head slumped forward, and his eyes fell shut.

Sveilis slapped him on the shoulder warmly. "Listen, don't you think you might have had a bit too much?"

Strauss came closer and put his hand on his other shoulder. "Young man, you can't go on behaving like this; you really can't. Go home now. Your father is terribly angry."

"Shut your mouth!" Rodolfs Lodziņš growled back. He pulled himself together and for a moment managed to shake off his crushing drowsiness. "My father? What the hell do I care about what he says... I'll go home when I want to. Do you understand? When – I – want!" He wanted to pound his fist on the table, but missed and went right past it. "We're celebrating Ziemelis's e-man-cipation..." He passed around his blank expression. "You haven't heard yet? His father kicked him out of the office."

Tilaks shook his head. "That was to be expected, that was to be expected. It just can't go on like this: late to work, lost bills of exchange, missing money almost every day at the bank... The whole city is talking about it."

"Yes..." Sveilis said. "Just recently... someone was telling me that from his father's desk, he'd taken..."

The whole city was talking about that too, and respectable people wouldn't deign to discuss an appalling event. Strauss hurried to interrupt Sveilis's blabbering. "Well, and what's he going to do now..."

"Him?" Lodziņš blinked and tried to push a piece of caviar toast into his mouth. "What does he care! He'll join the Crown Lands Council as a surveyor. He doesn't even need that old man of his..." To stand up he had to grip the edge of the table, which wobbled a bit. He pulled Sveilis by the sleeve off to the side. "Listen, lend me a hundred roubles..."

"What do you need it for? You'd better go home."

"Shut up and listen when I'm talking to you, You've got to lend it to me. I need it."

"But I don't have it - honestly." Sveilis didn't want to give it to him. An insane amount of money had gone into construction, and there were loans and guarantees almost every day. He didn't even really know how much Lodziņš already owed him. But there was no way of getting rid of him. He took fifty roubles from the buffet and gave it to him.

"Shake it off, you old bastard!" Bebrītis, noticing that Lodziņš had money, shook him by the shoulder and pulled him towards the buffet.

"Don't drink anymore." Sveilis leaned over, practically begging him. Then he beckoned over Juškans. "Give him a glass of tea with lemon. But make sure it's good and hot."

Ridiculed by his friends, Lodziņš drank two glasses of hot tea and did actually sober up a bit. He was bored with his friends and began to stand closer to the men from the bank. And when they got up and went over to Tilaks to play cards, he went along too.

Along the way they stopped in at Sveilis's construction site. It had been three days since Sveilis had visited it. They were all a bit tipsy, and so didn't care where they were going. They met Made and Old Mrs. Sveilis at the gate – the two of them had also come to see it. Made was wearing a modern coat stretching down to her heels, with an incredibly large and ornate hat on her head, pince-nez on her nose, a purse decorated with glittering sequins on her arm, standing straight and trying to look as dignified, serious and elegant as possible. Her mother was wearing a half-hat, half-scarf Made bought her and a black ribbon tied under her chin, and carrying an overstuffed velvet bag filled with who knows what hanging on a thin cord from her arm, while trying to mimic the way Made was carrying her purse.

They nearly ran into each other. The men lifted their hats as they greeted them, the ladies nodded their heads in a dignified fashion. Rodolfs Lodziņš wanted to say something, but Made shot him an angry, offended look and he turned away; she'd heard about their three days of living it up. Her mother smiled at the son of the building's owner to make amends for her daughter's rude behaviour, but at the time he didn't care about anything. He was just trying to keep up with the others in this excavated area that was strewn with nailed boards, piled high with mounds of gravel, and cluttered with stacks of bricks.

They didn't stay long – nobody was really all that interested. They went over to Tilaks. Tilaks wasn't married, which is why his apartment was fairly agreeable. They sat there for three or four hours. Sveilis lost forty-three roubles and some kopecks and borrowed two hundred from Strauss. Lodziņš played without any sense and lost everything. He borrowed sixty roubles from Tilaks and five with some change from Strauss. By the end, Sveilis had borrowed some more from him, too. As always, Tilaks won the most; he never got too excited and never took any foolish risks.

As they played, they didn't drink much. Getting thirsty, they finished and went over to Eiropa for some refreshments. There was almost no one there that night, so they moved on to Panama. They dined there and had quite a bit to drink.

Lodziņš ended up getting into an argument with a waiter there, so they all left and went to Café de Paris. Here they really had a lot to drink. They found a motor car and drove to Convent Cellar, but this German tavern didn't agree with them, so they talked it over and ended up driving to the Casino Theatre. They had a bite to eat and during the course of the entire show drank two bottles of champagne. Lodziņš was beginning to doze off, but when his companions woke him up, he began to fool about and made rude comments to the performers – making fun of the ballet dancers, arguing with the coupletists, droning out the singers. Sveilis, who was also half-drunk, joined in with Lodziņš's jokes, though a little less boisterously. Strauss and Tilaks, who were only slightly tipsy, couldn't stand the stares and whispers of the elegant public. Before the show had reached its end they started to leave. Sveilis and Lodziņš didn't care; they'd seen this performance at least ten times already. Strauss paid the bill, and they all got up and left.

The entire time, in the jumble of stifled speech and laughter behind his back, Sveilis had felt again and again that he'd heard a familiar voice. But in his drunkenness he hadn't listened closer and had thought nothing of it. Now as he walked across the woven hemp rug towards the exit, he again heard the echo of stifled laughter. He casually looked up. Towards the back, through the gap in the curtain pulled across the middle box, he could see Roberts's face twisted in laughter. He must have been holding the curtains shut at the bottom, as above him two tiny female hands were trying to tear them open. Sveilis saw, but was neither surprised nor thought anything of it. His head was too foggy.

He then went over to the Viktorija, where he met up with Blics the lawyer and Padegs the high-school teacher. Padegs was apparently uncomfortable in the company of people who'd had quite a lot to drink and so left. Blics was half-drunk and stayed. No one was interested in the cabaret shows. Tricot and racy couplets couldn't seize a hold of and excite their alcohol-dulled senses. Nobody was saying practically anything at all anymore – their tongues were stiff and what they had on their minds and what interested them was clear without needing to say it out loud.

The artistes had sat down all around the room. The more attractive ones had already found a spot in the company of drunk or half-drunk men. They were saying all manner of double entendres, flirting, allowing themselves to be pinched almost publicly and further enflaming the already animated men. The waiters dashed around with bottles wrapped in napkins or sitting in ice buckets. Ten roubles were nothing here... The women followed every twenty-five rouble note greedily with their eyes as it was taken by the waiters over to the buffet to be exchanged. This was especially true of the older and uglier ones who didn't have an escort of their own and who walked back and forth across the room by themselves for no apparent reason.

In the dimly lit back room some of the men were reclining comfortably with the women sitting on their knees. Sveilis walked through, then came back and sat down again. His lips were half-open – soft and moist as if they'd touched something delicious, but hadn't been able to partake of it. His eyes were narrow, tired, glassy, but still strangely burning... He shot a glance at his other companions and knew... They felt the same. Lodziņš sat down next to a dancer who was dark-complexioned, unattractive, and looked like she might be a Gypsy. But he must have been too forward; the Gypsy woman blew a cloud of smoke from her cigarette straight into his eyes, then went and sat down on the far end next to her associate who was sitting by herself.

Staggering, bumping into tables and the people sitting around them, Lodziņš returned. He didn't apologise and must not have seen any of them. There was coffee with Bénédictine on the table. But he couldn't drink anymore. After gagging on his first attempt, he tried again and managed to swallow some coffee, but just couldn't drink any of the liqueur. He'd toast, spilling it onto the white tablecloth and then, bringing it up to his mouth, would pour it onto the floor each time – drenching his and Sveilis's boots. He'd put it up to his lips, but couldn't swallow a single drop. When the powerful aroma hit his nose, he'd grimace painfully every time – that's how repulsive it seemed to him now. He became even paler. His mouth contorted as if he were either about to start crying or laughing in some half-witted manner. He began to hiccup and it was clear that he was struggling to keep down everything that had been poured and pushed into him for the last three days and nights... Tilaks whispered to the waiter and he led Lodziņš out the side door. The women sitting closest laughed derisively as he passed by.

When Lodziņš staggered back in through the side door, the others had stood up. The bill was paid, the waiter scowled as he cleaned up the table and floor covered in spills and stains. Time to go again. Lodziņš didn't care about the destination.

He did notice, though, where he was being taken – it wasn't the first time. But he felt neither particular joy nor particular disgust. It was hard for him, indescribably hard, he fell asleep standing up. He drank more hot tea with lemon – in great amounts and with gusto. He heard music playing somewhere, saw the faces of his companions and of strange, sneering women. Then they were all sitting in a small room with a bed and washstand. Men he knew, women he didn't, all of it a jumble. They drank coffee with cognac, the men smoking and talking bawdily, the women changing clothes and shrieking with laughter... He slept for an hour or so, hanging over the end of the couch, after which he was able to get up again and rage on with the rest of them. In this house his alcohol-induced dizziness soon scattered, and was replaced by a different flavour of it – stronger and even more senseless...

Sveilis and Tilaks stepped out onto the street in the grey autumn-morning light. They both assumed that Strauss and Blics had already left a little earlier, but they weren't sure. That Rodolfs Lodziņš was still exactly where he'd been, they knew.

They tried in all sorts of ways to bring him outside, but were unable to. He'd slept a bit and was now extremely ecstatic and absolutely didn't want to leave that hospitable place. He had the kind of nature whereby once he got going he lost all sense of what constituted acceptable behaviour. After all, it was no one else's business... Sveilis and Tilaks walked quietly down the street, their necks pulled down into their coat collars as they shivered in the chill of the morning. They didn't want to say a word. They loathed each other's proximity; they loathed the sensation of their own clothing touching their naked flesh. Sweaty, wrinkled collars sticking to their necks, fingers damp with a mixture of sweat, coffee and liqueur all gummed together. Dust and sleep stinging their eyes, they felt like all they could do was stagger... Eh, what a dreadful night!

Without looking at each other or saying a word, they both quickly shook hands and then pulled them back again. Each of them sat down in their own cab and went home to sleep it off.

But how long can a person sleep – during the day. At around ten, Sveilis was already up again. He washed for a long time – soaking his whole head with water. He looked in the bathroom mirror and then poured more water over his head. His eyes were bloodshot with blue swelling underneath them – his whole face was strangely bloated. As he put on his shirt front and collar, he stared into the mirror again. It was strange how he'd become so chubby in such a short time! His cheeks used to sit so nicely with his bushy, flaxen moustache which created a semicircle around them. But now he was putting on a bit too much weight. Towards the bottom, near his mouth, his face now was noticeably wider than up top. His neck too was oddly swollen; moving his palm down from the back of his head, he couldn't even feel the indentation in the spot where his back began – all of it was smooth, soft and white. But now, moist from the cool water, it shined with a strange, unattractive blue colour. Sveilis found his tin of cream which he rubbed generously over face and hands.

Almost as a response to the gentle aroma of reseda, he noticed an unpleasant taste in his mouth from all that he'd drunk, eaten and smoked the previous night. His breath was foul and stank horribly. His tongue was heavy and sticky. He tore open the bottle of mouthwash and rinsed his mouth furiously.

He got dressed and went out onto the street. A new cigarette drove away the unpleasant taste. Fresh, fragrant smoke and cologne cooled his nose refreshingly. But his bones were still stiff and his head was befuddled. There was a quiet hum in his ears and now and again a sour eruption would force itself up from his stomach into his throat. His perception and sense of time was hazy. Only by forcing himself to think could he understand that it was morning and that later on he had to go to the bank for money to pay for the building work. At times it felt like he was moving too slowly and that the street was endlessly long, while at other times the corner of a familiar building or store would quite incredibly appear out of nowhere. He couldn't take a cab – otherwise his head might truly start spinning and he might get quite ill.

He went into Tilaks's restaurant. Tilaks had already left. Sveilis had a drink by himself and struggled to eat something. He began to feel a bit better, and ate and drank some more.

All three Unity directors were already at work when Sveilis arrived. All of them were feeling ill, bad-tempered and silent. Lodziņš sat in his place, his brow furrowed, leafing through a thick cash book, and didn't even notice Sveilis's outstretched hand. Strauss was looking through the letters that Lodziņš had opened and read. Tilaks read through the submitted requests for credit, which were marked for decision today. Sveilis felt uncomfortable. He quickly took care of his business, walked out and received eight hundred from the cashier.

When he came back to the directors' office, Skrastiņš, who was nicely dressed with a well-groomed beard, invited him in and came towards him, greeting him very deferentially. Sveilis was pleased to know that he'd got this man where he wanted him. Maybe it was nice to know that this man was grateful to him. Sveilis was verging on the jovial now that he was in the directors' office.

A short distance from the directors' desk a man of small stature, wearing a worn coat, its collar turned up and holding a round brown creased hat in his hands, was shuffling his feet uncomfortably. Just as before, the two directors were seated and the secretary had turned towards the client.

"I'm very sorry, Mr. Lieknājs," Lodziņš was saying. The tone of his voice did sound truly sorry, but his face was stern and his eyes were fixed on an open book. "I'm very sorry, but we can't help you. The collateral you're offering appears to be insufficient."

"But you haven't even gone to look." Lieknājs replied. "I have an entire basement – inventory for fifteen thousand. How can that not be enough?"

Lodziņš shrugged.

"Well, it's the kind of inventory that..."

"If those books of yours are sitting in the basement," Tilaks yelled rudely, "then it's obvious that they don't have any value. Good books are sold; those that nobody needs get put down in the basement."

"Excuse me!" Lieknājs shifted again and gave him a pained smile. "It's actually quite the opposite. The worthless ones sell out much faster. Pulp publishers sell out their production in a single year, good books sometimes have to sit around for ten years. But their value doesn't evaporate, and they're gradually sold off – their readership slowly increases..."

"And what do you think," Tilaks interrupted him again. "Do you really think that we're going to wait for ten years? Credit institutions can't gamble or take risks. Banks require regular payment and security."

"Are you gentlemen claiming that I don't make my payments? Look in your books! The year before last I had three hundred in loans – did I miss a single payment?"

"That was with guarantors," Lodziņš snapped back. "I'm very sorry, but we can't." He sat back as he had been a moment earlier and turned to a new page.

Lieknājs slowly turned around and left without saying goodbye. Sveilis felt sorry for him.

"Was there really no way?" he said. "He seems like an honest man."

"Honest..." Strauss stretched the word peevishly and shoved the folded letter back into its envelope. "They're all honest – until they borrow money. Later on, we're lucky if we can get it back through the courts. What does he have for collateral: books! Who's going to buy those books right now?"

"And what kinds of books does he sell!" Tilaks added. "Mostly socialist works. Let the Socialist Party give him a loan – they've got plenty of money."

Lodziņš lifted his head and exchanged a hostile look with the rest of his colleagues. Sveilis felt rather uncomfortable. He couldn't understand what was really happening here.

"That's what I've said and those are my thoughts," Lodziņš said, emphasising each word in its turn. "We should've given it to Lieknājs. A decent man who always pays up. Four hundred – he deserved that much without any collateral."

Tilaks unintentionally let out a scornful laugh.

"Well, who doesn't deserve it! There's no shortage of takers. Four hundred to this one, four hundred to that one... And then when those who absolutely need it, those with construction projects come to us... then the bank will be empty. Then there won't be any money left to give."

Lodziņš sat up straighter. Despite its hard edge, his voice trembled a bit as he spoke with barely contained agitation.

"Well, gentlemen, I'll tell you this... It can't go on like this much longer. Is this a public institution or a private corporation? The entire nation brings us their money and deposits it here, but we're the only ones who use it."

"What do you mean – we?" Strauss called out angrily. "Am I building anything? Are you?"

"The nation deposits their money here and in exchange receives six percent interest," Tilaks noted.

But Lodziņš seemed not to have heard him.

"We turn down one, and another, and another – whoever comes here, we turn them down. Do you think that the public won't find out about that? Soon they'll be writing about us in the newspapers. The shareholders are becoming nervous. Just yesterday I heard talk of a new bank being established."

Tilaks fell back laughing.

"I've been hearing that kind of talk for ages... Paeglītis, Sietiņsons – they're the founders. Let them try, they'll see who brings them money."

"I've said," Lodziņš repeated emphatically, "it can't go on like this. I can't agree with it. If my name carries no weight here at all, then I will resign. I don't need this. I don't want to be in a place where a public institution is turned into the property of a clique. All this talk of needing to be careful doesn't seem to come up for us – this year not even ten thousand has been loaned to others..."

They were interrupted by a new arrival. Rodolfs Lodziņš... His coat hung wide open, underneath it his jacket was covered in stains and a torn coloured ribbon hung down over his trousers. His face was lined and bloated, his eyes were narrow and bloodshot from drinking and too little sleep. A fat cigar, which had gone out, was hanging from one of the crusty corners of his mouth... He staggered in through the door, his hands shoved deep into his coat pockets, wearing galoshes, smiling stupidly, blinking against the light, and trying to see everyone who was seated in the room. It was clear that he didn't really know where he was or what he needed there.

Old Lodziņš's eyes flared up.

"Well? What are you doing here?"

Rodolfs looked with dumb eyes at his father. He did recognise him, so he tried to focus and remember how he'd ended up there. He dug around in his pockets and pulled out his left hand while holding the edge of his coat. When he pulled out his hand, the others were wide-eyed with surprise. Tilaks hunched his shoulders, Sveilis just barely pushed his hand in front of his mouth and stifled a laugh, but Old Lodziņš gasped and in an instant his face turned bright red... Rodolfs had a woman's suspender belt around his wrist like a wide puffy blue bracelet.

A few seconds passed before Lodziņš jumped to his feet, reached across the corner of the desk, and slapped his son across the face with a firm, forceful hand. It made a soft smacking sound as if he'd hit something lifeless and numb. Without a single sound, Rodolfs fell back against the other corner of the desk and caught himself on it with his free hand. His head was hanging in the other direction from the force of the slap, his cap slowly slid down over his eyes and as it fell it knocked the cigar out of his mouth. It fell down onto the desk and kept rolling until it was stopped at the far edge.

Red, completely apoplectic, his fists clenched, Lodziņš attacked his son.

"You fiend! You degenerate! I'm going to kill you!"

But Tilaks stood between them and stopped him. He held the angry father's arms and sat him back down in his chair. Strauss rushed over and closed the open door to the cashiers' area through which the employees were looking with curiosity.

"Mr. Lodziņš," he said reproachfully standing with his back towards the door as if he were trying to hide the shame of the Lodziņš family from the world. "In a public place..."

"That's a bit too much..." Sveilis added as he regained his composure following the surprise of all this excitement.

Tilaks took the crumpled cap and put it back on Rodolfs's head. He took him by the arm.

"Of you go!" he said quietly. "Get out of here!"

Strauss also signalled – with his eyes and expression – that he should leave. Rodolfs tried in vain to find his footing. Blinking dumbly he looked around as if he were searching for something. His father's fingers had left four bright white stripes on his left cheek and now a fiery redness was beginning to glow around them. Just then his head seemed to slump forward, his eyes blinked more often and then tears began to flow copiously.

His eyelashes had stuck together and now large, clear tears squeezed out from under them one after another, some fell on his coat and then straight onto the ground, others flowed slowly and slid across his cheeks and chin; they dripped along the corners of his mouth around his lower lip which was hanging open. They flowed quickly and showed no sign of abating, as if they'd been collecting somewhere all this time, like water from a blocked spring that had suddenly broken free. Large, glistening tears held back since childhood. He cried quietly, without sobbing or feeling ashamed over his tears or trying to stop their flow. To all appearances he didn't even notice he was crying; he was just musing to himself as if he had caught a glimpse of something for the very first time. He didn't seem to be thinking about who had hit him, and perhaps he hadn't even realised what had happened to him. There was no sign of anger, pain or offense in his face. Its transformation was wondrous. This was no longer a fully grown, ruined person intoxicated by alcohol and degeneracy, but a drowsy child who had been woken up too early from sleep and who wanted to crawl back under his warm blanket – a helpless, weak, innocent child who is only capable of feeling his pain, but unable to understand its cause.

For some reason it was unbearable to look at this large tearful childlike face. His eyes were downcast in profound, overwhelming shame. Lodziņš rested his elbows heavily on the desk and groaned as he gripped his head with both hands. His solid body was bent and broken. Tilaks carefully took Rodolfs by the arm.

"Come... Let's take you outside..." His voice sounded so odd – exactly as if he were actually comforting a crying child. And carefully supporting him, he led him out of the room.

Lodziņš brushed his palms across his face, then let his hands fall heavily onto the desk. He took a deep breath and got up.

He looked at Sveilis and then at Strauss. They shuddered – there was such burning hatred and revulsion in this look...

"Swine!" he said bluntly, while looking directly at first one and then the other.

At first they stood there, as if they'd been hit straight in the face, then slowly looked at each other. Sveilis was as always confused, but Strauss's face was grotesquely contorted. "Who? You mean us? You mean me?" he said.

"You! Both of you! All of you!" Again with blunt and direct verbal slaps to the face, he cried, "You're middle-aged men... Aren't you ashamed to be roaming around brothels and the devil knows where else... and taking those young men with you!"

Strauss had already regained some of his composure as he took a step closer. "You're crazy!" he seemed to emphasise the last word with his fist in the air. "Crazy – there's no other word for it. Why are you causing all this commotion in here... when all the employees are watching... There are so many strangers at the bank. Why is my wife any business of yours? Why is any of that your business? How dare you use such rude language with me?"

"Rude language – with you?" Lodziņš was speaking even louder on purpose. "What else am I supposed to call a swine if not a swine? As far as I'm concerned, half the city can hear us. You're an embarrassment to our credit institutions, a laughing stock for our whole nation! And I don't want to be in here with you one day longer."

"No need to..." Sveilis said almost unintentionally.

Strauss was becoming even more offended and outraged. "This is unheard of!" he cried. "Suddenly we're responsible because this man's son hasn't turned out so well and has gone astray. Is it our fault he has been spoiling the boy rotten since the day he was born? And yet he's blaming us! This is boorishness in extreme!"

"You're the boorish ones!" Lodziņš screamed. "A bunch of degenerates! I don't want to have anything to do with you – not a single day longer! I don't need your bank, I don't need any of you..."

He ran out into the cashiers' area and left the door wide open. The employees sat staring down at their desks without lifting their eyes.

"Please, Mr. Director..." A grey, little man with some paper in his hand was leaning over the counter in front of him.

"Leave me alone!" Lodziņš shoved away the hand with the paper roughly. He pointed back across his shoulder. "Go and see them. They can deal with it."

His steps loudly echoing across the parquet floor, he hurried off and disappeared at the far end.

Strauss closed the door again carefully. "Crazy – utterly crazy..." His eyebrows arched, he looked down as he stood at the end of the desk and nervously rifled through papers. "We can't tolerate him here any longer. He has to be thrown out."

Sveilis moved placidly and agreed, "Of course, we must throw him out. If there's no unanimity among the directors... Boorishness cannot be tolerated..."

Half an hour later he was sitting with Blics at Café de Paris in a private room drinking Muscat and eating asparagus with sauce. In surprisingly high spirits they were discussing how Lodziņš could be thrown out of the bank. The man was rude and conceited, and always stood in the way of everything. If Tilaks and Strauss want to act one way, then you can be sure that he'll say the opposite. Old and stubborn – and too risk-averse. If he got his way, then none of them would be able to a borrow a single rouble. If there's no unanimity among the directors, then the bank can't grow; if it can't grow, the bank can only go bankrupt...

Strauss would take over Lodziņš's position and Sveilis – well, Sveilis could become one of the directors. Bank transactions were on the increase, and it couldn't hurt to have a spare director... These were the prospects for the future. Four or five thousand in income – and then credit on top of it! Unlimited credit – oh, there were many ways of doing that... There was no reason to run afoul of the statutes or the law. Blics knew those things very well. The morning's unpleasantness had been carried away on the wind, Sveilis felt, and laughed and talked breathlessly while he gesticulated. He slapped Blics on the shoulder and gripped his sleeve. He leaned out through the brown fabric partition.

"Waiter!" he called out loudly and beckoned with his hand. "Another bottle!"

Afterwards his feet felt strong and sure as he walked alone down the street as he usually would to erase a hangover. It's true that his head still was a little dizzy, but all his joints felt agreeably vigorous and his heart was happy and eager. Just as if he were reliving the enjoyment of the previous night, as if he were filled with the vigour that came from plentiful amounts of good food and drink, as if he were buoyed by the fantasies arising from bright prospects. He still hungered for something – for something ill-defined, something mysterious and yet it still piqued his desire.

Not thinking about anything in particular, he walked into his wine shop with a smile on his face. Just like last time, Miss Zvaigzne was standing on the steps, and Timma was idly handing her bottles as they casually chatted about this and that. Seeing their boss, he fell silent and bowed to greet him while holding a bottle wrapped in blue paper in each hand. But Sveilis didn't see him bowing or the blue bottles in each hand, or even him. When he came in he looked straight at the salesgirl as if he'd just remembered something. His mouth was half-open, his round, soft lips instinctively formed into a smile, his eyes were narrow and fiery, fringed by semi-circles of a thousand tiny wrinkles.

Without a word, he went behind the counter, took the first bottle that came to hand and squeezed between the shelf and the underside of the steps on his way to the back room. Aina let out a feminine yelp, pulled back the corner of her skirt that had brushed immodestly across her boss's face, and apologised. But he wasn't bothered by it; he smiled as he walked into the back room.

He went in and immediately appeared again in the gap in the door.

"Listen, Timma..." Timma leaned over into the space between the shelf and Aina's steps. Hooking his finger into his mouth, Sveilis gently sucked on one end of his moustache while he looked at the salesgirl. He must have forgotten what he was going to say. "Y-yes... Take... two bottles of Zubrovka... yes, and two bottles of Pomeranz to Mr. Juškans at Baltika..."

"Two each?" Timma asked and quickly grabbed them from the shelf. "Does he need any Ryabinovka? He only took four over yesterday."

"Yes, yes, definitely! Two bottles of Ryabinovka, as well."

Sveilis disappeared again. They could hear him handling a bottle and glasses. Aina climbed down and put the steps away in the corner, now that she didn't have anybody to hand things to her anymore.

"Miss Zvaigzne!" Sveilis called. "Please, just one word."

Not thinking anything of it, she went in. In the dim lighting she could barely see where Sveilis was sitting. He looked at her without saying anything – all she could see was the shine of his white teeth. She began to feel uncomfortable.

"What did you want?"

He laughed quietly and filled two glasses.

"How are you doing, Miss Zvaigzne?"

"Me?" she looked truly surprised. "Alright."

"You passed that... exam?"

Aina shuffled her feet; no, he's not such a bad person after all. He also thinks of his subordinates. There is a difference between one employer and another.

"I passed it. And largely thanks to you. For a whole week I missed two hours a day."

"Nonsense!" He dismissed this and laughed it off; his laughter sounded a little hoarse. Then he grabbed her hand and squeezed it tightly. "I wish the new teacher good luck... Now you probably won't want to work here with me anymore. But, let's drink to this good result. Well, please, please!"

With his left hand he brushed across her hand in a strange way – from her wrist to her fingers. She was a bit confused by this unusual kindness. She didn't remove herself from the situation as quickly as she should have and as a result Sveilis became even more secure but also cautious. He didn't take his eyes off her face, lifting the glass containing the red drink towards her.

"To this good result... Please!"

He was so benevolent that Aina didn't want to offend him. She gripped the glass, toasted awkwardly, and lifted it to her lips. But she had barely put down her glass before he was pouring more – carelessly, generously, the fuller the better. It spilled over – the red liquid flowed onto her hand; it was unpleasantly sticky between her fingers and dripped loudly onto the floor.

"Thank you, no more. I won't drink it..."

"Why not? Drink! As much as you want, every day... I've got plenty! Whatever you like...Whatever you like...What does your Lausks do then?"

Just then she saw a flushed face with eager, round lips and piercing, bloodshot eyes, and he leant in close to her in an unsavoury manner. She pulled back instinctively and lifted her hand in front of her face in defence.

Then two powerful male hands grabbed her, one from the back around her waist, the other around her breasts. She only barely noticed the one around her waist, but the other one squeezed her like a metal vice – ever more tightly. It pressed down her arm and painfully constricted her breath. As if in the clutches of a wild animal, her head began to spin and she saw greenish-yellow circles rotating before her eyes. A hot, sweaty forehead hit her own and roughly pushed her head back as if it were some inanimate object. The back of her head hit the sharp corner of the shelf painfully and from there she slid down onto the pile of bottles. Something rolled away with a crash and immediately began to drip somewhere, like blood from a slashed vessel... Hot, stinking breath singed her face, tremendous weight bent her body back and pushed it closer. She heard repulsive, incoherent muttering and felt how these powerful male hands gripped her ever tighter and more indecently.

Her disorientation lasted for only a second. Then she came to her senses and understood. With superhuman strength she leaned back and tore herself away. Something cracked in her back and her side stung with pain from overstretching. Her arms had gone to sleep and felt heavy, but she used them to hit and push – she wanted to tear him apart, to bite him with her teeth... But suddenly she was overcome by weakness; fearing that she would collapse and end up in this animal's clutches a second time, she turned around, covering her face with her hands, and sobbing hysterically, she ran out of the shop.

Sveilis came to his senses. Dammit! What had he done now... It was as if he'd completely lost his mind. Who knows where she ran off to... Hopefully, there won't be trouble... Dammit, who could've known that she'd be so fragile? So sanctimonious. But still, she does live with Lausks... He'd started this thing too hot; he should've taken it more slowly and with more forethought... He spat and walked out to where Timma was. What should he say to him? Her coat and hat were still hanging there, but she was gone...

He grabbed a few things and lied to Timma. Then he left and hurried over to Baltika. This nasty, unpleasant feeling just wouldn't leave him. He did manage to forget it for a while once he found himself at the restaurant among friends.

Bebrītis, without his jacket in just a waistcoat and shirt with broad white sleeves, looked serious and slightly anxious as he told the others his story.

"Completely drunk... We took him up, laid him down in Room 10. He can't see or feel anything. Pauls was putting on cold compresses. His cheek was swollen like this. His eye completely shut. But that old man really is crazy though... what a punch! Completely crazy."

"Of course, he's crazy." Strauss agreed. "Just an old fool, nothing more..."

He stopped talking just as Paeglītis came in from outside. He didn't come up - just lifted his hat a little from a distance, went moodily over to the buffet, looked into the billiard room, and then pointedly went outside again.

"Look at him run around..." Sveilis growled sarcastically.

"Let him run!" Strauss said mockingly. "The founder of a new bank... Let's see who takes their money over to him. There are too many credit institutions as it is - several on every corner. He thinks that just because he voted with us, we'll give him as much as he wants based on nothing but thin air backing him up. We made him wait... Now the money isn't even flowing that quickly anymore. Silly people scared by these fairytales about wars. We paid out twenty-seven hundred again today... Dammit, how will we finish the construction on those buildings?"

"We need to try to expand our operations." Sveilis answered cautiously.

"Like I said," Strauss started again, "Lodziņš is out if he doesn't quit himself. We don't need an old clown like that. Then we hold a special meeting and we put you in his place. And add two new ones on. It's absurd: one of the best credit institutions and only three directors! Three can't manage all the work - each one of them just wants to take it easy... Blics and Zīle should be chosen. We have to make sure of that; nothing can be achieved when the directors are not on the same wavelength... And at the next regular meeting, we'll propose turning it into a credit union. Then we can do so many other things."

"May it be so!" Bebrītis lifted his glass. "Then, my first order of business is discounting a bill of exchange by five hundred... Absolutely - the first order of business. Cheers, gentlemen!" He drank and wiped his moustache on his shirt sleeve. "But now I have to take up a drop of oil to pour into the wounds of the one who fell into the clutches of thieves on his way from Jerusalem to Jericho." He walked off carefully carrying a glass that was filled up to the edges, making sure that not a single drop would spill out.

Sveilis became more jovial.

"We definitely have to do this, otherwise there's no way that we can finish our building projects. You know, the Seventh Credit Union is absolutely refusing to raise my credit any higher. I've had my fill of their miserliness."

The friends sat closer together and began to discuss private matters in quieter voices.

Aina didn't know how she'd made it home. She was insulted to the depth of her being. Angry and ashamed, her inner pain made her forget the rest of the world and the sharp stinging pain in her sides. Only when she began climbing up the steps did she notice it again and, moaning quietly, press her hand to that painful spot.

She stopped for a moment at the door and tried to collect herself as much as possible – to keep from scaring her mother. But her mother was startled anyway, seeing her daughter at a strange time without her hat and coat, hair askew. Her red eyes were swollen from crying.

"Child!" she took both of her hands. "What's wrong? Where are your hat and coat? Why are you home so early?"

Only then did Aina realise that she'd fled without her things. But now her hat and coat seemed like such trifles that they disappeared from her mind the instant after she'd thought of them. Now there was something greater and more significant. Suddenly she remembered everything, even the tiniest details. She shivered and pulled away, as if she were being touched a second time by those powerful, shameless male hands. She pulled away and immediately cleaved tightly to her mother. She pressed close to her and sobbed, as if she were begging for help, pressing her burning face into her mother's breasts.

"Child... child..." Her mother stroked her head and couldn't keep from crying herself. "You're ill..."

"Yes..." Aina latched onto these words. Now it was more important than anything for her to avoid frightening her mother too much. "It hurts – here... Help me undress."

Like she had many years before, Mrs. Zvaigzne undressed her child and laid her down. She wrapped her warmly in blankets and sat down at her bedside. She held a cool, solid hand against her hot forehead until her daughter fell asleep. Then she sat quietly, her hands in her lap, and looked at Aina's burning face. Ill... But what were these strange, pained lines across her usually smooth, white forehead? Why are her lips pinched together as if she were enduring some grave spiritual pain? And why is her head shifting uneasily from side to side and why are palpable shivers running across her entire body every few moments? No... She shook her head and sat gloomily, waiting for Aina to wake up.

She woke up after a short while – less than half an hour. With a heavy sigh, which sounded more like a moan, she opened her eyes and was met by her mother's gaze. And knew in an instant that she didn't believe her stories about illness and wouldn't leave her alone until she knew the truth.

Moving through the suffering she felt as her initial pain retreated, Aina fought to control herself, in order to spare her mother, she tried to find calmer words with which to tell her.

Her mother looked at her daughter's face with wide eyes and didn't take them off of her mouth. And when she had finished and was lying there again with a pained expression and pinched lips, her mother still didn't say a word. As if she were recovering from a powerful blow.

"Scoundrel... what a scoundrel!" finally slipped from her mother's lips.

Along with his moaning, her father's long, rattling cough could be heard coming from the kitchen. Her mother was sitting stunned, stooped and wrinkled, her lip twitched at the thought of her daughter's shame. Aina lay there feeling humiliated and powerless, as well as a profound and stinging bitterness about the unjust burden of poverty that pressed them all under the feet of the wealthy – down into the mud and humiliation. She'd never yet felt so pointedly degraded and offended and never before had her human dignity risen up so powerfully against these feelings. She had an unquenchable thirst for openness and freedom – for work of her own choosing, which respected human dignity, and for a life filled with the beauty of the struggle...

"My daughter, it's because of you living with Lausks like that," her mother's words suddenly wrenched Aina from her heavy thoughts, and returned her to topics Aina found most unpleasant and was tired of hearing about.

"What are you talking about!" she yelled back, insulted.

"That's why, that's why," her mother stubbornly repeated. "If you were a married woman, nobody would dare touch you. But living like this... they think if you can do that with one man, anyone can have you. They take you for a prostitute."

Hearing these words from her mother's mouth was a no less painful offence than her earlier experience, but Aina's feelings were still dulled by what had happened earlier. She moved ever closer to the wall.

"No, that's not why," she protested adamantly. "How many married women are out there living lives worse than those of prostitutes, and how many unmarried women aren't faithful to their husbands to the grave... How many times do I have to tell you that marriage is just an external rite, a stamp that you can mark yourself with and wash off later as you wish."

"Don't talk, don't talk!" her mother said waving her hands as she began crying. "Until you're married, you're not any kind of a wife, but... just someone sleeping with a man! Do you think he thinks of you as his wife? On the outside – maybe, but in his heart he values you much less. Without a blessing you're not his wife, and you won't ever be. You're just a little person who others trample on... A lost little woman, whom no man takes seriously."

Pity and the love of a child for their parents struggled within Aina against her self-respect and pride in her beliefs. Just like countless other times, an immovable realisation concerning the nature of the world had come into serious conflict with an ancient moral belief based on family instincts which could not be ignored. If they couldn't be ignored, they still had to be gradually pushed off to the side and silenced.

"No, that's not why... It's because we're paupers. Paupers - without rights or power. That's why the rich step all over our living flesh with their gold-nailed boots. Those who have gold don't need marriage or commandments; they don't need any of it. Gold is the ruler of this world and its god... You know yourself that Strauss has a wife and children, but he lives with other women - and still if you see him on the street, you greet him obsequiously, and don't think at all about his immorality or sin. The factory-owner Eisners drives by here every single day in his convertible with his mistress and have you seen anyone smirk at him or dare insult him or his ballet dancer? He has gold and power, and honour... and everything else. We don't have anything and so anyone can push us down into the mud."

"No one will push a married woman anywhere," her mother stubbornly refused to budge. "You're looked at as a lodger and a prostitute..." Her old mother angrily tried to rub away her disobedient tears. "And what else are you other than a lodger? Lausks's lodger!"

"Until now Lausks had always been my lodger."

"Both of you... You're both the same. Each as bad as the other. That shame falls on you both, but twice as much on you as him. You're a woman... A fistful of mud is invisible on a man, but when there's a speck of dust on you, everybody can see it."

"It's because I'm poor and don't have any silk clothes; I don't have gold to blind everyone with its shininess. We're both poor, that's why you complain the way you do... Mother I'll tell you straight, that you wouldn't cry or scold me I went off and became a mistress - today for one, tomorrow for another - as long as I had the sense to find rich ones who had plenty of gold. If Lausks could give me expensive clothes and glittering jewels and a comfortable, warm apartment for you with good food, I'm sure that you'd find a reason to excuse us and be content."

"Of course, daughter, just keep talking like this." her mother replied mournfully. "Carry on... I'm just interested in myself and my own interests. I don't have a mother's heart after all, and I'm not sorry for my child..."

She began to cry so pitifully again that Aina couldn't stand it anymore. She turned towards the wall and pulled the blanket over her head, so she wouldn't have to see her old, grey face contorting into pained wrinkles or listen to the plaintive weeping.

Her heart became heavy, very heavy. Well, why did she need to upset herself for no reason and try to convince her? How many times had she tried already, only to realise that it was all futile. Every wise and convincing word bounced off her like peas thrown against a wall. It was due to a seemingly deliberate lack of understanding, opinions raised up in a different world, beliefs formed by a different life, realisations prompted by different circumstances, feelings ripened by different impressions. She had decided it was better to be quiet and to just live her own life. But her character was too weak – she couldn't. She couldn't stay quiet, she would get pointlessly upset, argue, strain her nerves and make her own heart ever heavier as a result.

But how foreign her mother was! How few – painfully and pitifully few – of the things her mother had tried to cultivate within her had she retained. These were things her mother had taught her throughout her long childhood and youth, hammered into her with scolding and spanking, supported with examples, and strengthened with the word of God. Five years of work spent among conscientious working people, five short years, though difficult years filled with toil and suffering had completely overwhelmed everything she'd inherited from that old world. And with every passing day what little was left was gradually overshadowed and eradicated. The weak and feeble inherited parental love in place of the new, great and expansive love of thousands of brothers and sisters, the love of all the poor and humiliated. Her parents' sweet love touched her heart for a moment like a gentle breeze. But in a troubled hour of heaving emotions, repulsive thoughts and pain, a child flings their arms around the parental neck like a dying person, but this merely delays one's own independent struggle, while the parents' tearful lament melts. She couldn't let herself melt or surrender. Her own silent pain was something to be carried and suffered by her alone, but her will was held like a link in a chain by a thousand others, it couldn't relent, melt or drop to the ground. Her wants were not just her own. She was alone on a difficult forest path but she wasn't afraid of getting lost; others had gone before her, and as she walked she was stepping on fresh, strangely familiar footprints. Behind her she could hear the rumble of countless other steps following her.

And still it was good to lie there quietly for an hour in peace – half asleep, half awake. Without thinking, without yearning or suffering, she was gently aware of the pain sweetly twinging through her heart and the fatigue binding all her joints with its soft tethers... Aina pretended to fall asleep again, so that her mother would leave. She lay there with her eyes closed listening to her own shallow breath.

She heard Lausks come home. He went into the kitchen where her father and mother were, and immediately she could hear the sound of excited voices, maybe also crying. And then she thought again of the day's events, and she understood right then that what had happened wasn't just between her and Sveilis, but also between her and Lausks – between her and Lausks most of all. She sensed that...this...was just the beginning, that the most important and perhaps most awful thing was yet to come... In a moment Lausks would come in, come up to her and ask her. She would have to answer, firmly and decisively. But she couldn't snap back, for a moment she couldn't think of what to do.

He came in. She saw the door open, in the twilight she noticed his familiar lithe form, but she couldn't hear his steps over the blood thundering in her ears. She waited nervously. But he quickly walked across the room and sat down at the table. He didn't come over and didn't look in her direction. She caught sight of his cool, almost hateful face and felt something in her heart freeze over. And she knew she had nothing to be afraid of, she didn't have to tell this man anything.

Lausks sat there for a long time staring at the lamp, and then walked over.

"What's wrong with you? Are you sick?"

Aina heard his cold, almost hostile voice. The sideways stares he threw at her felt like sharp-edged shards of ice as they hit her. And she immediately felt the burning pain in her side, but pretended not to notice it.

"No," she answered bluntly, looking straight into his eyes.

"Why are you in bed then?" Lausks asked even more sharply, irritated by the fearlessness in her eyes.

"I felt like it," she answered.

He moved, but thought better of it and stayed where he was.

"What have you been up to over there... with that Sveilis?" he said through gritted teeth. It was plain to hear how difficult it was for him to speak. Every word seemed to hurt him.

The hostile stares and crisp, formal questions felt to her like a cold hand running across her entire body. The entire time she kept waiting for him to treat her like he had other times: sit down, hold her legs, stroke her and comfort her. And together they would try to overcome and forget what was so hard for either of them to do alone. He knew after all... What did her mother tell him? And yet he kept asking her more? Poking at her delicate, bleeding wound again with rough fingers...

"Nothing..." she answered and surprised herself by how cool and strange her voice sounded.

Lausks just hissed, turned around and walked over to the table again. Not upset, just surprised, Aina watched him. How could he still be angry? What is offending and insulting him? Was that her Lausks – the Lausks whom she'd been living with this whole time and from whom she didn't hide even the tiniest thing? He'd been able to read her heart like an open book but now he didn't understand and didn't want to understand. Now when she needed understanding and support more than ever! But he was acting towards her as if she'd somehow transgressed against him. As if she were guilty. It must be because she's poor, because she has to submit to serving the wealthy and suffer humiliation. She remembered his earlier foolish jealousy, his silly suspicions – a thousand little things she had laughed off as an unnecessary manifestation of deep, blind love. And now when his heart should have opened wide, when hot, irrepressible love should have flowed like a stream, engulfing and warming her – now he coldly turned his back on her and went and sat down at the table! She clenched the edge of her blanket between her teeth, to repress a loud pained scream. She closed her eyes so she wouldn't have to look at the collapsing edifice of her joy. But she saw it nevertheless.

He got up and came over. She shivered in anticipation: maybe he's realised his unfairness and cruelty and he'll come over and everything will be good again. But no, he walked out into the kitchen, to her parents – without looking at her.

She stayed lying there with wide eyes and stiff joints – as if on the operating table. Outwardly calm, but watching with profound inner horror, as an ice-cold knife twisted in her brain and freezing shivers ran across her nerves.

Not out of depth, but instead out of shallowness of his love, did all these small, petty qualities arise. She'd always teased him about them and laughed carelessly. His trifling concerns regarding their daily bread, worry about what others were saying, fear of her parents' curses and maybe also of sin and its threatened punishments. All this time she'd thought that she was gazing into the depths of a lake where the bottom was clearly visible only because the water's clarity and calm. But it wasn't a lake, just a shallow puddle and the mud at the bottom could be reached with a little finger. And hungry leeches and the slime-covered mud worms, and lazy snails squirmed in that shallow, warm ooze.

Aina was laid flat underneath an insurmountable burden of disgust and shame. She'd associated herself with this person without thinking or reason. He hadn't really understood anything at all of what was most real and valuable in her. Just like every strange man on the street, he'd only seen her exterior, he'd desired her body and nothing else. He'd taken her while she was still immature and not yet hardened. And when she slowly awoke, when her views gradually formed and her will became solid and unbendable, he began to sense and understand, but she was hiding from herself. She'd really given up too much to part ways now in peace and go her own way. Now she knew: in arguing and becoming angry, she was hoping that it was just a momentary misunderstanding. She was ashamed of him and herself, she had tried to awaken his masculine self-respect and waited for him to become aware. Now it was clear that this was all in vain! This was the end. He'd gone to talk to her mother. He could understand her better!

Lausks came back. Slowly, staring at the ground, he came hesitatingly up to the side of the bed. She huddled closer to the wall and avoided the arm that wanted to hug her. And yet she was still waiting for it! Perhaps... a woman can never forget the one she willingly belonged to.

"Don't you worry," he struggled to say. "Me and him – I'll demand an explanation from him."

"Who? Sveilis? What explanation?"

He was confused, brushed her off, got up and began walking around the room, faster and faster. His steps painfully punctured her tortured brain.

"I'll show him – that scoundrel!" he clenched his fists tragically. "I'll pound him into dust! How dare he lay a finger on you! Oh, he thinks he's the boss and so he can do whatever he pleases..."

"Don't get so carried away. Hasn't your Blics ever insulted or demeaned you before?"

"Blics –?" Lausks was caught off guard, but then summoned up his nerve again. "What Blics has done to me is something completely different. Blics can't do anything to me. But I'll show that Sveilis. I'll show him! You're a woman..."

"And ladies must be treated chivalrously..." Despite all her spiritual pain, she almost wanted to laugh: he looked so ridiculous right now – dishevelled hair, a furrowed brow, clenched fists. "Calm down. You won't show him anything and you can't anyway."

"But... what do you mean?" He spread his hands. "Then he'll think he can always touch you. Then he'll – devil knows what he'll think."

"Let him think what he wants. But he'll never touch me ever again."

Lausks looked in bewilderment at Aina.

"What are you saying?"

"I'm not going back there again."

She didn't look, but there was no immediate answer. After a moment Lausks began to pace again. He cleared his throat twice.

"Y-yes... of course... That kind of rudeness... that kind of shamelessness can't be tolerated. We're servants, but not slaves... Still – I don't know, wouldn't it be better... Be that as it may, I could make him understand... I'll go and talk to him, I'll tell him that you're effectively my wife and that we'll be married soon..."

"Effectively – your wife..." she repeated, propping herself up on her elbow. And her face strangely contorted – and it wasn't clear if it was from laughter or tears.

"Fine, fine!" He interrupted her peevishly, fearing that the conversation was moving away from the main topic to more delicate and peripheral matters. "I'll talk to him. He's a scoundrel, it's true, but which of them is any better? They're all the same. We'll always still have to earn our living. It's time to stand up to them sharply and bluntly once and for all..."

"But I can't be that way!" she interrupted him almost

screaming. "I like to joke around... have a little fun..." And again it wasn't clear whether it was suppressed tears or laughter, which were attempting to force their way out and contorting her face so hideously.

Grimacing, he glowered at her.

"Go ahead and joke – but my heart is a shambles... It's an insult – it's vile and obscene. Oh, what a working person must endure... I told you: Blics wants me to join their cyclists' association as a watchman – he thinks I'm thrilled about this, but what can I do... And then – they're planning on throwing Lodziņš out of that Savings and Loans. Sveilis is joining the directors. If you do that, if we begin feuding with Sveilis, then nothing will come of that place for me – that's for certain, nothing will come of it."

She lay back down and let out a wicked laugh. She laughed and stopped, probably because it was too easy to hear her tears through her laughter.

"Nothing will come of it," she repeated in a strangely transformed voice. That voice and her laughter alarmed Lausks.

"What's wrong with you?" He leaned over her. He looked into her strange, cold caustic eyes. It seemed like Aina hadn't heard the question; she wasn't thinking about what she had just been thinking about anymore.

"Effectively my wife..." she spoke in a dry, quiet voice. "Listen, Lausks... Aren't you ashamed that you've been living with a prostitute for so long?"

He pulled back, but immediately leaned back down again – even lower.

"What's wrong with you? You're ill..."

He tried to examine her forehead. But she pushed his hand away with such force that it knocked loudly against the side of the bed.

"Don't touch me! I'm becoming healthier than I've ever been. Go and leave me alone... Go!" she yelled loudly when he hesitated.

Defeated and miserable he dragged himself out into the

kitchen over to her mother and father. Late into the night she heard the soft sound of their worried voices.

Aina lay there the entire night without sleeping. Again and again she'd plan out her entire life and would always come to the same conclusion, one which had long been germinating inside of her but had only just blossomed. With the approach of morning, when her brain grew tired and was wrapped in a fatigued fog, she felt the powerful twinge in her sides, it seemed like all her muscles had been ripped to shreds, all her bones pulverised. But the pain in her body covered up the spiritual anguish she was only half aware of. The autumn wind was still banging against the crooked, rotted out windows, the room was cold and damp. But what was the chill in this room compared to the frost that was slowly freezing her heart... Where there had recently been a garden of asters in full bloom now an icy breeze was blowing. The heavy stems bent and broke with a sorrowful twang, and that destruction was soon covered by frost... bluish-white, but clear, crystal clear...

Good – after getting up in the morning, Lausks didn't come in, he just went straight to work. Aina couldn't be sure that she'd have been able to hold firm. When her mother came in, she pretended to be fast asleep. She'd reached the end, but also found clarity, and yet she wanted to be certain – to weigh and examine every detail one more time, to bring it all together and shape it tightly. So that she wouldn't need to be in doubt for a single moment longer, and that as a result of this certainty she would never make another misstep again.

In the afternoon she was suddenly startled out of her contemplation. Someone was banging on the door. She didn't know for certain, but sensed something bad. She listened, yes it was. And her mother immediately, a little confused and bashful, pushed her head into her room. "Sweetie... it's that gentleman... Mr. Sveilis."

"Get him out of here," she answered bluntly.

Her mother shuffled uncomfortably. Sveilis's overheated,

unhappy face appeared over her shoulder with its round, slurring lips and the semi-circle of tiny wrinkles fringing his half-closed eyes.

"Forgive me, Miss Zvaigzne..." he stuttered. "I didn't want to disturb you... I was just... saying to your Mum..."

"Get that brute out of here!" Aina yelled even more loudly. She reached over, pulled the chair closer, and wielded the heavy clay cup that had been sitting on it.

This kind of rudeness frightened her mother, who gave Mr. Sveilis a look that was both begging and apologising. But he was savvier and leaning closer to the door, he said, "If she doesn't want to..." he crouched over and whispered something in Mrs. Zvaigzne's ear. The heavy stench of alcohol and some kind of stinking cheese flowed over her. "Let her sleep, let her calm down. Can we... Where can we go and talk...?"

"Please, sir..." Mrs. Zvaigzne moved to open the kitchen door. "If you don't object. Our kitchen is really not clean at all... That's my husband..." she pointed to the corner where an incredibly emaciated old man wracked with pain grabbed at a blanket with bony corpse-like hands and pulled it over his bare hairy chest. Bashful, timid eyes looked out at the splendid gentleman from deep, black hollows. "Please, sir!" Mrs. Zvaigzne dusted off an old Vienna chair with her apron and pushed it over so Sveilis could sit down.

"Thank you," Sveilis said gratefully. He'd prepared himself for a completely different reception. He wasn't as worried about the daughter as he was about her parents. But they didn't seem that foolish at all. He could talk to the old woman. But – that kitchen! What terrible filth... on the ground next to the bed was a tin can, half full of the sick man's spittle... and there was an unbearably repulsive stench coming from the corner. But he had to endure it, there was nothing else to do. He sat down. He pulled out a scented handkerchief and blew his nose in it for a long time.

Mrs. Zvaigzne shuffled nervously – feeling both offended and insecure. She had to talk to him... But how could she scold such a fine and wealthy gentleman. The old man in the bed tried with all his might to hold back his coughing – his chest heaved, his throat seized up and his eyes seemed to bulge out of their hollows. To make it easier, he kept moving his head from one side of the pillow to the other.

"Sir, you really..." Mrs. Zvaigzne, wrapping her hands nervously in her apron and looking out the window, finally managing to get it past her lips. The sick man backed her up with his glances, lips, and movements of his head. "How could you... She's the only child we have..."

Completely as if it didn't apply to him, Sveilis, but instead to someone else, her statement sounded more like a strange kind of pleading than an accusation. That's not how an outraged mother spoke, one who felt her rights and maternal sensibilities deeply transgressed against, but the words of a submissive, frightened victim. Sveilis immediately understood his circumstances. He threw open his coat so that the brightly-coloured plush lining shone brilliantly and the gold chain hung prominently across his chest. He shoved his handkerchief back into his pocket and looked intently at the befuddled old woman.

"You really – what? What are you talking about?" It came out sounding quite lordly and dignified. Mrs. Zvaigzne became even more fearful. Sveilis was completely at peace with himself and the impression he was making.

"Sir, don't you know...She's our only child..."

"A-ha – you're speaking of Miss Aina... You see, Mother Zvaigzne..." He leaned in closer. "That's also partly why I came over... Yes, to assess – to find out... why she isn't coming to the shop... Is she very seriously ill?"

"No, no, it's nothing too terrible at all. She'll be able to go back to work again tomorrow. Don't worry. She's just a little worn out... and afraid... Sir, what you did... You really shouldn't have..."

Sveilis grabbed his handkerchief again. Cheap, wet firewood was smouldering in the stove. There was a torn piece of coat hanging out from underneath the pillow. The pained shining eyes stared and stared at him from their black hollows and he couldn't avoid them... Dammit! How difficult it was to remain dignified... He felt beads of sweat forming across his forehead again.

"I came because... to tell you, because you're her mother..." It felt like his tongue was grasping for a word it couldn't say. "I have to apologise. I know that it wasn't right. But I didn't mean anything bad... I'd had a bit to drink – and you know, Mother Zvaigzne, how it goes..."

Yes, she knew. She'd known right away that it wouldn't have been as bad as Aina made out. A man gets drunk – and the foolishness he gets up to! Drunkenness – it's practically the same as being asleep. But Aina must have that kind of nature: where there's a molehill, she makes a mountain... A wealthy and generally polite person... Mother Zvaigzne – she liked the sound of that very much.

"Well – I'm not saying anything... But Aina... you saw what she's like. She always gets upset about nothing."

"Yes, yes!" He agreed with that wholeheartedly. "You can see it yourself, Mother Zvaigzne. I'm not that kind of a person, I am always mindful of my manners. Me – what rubbish, Mother Zvaigzne!" He waved off the idea dramatically and shivered. And in his gesture and expressions one could see that the greatest insult of all was that anyone could have had such ugly suspicions against him. "Making mountains out of molehills. That's why I came over. So she doesn't let her imagination run away with itself... so she doesn't do something foolish. You tell her...to put it behind her. She better not think about complaining...or getting the police involved. Nothing at all will come of it. All the gentlemen are my friends, I'm with them every day. She'll end up getting into trouble herself... Think about what sort of losses I make when my cashier arbitrarily abandons her job. It might be a hundred roubles, maybe five hundred... I can make her pay it."

Mrs. Zvaigzne became even more upset. "Oh, sir...She'll be back again tomorrow. I'll tell her – absolutely, I will."

"Yes, yes...You must tell her. I'm not wicked, I've always treated my employees decently... Tell her that I'm taking her back – just make sure that she comes tomorrow. What's past is past." He looked around as if he'd only just come in. "I can see that you're not doing so well here. And with that sick patient to look after... Tell Miss Aina that I'll add five roubles a month to her wages... Five roubles."

Mrs. Zvaigzne practically collapsed with joy.

"Thank you, sir, thank you! And please don't be offended that she's acted this way...That's how it always is with her. Hot-headed... Thank you, sir."

Sveilis motioned regally with his hand.

"It's nothing at all, Mother Zvaigzne." He hesitated for a moment, then reached into his pocket for his wallet. He lifted out a golden five-rouble coin by its edge and held it in front of Mrs. Zvaigzne's eyes. "And this is for the old man's medicine..." The shimmering yellow disc came to rest on the worn sideboard.

"Thank you, sir, thank you!" Mrs. Zvaigzne's lips trembled as tears rushed into her eyes.

"Tha-a-ank you, sir..." the sick man moaned, as well. His hoarse voice with its dry metallic undertone sounded more like a dog barking than human language.

Sveilis flinched hearing that unpleasant, alien voice. He couldn't stand another moment in this ruined and poverty-stricken hovel. He got up and buttoned his coat.

"Alright then – just make sure she doesn't do anything foolish. Nothing will come of it anyway. She'll just end up getting into trouble herself. All these gentlemen are my friends. Let her sleep and then come back to work tomorrow. But I'm giving you this money regardless..." He lifted up the five-rouble coin again and tossed it down onto the table. "I won't deduct that from her salary... Where is the door?"

"Right here, sir, right here..." Mrs. Zvaigzne trundled over to open the door. "Please forgive us – we have so little room ..." As Sveilis quickly moved down the steps, she looked on elated. The outer door collided with the body of a slender, fairly attractive girl. She was swinging a bundle of books by the small strap that held them together, and she must have been coming home from school. She screamed, though she didn't seem too afraid. Then she pulled back and curtsied coquettishly when Sveilis lifted his hat. She smiled – and the little gap between her front teeth looked very pretty on her.

Sveilis looked back again from the gate. Of course – she was looking back at him too and disappeared inside in a flash. Sveilis was tickled with laughter.

A lively girl... and it seemed like she knew him.

Back inside, Mrs. Zvaigzne examined and gently handled the unexpected gift in her hand. The sick man coughed violently and moaned, but after he'd finished coughing and spitting, he also wanted to look at the coin. He clutched it in his sinewy hand for a moment, then settled down and closed his eyes with relief.

Wrapped in a large woollen shawl, pale but already looking fairly strong, Aina came in.

"It's cold," she said and sat down by the stove. But her parents knew she wanted to know what had been discussed.

Her mother didn't look over and was in the midst of some feverish activity by the side of the bed.

"Well, just pull yourself together," she said in an artificially peppy voice. "Get some sleep today, then you can go back to work tomorrow."

"I'm not going back to Sveilis." she answered.

Her mother spun around. "What do you mean – you're not going back? What kind of talk is that? What will you do then?"

"I don't know yet. But I'm not going back there – never again."

"Daughter, dear!" her mother called out; her voice was tinged with bitter accusation, nervousness, and dread. "What kind of talk is that? So, having no job again would be better? Haven't we suffered enough? What are we going to do with your father when you can't earn anything anymore?"

Aina shrugged her shoulders. These tiny, trembling fears were buzzing around her like a tenacious wasp.

"The three of us will starve to death. And that would still be more dignified than letting a drunken, depraved scoundrel touch me."

"Don't speak so disrespectfully!" her mother yelled at her indignantly. "He's not like that at all. Sometimes drunkenness... Being drunk is practically the same as being asleep."

"Well I'm neither drunk, nor asleep. My head is clear, and I can't submit to that. I'm not going to a brothel: I'm going to find an honest job and will receive a salary for it. He can pay for my labour – but my body and soul are not for sale."

"Don't talk, don't talk!" Her mother said waving both of her hands. "You're just a tramp yourself, nothing more. That gentleman isn't bad. He's promising to pay you five roubles more a month."

"Oh really?" Aina drawled and let out a rasping laugh. "So the haggling is already done. But this time the stock animal won't let itself be sold – oh no. That price is too low. At the brothel he pays five roubles for every night."

"Good lord, what a shameless mouth!" Her mother blushed. "You tart – is this what I taught you?"

The sick man moaned something and shook his bony fist. "Ta-a-rt... I'll knock your teeth out!" He opened his fist. "Look at this. It's from him and it's for me." His coughing broke up his speech. He spat pink mucous into the tin can as he wheezed.

Aina shot up and grabbed the gold coin, just as if someone had yanked her by the arm.

"He – this? Now? For what?"

"For your father... He said it's for the old man's medicine."

Aina's arms dropped down by her sides; it was as if a stone and not a thin yellow disc had been tied to her hand. Her mouth twitched, her face took on a strange appearance and her legs visibly buckled.

"And you! You took it? You didn't spit in his face and push

him down the stairs. Mother, mother! That's blood money... Didn't you notice how it sticks to your hands? For five roubles you sold your daughter to a drunken lout..."

She pressed her fists to her temples, hunching her shoulders and rocked back and forth as if in terrible pain.

Her mother slumped down onto the chair and began to cry.

"You godless child, what appalling things I have to hear from you!"

The sick man lifted a terribly emaciated, yellow, blue-veined corpse-like hand.

"Tramp! Your teeth, I'll..." His coughing robbed him of his voice again.

Aina suddenly tore her fist away from her temples. Her palm was burning. A gold coin – no, it was a glowing piece of coal ... Before her mother could realise what she was about to do, she tore open the tiny misted window pane and threw the coin out of it. The yellow disc rolled tinkling faintly across the roof of rusty corrugated iron.

Her mother's tears had stopped. With eyes transformed by blind fury she stared at Aina.

"Crazy, utterly crazy!" she finally managed push past her lips.

"Clearly crazy," her father wheezed and then started moaning deeply.

Aina slumped onto her seat – broken. She rested her elbows on her knees and held her head in her hands gazing at the red sputtering flame... The excitement settled down. She wasn't angry at her parents anymore. After all, they weren't to blame for the circumstances in which they'd grown up. Different types of trees grow on a solid mountainside – bent by the winds from all four directions – than in a swampy mire. They were forged by the mire and they'll stay in that mire. Who knows, maybe she would too... if a bird doesn't suddenly appear and carry her up the mountain... No, she didn't want to be angry or feel hatred: an old, rotting tree could no longer be bent, nor could it be replanted somewhere new... If only they'd left her alone, if only they hadn't complained about her or argued with her day in and day out. She felt sorry for these enfeebled, broken people – more than for herself...

Sobbing again and pushing her forehead against the foggy pane, her mother tried to see.

"We should go down there," she said breathing heavily.

"Maybe nobody's picked it up yet."

"Such a pretty little coin!" the sick man moaned.

"Leave it..." Aina replied sounding glum and weary. She crouched down even lower. The red flame lapped lazily at the damp fir cuttings. Peculiar thoughts flashed across her mind as she stared. "It's beautiful... that gold... because it has been washed in blood and rinsed with tears. It's heavy, because so much pain has been melted into it. Chimneys puff out smoke and machines rumble all day long for its sake, working people in their millions sweat and labour for it, all living creatures fight and suffer for it – all of that has been melted together and forged into heavy golden discs. They jingle with their wicked laughter as they wander around the world, and everyone grasps at them eagerly. People push each other out of the way, walk over each other... brothers forget brothers, parents give up their children..."

She stopped as she didn't wanted to talk about this anymore. Let it be – they won't understand, it will just embitter them more and make it more difficult for everybody... She stared into the lithe, red flame...

A small red campfire is burning – somewhere a thousand versts away in the Siberian taiga... There is a windbreak on the mountain slope, but up above, the cold morning wind howls powerfully through the thickets of knotted cedar, red pine, and grey fir. The light from the fire spreads only about ten steps around. Further out, the darkness is like a black wall – reaching up to the tops of the giant trees and even higher up to the invisible, starless sky above. Next to the dying fire sit two people – an escaped deportee and a convict who has served his sentence of hard labour – both of them secret, stealthy gold diggers. They're not free; the threat of a harsh punishment hangs over their heads, but could anything quench their thirst for gold? For weeks they've waited half-starving in the freezing cold. Ten of their comrades dug in vain, but eventually their luck came in. Each one of them gained a handful of yellow sand in a little bag hidden under their clothes... But when the fire goes out and the coals smoulder as they cool, when the taiga is fast asleep and its heavy breath can be heard above them, that's when the man's beast and master awakes and raises his slave to his feet. He stands, shaking from fear and pale from shame, filled with uncontrollable desire. The axe glints in the glow of the coals, and a red spray of blood extinguishes their final shine... A sharp knife cuts off the worn, dirty rags, bony fingers grab and rip like the claws of a wild animal, they tear, and search... And then that man steals away with his loot over the taiga – moss giving way under his feet as if it wanted to swallow him up, dry sticks screaming loudly as they snap and stiff branches scratching at his head like hands reaching down from above. A startled owl lifts up from the thicket shrieking loudly. It flaps its wings fleeing from the one who betrayed and murdered his comrade. Back at the campfire, there's a threatening growl in the dark and somewhere far-off, a sorrowful moan... The man lies on the ground and around him greenish flames flicker in the eyes of wolves who've smelt blood... They keep moving closer... But the other man is fleeing across the taiga, clenching an axe handle speckled with red, and feeling his flesh burning in two spots next to the heavy yellow sand...

Aina fell quiet and took a deep breath. Whom was she telling all of this to? Probably just herself... She looked back. Her mother had pressed her forehead to the window pane again. Her father was moving his head from one side of the pillow to the other... She couldn't stand this any longer. Aina got up and went back into her room.

Irritated and gloomy, Lausks came home in the evening. He slammed the door and angrily kicked away Milda's galoshes;

she always put them in his way. She just threw them down without thinking about it – she had no sense of order. Spoiled girl!

Someone was scratching at the front door again. Lausks opened it. Roberts Sveilis...

"Is Miss Caune at home?" he asked, putting his hand on the brim of his hat and bowing gallantly.

Lausks's anger exploded. As if this boy were the only one to blame, he held the edge of the door and didn't let him by.

"Miss Caune is home, but what do you need?"

"That's something only I can tell her," Roberts puffed out his chest.

Lausks stepped over the threshold and closed the door behind him. He shoved the guest back with his shoulder and then stood threateningly in front of him with raised fists.

"You've got nothing to say to her. Understand? No more running around – understand! You've got no business with that girl – from this day on. Understand?"

Roberts looked into Lausks's eyes. His face twisted into an impertinent expression. "Excuse me, young sir... Perhaps you've misunderstood. I've got nothing to do with Miss Zvaigzne, that's your business."

Pushed suddenly, Roberts spun around. Pushed a second time in the back, he darted quickly down the stairs. His heels echoed as they hit the wooden steps. His palm whizzed along the smooth banister. "Hooligan!" he screamed furiously.

"Get out of here!" Lausks stamped his foot standing above.

"Will you be quiet!" Milda ran out and pulled him away from the top of the stairs. Too late! Roberts was downstairs standing there breathing heavily and had just slammed the door. "Hooligan! How dare you, this is none of your business!"

Lausks's face twisted with anger, his hands were clenched and he stamped his foot. He could barely keep himself from shoving her down the stairs too. "Yes, this is my business! This isn't a hotel or a brothel. Go out onto the street... go to the forest!"

"Why don't you go!" Milda snapped a second later. "Why don't you and your Aina go to the forest! I've paid for my apartment – you all live off of what they bring me from the country. Do you think I don't know that? And then nobody is permitted to come and see me. You're all living like Turks – and I'm not allowed to see anybody. But it's fine! Very soon, I'll be moving out to live with Mrs. Bērziņš. My mum is at the inn..."

"You and your mum can go to hell!" Lausks screamed back and left Milda standing out front quickly putting her coat on. But when he went into the kitchen, he felt tired. What had he done: Sveilis's brother! Lodziņš had resigned; Sveilis would be one of Unity's new directors... That boy would complain and his good spot at the bank would be gone... And what would it have mattered if he had come inside, let him and that spoilt girl do what they like... He couldn't eat, or even sit still after all that unpleasantness – all he could think about was his own anger.

But that wasn't the end of it. Half an hour later Milda returned with her mother. This fat wife of a country estate owner was furious. Aina had locked her door, but Lausks and her parents were forced to sit and listen. They listened for an hour as she pummelled them like a filthy rainstorm. No one was spared. She wasn't afraid of naming names and being explicit in her insults. Plainly, directly and according to the custom of country folk, she cursed each of them in turn and then all of them together. Everything she'd brought here – they'd all eaten themselves; this whole gang of theirs was living high on the hog, while her child was starving to death. So pale and clearly almost done for... These city hags were so ruthless they'd practically tear out someone else's eye. The old man is sick and who knows what kind of illness a person could come down with here. And as for those two – how shameless and indecent! This is a brothel, not an honest boarding house...

A muddy stain was left where each of her words had struck. For an entire hour Lausks sweated like he was sitting in a sauna – until Milda and her mother finally gathered up their things and left. Offended to the depths of his being and full of rage, he went in to see Aina.

"Well, did you hear that?" he asked angrily.

Aina shrugged her shoulders. "I wasn't listening. I've always known that women like that know how to curse."

"I've kno-o-own, I've kno-o-own..." Lausks repeated mockingly. "Why do you think that is? Isn't this all your fault? You don't even know what you're doing because of your obstinacy and vanity. Your ideas..."

"Don't talk like that. You're in my apartment, not your own. Take your things and get out of here."

He stared at her wide-eyed and looked around cautiously. And there were his things, all thrown together. His rage disappeared in an instant and something else, which he couldn't quite understand yet, appeared in its place.

"What kind of nonsense are you talking? Why are you fooling around like this?"

"I don't have an apartment for you anymore. Gather up your things and go – just like Milda did."

And right away he understood all too clearly that this wasn't any kind of a joke. It was as if someone had lifted him up by his collar and hung him over a high wall – and he was pointlessly shaking his legs and grabbing with his hands without any footing or place to grab a hold of.

"For what reason?" he asked feebly. Tears could be heard in his voice.

She shifted and impatiently brushed him off.

"Oh, don't ask anymore. You already know. We're disappointed in each other; we became involved by accident. Both of us have suffered. Let's part ways now without harm or hatred. And without a long speech – don't talk!" she interrupted him. "That's all I ask. You'll go to your bank and your Cyclists' Association, and I'll stay with my parents – I'm sure we'll all be fine."

Offended and humiliated, he hobbled over to the chair

and grabbed his things as if he were trying to flee a fire. There wasn't much there: a pillow, a sheet, a worn little quilt, a suit and a couple dozen books. But he had to speak up, because his heart was too full.

"So this is the great love that I always heard about... caprice and suspicions. Talk and petty arguments, and humiliation... It all begins with caprice and ends in humiliation..." He became quiet. His tears began to shake his voice too much. More than anything, he was trying not show any weakness or pain.

"It's pointless to talk about it. Can't you see that?" She spoke calmly and considerately without hatred or agitation. "So much has been said during all these years, now all that's left is to remember it. To remember it and move past it." She stirred driven by the boredom and the fear that this intolerable moment of their parting would be pointlessly prolonged. "We've disappointed each other and we're both disappointed. We've walked the same path, but each on their own side. Why should we accuse each other of anything? I don't have anything to accuse you of. Maybe you do. Let's part as if we were travellers who'd met accidentally and walked the same path together for a while – without hatred or bitterness. Can we do that? Give me your hand."

But he didn't give it to her. He turned away angrily. "You're mad! What do you think you're going to do when you have – the child?"

"It'll be my child," she answered bluntly and also turned away.

"And mine!" he shot back.

"Only mine! Don't worry about me... or about him. He's better without a father than with one like this. It'll be better for him if I'm there for him by myself."

He was angrily trying to tie his things together into a bundle and wasn't able to.

"You could at least think of your parents. They've done nothing to deserve this kind of shame. When your mother sat nursing you, could she even have imagined it... When your father worked every day so you'd have bread, could he have known he'd have to see this as he lay at the edge of his grave? No matter how grandiose your ideas may be, blind disregard of one's parents' feelings never turned out well. Mark my words! You'll have no peace from them."

"Oh I will!" she laughed unkindly. "Don't you worry about that, choirboy. I've suffered their tyranny long enough." She stated at Lausks. "Nursed... worked...Whoever brings a child into this world has a responsibility to raise and feed them. I won't abandon them while I live; nobody will have to starve or go and live in the poorhouse. They can expect bread from me, but nothing more. What else have they given me? An elementary school education...beatings in great amounts and without warning, whether I deserved it or not; they've made me pay for their anger resulting from their own ignorance and mistakes. They filled my head with all manner of musty nonsense, and they've strangled and crippled my healthy spirit. For ten years I've fought with myself and with bloody fingers I've torn everything out at its root and fibre – everything that they planted deep inside me... Now at least I'm clear of it and clean!"

She spread her arms, and tossing back her head, took a deep breath. He didn't want to look, but he couldn't help it. He tried not to, but he still felt hot just looking at her. She was so attractive in passionate moments like this.

"Aina..." he said slurring his words. But his eager, breathy voice only cooled her down and pushed her even further away. She glanced at him with a mocking smile.

"I've walked around as if I'd had a millstone around my neck this entire time. I had to take it apart grain by grain. I tossed those grains to the ground and you kept gathering them all together and trying to put them back around my neck. Yes, you were their eager helper. That's why you have to go, so that I can live freely according to my own will and understanding. I'll be able to deal with father and mother, if I was able to deal with you... They can ask for bread from me, and they'll get it. My life and work belong only to me. Let them think what they want, that's their business. And if they think that I'm going down a wrong path, if it hurts them, so be it; they've earned it and it's their destiny. I can't and don't want to help them there. My entire life is still in front of me, and I have so much work to do! Am I supposed to listen to the moans of two old people who already finished living their lives long ago? When they were raising and feeding me... and beating me, did they ever ask what I thought or what my mind yearned for? Now our roles are reversed. I'm not going to give up mine. Never! Go and tell them that – since you get along together so well."

"Aina..." he was almost sobbing.

"What?" She became angry again. "What are you still waiting for? Go!"

He trudged out the door holding his bundle and his appearance was one of utter dejection.

Aina followed him and locked the door behind him. She turned around and looked around the room. Alone again – free and independent like long ago! Feelings of joy and strength washed over her like a wave. The old dregs and grime sank heavily to the bottom. But it was cool – and after the shock she had just experienced her nerves felt weary and sensitive towards this onrush of all that was fresh and new. She needed to rest – until tomorrow... She sank heavily onto the chair and held her burning head with both hands...

In the Unity directors' office, Lieknājs the bookseller was standing a step away from the table once again, glumly turning his hat in his hands.

"So – nothing, gentlemen?"

Strauss shrugged his shoulders and gave a bored look to his colleagues.

"I've told you: it's not possible for us. Not – po-ssi-ble!"

Sveilis nodded as he pushed a cigarette into his holder. "If we could – we'd do it without a second thought."

Blics was writing something. Without lifting his eyes, he nodded indicating that he was in agreement with the others.

"We have our directives from the board and the shareholders, and we can't go against those."

"But why can you do it for others? Zaķītis got approved just the day before yesterday. Beitans the engineer was in Bramberģis's faction – he was approved... Am I not a member just the same? Have I ever missed a payment in the past? I give you my word: not a day past Easter. On Easter I'm receiving two pamphlets from the printer – eighteen and twenty pages – then I'll have money again. But right now I really need it: I have to pay for paper, for the printing..."

"Yes, but who is buying those books right now..." Sveilis answered snidely. He wasn't at all sorry for this threadbare person anymore. His position as director had considerably desensitised him in a very short time. And even before that, he hadn't been that sensitive. Of late he'd grown careless of other people's needs.

"We haven't the slightest doubts about you as a person," Blics said warmly. "But we are forced to act according to our directives... and to be measured in the use of our resources. Wait for two or three months until we've received confirmation. Once we've become a credit union, we'll be able to act with greater latitude."

"Who are the ones who require greater latitude? Are they the ones with construction projects, the ones with seventy or eighty-thousand-rouble debts? Savings and Loans has enough for my seven or eight thousand. But when it doesn't want to, it can't. It is, after all, like they say: the large ones who have enough already, they get hundreds of thousands, but the small shop owner who really needs that credit, can't get a couple of roubles..."

Deeply offended, Lieknājs put his hat back on right there in the directors' office and quickly rushed out the door. Skrastiņš came in, obliging and pliant, and swept where he'd been standing as he hadn't worn galoshes and his boots had been covered with snow.

"An unbearable character," Strauss said crossly after the man had left and he began to stir his tea, in spite of the slice of lemon which was floating on it. "How many times have we told him – and yet he keeps crawling back. Skrastiņš should stop letting him in, and then we'd be done with him."

Blics shook his head in protest. "Not like that; that would be tactless. Don't forget, gentlemen, how the opposition treated us at the extraordinary general meeting. And they're working even more diligently in advance of the regular shareholders' meetings, of that you can be absolutely certain. A fifty-vote majority – that's not much. And we can't predict how the governor will deal with those complaints. Our situation isn't that secure."

"They won't achieve anything through the governor," Strauss said categorically. "They are no grounds for their appeal. Lodziņš voluntarily resigned, nobody forced him out. If he had something to say, why didn't he appear at the extraordinary general meeting? Why didn't he give his reasons plainly and clearly? We have the document," he hit the table with his fist, "due to illness and shortage of time!"

"Yes..." Sveilis said mockingly, as he leaned back in his chair and watched his cigar smoke rise in swirls.

"And the same with the rest of it... Arbitrariness, invalid authority, the destruction of ballots, defamation: all of it gossip, utter gossip. But where's the evidence? There's none – not even a little! It will be rejected, and that will be the end of it."

"And at the regular shareholders' meeting, we'll have forty new, trustworthy members," Sveilis added.

"That's true. I don't envisage that anything will catch us out on that count. Legally we're completely secure. But, gentlemen, a credit institution's greatest security lies in the trust the community places in it! And as far as we're concerned that has been shattered... or at least weakened. All of that gossiping, complaining, counter-campaigning and divisions within our own faction have not passed unnoticed. Just in yesterday's paper... did you read it?"

Sveilis brushed it off.

"The things they write in those papers! Didn't they write the exact same things before the meeting? We have nothing to fear from these scandalmongers in the press, as long as our membership is secure. And if we don't let slanderers anywhere near us! That Sietiņsons needs to get two or three months himself. Then he'll know not to curse. Just don't miss the deadline."

Strauss was becoming agitated again.

"The court's decision must be appealed in any case. So this matter goes to the Senate. The Senate can decide in principle if it's permitted for representatives of community institutions to be called crooks and swindlers in public places. And if there is a right to sue for at least those material losses which arise for the bank as a result of this kind of shock to the community's trust."

"Blics will need to go to Petersburg in person," Sveilis motioned with his head.

Blics didn't get a chance to respond; he got up and went over to the telephone, which had just started ringing. He spoke, returned and put on his galoshes.

"Excuse me, gentlemen... I have visitors from the country. I need to go with them to the Land Registry." He put his papers into a folder. Already wearing his coat and with a high karakul hat on his head, he came back to the table. "We can and will manage to do all of this. But the most important thing is the trust of society at large. And that has been weakened. Take a look at our accounting from the last month. Our deposits have significantly decreased and that's a bad sign. I don't want to offend anyone, so I'll just say: in the future we must limit our own building projects and borrowing and give more access to other members. One way or another, we've got to give up being something of a clique here. That gives ammunition to our opponents. At the shareholders' meeting we'll be forced to endure vicious attacks, you can be sure of that."

Blics left. The remaining two directors stared at each other for a long time. "Hoo..." Sveilis spoke first. "And now we see what kind of bird he is!"

"Do you think he has been bribed?" Strauss shrugged. "If there isn't unanimity among the directors then how can the community trust us. He's more harmful than the entire opposition. We can't tolerate people like that on the board."

"He should be thrown out, just like Brambergis. If he doesn't want to be here, we don't need him..."

The friends pushed their heads together and discussed something quietly but intently.

Humble and slick, Lausks opened the door from the cashiers' area and pushed his head inside. "Excuse me, Mr. Sveilis, but that craftsman that you asked for is here..."

Sveilis had already known that his carpenter, Rozentals, was sitting out by the cashiers. He'd been waiting since ten. He'd waited yesterday and was waiting again today. But what could Sveilis do? Where was he going to get those three or four thousand now? His credit was spent to the last rouble and he wouldn't be able to get any more before the shareholders' meeting. Blics was completely against it. Without the legally required security... He owed interest payments for three terms... He hadn't even paid his membership fees yet... Damn it!

He got up and went out into the cashiers' area, attempting to put on an indifferent expression as he walked. Rozentals the master carpenter immediately got up from the lacquered bench on his side of the counter. Holding his hat in hand, nervous and burdened by worry he leaned over.

"Well, how was it? Will I be able to get it today?"

"Oh, today..." Sveilis said casually, pretending to have completely forgotten that the day before yesterday he'd said yesterday, and yesterday he'd said today. "Yes, yes... of course... I'll go and see."

He walked over to the till on the far end – as if there were something to see or discover there. He stood for a moment.

Today a great deal of money had been withdrawn again. Whole handfuls of gold had poured out through the little window. Of course, others came in to make a deposit, but judging by what he'd seen, there were far fewer deposits than withdrawals. The employees would calculate the interest as they lazily leafed through the thick books without any hurry, drinking tea, eating a bit of pastry along with it and looking out the window. But the clients waited patiently behind the counter with their deposit slips and passports in hand and watched every page, every bit of pastry. They had to pay... And the gold streamed constantly out of the little window.

Just then Lausks threw the deposit book back down onto the counter with a loud thump, along with the grease-stained, dirty passport tucked inside of it.

"Well, why are you coming here? What do you want?" He went over to his seat and sat back down again. The old man with a thin nose like Ķencis shuffled his documents unhappily.

"What is it?" Sveilis asked.

"Doesn't know how to sign..." Lausks answered and glared belligerently at the old man.

"A-ha...," Sveilis puffed out this chest and turned harshly towards the offender. "Without a signature we can't pay anyone anything," he said, and then, without listening to what the old man was mumbling, he turned and walked back.

His hat in hand, Rozentals approached the counter again. What could he say to him? His head down, Sveilis made a motion with his hand as if he'd forgotten something and had just remembered, and quickly went back into the directors' office as if he wanted to check something one more time.

But how long could he stay there. Rozentals was waiting out front. He had to go back again. He returned and tried in vain to look indifferent.

"It's a hell of a thing..." he said with a furrowed brow, supporting himself on his elbow and leaning over close to Rozentals across the counter. "There are so many fixed payments... the bank won't have the money."

Rozentals started to button up his coat and then began unbuttoning it again.

"Maybe it'll come in..."

"Maybe, but there's little hope. We already know how much to expect – it's all been calculated ahead of time. Today I won't be able to. Tomorrow, maybe, the day after for certain..."

"But I can't... Look, you have to see from my side. The workmen have been waiting for an entire week. They have to eat... what are they supposed to live off? All the windows are already done, the doors next week... If you can't do three thousand anymore... well, at least do two!"

"Like I said: today I can't even do two hundred! It's all become so complicated and involved... There was no great need for those doors yet, they could've been put in later. But I think it'll work out for me. I had been counting on the Seventh Credit Union to increase my credit to ten, fifteen thousand – but they didn't. They won't extend the old credit I already have. The Twelfth Credit Union, treating me like a fool, two thousand...The Fifteenth Credit Union didn't even see me. I already know why: they are all Lodziņš's relatives and now they're biting me back. And the branches of my shop are not doing well either: everybody is going to taverns, and nobody needs anything from retailers... After the shareholders' meeting, then there'll be money by the handful again..."

He wanted to encourage Rozentals with a friendly smile. But the friendlier Sveilis became, the more the master carpenter scowled.

"You're not listening to me: what are the workmen supposed to live off? How am I supposed to live? Not a rouble for over a month..."

"What do you mean – not a rouble! What about those two hundred last week?"

"Two hundred..." Rozentals laughed angrily. "What can you do with two hundred?"

Sveilis knew that two hundred wasn't enough to do anything. This situation was intolerable. At that moment he had only one thought: how to rid himself of this person as quickly as possible. He noticed Raugs the architect, who was standing not far from them looking at his prize-winning plan for the new bank building hanging from the wall in a glass frame. Sveilis quickly hurried over. He greeted him and leaned over the counter on his elbow in the same way. They spoke for a moment. Raugs wished to know whether it was true that he was overseeing construction of the new bank building and whether he knew anything about the industry. Sveilis boasted that in his youth he'd worked as a bricklayer and that he had come to an agreement with the board – and if the shareholders' meeting approves the credit and gives the directive to begin work, then they'll end up working together. Smiling self-importantly he looked the architect straight in the eyes and squeezed his hand warmly. It was always very enjoyable to spend time with educated people.

Strauss opened the door. Sveilis needed to come to the telephone.

Some strange man had come. He won't come to the bank, but won't leave either. At any rate, he had to meet Sveilis as soon as possible... Sveilis knew who he was. Not the bank, he couldn't come here. This matter wasn't to be discussed or resolved at the bank. Today? He looked over at the wall calendar. Yes, he could. How could he have forgotten that deadline! He quickly threw on his coat and galoshes. This matter couldn't wait. Hopefully it would turn out all right... Waking up at night, sometimes he couldn't fall asleep again thinking about it. Total nonsense! The devil himself had pushed him into it back then!

Tilaks was coming up the stairs towards him... He couldn't forget that tonight is Strauss's forty-fifth birthday... Where is he off to in such a hurry? Sveilis extricated himself from that conversation as quickly as possible. He sat down in a cab and rode home.

Motor cars moved up and down past his cab. He had been counting on getting a motor car himself in the spring. But if things are still pinching as much as they are now, then who can say whether he will. Damn it, how did everything become so complicated! At first it was all going smoothly. The hotel made a tidy profit, and the land sold to the bank earned eighteen thousand. Credit was everywhere and as much as he needed. Money came in by the cartload... But then gradually it began to slow. The branches didn't do well – the one in Pārdaugava had to be shut down after just three months, the one on this end was only barely holding on, and the other one was halfway successful. The main wine shop was also only just barely scraping by. A few payments were delayed and then immediately there were problems: it was difficult to get stock on account, especially from foreign firms, and even if he did, it was only for a short time and on disadvantageous terms. The shop was missing this and that. The Christmas advertisements had not been paid yet and the newspapers were refusing to accept new ones. There were fewer customers, that was easy to see. Timma and the new cashier weren't completely trustworthy either anymore. There was no hard evidence, but he had strong suspicions.

At first money had been coming in all the time, but now he was only paying out.

New deadlines every day, extensions, interest... Three times now he'd narrowly averted a dispute on a bill of exchange. It was difficult to get anything from those who owed him money; he had to borrow a hundred, two hundred, or even just twenty-five at a time. He felt ashamed – but there was absolutely nothing he could do about it. He had no other resources. He could no longer meet with some acquaintances. Unpleasantness of one sort or another every day. It was practically impossible to live it up without a care. It was a constant weight on his heart.

At least Unity was able to delay his interest payments. On the one hand, good, but on the other, bad. That just meant that huge sums were accruing, which would one day have to be paid. And the opposition – all those who were thrown out, didn't get in, or were dissatisfied – were spreading dark, ugly rumours. Allusive articles based on hearsay were appearing in the hostile newspapers, though it was abundantly clear who and what they were talking about. The bank's good reputation in the community was being ruined both openly and behind the scenes. Those who were jealous and wished them ill were hard at work. There's never been a shortage of wreckers and instigators. A Latvian never wishes another Latvian well...

Blics was agitated and concerned. They'd made a mistake in letting in this little lawyer. Anyone who is so very sensitive and worries so much about their good name, had best not join a bank. The directors had to be in solidarity with each other – this was a widely-held view and not some kind of personal swindle. And it wasn't really even that bad. Every bank had to weather crises until a trustworthy membership can be established and the community calms down and becomes accustomed to it all. Once the new building was finished, renewed trust would immediately follow. Money would flow in again. A publicity campaign could be paid for at one of the larger newspapers in order to create the right impression. So much was possible now with the help of the press.

Sveilis tried to comfort himself, but didn't feel comfortable. Who hadn't been in such a fix at some point in their lives? Hadn't Strauss, and Tilaks... and Lodziņš? Every one of them spoke from experience. And still they overcame it, got through it and adapted. Let anyone try to lay a finger on Strauss or Tilaks now. It'll be the same for him... He just had to make it to the shareholders' meeting... He'll receive the directive for the construction of the bank building – and he'll be able to get an advance right away. He'll pay off a part of the interest and there'll be some left over for him. His house will be ready in the summer – he'll take out a mortgage on it and immediately rid himself of the expensive credit. That high interest was enough to ruin people just on its own. He'll receive money for rent and won't have to pay for his own expensive apartment... In the end he'll be able to sell that wine shop and its branches;

Tilaks already had a buyer. And then, together with Gailis and another foreign expert, they'd open a cinema. Now that kind of an establishment has a future, and one can still make money from it, as long as one doesn't skimp on the advertising. Print flyers and distribute them across the city every morning. Good-sized with attractive drawings, pasted onto boards, and get a few draymen to take them on their rounds. In the newspapers – on the front page of every issue and once a week in the editorial. Those editors will print anything if are invited often and fed well. The devil himself dances for money...

The long-term outlook was good, but these momentary complications were bearing down on him. If only he could somehow make it through this awkward period... An unpleasant thought had wormed its way into his head and it just kept nagging him.

Who was really to blame? Was it him? No, he couldn't admit that. Everyone knew how effortlessly money could continuously circulate. And it did so to everyone in the same way: he would've been a fool if he hadn't grasped the opportunities. It circulated – and then suddenly it stopped... But why was that so? He felt hurt and undeservedly saddened. He'd wasted some of it, of course, but who hadn't? Hadn't Tilaks or Blics or Gailis done the same? Each of them had dropped a hundred at the restaurant or on girls, and lost the same playing cards. Losing a hundred once, winning fifty the next time – one couldn't get ruined or fall into debt just because of that. Of one thing he was certain: he'd been too willing to guarantee and loan money to anyone who asked. In that sense the others had been more careful. Made and Roberts had also spent quite a bit... But was it so bad that he'd helped others? Was that the reason he had to suffer these difficulties now? This was his reward... He knew he'd only meant well, that he'd done good, and now was undeservedly affected by all this and made miserable. He could feel it in his thoughts, in his heart, and in his very nature that he was becoming hardened and less kind, that with every day all the others were becoming more distant and unfamiliar, and that foremost on his mind was the degree to which his own situation was good or bad. He realised he'd begun to evaluate his closest friends – yes, even them – only based on how much he could borrow from them... how much they'd be willing to lend him... Drinking and living it up, he used to love doing that – always. Earlier he'd been more tolerant and helpful, he wasn't suspicious of anyone and only felt hatred for someone very infrequently... He was sorry for himself – and that made it even sadder and more difficult...

But at home everything went well – even better than he'd thought. The most important matter of all had been seen to, at least for a couple of months. And how things would be after that, no one could say. Would they be worse – certainly not... And immediately his heart became lighter and merrier. A temperamental person, quick to become upset and quick to calm back down again... After taking the strange man outside again, he rushed into his office.

Lonija had just been cleaning, her sleeves rolled and pinned up to her shoulders, when she came out of Roberts's room and towards Sveilis. She probably wanted to ask him something. But he, feeling jolly and bold, grabbed her above the elbows and pushed her into the corner, as was his habit.

"Mr. Sveilis!" she said under her breath and tried to free herself.

"Don't scream, are you crazy..." he laughed, scolding her. He held both of her hands with one of his and with the other one pawed her as usual. But he quickly pulled back and turned away in confusion; his mother's head disappeared through the open kitchen door. Damn it! He shot a condemning glance at Lonija, as if it were her fault, and went into his office.

Moments later Made came in after him. In a dark silk suit, her hair styled up high, with a gold chain bracelet – she looked serious and distinguished. Each of her movements sent forth a powerful cloud of perfume.

"Where do you live, because I barely ever get to see you?"

Sveilis gently shrugged.

"You think that I have free time..."

"Yesterday I was at the Ladies' Committee meeting at the Poverty Aid Association – nothing came of it. The interesting news is that Mrs. Strauss announced that she's leaving..."

"Yes, she and her children are going abroad."

"Oh, abroad... But when there is no director or assistant, the meeting can't be held. And where were you yesterday? At lunchtime you left me guessing."

"Oh, leave me alone with your meetings!" He gestured crossly that she should leave him alone. "I've got so much work on. Complications..."

But she didn't have the least bit of interest in knowing about her brother's complications. She had something more important on her mind. She hesitated for a moment. "What's that young Lodziņš doing now?" She wanted to make sure the sarcasm could be heard in her voice, but her suppressed bitterness was stronger.

Sveilis shook his head and sighed. "Things are in dire straits for that young man. Things like that can happen; we all make mistakes... But this is a little too much. The entire city is talking about it. His mother had a stroke or something like that from the worry. I don't know about the old man... he's as tough as he is sanctimonious ..." He changed his tone. "He can break his neck as far as I'm concerned. I shouldn't have loaned money or been a guarantor for him. Now I'm being asked to pay it..."

Made too had become used to a life of asking and taking from him. Always with a fist full of money – she couldn't imagine her brother in any other way.

"You're all the same," she said, becoming increasingly agitated. "Boozing all day and night. I don't understand where you put it all, or why you don't get bored."

"Boozing..." Sveilis stretched his lips into a sneer and wanted to tell her. But then he looked at Made and thought better of it. She'd fallen for that boy. Nonsense, of course, and nothing could come of it. But let her fool around – why should she know... He buttoned up his coat. "I have to go. All kinds of complications..."

"When you see him, tell him..." But she stopped and didn't go on, deciding it was better to keep it to herself. "Such a shame – an educated person, living like the most menial factory worker..." She wiped the tears of anger from her eyes. "Those twenty-five roubles..."

Sveilis started to search through his pockets. Another unpleasant situation.

"Yes... but can't I give them to you tomorrow? I have to make some payments today..."

Made looked at him wide-eyed in disbelief. This was the first time she'd heard him refuse.

"But I'm scheduled to have a seamstress come over. She's been waiting an entire week – I scheduled it. You said so yourself, today."

Sveilis felt guilty. He shoved his hand into his pocket towards his empty wallet, but then pulled his hand back out again. To hide his shame, he pretended to be annoyed.

"I can't today. Right when there are payments due on my bills of exchange... Tomorrow!"

Without listening to whatever else Made was saying, he pushed her aside and hurried out of the room. But his mother, who had poked her head out through the kitchen door, was already waiting for him there. She was looking somewhere off to the side and he felt increasingly uncomfortable. He tried to stay calm.

"Augusts, dear, we don't have any more firewood," his mother said. "Father looked down at Daugavmala – there's some nice birch firewood there."

"Yes," his father's voice came from somewhere further back. "And eighty roubles per fathom. Now that it's the winter –"

"And Lonija is asking for ten roubles," his mother added.

Damn it! And it was nothing really; he simply didn't have it and should have said so. But he couldn't – he couldn't! It was so unusual and unpleasant for him... He was so upset that he even forgot to take a cab. Breathing heavily, he hurried up the street. His coat was heavy and warm, his galoshes slid across the smooth pavement. And the weight of his body increased noticeably with each day. He would overheat quickly; it was hard for him to catch his breath; his heartbeat would sometimes seem irregular... For a few days now he'd been drinking only seltzer, but he wasn't sure how long he'd be able to keep that up. Next summer he had to start being serious about swimming in the sea and playing sports...

He caught sight of Roberts. He was coming down the other side of the street with a girl he felt he'd seen somewhere before. Noticing him, they parted, and Roberts hurried right over to him – the girl stayed where she was, watching and fidgeting. A smart young man – in a karakul collar, grey clothing, half-length galoshes, a hat on his head. His fuzzy face looked self-confident; he had a cheeky look in his eyes... Sveilis's earlier anger hadn't completely passed yet. Money, what else could he want – Sveilis thought.

"What are you slinking around for?" he screamed at his brother, not letting him speak first and not paying heed to any strangers that might hear. "Don't you have any work at all? How long do you plan on loafing about?"

Roberts blushed, searched around in his pockets for a handkerchief, and blew his nose.

"Today... homework..."

"I know your work!" Sveilis yelled back, trying to seem angrier than he actually was. "Slinking around the streets, begging! Who's that girl with you?" he pointed across the street. "Shame on you, boy!"

He spun around and hurried away. He was quite satisfied with himself; after walking a short distance from there, he got into a cab. Roberts wasn't really his problem! He could break his neck as far as he was concerned – as long as he didn't ask for money.

Tilaks's restaurant was practically empty. He wasn't home

yet himself. He waited around for a moment and spoke with the buffet attendant, then drove on to the Baltika.

There weren't many people at the Baltika either, but there were still more than at Tilaks's restaurant. Sveilis's restaurant had never been completely empty. Right by the doors, hunched over an empty table, was Rodolfs Lodziņš – deadly drunk, pale as a corpse, his eyes almost completely closed.

"He's been here since we opened this morning," Pauls said rushing up to his boss. "I wanted to take him upstairs – but he wouldn't go. He tried to hit me."

Sveilis already knew the cause of Lodziņš's malaise. Sveilis was feuding with the father, but was still friendly with the son. He slapped him on the shoulder in a familiar fashion.

"Well, young man, how's it going? Badly?"

Lodziņš didn't see the hand extended towards him. His coloured cap had slid down over one eye. He blinked the other one tearfully and closed it again.

"A hell of a thing!" he grunted and then shook himself off. "I drink...and drink...and drink...all night long... One day and two nights, but I can't get drunk."

Sveilis sat down next to him.

"Listen, be sensible. What good will come of this constant drinking? You should stop at least for a little while. Later on, you can go back to it."

"I want to get drunk!" Lodziņš seemed to be wailing more than speaking. He hit the table so hard with his fist that the ashtray tumbled onto the floor. "Why won't they give me any more?" He watched in horror as a large red drop welled up on his injured fingertip.

"Be sensible..." Sveilis comforted him very seriously. "Drinking and carousing don't help. You need to stop – for a while. And go to the doctor. It's nothing dangerous. With all these new medicines, everyone can be cured."

"I'll shoot her, that... damned..." He used the actual uncouth term. "I know who she was... I'll go and shoot her... and that'll be it!"

"Don't talk nonsense!" Sveilis rebuked him sharply and turned to see Bebrītis coming over from the billiard room in his shirt, jacketless and a cue over his shoulder. He took a sip from his glass, which he'd started drinking earlier, and said, "Be so kind and take him upstairs. He needs to sleep it off. What's the point of him sitting around here boozing all day long?"

"I'll drink... and drink... and drink..." Lodziņš wailed and tried to hit the table again, but missed it.

Bebrītis smirked and tossed the cue over his other shoulder. "We'll heal that wound," he laughed taking his friend under his arm and standing him up. "Let's go!" He pushed the doors wide open. "Make way, cruel world, the plague is coming for Vidzeme..."

"I'll shoot her..." Lodziņš said, slurring his words as he staggered out the door.

Young Skrastiņš, with heavily oiled hair and wearing a shirt front without a collar, came out of the billiard room with chalk-covered fingers. "Excuse me, Mr. Lodziņš once again ended up not paying one rouble fifty-seven kopecks yesterday. Four parties... two carafes for twenty... six for lampreys..."

Sveilis shrugged indifferently. "None of my business. Speak with Mr. Juškans. Why is he bringing any of that to types like these?" He turned his back and went up to the buffet. "Listen, Juškans - do you have anything in the cash register over there? For just a moment... I need some."

Juškans's pockmarked face scowled. How many days had it been now that the boss took the last kopeck... He reluctantly opened the little drawer, lifted up the banknotes, jingling the coins together as he counted them.

"Six... eleven... twelve... fifteen... What's here: twenty at most. We've already ordered the pork chops... and the fish will be delivered today - we'll need to pay for it."

"Well, we'll make some more today... Give me ten roubles - I need it. I absolutely need it... Eh... give me ten roubles from the cash register..." He threw a piece of eel on the plate and motioned with his finger that it was better for Juškans to give him the money than talk about anything else. "Pour me a Ryabinovka."

Juškans reached for the bottle, but didn't give him the money yet. After pouring it he spent a good amount of time pushing the cork back into the bottle. "I need it too... I haven't been paid for a month and a half..." "Yes... yes... yes!" Sveilis agreed and with each "yes" pushed a piece of eel into his mouth and nodded his head. "Tomorrow or the day after – absolutely. But today I need it." He leaned over the buffet and took the money himself from the open drawer. "Ten? – well let's say thirteen... I need it. Tomorrow or the day after, when there's money again, as much as you need." Leaving half a piece of eel on the table, and sticking a handful of banknotes and silver coins into his trouser pocket as he was still chewing, he went off on his way so he wouldn't have to listen to whatever else Juškans was about to say. He heard what sounded like familiar voices and laughter coming from behind the curtains. He turned in that direction.

Little Flame, Fricis and Gailis. Little Flame was sitting with Fricis close by her side. Gailis was facing her. Little Flame had one elbow on Fricis with one elbow and had almost pushed him down onto the table, while Gailis had stretched her other arm across the table and was squeezing it, but also pulling off the rings on her fingers and putting them back on again. Fricis was using all of his might to keep his nose from ending up in his beer glass. Gailis fooled around by brushing his white beard like a broom back and forth across Little Flame's arm. All three of them were fairly drunk – Gailis was red-faced, Fricis smiling as always also seemed incredibly sleepy and Little Flame was clearly bored with him. She lay on him with all her considerable weight without taking into account the difficulty she was causing him, while watching Gailis and laughing so artificially at all of his moves that it sounded as if she were practicing her laughter for a performance. Her face was noticeably swollen, her cheeks looked as if they were about to begin sagging due to old age and her eyes had become paler but were still bright.

Pauls nudged Sveilis from behind and whispered.

"She's caught that old one, and is letting him pay for everything. It'll be about ten roubles already... She hasn't let Fricis go home for two nights and he doesn't have a single kopeck left... Yesterday an older lady came in, his mother or aunt, and asked if he'd been here! If he comes in, she said, could we please send him away. I said yes, but would he listen to me? Maybe you should tell him, sir..."

The boss and waiter exchanged knowing glances and smiles. They both knew what aunt or mother it was that had come looking for Fricis...

"Have a seat, director!" Gailis called out from a distance. "We're having a little drink here... What do you say? I'm saying that this young lady is wearing an engagement ring, but she denies it."

"Absolutely an engagement ring!" Sveilis announced and sat down next to Gailis. It was very comfortable being in this kind of company. All of his troubles drifted away.

"Blabbermouths!" Little Flame tried to flirt innocently. "Who would marry an old girl like me? Mr. Gailis would suit me, but he already has a wife at home."

"Just one, just the one!" Gailis said, tickled with laughter.

"But what about Fricis? Does he have a ring on his finger, too?" Sveilis was about to look.

"Yes, yes, doesn't Fricis have one, too?" Gailis said. The old man's wrinkled, bluish fingers shook as they clutched the chubby, pampered woman's hand. "Haven't they been on a honeymoon in Riga together these last two nights?"

"Yes, before the wedding's even happened," Sveilis added.

"My goodness, gentlemen!" Little Flame grimaced. "Who would say something like that... How rude..."

Her elbow had lifted a bit. Fricis took advantage of the situation and sat up almost completely straight. With pleading eyes, he looked across the table and smiled weakly.

"I'm so sorry... But I need to go home now ..."
"Stay where you are!" Little Flame rebuked him. Half-jokingly, though somewhat unkindly, she slapped her companion across his bald head with the gloves she was clutching tightly in her hand. Both of the men on the opposite side of the table laughed with gusto. Little Flame also started to laugh. Her bare, heavy elbow once again pushed down her unhappy, weakened companion. He slumped down once more with his nose in his beer glass.

"Listen, director!" Gailis leaned over closer to Sveilis. "Listen to an old expert: close down that wine shop and all of its branches. What joy could it bring you to have to keep paying for it? And then we'll open a cinema called Venezia, Columbia or Ganges... That's the kind of business making money now."

But Sveilis wasn't interested in talking business right now. He had something else in mind.

"Yes, yes..." he replied hurriedly and then leaned over the table, closer to Little Flame. He was powerfully jealous of those hands, which Gailis was using to squeeze and stroke as much as he liked. He wanted to tempt away that white elbow, which was pressing down so heavily on drunken Fricis. "What do you say, miss, should we switch to coffee? Yes?" And seeing the answer in her eyes, he beckoned with his finger. "Pauls! A pot of coffee and a bottle of Pomeranz... give me that one for..." He lifted up three fingers.

But before the waiter had time to bring any of it, something ugly and unpleasant happened. An older, but still rather well-maintained lady, came in from outside in a dark suit with a rustling silk dress under an old-fashioned fur coat. Her winter hat was in the style of the year before last. She looked into the front room and then the alcove where the buffet stood, and was just about to turn around. But the waiter, whether on purpose or not, motioned with his head towards the back, and she looked in past the curtain.

She came over, looked and stopped for just a moment. Just

one short moment. With a strong, slender hand she shoved Little Flame's arm off of Fricis's neck, grabbed him by his crumpled collar, and pulled him up to his feet.

"Swine!" she whispered in German. "Forgotten where you live? Why are you boozing here with these drunkards! Wasting my money?"

She pulled Fricis into the middle of the room, but he was too drunk and couldn't manage to stand on his feet – or maybe didn't want to. The lady grabbed him under his arm, held him, but couldn't lift him up.

"Crazy hag!" Little Flame cursed coarsely as she slumped back, furious, her eyes shining.

But Sveilis shook his head at her threateningly and hurried to help the strange woman. For some reason unknown to him, he immediately felt great respect for her.

"Allow me... I'll help you. He had a little more than..." He took the drunken man under his arm and helped lead him over to the doors.

But Fricis also couldn't or didn't want to sit down in the sleigh. The lady tried holding him with her arm around him in vain. His eyes were closing, his head was lolling around and his entire body kept slumping out the open side. Nothing else could be done: Sveilis sat down on the other side and supported him. Now Fricis was leaning forward on purpose – nudging the driver's back, but he couldn't fall out.

It was more difficult still getting him up the five steps to the old-fashioned porch and in through the doors with the discoloured bronze plaque engraved with: Frau Hofräthin Wilde... But eventually they got him inside. They led him into the bedroom with its dark, plush curtains, green marble wash basin, giant glass case, crucifix on the wall, pink lamp hanging from the ceiling, thick carpets and two mahogany beds placed tightly against each other covered with a blue Atlas blanket. Fricis staggered and fell back into one of them. He groaned painfully and angrily, falling diagonally onto his back, so that his feet were sticking over the edge. But the ruffled white pillow case slid under his head; Mrs. Wilde began to unbutton his clothing and took each piece off one after another. Sveilis began to feel awkward. He quietly backed out through the nearest half-closed door.

A small parlour with three windows facing the street. Sveilis looked around in surprise. He had a rather fancy apartment himself, and had been the guest of wealthy people, but this level of luxury he had yet to see... No, it wasn't just luxury that surprised him so much about this room. Shiny, thick, leather-like wallpaper... Windows almost completely covered with striped double curtains... Unusual furniture made according to a style he'd never seen before – light, thin, white lacquered, gold-striped wood with blue floral covers... The place of honour on the wall was taken by an old-fashioned oil painting of a corpulent gentleman in the uniform of an official, white tufts of beard below his ears and a smooth-shaven chin. Beneath the bronze frame under glass on a black velvet pillow, there were three golden rings and a cross with ribbons in various colours. Here and there were a few more faded prints... Dignified, old-fashioned luxury seemed to exude coolness from every corner, from every item.

Sveilis began to feel uncomfortable. It would have been better if he'd fled immediately through the other door, which was completely closed, but he thought that this wouldn't be polite or refined. He stayed and waited. He could hear noise coming from the partially closed door to the bedroom. There was laboured breathing and sighing – groaning and what seemed like quiet arguing. There were even a few suspicious bumps. Then silence. Mrs. Wilde came out into the parlour.

Out of breath, overtaken by profound sadness, she came in and slumped heavily into the soft chair. She sat and breathed heavily, holding her hands on her lap with her head down. Sveilis felt like he was standing on a bed of hot coals. Didn't she see him at all? Yes – and why was he still there? He quietly moved towards the door. But it didn't seem right to leave that way either: it felt like he had some part in Mrs. Wilde's sorrow.

He coughed. Tears began to stream down Mrs. Wilde's cheeks. "He hasn't been home for two nights…" she complained quietly. "I can't sleep; I'm not used to it. I drove around all day yesterday, and did the same today… He's wasting my money on those tramps…"

A little confused, listening to the oddly candid tale, some things he had often heard in the past became clearer to Sveilis. And he became even more uncomfortable. Two beds next to each other… As should be the case in a proper marriage…

He muttered something as if defending Fricis.

"Don't say it!" Mrs. Wilde shook her head mournfully. The tears began to slide even more quickly down her cheeks. "I know where he was morning to night. I'm not sad about it – he can live, he can spend my money. My dear departed husband had a little manor in the country and a two-storey house in Cēsis. Now all I have left is this house…"

"Yes, but how many thousand in the bank?" Sveilis asked inadvertently. He had heard many times about Mrs. Wilde's astonishing wealth.

But she was overcome by her sorrows and wasn't listening.

"He can go, I don't say anything. But by eleven at night – he needs to be home. That's what I was accustomed to with my dear departed and I get a headache if I stay awake any longer." And then she wailed. "I can't… my nerves can't stand it any longer."

Wiping away her tears, she brushed her palms across her cheeks. Sveilis didn't have a chance to comfort her or say a word. Fricis staggered into the parlour from the bedroom. He was missing his hat and shirt front, his waistcoat was open, and he'd tossed on his jacket in such a hurry that he hadn't put his arms through its sleeves. He seemed to have slept off half of his hangover in ten minutes…

"You think…" He said rocking from foot to foot and against the wall. "I'm your slave – right? You've bought me – right? I'm to stay here like a prisoner – is that it?" Having put on his jacket he was shaking his fists at Mrs. Wilde. "To the devil with you, you old bitch!" He spat – he spat on the expensive red carpet and then shoving into one and then the other side of the doors, he ran out.

Sveilis could've laughed now. But he stopped himself and showed a rather sympathetic face.

"Don't worry, madam... I'm sure I'll be able to bring him back. I'll find him and bring him."

But Mrs. Wilde wasn't crying anymore.

"No need, let him run... He's wasted enough of my money on all that swill..." It seemed like she'd only just noticed the presence of a stranger in her parlour. With the apparent shyness of a young girl, she got up, and with seductively arched arms she fixed her hair. "Excuse me for disturbing you..."

Sveilis wasn't certain though in exactly what way he'd been disturbed. His mood was strangely altered. A little uncomfortable, because of what he'd just seen and heard. A little amused by the flirtatious glances Mrs. Wilde was giving him with her half-closed, tear-stained eyes. And behind it all this strange, overpowering respect for her fantastic wealth, which exuded from every object in the room. Respect and desire, and also something else... he couldn't grasp or understand it right away. Almost as if he had accidentally wandered in here for the first and last time. As if he needed to stay here, to help Mrs. Wilde endure her sorrow... She wasn't that unattractive at all – a little old, yes, but fairly well-preserved for her age. And because of this odd naivety and foolishness, he felt all his shyness and boredom evaporate in her presence. But this time he couldn't stay. She was already extending her hand.

"Good day, madam..." he whispered enthusiastically, then, for reasons not entirely clear to him, he leaned down quickly and kissed her limp, warm hand.

"Auf Wiedersehen!" she replied and watched him through the gap in the door as he left.

On the street, the winter cold engulfed Sveilis once again. He was back in the city crowd, back with his debts, deadlines, bills of exchange and all of his other problems. But there remained... yes, a somewhat old, but still rather attractive and warm-hearted lady... a warm, luxurious room and hundreds of thousands... There's nothing a person can't do if he has all the money he needs! Sveilis looked back. The door still seemed slightly open, but perhaps it wasn't. As if someone were looking through it – but also perhaps not...

Sveilis sat down pensively in the cab and rode back to Baltika.

Gailis and Little Flame were drinking coffee. Gailis had sat down next to her and become even more intemperate. Sveilis didn't like that: it was his coffee and Bénédictine, and his hotel. He had a respectable hotel; he couldn't allow these sorts of things here. He drove Gailis away and sat down next to Little Flame...

But today, for some reason, she didn't want to have anything to do with Sveilis. She seemed tired or cross. When Tilaks arrived, she took the opportunity and disappeared completely.

Tilaks agreed that having Blics on the bank board was intolerable. If there isn't unanimity among the directors, then such a large public institution can't exist. The directors must be in solidarity with each other. Wreckers can't be tolerated. But if they throw him out, there will be another scandal. He won't stay calm. He'll campaign against them at the shareholders' meeting, he'll create a scandal and cause trouble. They had to know ahead of time how to silence him. They needed to get Padegs and the other better speakers. And they had to hire a different lawyer: this one will miss all the deadlines for their appeals and will harm the bank's interests in all kinds of ways... A whole score of new worries. Those outside the business had no idea how many problems, difficult decisions and hard work comes with positions in large financial institutions like this one...

Gailis began to nod off and there was no point demanding the old expert's attention. The directors weren't listening to his babbling. Finally he understood that he was rather drunk and left. The directors ordered another round of coffee.

The waiter brought the coffee and announced that a lady wished to speak with Mr. Tilaks. She was waiting outside in the corridor and didn't want to come inside.

Tilaks was very offended.

"You tell her... The corridor isn't my reception hall. She can come see me at home between six and seven. Or tomorrow after eleven at the bank... If not, then she can come in right away."

And she came in... Both men turned their heads and smiled at the same time. Well, she wasn't any shrinking violet! Elegantly attired, slender and on the pale side, with black hair and dark eyes – not exactly beautiful, but piquant, interesting. Maybe it was because of the stories people told about her around the city. Sveilis and Tilaks recognised her. She was the widow of Bērziņš the bookbinder. A year and a half ago her husband died – and she'd continued to run her husband's shop, but it just didn't work no matter what she tried. She went to all the banks looking for money. Companions, on the other hand, were something she didn't need to look for at all. Over a year and a half ago she had become great friends with a student who was later arrested due to events connected with the revolution, and after that she lived with the bookseller Āķis, who went bankrupt and fled. They say that he took a large part of the deceased bookbinder's savings... Now Mrs. Bērziņš was going to all the banks looking for money.

Both directors rose to their feet and greeted her with a smile and a bow.

"Hello, Mrs. Bērziņš!" Tilaks squeezed her hand.

Mrs. Bērziņš apologised and smiled. Her flirtatious smile did not completely disappear from her face. And, as he looked at her, Tilaks also felt compelled to smile back at her in the same way... An interesting girl! The directors wanted to make her sit down.

"I won't be sitting, gentlemen..." She took off one of her gloves inside her hand-warmer and brushed some hair back behind her ear under a large, rust-coloured hat. "I was at the bank, but it was too late. I was told I might find you here. Is there any hope for me at all? I'm in real trouble."

Tilaks became pensive.

"You see, Mrs. Bērziņš... I completely forgot about that today. It was only a trifling amount you had there – if I'm not mistaken, a little more than one hundred roubles..."

"One hundred twenty roubles."

"Hm... perhaps we could. I'll speak with my colleagues. What does Mr. Sveilis think about this matter?"

"For Mrs. Bērziņš – always a pleasure ..." Sveilis had not taken his eyes off her. But now he refocused his attention, and added, "That is to say I have no objections. But the two of us can't decide alone. We must discuss this... Please sit, Mrs. Bērziņš, won't you!"

"Thank you. I would love to... but my boarder – she's waiting for me outside."

Another young lady? Both directors became even more keen and jovial. Why doesn't she bring her inside to warm up? Then they could discuss these money matters... When Mrs. Bērziņš went outside hesitatingly, they both looked at each other, as if they were telling each other something they already knew.

The young woman was brought in, but blushed as soon as she saw Sveilis. He looked at her and couldn't remember where he'd seen her before. Finally, he remembered. Ah – the same one who was with Roberts this morning! Milda Caune? Yes, yes. Smiling a little absurdly, he sat the girl down next to him. Mrs. Bērziņš sat down closer to Tilaks.

They weren't here to sit and drink with these gentlemen – they were passing by and had just sat down for a moment. All signs pointed to this: their poses, the hats they had kept on their heads, their hand-warmers still on one hand. It was clear that these women weren't carousers or anything of the sort. Mrs. Bērziņš, supporting herself on her arm, tried to force a serious expression as she spoke with Mr. Tilaks about money matters. Milda was sitting on the chair, her head thrown back, staring at the frescoes on the ceiling with pursed lips, as she tried not to smile at the jokes that wealthy Sveilis was telling her as he leaned closer. She felt a little afraid and also rather gratified sitting with this attractive, wealthy man about whom the entire city was talking. This one was completely different from his brother... But she didn't want to seem like a dumb little goose and so remained very serious, almost as if she were slightly irritated.

"Are you trying to get me drunk!" She pushed away the little glass of Bénédictine which had been filled for her.

"My goodness, Milda!" Mrs. Bērziņš scolded her. "How can you speak so rudely! Go ahead and drink just one..."

She drank one, then another... They all got to know each other and became fast friends...

When the women left, Tilaks took Sveilis over to his restaurant. Bebrītis, Taube, and Dr. Zīle were already there ahead of them. They all went to Tilaks's apartment and began playing cards. Sveilis wasn't having any luck and nearly lost his last rouble. But then his luck changed and he won sixty roubles for a few kopecks. Zīle and Bebrītis lost the most. Bebrītis borrowed thirty roubles and then lost those. He became angry, pulled out his silver pocket watch, and threw it down on the table so that glass shards and fragments of watch hands went flying all over the place. Then, he wanted to tear the lamp from the ceiling, but they calmed both him and Tilaks down with some difficulty. Tilaks was extremely angry and was determined to teach the student a lesson. But Ziemelis arrived in Strauss's motor car and took them all to Pārdaugava to celebrate Strauss's birthday.

Strauss's house stood in the centre of a park filled with old trees and surrounded by a high fence. It was a wooden structure, reminiscent of a summer cottage, with two five-sided rounded brick verandas. During the summer, a peacock would walk around on its neatly-trimmed lawns, while a pair of swans swam in the pond. Now the pond was frozen over and the fountain was unattractively ringed by dead grass and a few plaster statues covered with mould. It was an old, aristocratic property, and Strauss had become its owner by marrying a German wife. In truth, he only had a general power of attorney, though he never failed to invoke it.

Mrs. Strauss and the children had sent their felicitations by telegraph from abroad. The little paper covered with German writing, passed from hand to hand – the guests showed it to each other, read it and were gladdened by the strong family ties that even a distance of several thousand versts couldn't sever. And, in addition, each one of them knew that here in the city, Strauss had another wife and several children... A man with two families! But he was a wealthy bank director. Distinguished citizens and old enthusiasts of strict Christian morality did not hesitate to seek his company, shake his hand, wish him well and smile kindly about the warm greetings from wife and children. Gold can do anything!

"Today you're a bachelor too," Tilaks laughed and clinked Strauss's glass, "we're all bachelors. Gentlemen, I want you to feel like you're at a bachelors' club!"

And that was how the gentlemen felt. Not a single lady – so there was no sense in being coy. Right from the start, this evening had a relaxed, more intimate quality, which engendered loose talk laced with double entendre. Every congratulation, toast and song had a slightly piquant quality to it, even if it was nothing more than a meaningful gesture, a brazen smile, a passing wink. And the more time passed, the looser and louder they became.

After the official dinner, the guests scattered. The three large rooms and one small room were full of people. In the first room, the guests sat around the long, half-cleared dining table and were simply enjoying themselves. In the second room, those who liked sarcastic, juvenile stories were gathered around a pair of the more skilful storytellers. In the third room, the more clear-headed and wiser crowd discussed campaigning, the intentions and prospects of the bank leadership and opposition, and how various business matters stood in relation to them. In the small room three parties were playing cards around three tables, and around them were three more groups of people composed of those who didn't have a place to sit, those who had less money and those who just wanted to watch out of curiosity.

Beer, champagne, foreign liqueurs and cognacs flowed without measure. Crude anecdotes and increasingly loud roaring laughter resounded without end.

"Listen, you there, the journalist!" Blics pointed his finger across the table directly at Kārlis Roblapainis's face. "What kind of rubbish are you printing in that paper of yours! That story – well, who did it come from?"

"What do you mean – rubbish?" said Kārlis Roblapainis, clearly agitated by the sudden attack. "A scene from our present-day civic life portrayed evocatively..."

"Literature does not mirror life; you won't convince me that it does. Art is not a substitute for life. Either it discusses universal and timeless or historical and mythical elements, or it doesn't exist at all. We don't have any literature yet; we only have fiction dealing with the questions of the day, journalism written in a fictionalised style. All of our literature is just a product of topical satire."

"If you'll allow me!" Kārlis Roblapainis closed the top button of his coat nervously. "The universal and eternal don't stand alone and apart from life. All that occurs in everyday life and within the man of today –"

"Cheers!" Blics clinked Zīle's glass and, not taking his eyes off his opponent, rose to his feet. He puffed out his chest with its deep-cut waistcoat and white, pleated shirt front. "Trends in literature aren't literature. What are you complaining about: our citizenry doesn't appreciate literature! Where is it then? Give us true artistic literature. We don't need popular editorials; we already have plenty of lightly satirical chatter..."

A loud wave of laughter, flowing out through the doors of the adjoining room, overpowered Blics's voice. There, a stout older man with a clean-shaven face and a garland of light hair ringing the bare, shiny top of his head, his hands pressed against his knees, his eyes half-closed, waited for the noise to subside a bit.

"And anyway, in our day mothers were younger than daughters. Liquor, yeast, and original sin were all twice as strong in the old days! And if a son-in-law is forced to choose between his wife and mother-in-law..."

The sound of Padegs's raised, solemn-sounding voice came from the third room.

"Those who campaign to limit the bank's operations are either simpletons or blatantly wish us ill. Capitalism has now reached the stage of development where the central and leading role has been taken up by financial capital: banks and savings. Financial capital is capital – one could say – in its purest form, both the peak and distillation of capital simultaneously, the synthesis of capital. The signature characteristic of this kind of capital is its exceptional drive for growth. Larger capital mercilessly absorbs small capital..."

Thwack! Thwack! In the small room the cards slapped down on the green cloth covering the tables, and handfuls of gold coins jingled quietly as they changed hands...

After midnight, only the most resilient remained in the four rooms. The older men had gone home, and those who were too drunk had been bedded down there so they could sleep it off. Gradually, those who remained left one at a time. Without any undue ceremony, without saying farewell – they moved towards the front, put on their coats, and got into motor cars or cabs. Only three or four lanterns still burned in the yard of the summerhouse; the chauffeurs napped, huddled on their masters' seats, the idling engines hissing softly.

At last, most of the rooms were almost empty. Only the very closest friends remained. There were ten people in the large back room, and six in the smaller one: Strauss, Tilaks, Sveilis, Blics, Bebrītis, and Taube. Four of them were playing cards, Strauss was rolling around on the sofa half-drunk and Taube made sure there was no shortage of drinks.

There was plenty to drink, but an absence of something else was palpable. They drank without sense or measure; they played until their nerves were dulled from excitement; they laughed until their jaws hurt and they were so bored that even the sauciest anecdote seemed dull and grey. But of all this, something rather subtle and unfathomable remained: it congealed and rested in the depth of the soul until with a thousand quivering feelers, it moved outwards softly and slimily but also carefully and relentlessly. It had been waiting quietly, coyly, shrunken in the large crowd and din. But now it began to rise to the surface. Memories of vulgar anecdotes, games leading to overstimulated and jittery nerves, swirling alcoholic vapour – they all supported and encouraged it. It was now moving as if it were rushing up steps. Flushed faces glowing deep red, glassy eyes were blazing brightly, trembling fingers fluttered bashfully, but it was no longer hiding, but begging to reveal itself in gazes and overtly in speech.

A degenerate fantasy craves something unique and unfamiliar, like desserts that are specially selected to suit various after-dinner liqueurs and champagne from abroad. The desire for gold, the all-powerful enslaver of men, yearned for something impossible, for something which had never yet existed, which no other hand had held. There's a strange satisfaction in stepping with a muddy boot onto freshly fallen pure white snow, or pouring dregs from a glass onto a newly opened blossom. Three expensive vases had been tipped over on the dining table, and there were giant bouquets of roses soaked in red wine as if lying in pools of their own blood...

Tilaks and Sveilis whispered to each other, and winked mysteriously to the others as they got up. They didn't ask; the abilities of both friends were tried and tested in such matters. They listened as a motor car whirred past the windows. They spoke quietly and waited. They waited and drank. They drank and slowly began to grow impatient.

But then the motor car disappeared past the windows again. And a moment later the doors opened wide as two women came in accompanied by Tilaks and Sveilis. One of them was young, slender and graceful, with a thick braid over her shoulder and the black apron of a high school student in front. The other one was politely reserved, smiling shyly as if she had been pressured into coming, but that was exactly what made her so attractive and valued... Mrs. Bērziņš and Milda Caune...

Clutching the sides of the tables, pushing against their chairs, all of the men rose to their feet, attempting to look dignified as they stood up and bowed. They greeted their pretty guests with exaggerated chivalry.

Milda didn't notice that the two of them had been separated into different rooms. She didn't notice that Tilaks, the last to come into the room, quietly locked the door behind him. She didn't notice whether she undressed or was undressed by others... She only saw that one gentleman had slipped her jewellery into her hand-warmer, and another had her coat around his shoulders. Her galoshes were on the card table and a student with a thick, black moustache was attempting to stick two wine glasses into them like the blood-soaked rose bouquets.

She was sitting in a simple white wool dress on the table and six pairs of probing eyes stood around staring at her. She began to feel terrible; her breasts lifted and sank, her eyes filled with tears... But she composed and restrained herself. She didn't want to seem dumb. And there was really nothing to fear from all of these kind, refined men...

"Please, miss!" someone sitting down next to her thrust a small, narrow glass into her hand. Another sat down next to her on the other side.

"You want to get me drunk?" she responded shyly. But on realising that what she had said was impolite, she took it and drank. And smiled – at one and then at the other one...

Roberts, a pair of skates tied together and thrown over his shoulder, opened the door to his brother's office. He wasn't there. He walked over to his brother's bedroom door and opened it. Yes...still lying around in bed.

"Could you give me a little money – about – ten, fifteen?"

At first, Sveilis pretended not to have heard him. But then he opened his bloodshot, sleep-filled, furious eyes.

"What? Money? Again! Have you gone crazy! Money every day! Where do you put it?"

Roberts got angry. His brother's unkindness surprised and hurt him. He had asked this same question so many times, and his brother had never said "no" to him, never said a word, just found his wallet and gave him the money. He was so used to getting it every time he asked, and getting the amount he'd asked for, that he hardly believe this unexpected refusal. His brother's truculence could only have been caused by a bad hangover.

"Ten or fifteen..." he repeated. "I need it..."

"You need it?" Sveilis mocked him. His voice was harsh and flinty from the previous night's drinking. "You all need it! Money, money! That's all I hear all day long. You've cornered me like a pack of dogs. Where am I supposed to get it from!"

Roberts slammed the door angrily. "Monkey..." he hissed to himself. He almost knocked down Made, who was going from the kitchen to her room. He didn't notice Made's tear-stained eyes or her anger, distracted as he was by his own, and didn't know that she'd had her own misfortune that morning.

He was incensed and couldn't shake off that feeling of annoyance. He'd really needed those ten or fifteen roubles. Yesterday he and Milda had seen an attractive two-volume book, A Man and a Woman at the second-hand bookshop and agreed to buy it today on their way home from the skating rink. What was he going to do now? Milda will make fun of him again: rich Sveilis's brother is suddenly penniless.

In his anger, Roberts reviewed his recent past and was forced to recognise that he had probably been spending a bit too much lately. There was one memory that came to mind. He'd asked for fifty roubles from his brother to pay the school, but had ended up spending it all on those girls and his friends. It was the time that Fatty got into an argument with a policeman and barely escaped, and Milda, who'd been very drunk, had sat down on a snow bank on the corner by the park. Later he was thrown out of school for non-payment... It was lucky that his brother was so inattentive: he had no idea he wasn't going to his classes anymore and no longer had the right to wear his uniform.

Art school – well, there's no big worry there. It was all just rubbish anyway; they didn't actually teach anything the least bit practical there, nothing. It would have made more sense to start taking courses to become a surveyor or accountant. Milda also talked about accounting; Miss Ziepēns had threatened her with non-promotion to the next grade and expulsion. What a goose... and what about her! Running around with students... and going to the Northern Lights tavern with young Lodziņš... and who knows where else! Accounting – what's there to learn? And you can get a position right away. Fifty, even seventy-five roubles a month and more later. Work three or four days and your evenings are free...

Roberts waited for Milda in the agreed spot. But she didn't come. It was long after the time they'd arranged to meet. He became angry again; lately he became upset and angry about every little thing. What can that girl be thinking? That he needs her; is that it? The streets are full of girls. As long as you know what to do and have money...

He stood there for another few minutes, then turned around and walked quickly towards Mrs. Bērziņš's apartment. He'll show that girl! She's not that special!

Mrs. Bērziņš opened the door only half-dressed, with unkempt hair, circles under her eyes, still drowsy from too little sleep, flushed and agitated. To his surprise, Roberts heard a strange sound further inside; it sounded like heaving sobs, like water dripping and the wash basin splashing... Old habit made him want to push Mrs. Bērziņš aside and go in. But she angrily shoved him back.

"Where the hell are you going! You've got no business here!" Roberts looked back wide-eyed.

"Is Miss Caune at home?"

"Miss Caune isn't here and this isn't your home!" Mrs. Bērziņš screamed back angrily, slamming the door, and locking it from the inside.

Roberts stood there for a moment, shrugged his shoulders, and slowly went down the stairs. What could be going on? She looked so utterly strange. Maybe Milda wasn't at home? No, it couldn't have been anybody but her that was moving around back there. And it definitely seemed like she was crying. Maybe she was ill? No matter, but he had to find out what was going on. He wasn't going to be treated like some kind of clown. Just then he remembered the time Lausks had shoved him down the stairs.

When he got to the main entrance to the flats, he straightened up, and then rushed back upstairs. He wasn't some kind of a clown. He had to know...

He rattled the door handle and Mrs. Bērziņš's shrieking voice could be heard immediately coming from inside.

"I'll drench your eyes with boiling water if you don't leave!"

On the other side, the door of another flat opened and strangers began to look out. Roberts got embarrassed and went downstairs again.

Pensive and angry he walked back home. A tantrum, nothing else. That girl just gets more capricious with every passing day. Why did he have to put with that! Anybody who knows what to do and has money can get it every time and as much as he likes. But did he actually have any money? His thoughts turned again to that point and he made a firm decision to ask his brother again. His brother had to give him money! What was his brother thinking? He moves him to the city and then suddenly stops giving him any! What's there to do here without money?

But Sveilis wasn't at home anymore; he'd woken up and gone to the bank. Made had also gone out. Roberts asked his mother, but she didn't have any either. He immediately became upset and began to complain that he doesn't get a single rouble from anybody anymore. Lonija was cursing like mad, promising to sue and leave. Tomorrow night there won't be anything to eat...

Roberts got bored listening to her. In his anger a strange thought occurred to him. If he doesn't get what he needs voluntarily, then he'll just have to go get it himself. And he needed it: nobody can live in the city without money. He quietly went into his brother's office and locked both doors from the inside. His brother sometimes took money from the desk drawers. He knew where he kept the keys; he'll just take a big stack so he has enough to last for a while. After all, his brother never really knows how much money he has. He won't notice a thing.

But this time there wasn't any. In one drawer there was a worn ten kopeck coin and seven kopecks in copper change. Furious, Roberts hit his fist against the floor. Bouncing and jingling, the tiny coins rolled around and off into every corner. He tore out the drawers one after another, emptied them out, mixed it all up, and pushed them back in. Just then a bundle appeared from somewhere in the back. Ah! Roberts seemed to catch fire. So, he kept things like that in there too! His fingers shook feverishly as he lined them up on the desk. A shiny card sat in his palm: an entire pile of obscene shameless pictures. Blushing and red-faced, trembling from desire and shame, he looked them over. Images formed in his mind wrapped in a haze filled with fantasies... He'd forgotten his mouth was still open and saliva trickled down his chin...

Clutching it tightly, Roberts spirited his plunder back to his room. And he didn't understand that it wasn't him holding those pictures, but them that had him in their powerful, burning claws. He didn't notice that he was now their life-long captive, a slave to the most base and vile tyrant.

But staring at the pictures, his imagination gradually tired and his instincts began to yearn for a concrete, tangible object for his feelings. Milda came to mind and everything he'd experienced with her. They had done a lot, but still not that last, that final step. Though ruined and spoiled, their childlike shyness and self-consciousness had protected them from taking that final step. They'd instinctively pulled back every time from that boundary, which separates men from beasts... But now the protective barrier stood broken. Now he was rushing headlong into a tempting, mystifying, disgustingly alluring world.

Roberts threw on his coat and hurried away again. His agitated blood thundered in his ears, his enflamed instincts swirled all sorts of thoughts and fantasies around in his head. Maybe that damned widow had locked her away and was tormenting her? Why didn't she let him in? He wanted to involve the policeman at the street corner, but decided he wouldn't be treated with the appropriate respect. So he ran over to see his brother at the bank and got there out of breath.

He didn't notice the sour faces of the directors, and called his brother out into the corridor. He told him everything and was visibly upset. He shared all of his suspicions and asked for his help, without perceiving that Sveilis was becoming somewhat circumspect.

"Some kind of misfortune, you think?" Sveilis tried to laugh facetiously. "It's just your imagination, nothing else. Both she and that Bērziņš woman are the same. That tramp hangs off of every man's neck. And that girl is no better. Both of them must have been out carousing last night."

Roberts became even more agitated. "Never! She has promised me."

Now Sveilis actually had to laugh. "There's not much bawdy girls like that won't promise you. Don't believe them. They'll pull one over on you a dozen times in a row. They'll swear up and down to you and in the meantime go around with somebody else. She's not pure – that's for sure."

Pure or not, Roberts didn't care at all. He just needed to see her. "I can't live without her..." he groaned.

Sveilis became more serious. "You know, don't get too tangled up with that girl. That's not good for you at all. You'll miss school, and then that's that. And she's a tramp through and through."

Roberts left feeling even more miserable than when he'd arrived. He didn't know where to start or what to do. But he couldn't just stand around. He wandered aimlessly around the city. He walked to Milda's apartment and stood on the other side of the street staring at the windows, but he couldn't see anything. So he wandered on.

When he came back again a while later he looked on with amazement as his brother came out of those same doors... He walked out with a spring in his step, turned up the collar of his coat, sat down in the cab, and was off. Roberts kept looking on after him and couldn't understand. Why had he been there? But... maybe he went to some other apartment? No, for some reason Roberts was certain that he'd come from Milda's. He couldn't understand a thing anymore. But it just seemed that something was binding and entangling him, winding around him. Soon he'd trip over his own feet and wouldn't be able to move his arms anymore, and would fall. He climbed up the stairs filled once more with dark foreboding.

The door was open this time and he didn't see Mrs. Bērziņš. Milda dressed in a white nightgown was kneeling on a chair, her elbows resting on the table. She was holding her head with both hands and was looking at an album. She must have recognised his steps, but only turned her head slightly. Roberts coughed at the door.

"Why didn't you come? I was waiting and waiting..." He wanted to seem upset and bitter, but his voice sounded weak and almost tearful.

Milda climbed off the chair and closed the album.

"I'm not going anywhere, leave me alone!"

He was shocked by the strangely dry and hate-filled sound of her voice. Now he felt like he understood even less.

"What's wrong with you? Are you ill?"

"What business is it of yours! I didn't want to come and so I didn't... and that's it!"

In the dim light he couldn't see her face clearly. But it seemed unusually pale, her eyes wide and strangely dark.

"I've been walking around here all this time... thinking that that Bērziņš woman was keeping you here..."

She looked at him with such scorn and hatred that it made him feel sick. If he'd known this would happen – he wouldn't have come at all...

"I-diot!" she hissed. "What did you drag yourself over here for! I want you out of my sight."

"Milda, sweetie... what's wrong with you?" He was choking back tears and trying to catch hold of her hand in its wide, open sleeve. "You're ill..."

But she yanked her hand away and moved it so quickly that all he felt was a gust of wind move across his face.

"Quiet, you clod! Don't lay a finger on me! I'll let you have it straight in the eyes!" And then she stamped her foot. "Get out of here – now! Or I'll call Mrs. Bērziņš."

Standing on the other side of the half-closed door he stopped and shrugged. He didn't know whether to laugh or cry.

"Crazy or drunk..." he said half-laughing, half-crying.

"Don't show your face around here anymore!" was the one last angry shout that came from Milda. Then the door closed and was locked from the inside. And then another one closed further in, the steps fell silent, and everything was quiet.

Roberts felt punch drunk, as if someone had hit him when he wasn't expecting it. He staggered back out onto the street. Pushed and shoved by those moving past him, he wandered around the middle of the crowd. He went a bit in one direction and then the crowd's motion pushed him back in the direction he'd come from. He couldn't focus and couldn't understand anything. It was so hard, so unspeakably hard. The river of desire cut off midstream rose up again and took his breath away. His legs wobbled like a drunk's.

He had no idea how he'd ended up inside the Baltika. He didn't have any money, but knew he could get what he wanted on credit from Juškans. Plus - young Skrastiņš would also gladly pay for him if he needed it.

Skrastiņš didn't have much to do at the billiard table today. He'd been out somewhere in the city, met someone, got a little drunk and was jolly, talkative and animated. He ordered a half-carafe of spirits and a couple of lampreys right away; they both drank and had a bite to eat. Roberts immediately felt better. Skrastiņš recounted his adventures from the previous night. Some drunk had started to raise a racket - they'd given him a good beating and handed him over to the police. He pointed to where he'd scratched him with his teeth... Then he started up about other things. Hadn't Roberts heard what had happened with that brother of his? Everyone was saying he'd be bankrupt soon. And nothing's going right for him, that's more than clear. He'd taken his last kopeck out of the bank. And wasn't paying anybody. Yesterday there weren't any pork chops. They won't give them to him on credit anymore. Today the agent from the brewery had threatened to cut off the beer - if he didn't pay by Monday. The cook had been cursing up a storm in the kitchen: beggars and cowards, nothing else! Wanted to live like lords - off other people's money. Washing the floors with champagne, but don't even have a bread rind of their own to eat at home. Their daughters pulling a hundred roubles out of their pockets, but they can't pay their workers ten measly roubles... Roberts heard it all, but couldn't be bothered to muster up any interest in his brother's money matters. Then the topic turned to more intimate matters. Skrastiņš told him about his newest adventures with women. But stopped when he remembered that lately he'd been thinking quite a bit about Made, so it was probably better not to mention it to Roberts. He began to ask him this and that, but Roberts had nothing to share about his sister. His own unhappiness kept weighing him down. He wanted to tell Skrastiņš about it and ask him for advice, but then he started up himself. He moved closer, laughed eagerly and began describing – embellishing it as he spoke – the previous night's orgies at Strauss's summer house. Even the tiniest details always come to light at the pub... Sveilis and Tilaks were the wildest of all... They'd taken the motor car and picked up that Bērziņš woman and her boarder... Like an ugly, disgusting, bewildering nightmare, Roberts watched this exaggerated, gaudy depiction of brutish debauchery unfold before him... He'd experienced, seen, and heard a great deal, but he could never have imagined depraved fantasies like these... And it was his brother! And the girl he'd thought was only his, the girl he wouldn't have let anyone lay a finger on! Her! Yes – he remembered what he'd just seen, he remembered that Bērziņš woman, he remembered Milda, he remembered his brother, and knew right away that it was all true. He had to believe every single word of it.

So, that's what his beloved was like, the one he pined for and protected! But that only made him feel a hollow kind of painful sorrow. Like a salty, green wave, boundless hatred rose up within him against his brother, the one who had stolen the only treasure he had from him. Wounded pride, grief about all he'd lost, and despair blew around like a winter wind through his mind and jabbed at him with their sharp icy needles. He drank and drank, but couldn't get drunk anymore. He got up and went outside.

He had a plan... Not really a plan. He'd listened to it all and knew right away what he had to do. It was as if his senses and brain were a mechanical device that some outside will using its strange fingers was manipulating as it wished. If his brother had happened to be right there on the corner, he would've pounced on him with his fists, choked him with his fingers, bitten him with his teeth... But he wasn't there. Roberts went home, undressed, lay down on his back in bed, clasped his hands behind his head, and listened. He waited for him to come home.

As soon as the door opened outside, he recognised him right away. And only then did he realise that he didn't have any kind of a weapon. He needed to buy a revolver, but all he had was a small penknife in his pocket... No matter. He'd strangle, crush, and destroy him with the weight of his hatred and disgust.

He shrank back. Could it be... that his brother was coming right to him? Here, where boundless anger and death awaited him... certain, inescapable and unavoidable death! But still he came. He turned the knob and it immediately became light in the room... A bit drunk, friendly as always and smiling, his brother stood in the middle of the room and looked at Roberts.

"Are you sleeping? Are you sick too?" He laughed gently. "It seems like that's the order of the day.... I went – where you told me about earlier – to see that Bērziņš woman. You know, it was nothing serious. Just a bit sour, the both of them; a hangover. If you'd only seen how the two of them were living it up last night! Maybe you've already heard; Tilaks brought them to Strauss's party... The Bērziņš woman is an old bitch, everyone knows what she's like. But that girl isn't any better. A tramp through and through..." He laughed again. But now his laughter had a strange, repugnant tinge to it. He must have heard it himself and fell silent.

Roberts listened as he lay on his back. The time had come... To get up, grab him, strangle him... But yet he stayed on his back. Not moving a muscle. A moment earlier he'd imagined it completely differently. But now, looking at this familiar, kind, smiling face, he couldn't... No, he couldn't move a finger. His brother... the same as before, as always... It seemed unbelievable that he'd ever have been able to do something wicked to him... He didn't know himself, his brother or Milda anymore. He moved feebly and groaned.

"All of you... I know..."

It would've been better if he'd stayed quiet... He immediately felt the last dregs of his anger and thirst for revenge scatter and evaporate. He felt his own body as a useless, worthless rag thrown on the floor, broken and trampled, powerless and weak. Nobody was to blame for it and no one could do anything to help. He felt incredibly sorry for himself. It felt like a lead weight was pressing down on him. Gritting his teeth, clenching his fists so that his nails dug into his palms, he fought against his choking tears.

Sveilis blew his nose and calmed down again. He came closer and spoke in an even kinder and friendlier way. "Don't worry about that...girl. You're naive and don't know city girls. You think all kinds of things, but she's put one over on you a dozen times already. The same kind of rat as that Bērziņš woman. She's already being thrown out of high school – wants to work the till at my wine shop. I told her to come – I've got no objections. Forty roubles, just like Miss Zvaigzne got..." He stopped talking. He thought Roberts had said something. But no. He must have misheard. "The streets are full of girls like that. Spit on them, nothing else... Listen. How are you doing at that school of yours? Not all that great? Well, all that drawing is rubbish, just like music. A person only gets ahead with a practical trade...Next week there will be a meeting – we're transforming the Savings and Loans into a credit union. Then it'll be a completely different story. Money will come in by the cartload. We'll need to double the number of employees. If you want... that is, only if you want to, there'll be a place for you. A hundred roubles a month – enough for a start, right?" He paused for a moment and coughed. "You think about it. It's not a bad thing... They'll complain, make a scandal, but the devil himself can't do anything to us. You'll see how we'll live... Think about it and tell me: yes or no. I'm not pushing – only if you want to."

He stood for a moment, then walked out quietly.

Roberts got up, turned off the light. He lay face down in bed and cried huge tears.

Sveilis had high hopes, but they just refused to be fulfilled.
Crisis followed crisis, as the money situation became more and more complicated. He could neither really work at the

bank anymore, nor give his attention to the shop. His entire time passed running around and ensuring that complaints weren't filed against his bills of exchange and that all of it didn't finally do him in. He was forced to get involved with dodgy characters, take risks on dubious operations. But there was nothing to be done. He was no longer his own master; he could no longer act according to his own desires and wishes. The same force which lifted a man like a splinter on a wave or plunged him into the depths, was now incessantly and inexorably pulling him forward, throwing him back and tossing him to and fro. Feeble and useless struggling – that's all he could manage now.

To restrain himself, to live more frugally? Nothing helped anymore. In the end, how much did he really ever spend drinking, playing cards and carousing? Where thousands were needed, hundreds mattered little. Profiteering, risking, stealing – all of that was nothing, the only thing that mattered was staying afloat. Just to keep the water from washing into his mouth, suffocating and drowning him. The more complicated his circumstances became, the stronger his will to survive – to have a chance to enjoy life again, to toss money around by the handful, and to show all his enemies and those who envied him what he was capable of... And he kept going – all day long, from morning to night. But it seemed like the ball of tiny complications couldn't be unwound and the mountain of tiny problems felt endless. Freeing himself from one problem, he'd become ensnared in another – and would become even more entangled than before. Various trifles, a hundred roubles grabbed from here or there, a bill of exchange obtained thanks to friendship – he understood that none of it was helping. He'd need tens of thousands to have his hands free again.

In all the less familiar banks, credit was shrinking or was cut off completely. He tried in vain, going to directors' meetings and making his rounds visiting private apartments. Nobody turned him down to his face, but later on in a roundabout way he'd find out that it was all in vain and nothing would come of it. He knew all too well: various rumours spread about him behind his back, which were composed of one-part truth and ten-parts malicious lies. Rarely could he identify the actual guilty party, but Sveilis was suspicious of almost everybody. He didn't even trust his best friends anymore, showing them a kind, smiling face, while secretly watching them. But it seemed like his friends now didn't trust him either – their friendships seemed artificial, a strange chill could be felt in their speech, something suspicious in their smiles and sympathetic handshakes. But, after all, he wasn't yet materially or morally bankrupt. Those unsuccessful branches – yes, they needed to be closed... Unpaid wages... Accrued interest... Delayed payments... Various risky combinations... Yes, but who hadn't had something like that happen to them in their day! Nothing illegal or punishable had been proven about him yet. And had he ever denied anybody anything or been jealous of anyone? Sveilis felt his current difficult circumstances as a profound, undeserved injustice. Deep lines formed across his smooth brow. So that he could forget for just a moment, he needed to drink and get drunk. His face swelled noticeably, and large, watery bags appeared beneath his eyes.

   He couldn't depend on anyone else, he had to grip on tightly to Unity. The appointed day when the Savings and Loans would be transformed into a mutual credit union approached incredibly slowly. But when that day finally arrived they would be able to expand and free up their operations by a factor of ten, as they'd be able to attract deposits again. But Bramberģis and Lodziņš, and Paeglītis, and the entire opposition wasn't asleep. The opposition campaign took on unseen proportions and was carried out with unprecedented ferocity. Stop this change, throw out the current clique, bring back the former men of honour – that was the opposition faction's slogan. Voices from the community, the press – they used it all, just so they could depose the current heads of the bank. Sveilis knew they couldn't sleep either. They couldn't allow this old, reactionary, decrepit gang to push aside men who have worked quite selflessly for the benefit of the public and have considerably increased the bank's balance over such a short time. All of their forces were being mobilised, all of their reserves used. Sveilis knew they had to be careful and not spare their resources, as the board itself lacked the desired unanimity: Blics had become suspicious and doubtful, and they weren't certain that he wasn't secretly supporting the opposition and giving away protected secrets.

Sveilis worked most enthusiastically of all. But now and then he noticed that he no longer had the kind of influence he once did. Others would speak to him, listen to him and then turn their backs. He no longer had his old moneyman's reputation or received the respect given to rich men. He couldn't be sure the elections would go his way. Nowadays a person couldn't trust his own brother. But nothing could be done about that. Sveilis hid his bitterness and dark premonitions deep inside and went along with the crowd. And seeing the way in which he sometimes still drank, caroused and frittered away money, a person less familiar with him would never think that he was up to his neck in debts, that bankruptcy was right around the corner for him.

Decision day arrived. The evening before, Padegs, the well-known expert on the national economy, a democratic public figure and high school teacher, gave a lecture at the popular social club on the importance of banks in the life of modern Capitalist economies and industry. He reviewed the history of financial capital, banks, and credit as a whole in Western Europe and then turned to the conditions in their homeland. He described the battles between the founders of the first Latvian bank with the organised capital held by foreigners. He showed the incremental growth of national credit, its formation and concentration. He proved convincingly and irrefutably that all capital and therefore also all Latvian national financial capital possessed an unstoppable tendency towards expansion throughout the structures found in the upper levels of the economy, and that it would reach ever deeper into all aspects of the nation's cultural and intellectual life. Then he moved from pure economics to national life and politics, tying it all together and painting it in attractive colours. With irrefutable statistics he proved that only thanks to the continuing expansions of bank operations had Latvian citizenry come to be what it is now. He spoke very convincingly about the high interest that small depositors received on their deposits at Latvian banks. He acknowledged that in a cultured democracy there could be no other way and that such a democracy must also acknowledge that the savings of small depositors are the safest and most productive in institutions run by their own people. He stated that it was vital to expand the domain of work done by credit institutions to its maximum possible legal extent as well as to attract as much of a proportion of all circles of society as possible and involve them in this work. This was because we live in the age of democracy, when all intellectual and material culture is democratised and therefore capital must also be democratised...

His lecture was followed by long, thunderous applause. The speaker had to step back up to the lectern twice to bow. Each time he would step back reluctantly, bowing seriously and coolly. Science paid no heed to whether it was cheered or jeered... It was made certain ahead of time that those deciding Unity's fate as well as its current leadership would be there to hear Padegs's lecture. The loudest applause of all came from the front rows where the members of the board and leadership were sitting with their close acquaintances. Inspiration had to lay the path for their march to victory the following night... Everyone applauded and then fell silent. No one was truly satisfied. Why didn't he say a single word about the important anticipated event? He'd talked at length on Western Europe, but uttered not a word regarding the shameless, un-Latvian opposition campaign... Bankers and experts didn't understand that in order to ensure victory, there was nothing more important than a carefully crafted psychological atmosphere. They also didn't understand that a party couldn't win if it showed all its cards to its opposition at the wrong moment. But no one doubted Padegs's abilities or intentions. If he hadn't spoken today, he would've spoken tomorrow.

And he spoke tomorrow as well. After several hours of terrible yelling and cursing from both sides, after one member of the board and three members of the opposition were escorted from the hall by the police, when five opposition members had attacked and he'd been defended by ten members of the ruling party, when it became clear that Blics truly had been a traitor and stood openly on the side of the opposition, Padegs climbed up to the lectern, slowly and solemnly, without any undue theatricality. Even the fiercest opponents and noisiest rabble-rousers stopped and began listening – so great was the respect for Padegs and the beauty of his speech.

Party divisions? Those exist throughout life and nature: no individual and no community institution can avoid them. One need only to look and consider whether these divisions are deliberate and desirable or unintentional. Who has suffered from these party divisions? Is it the person whom the old board didn't wish to give fifteen hundred, the person whom the current board was ready to loan twenty-five hundred, but who now wants a new board so that he can borrow thirty-five hundred? Isn't it obvious: if a new board promises him thirty-five hundred, he'll need an even newer one, that'll loan him forty-five hundred... L'appetit vient en mangeant – the more you eat, the greater your appetite. But that's like blackmailing the bank, and in such a case only children and simpletons can speak of party divisions... Applause and hurrahs interrupted the speaker. He waited a moment for them to calm down... Or perhaps it's due to factional divisions that the board hasn't allowed itself to be convinced and has begun to collect on a guaranteed debt before the end of its term. But any serious judge will see the board's admirable tolerance and impartiality in precisely this case. It has not considered the debtor to be less trustworthy than the guarantor, it understood that the debtor is the weaker party and didn't wish to burden the weaker party while sparing the stronger one. The borrower and guarantor were both members of the bank, and the board prudently did not wish to involve itself in their personal relationship with each other... Applause. Sietiṇsons, red-faced and sweaty, jumped to his feet somewhere in the back of the hall waving his fists and yelling: "Swindlers! Crooks!" The police took him out and issued a fine... Clique politics? If all of the wealthy property owners and honourable citizens who have gathered together at Unity are a clique – tell me then, where is a clique not to be found? In that case, every society and association which has been established based on a foundation of mutual acquaintance is a clique. Then the politics of every bank are clique politics. But that's how it must be and God help us if it ever were otherwise. If loans were made without any criteria at all, a questionable bond for one, an uncertain guarantor pulled from who knows where, then that would be playing around with money deposited based on trust, that would mean a dishonest use of the trust of the community. The board cannot act irresponsibly with the kopecks given to it by its little brothers, and it speaks highly of it, if it entrusts that money only to solvent individuals well-known in the community... Applause and hurrahs. Sveilis couldn't restrain himself: he applauded, jumped to his feet, and cast withering glances at those who might have thought differently... An illegal expulsion? Padegs raised his voice... Against such... individuals... who do not refrain from running to complain, who denounce and publicly defame honourable and well-known members of the board – indeed, someone who is not ashamed of behaving like a street thug and hooligan right here at the shareholders' meeting – against such individuals, no measure is too severe. The board deserves gratitude for its moral fortitude. And encouragement not to tolerate those who ruin the blessed unanimity among its members, who secretly act as Jesuits and traitors behind their backs... Applause – jeers – and even more thunderous applause. A terrible racket. Blics and Strauss leapt to their feet, ran at each other, shaking their fists, and seemed to be ready to jump on top of each other. But their friends and supporters pulled them apart by their coats, separating them again... Not to transform it into a credit union, so that the less wealthy would have easier access to cheap credit? At this time, when all capital is concentrating so quickly and expanding, when bank transactions have multiplied so impressively and their balances have grown! It would be foolishness, self-imposed defeat, castration. Who does it harm if capital accrues and profits increase? Nobody, not the wealthy, not the poor! Today is a historic day; the entire nation looks to the members of Unity and waits to see whether they will stay in their own narrow little corner or whether they'll venture out into the wide world of culture, taking themselves, their nation, and all of humanity towards a happy future...

Applause, hurrahs, stomping of feet and rattling of chairs... Jeers and hisses. But the noise from the supporters soon overpowered and defeated that of the opponents. The results could be seen. Padegs stepped down and slowly took his seat in the front row. Sveilis turned and kept vigorously shaking his hand and gazed into his eyes lovingly – as one would with a brother or bride.

The vote approving the transformation of the Unity Savings and Loans into the Sixteenth Mutual Credit Union passed by an overwhelming majority. The purchase by the board of the lot was approved as well as three hundred thousand designated for construction of the new building. With a fifty-vote majority, Blics was recognised as being harmful to the work of society and destructive to its goals, and failed to be elected. Padegs took his place. Sveilis kept his place among the directors with only a fifteen-vote majority – but he kept it nevertheless.

The victory was celebrated as was to be expected. Again, for two days there was no sign of Sveilis at home or at the bank. But after the initial jubilation came the hangover. The defeated opposition party complained, sent delegations, spread preposterous stories in obliging newspapers. For now, while these matters were being investigated, the meeting's decisions were not affirmed. Blics didn't show his face at the bank, but was said to be diligently travelling to Petrograd and who knows where else. For now, everything stayed as it was. Only new complications, new problems, and new debts were added on.

Skrastiņš was warned not to let anyone come into the directors' office unannounced or without warning. But there were some who didn't want to wait and couldn't be deterred – untroubled by the presence of employees or the public, seething and swearing like mad. Then Sveilis would throw on his coat and make his way out, down the back steps.

But he couldn't feel safe on the street either, as he might accidentally run into one of his creditors. It seemed like they lurked on every corner like dogs. Folding up his collar, sinking down into his shoulders, Sveilis walked quickly – as if he were in a tremendous hurry to reach an important appointment, as if he didn't have a single moment to spare. If he happened to have twenty kopecks in his pocket, then he'd take a cab and drive there. But he often didn't have that much... In truth, he didn't have anywhere to hurry off to, he didn't know which street to turn down and which not to. Home? But he wasn't any safer there. They came there too and there was no getting rid of them. His mother, sister, brother – they'd all been told to say that he wasn't home. They all lied as best they could, but they rarely fooled anyone. Nobody believed them and would wait around right there by the door. And it happened a couple of times that Sveilis, after two or three hours, came out of his apartment, and somewhere from the curve of the stairs or the bench along the side a threatening figure would suddenly appear ... The cinema specialist had fled, and so Sveilis and Gailis each owed five thousand... five thousand – for used equipment, and films, and the set up, and unpaid rent... Rozentals had sued... The shop assistants from the two closed branches had sued Sveilis for non-payment of wages...

He'd already lost two court cases and been sentenced. This week they'll be after him with a court order for five hundred roubles, next week for eighteen hundred... Utter madness!

Tired, nearly at his wit's end, Sveilis rode up to his apartment. He walked angrily past his mother and lay down on the sofa in his office... He couldn't understand who was to blame, but knew only that a great injustice had been done to him. It pressed down on him like a weight. He was tired of the whole world, which was having its revenge on him. He didn't really want to drink anymore, nor could he even get drunk. If only he could have laid down and gone to sleep, but not even that... His nerves were completely ruined, always worried and agitated. He didn't want to, but couldn't stop himself from listening for the bell to ring again.

There was still one way out - but only one. He wanted to try. He thought about it all day long. He weighed it up this way and that, and decided that it should work out.

Mrs. Wilde... She had money without end. He needed to try and get it. If there was no other way, then he would marry her... She wasn't that old yet, or all that unattractive. And even if she had been - as long as there's money. There was no time to think about anything else anymore. This thing should work... Fricis had disappeared without a trace - some said he was wandering from tavern to tavern in the outskirts of the city, others that he'd boarded a ship and left the country. And was he any worse than Fricis? How many times now had he stopped by and been warmly received by her, always warmly. He would have preferred it if she had been more distant at first and then gradually opened up and become warmer. That's what he was used to and that would be a sign that everything was moving in the direction he wished. But perhaps the customs are different in more exalted circles... When he happened to have a rouble on hand, he'd send a bouquet of flowers to Mrs. Wilde. He'd pin his business card to it - only that, nothing else: Augusts Sveile, Jr., Director of the Sixteenth Credit Union. It should work- he couldn't imagine why it wouldn't. But now was his last chance, there was no more time to waste.

He got up, washed, oiled his hair, and put on cologne along with a clean collar and a white cravat. He put all of his rings on his fingers, the pin from the Cyclists' Association on the silk lapel of his jacket. He laboured over his moustache, then examined himself carefully in the mirror. He hadn't looked at himself so closely in some time and only now noticed how much he'd changed. He'd become fatter, much fatter – he could barely button up his brightly coloured waistcoat. It wasn't completely clean anymore either, he'd needed a new one long ago... His cheeks were too flabby and sagged down, his eyes seemed to somehow have narrowed. And his hair was much thinner – the dull sheen of his scalp was beginning to peek through. So that was the reason his mother had patted his head several times, sighing... Eh, he was angry at his mother, his father, the whole world... He'd grown old. But still...compared to Fricis... Sveilis puffed out his chest and pulled his head down towards his chest, so that his double chin dropped onto the snow-white collar.

But then he started looking around in his pockets. He couldn't find anything in his new suit. He looked in his old one. Without even opening it, he threw his wallet down onto the chest of drawers. He had a few silver and copper coins in his waistcoat pocket. He didn't count them – what for! A rouble and a half, it made no difference... He sank into the heaviness of his thoughts for a moment. He opened the door and stuck out his head.

"Mum!" He tried to call her in a gentle, kind voice, but surprised himself when it came out sounding stern and cold. They were all having their revenge on him. He was supposed to feed and support the whole lot of them. They all knew how to spend money, but not one of them earned a single bit... He hadn't even admitted to himself that he was ashamed that Lonija had left and now his mother was doing the maid's work...

His mother came, wiping her hands, which were still wet; she'd been washing laundry in the kitchen... Sveilis knew that she was doing the washing – but was so ashamed that he didn't want to admit it. And he was angry at his mother and the entire world.

"Just a second, just a second..." his mother murmured timidly. "My hands are wet: I washed the dishes a bit..."

Sveilis looked out the window as he tapped his fingers against the pane.

"Do you have... Did you spend that entire rouble yesterday?"

His mother began to wipe her hands on her apron with even more determination.

"Yes, all of it... Four pounds of salt for ten kopecks... We were completely out of tea – so twenty-five for that..."

Sveilis was taken aback and realised that he'd made the wrong choice in asking his mother. This made him even angrier.

"Never mind. I was just... You can go."

His mother wanted to go, but stayed anyway.

"Just now someone was looking for you again – that one with the grey beard and glasses. Terribly angry, promised to do all sorts of things..."

Sveilis forced himself to laugh mockingly.

"Let him promise. No real concern of mine. I'll be wrapping them all around my finger again soon... You always listen to whatever anyone is babbling on about and think who knows what."

"I don't think anything, son," his mother said sorrowfully. "But I do see that it's not easy for you. All of us depending on you. None of us earning anything, only spending...Made, she's completely crazy... Running around with these boys! She's getting to live like quite the young miss, so then you have to keep a maid. It's shameful! Don't allow it! I'm telling you: all that silk rubbish of hers is just dropped on the floor, and as for getting her to do something in the kitchen! Going down this road, a person becomes a complete waste... As for that boy... You know plenty of people here would have him work in a shop or as a clerk. He's an adult, let him learn how to earn his living."

"Him - earning a living..." Sveilis muttered angrily. "Running around with girls - that's all he knows how to do..."

"And us..." His mother's voice faltered and she turned even more to the side. "Your father and I have practically no life here. We have no work, no people to see... No church we can go to, as befits a Christian person. It's like we're lost in the middle of the woods... It would be better for us to go back to our little town... Your father still knows how to sew, I can wash the laundry of the gentlemen, I'm sure we'll earn enough so we don't go hungry. How much do the two of us, a couple of old wrecks, really need? Here we're just in the way..."

His face turned towards the window, Sveilis didn't see how she dabbed first one eye, then the other, with the corner of her apron. He'd heard what she'd said, but thought only one thing: it's all because he had run out of money... When he had money, everyone was happy... Damn it! He was sick of them all!

"I'm not asking anything from anyone," he snapped sharply, "and not forcing anything on anybody. Everyone can do as they please. If anyone doesn't like it here - please, there's the door. No one is tied down here..."

His mother moved quietly through the door. Sveilis shuffled around angrily for a moment and then tried to calm himself down. He looked his suit over one more time in the mirror, then left.

Walking through his office, to his great surprise he saw two red, unbelievably crumpled pieces of paper lined with countless small folds sitting on the table. He looked closer. Two paper ten rouble notes... He looked at them from one, then the other side - yes, incredibly crumpled, but real. Just when he needed money as much as food. It was a good sign. He sensed where the money might have come from, but none of it mattered to him now. As long as he had it! He smoothed them out, folded them up, and slipped them into his waistcoat pocket.

At the flower shop he selected an immense, white, fragrant bouquet of flowers and had it sent to Mrs. Wilde. He waited around for a bit, then stopped off at the beer shop on the corner to fortify himself. He drank three bottles of beer and ate two sausages and half a bun. And then he left.

His heart was pounding as he opened the door. But there was nothing to fear. Warm as always, Mrs. Wilde came towards him and invited him into the parlour. Yes, there was his fragrant bouquet sitting in an old vase tinted a light rose colour and on the other table a glass serving tray with a bowl of sweet, dry cookies, three teacups and three wine glasses... Who was the third one for?

He was having a hard time speaking, as always. Sveilis kept tripping over his own words and their conversation seemed to run out of steam a dozen times. A half-dozen of his cards were pinned onto a brass nail – their edges cut at angle, smoothed, and coloured gold. Augusts Sveile, Jr. – and then right after it, an ugly torn rip with the yellow nail shining through... He didn't know why exactly, but he felt ashamed when he looked at it.

"Excuse me, Mrs. Wilde..." Sveilis stammered. "But...I think...we've known each other for some time. We've met, spoken and come to know each other..."

Nibbling on the sugared sweet, stirring her tea with a spoon, and watching a melting sugar cube, Mrs. Wilde nodded.

"You are an honourable woman..." Sveilis became more secure. "No matter about your reputation in the city... I've never said a thing. I don't believe a word of the gossip that people say... To me you've always been a distinguished lady. I know your golden heart and say so to everyone..."

She had barely said a single word; he couldn't keep going on like this on his own. But no – she put the silver spoon to her lips and seemed satisfied, but not upset, not particularly interested and nodded. She pushed the crystal vessel containing strawberry jam towards him.

"Please, have some jam, Mr. Sveilis..."

But he didn't. He was blushing, but continued, though he didn't know what he was saying anymore.

"You are well-known as a humanitarian, charitable lady. Indecent people take advantage of your good heart. He... has squandered so much of your wealth... I have status in society and real estate..." He sensed too that his speech was veering off in the wrong direction, but he couldn't do anything about it. "In a month or two, I'll have money again. But right now I need...ten thousand, and no more..."

Damn it! What was he blabbering about! He should have offered his heart and his hand first, not ask for this. But now, whatever would be, would be... He took a sip of the sweet tea but couldn't swallow it. He looked with incredible tenderness at Mrs. Wilde.

She remained just as calm and composed as before, and kept sipping her tea somewhat absurdly by the spoonful. Only, she was no longer nodding her head – now she was slowly shaking it.

"Ten thousand? No, that I can't do."

Then the door to the bedroom opened wider and Fricis entered freshly bathed and smartly dressed, though his waistcoat was unbuttoned and he was still tying a new cravat behind his neck.

"That we can't do," he confirmed without anger, but also without much friendliness. "Ten roubles, that we could certainly do." He sat down and took his glass.

"Please, have some jam..." Mrs. Wilde pushed the strawberry jam towards him.

Sveilis endured this for another ten minutes. He apologised about something, gave an awkward farewell, and rushed out the door. It was all dignified and serious just like any other time. But it seemed to him that the picture of the official on the wall was mocking him, that the cards pinned on the brass nail were shaking with barely restrained laughter, that the bouquet was craning its neck and continued to follow him with its gaze as he left...

Was he at fault or was someone else, he didn't think about it and couldn't say. But he had been awfully foolish. He remained in a hopeless situation. Shame and anger sent another thought swirling around his head... Not a thought, but a kind of hidden, preposterous premonition, which frightened him. He touched the spot where the weight of the revolver in his inner pocket was pulling down and buttoned his coat tighter. Afraid to live... afraid to die... pointlessly afraid of himself...

Sveilis stopped at the first beer shop and drank – until the evening, until he could no longer stand up...

Resting her elbows on the windowsill, pressing her forehead against the fogged over glass, Made looked down at the street. Her room was already fairly dark, but outside it was still light.

She stood there just as she had on countless other nights. The twilight outside gradually grew thicker and with it, so too did the weight of her endless sorrows. She felt a longing made helpless and weary by worry... An unquenchable thirst for a life not lived... A dim glimmer of a happiness, which she'd seen from a distance, grasped at for so long, but could never quite reach... And boredom, stifling, unbearable boredom, which made it difficult to breathe and which brought tears into her eyes... There, in the cold dark miserable little room standing by the washing tub, she had never felt as overwhelmingly, as endlessly empty and unhappy. Silk would rustle when she moved, even a little bit; she only had to turn a small knob and the room would be illuminated by electric lights. But she still felt so poor and the twilight, which fogged up her eyes, that darkness which poured into her heart like an unending stream, no lights could scatter. She had grabbed at a golden cup holding a sparkling drink, but it kept slipping out of her hands, and her dry, parched lips could only sip the empty air in vain.

Just then she collapsed forward with her entire weight. The thick glass just barely supported the strong pressure from her forehead. Down on the street, going in the other direction, it was him – Rodolfs Lodziņš. In the dark, in a crowd of a hundred people, she would've recognised him. And that figure – tall, slender and straight, as if carved from wood – which was walking with him under his arm. Miss Ziepēns... A quiet moan passed over her lips, but she didn't hear it herself. Her hands slipped weakly from the windowsill. For a moment she stood there like that with her head downcast. Now there was nothing to look at anymore. Now the street was empty and dark for her.

She sat down in the chair and remained there somewhat stunned for a moment. She came around only gradually and then, as if she'd only just woken up, she leapt to her feet. That woman looked all dried out! Like she was carved out of wood! Made would take him away from her! She couldn't let it happen! She'd heard rumours, sensed he was avoiding her and hiding. She'd controlled herself and tried to convince her foolish heart that it couldn't be, that it was impossible. All in vain. A reckless, blind instinct stronger than her will. She had to go, find them, take him away from her, trample her, destroy her... She didn't know for certain what she would do, but she had to go.

She put on her scarf and threw on her coat. She forgot her gloves and galoshes – she went out in just her shoes.

The kitchen door was open, so was the back-room's door further on. Right then her father was dragging his sewing machine outside and behind him her mother, crouched on the ground, was busying herself around her baskets of knitting and balls of yarn. Made didn't care about anything else now. The rail baggage handler had just arrived at the front door, but Made didn't care about that either.

She wandered aimlessly down the street. To where – she didn't know. She only had one goal in mind: to find them both... She forgot herself and the rest of the world because of it. Her coat was open, the corner of her woollen scarf was flapping in the wind, her hands were cold, her boots slipped and slid on the slippery snow-covered pavement – she didn't notice any of it. She hurried along, almost running, as if she had to catch up with them and was afraid of missing them. She paid no heed to those coming towards her, but she would notice the two of them no matter what.

She walked until she no longer could. She was tired, but took no notice of it and didn't despair. She had to find them and she knew she would. And she did, after accidentally turning down a small, dark side street.

Rodolfs Lodziņš, speaking animatedly with a friend of his, was coming down the middle of the street. Miss Ziepēns was no longer with him – he must have just taken her home. He was deep in conversation as she approached and didn't even look over. But he turned instinctively towards her, was confused and stopped. He looked over with a furrowed brow and wanted to keep going. But that was impossible. That dishevelled woman on the pavement was standing in such an unusual, provocative way that he felt compelled to come over. It seemed like if he didn't, she would scream and come after him waving her arms... Lodziņš said a few words to his friend and slowly approached.

"Well?" he asked harshly and looked angrily into Made's eyes.

But she was already walking alongside him, satisfied, almost jubilant.

"I wanted to meet you..." she said slurring her words. And then thinking for a moment looked over. "What did you do with... her...?"

"Miss Ziepēns?" he asked reluctantly and became more tender, more cautious. "I took her home..." The tone and manner in which he said these words made it clear that this subject was to be spoken of with respect or, even better, not discussed at all. But Made didn't notice anything. Her heart was full and bursting.

"You're always with her. Why should you be taking her anywhere? Maybe it's true what people say: you're engaged to her..."

"Engaged? Who's saying that? That's certainly not true." He clearly wanted to add something else, but, glancing over, thought better of it.

"Well – why are you taking her around?" Made asked him even more obsessively and loudly. "Thin and dry like a fence post... She can run around on her own. You think these city girls are worth much? Now she's soft and cuddly, but you'll see later on: she won't care a bit if she's got a husband – she'll be running around with strangers."

It was extremely unpleasant for him to have her stomping alongside him – heavy, awkward, dishevelled, wet and muddy – and pressing up to him so closely. He was angry that refined people were giving the two of them looks filled with astonishment and mockery. But still it made him want to laugh that this spinster was meddling so absurdly in his intimate affairs – as if she had any right, as if she'd been his lover. Oh, he knew well what she hoped for and what she needed... In the end, it wasn't all that bad to feel desired by women, caressed by sensuous, unspeakably tender gazes.

Lodziņš chuckled. "What are you so angry about today?"

This made her even angrier, as if he was only listening to her as a joke.

"Why don't you come see me anymore? I wait and wait and wait... but you never come. You've got no time for me."

"I truly have very little time now..." But then it occurred to him. "What do you mean, I never come? Wasn't I there last Sunday? Or the Sunday before that?"

"Sunday... What do you mean Sunday! And what day is it today? I know – you're bored with me. You're running away from me – running after those educated girls..."

Half-moaning, she was speaking at full volume. Absolutely scandalous... Lodziņš looked around timidly and nudged her towards the coloured glass doors. She didn't care, as long as he was with her.

Through a dimly lit corridor they entered an asphalt-covered courtyard. And from here they went through a second entrance into the fancier rooms of a fine restaurant. An obliging waiter opened the doors, and they entered a small room in which there was a small table in the centre covered with a white tablecloth, two chairs on one side and a longer wicker chair made for two. A Smirnoff poster on the wall; an electric lamp hanging over the table with a large blue shade, still and warm...

Made sat down in the chair. Elbows on the table, her chin supported by her hands, she gazed at Lodziņš. She couldn't take her eyes off of him, and she kept looking longingly at him. He had changed quite a bit – he was thinner, seemed to have become greyer... his eyes were sunken, somehow dull and afraid. An occasional white follicle had sprouted on his upper lip and as a result he looked older – less familiar... But still dear, a hundred times more so than before! When he leaned over the table to fill their glasses from the bottle of mulled wine wrapped in a napkin, she could see that behind his high, modern collar, a soft, white cloth was wrapped around his neck and under it were some kind of wounds or boils... But what business was that of hers!

Her intrusive, melting gazes were making him uncomfortable. He hurried to make a toast.

"Cheers! Let's have a drink and see what comes of it..." A moment later he reached over, took her by her hand, and pulled her over next to him. "Sit here – next to me – that'll be better..."

That was fine with her, it was as if she'd been sitting like this for her entire life. She stroked his hand and looked at his face from the side. His pink lips moved whispering something she couldn't hear; her face beamed with such bliss that Lodziņš was suddenly terrified... This crazy girl could drive a man crazy, too... Lodziņš drank and urged Made to do the same.

He had found her a little off-putting from the very start. But her naive trust and her frank, undisguised pushiness were difficult to resist. And her irrational love held within it so much warmth and tenderness, that he only needed to rest against her chest, to lean into her embrace, for her to rock him like a child. This simple, country woman seemed so strange and unusual in the midst of city life and culture. To live with her – no, that could never be, but to forget himself for a moment and rest...

For a long time neither of them said barely a word. They sat, pressed close together, and drank. Lodziņš didn't notice when his head pressed against Made's shoulder, how it slid down along it into her lap... Clasping his head with both hands, she held it and with a warm, profoundly tender hand stroked his forehead and his thin hair. He looked up at her. The corners of her scarf hung over, obscuring the piercing brightness of the electric light, and cast him in gentle shadow. He felt so relaxed and at ease, and also sad – sadder than he'd felt in a very long time.

"You're not going to marry her, are you..." he heard a strange, distant question.

"No, no..." he whispered. He wasn't lying; what his parents had decided and what he had now agreed to seemed truly reckless and impossible indeed. What was Miss Ziepēns to him anyhow? It was good for him right here. He didn't need anything else.

Made's hand stroked his head even more tenderly.

"You've got such thin, soft hair..." She took the glass of mulled wine and helped him drink it like a child. He took a sip – and right away a gentle warmth flowed across his entire body, embracing all of his senses. He pressed his face into her clothing.

"I can't...her..." he said slurring his words. "I can't marry anyone... Made, dear – I'm sick... I'm finished. A wife, how would I...what would my children be like..."

She noticed that he was beginning to sob, but she didn't think about it. He was lying in her lap, calling her by a loving name, that was enough for her. She held his sick neck more tightly, leaned over, and breathed her warm breath onto him.

"My love... My love..."

At that moment he shuddered as if he'd been stung. He pushed her away and jumped to his feet. Choking sobs or perhaps restrained mad laughter had disfigured and transformed his face. With clenched fists he threatened something in the empty air. A completely different, unfamiliar person, not the one who had been there just an instant before.

"Get thee behind me, Satan!" he rasped hoarsely. "Leave me be, you witches! There's no escape from you... I'll strangle you... all of you!"

He rushed towards the locked doors, completely out of his mind. He straightened, turned the key, threw open the door. Excited voices – the sound of another slamming door, then silence.

As if awakening from a trance, Made slowly rose to her feet and looked around. Alone. Empty and quiet. From the knocked over glass, dark red fluid moved across the tablecloth and downward in little rivulets, crying tiny, poignant tears as it dripped onto the floor.

She grabbed her head with both hands, and doubling over she began to wail like a child.

"Ooo-hoo-hoo-hoo!" the sound of her sobs echoed hideously down the corridor and through the half-empty rooms.

The waiters and guests ran in. And how else could they have understood her misfortune? Fearing a scandal, they comforted her as much as they could, and quickly led her out through the garden gate.

Staggering as if she were drunk, she let them. Her coat, hanging wide open, dragged along the ground. The corners of her scarf had slipped out and, like the broken wings of a great white bird, they dangled down across her shoulders.

"Ooo-hoo-hoo-hoo!" the terrible sound echoed across the yard enclosed by grey walls.

PART THREE

Bebrītis and Taube were helping Roberts Sveilis walk, holding him by one arm on each side. He wasn't even all that drunk – and as the morning approached he had even slept a bit. But that's how it had been. Ever since Director Sveilis had entrusted his brother to them, they had hardly ever left his side. Going to the taverns and also to a certain other place, they'd always place their charge in between them in the carriage and bringing him back would take him by the arms. Mostly this was because they had much to amuse themselves with, watching his comical awkwardness and bashfulness.

But now he was starting to get accustomed to it all and there were fewer amusing missteps. He'd become attuned to night life in the big city astonishingly fast. At first they'd dragged him into all kinds of delicate situations, abandoning him there, having a good laugh and then returning in the nick of time to rescue him. But now he was beginning to figure it out himself. He'd let himself fall for some of their jokes, but other times would put one over on them. Jokes played on each other around the beer glass – he knew all of them now and was almost as adept as his protectors.

"Will they let me go?" He pulled out one, then the other hand and nimbly stepped off the street and onto the pavement. "Nursing school is over. My nannies can retire."

The students winked knowingly at each other.

"That lad... Pretty soon he'll be bettering us."

And truly they were less fleet-footed than Roberts. He lit a cigarette, but didn't offer one to his companions. There were only two left in the pack. He would need them himself...

On the corner he bade his companions and competitors from the previous night an indifferent farewell. His walking stick under his arm, he pulled his white, creased hat down over his eyes, and shoved his hands deep into the pockets of his light-coloured, striped coat. He yawned and shuddered. He'd slept, but not enough after that crazy night. The fatigue was weighing heavily on all his bones. Still, he couldn't really say that he was sleepy, and he hadn't thought at all about going to sleep. He didn't want to look like an oaf who couldn't make it one night without sleep. He didn't want to seem like that to himself either. He was developing a sense of pride – the pride of a hardened carouser.

Though it was still early, the late spring sun was already rather hot that morning. It pierced through the holes in the weave of his straw hat and poked at his face like tiny red-hot needles. His eyes closed making him look bashful and he would try to keep them open with all his might if a young or pretty woman came towards him. Whenever a tall building cast its shadow across the pavement, cold shivers would run across his soft body.

Maids would open windows and beat their dust rags against the windowsills. For the most part they were old and ugly. Roberts would look with interest and smile impishly only at an occasional one. Here and there, a drowsy face... Some wilted lilacs in a vase... Roberts yawned and lit another cigarette.

He felt some fatigue and heaviness in his joints, but practically no hangover at all. When he'd drunk a lot of Bénédictine with coffee, the next morning his throat felt like it had been scalded and his chest felt congested. But last night he'd mostly had white wine and beer. His head didn't hurt and he didn't have any unpleasant memories either. He pushed his hat further towards the back of his head and began to examine those coming towards him more carefully.

He wasn't interested in the men – only the women. The most important thing wasn't something you'd find in a woman's face. As long as she wasn't too ugly or old... or skinny. Old and skinny, that's something he couldn't stand. He liked the ones who were more full-figured. He looked for well-fitted, light-coloured summer suits and imagined the rounded shapes beneath them. Oh – he wasn't that same foolish boy he used to be! Like he was when he and Milda...

He could smile now remembering how upset he'd once been over Milda – he'd wanted to kill his brother or even himself... Certainly, Augusts was a pig and he would continue to repeat this whenever he wanted. But the whole thing wasn't nearly as tragic as that. He had become accustomed to her company – and this was why he had convinced himself that he couldn't live without the girl. But that's not what it's like at all. After all, they're all more or less the same – as long as they're not old or too skinny... He remembered how excited he was to be alone with Milda, hugging and kissing her in some quiet corner. Total rubbish! Boyish dreams! She wasn't that fantastic, nothing much there... Lasted just an instant... Oh – nobody was going to fool him like that anymore. Now he knew how things stood. But this new life of living it up with educated, clever companions appealed to him. It was completely different than it had been with those schoolboys and dumb little girls. He didn't like being with them anymore. He avoided them as much as he could. And he didn't like going home much either. But it all cost so much money...

He paused for a moment by Sveilis's wine shop. Why not stop in for a laugh and look to see what that young shop girl is doing there now? She'd probably get flustered, wouldn't know what to do, what to say. He didn't care about her hardly at all anymore. He'd seen her a couple of times from a distance, but hadn't said anything to her. And whenever he'd thought of it, he would toss back a few shots and forget about it. He wanted to forget and so he forgot. So she doesn't think he's sorry or broken up about it. The streets are full of girls like that... He looked in – the shop doors were shut. There was a sign with "Closed" in Russian and German. That made sense; it was Coronation Sunday.

At the same time, he remembered that the men from the bank were organising a motor car trip to the country today. He had to go with them. He had neither the slightest desire nor intent of staying home. Wherever they go, they always live it up. There'll be drinking and all kinds of fun. But he needed to sleep a bit before lunch time – so he's more refreshed when evening comes. Home – no, he only went there when he had no other choice... He turned in the direction of the Baltika.

The Baltika was also closed, but Roberts knew how to get to other entrance through the gate in the courtyard. The caretaker lifted his hat respectfully; he affably, but with evident self-confidence, returned it. The cook with her sleeves pushed up on her plump, red arms, moved to let him by. Through the kitchen he entered the billiard room. The room smelled as if it had just been cleaned, and this mixed with the unpleasant stink of yesterday's tobacco smoke. Both windows were open and there was a nasty draft blowing through them. Roberts moved in the direction of the small room.

Yes, young Skrastiņš was still asleep. He was stretched out on his back, his blanket only pulled over him halfway. His hands were clutching the stained blanket, and he appeared to have only been sleeping for three or four hours. His head had slipped off the pillow and onto the bare corner of the red-striped mattress, his mouth wide open, his breath rattling continuously. It was clear that he'd been really drunk. On the small, scuffed table, there was a dirty, pleated shirt front, a beer-stained collar, a plate with the remains of some smoked herring, a half-filled shot glass, an opened but still completely full beer bottle. On the windowsill there was a boot brush and an assortment of rags... The whole room was filled with hot stinking air.

Roberts carefully opened the door and hung up his walking stick on the nail. He quietly pushed the sleeper's covers down to his ankles and left him lying there in his underclothes. Then he took the shot glass, and, holding it somewhat high above him, began to drip its contents into the sleeper's open mouth. He had poor aim. One drop would fall too low and drip across his chin onto his neck, another would end up too high and would flow towards his eyes. The sleeper moved his lips around as he slept and grimaced amusingly when he'd catch a drop or two. Roberts held back, but then started to laugh out loud. He poured all the rest of it in a single burst into his half-open mouth. Skrastiņš woke up, coughing and sputtering, and jumped up to a sitting position as he rubbed his eyes with his fists. Sneezing and cursing, it took him a while to recover.

But Roberts didn't care. Tearing off his coat and throwing it onto the nail, he pushed himself onto the bed along the wall and forced Skrastiņš out completely. It felt good to stretch out after all that effort... Crossing his legs at the end of the bed, his eyes closed, he lay there and told Skrastiņš about his adventures the previous night. He gradually calmed down. Staggering about, finding one and then another piece of his suit with difficulty, he got dressed, and slowly became more interested in what his friend was saying. He backed up his vulgar stories with even more vulgar comments, the two of them roaring with laughter at the lewdest ones. Then the clanking of dishes coming from the kitchen stopped for a moment, interrupted by angry, shrill voices; the women must have been listening too.

On the other side of the wall, in the presence of strangers, these young men knew how to behave politely and speak properly. There, language and everything else had its clear boundaries, which even the greatest cynic couldn't overstep. But here, on this side, in a tiny room stinking of dirty tobacco smoke, alcohol and the sleeper's breath, the rawest and dirtiest things seemed to emerge as of their own accord. Skrastiņš didn't have much money. He couldn't manage five roubles - a rouble, a half rouble, at most. He listened to Roberts's stories of high living with an incredible craving. Because of his jealousy, he tried to embellish retellings of his own adventures with all kinds of additional events, which never occurred... Again and again, raucous laughter would echo from the small back room. But behind the wall a broom moved swiftly and sent a cloud of grey dust wafting up along the window.

Now dressed, Skrastiņš went out to see what food he could find to tame his hangover. He could be heard arguing angrily with the women in the kitchen for a long time. But Roberts dozed off for a while. It was so nice to rest after the night's frenzy and exhaustion... Smiling and yawning he had barely opened his eyes when Skrastiņš returned with a steaming tray piled high with food...

After lunch, Augusts Sveile Jr. sat with his private secretary and Lausks, the clerk from the Sixteenth Credit Union, in the back office at the Baltika. Sveilis, half-reclining on the modern sofa, supporting himself on his elbow and casually crossing his fully extended legs one over the other while his patent leather boots lightly rubbed against each other. He was smoking a cigar which gave off a pleasant scent. In front of him was a half-bottle of foreign cognac and a glass of yellow lemon candies, a new briefcase with silver fittings and a rather large white metal box filled with money. Lausks was sitting by the window writing in an open book which lay on the table. Next to the book was a steaming glass of tea, a plate of sandwiches and a half-empty glass of cognac.

On the other side of the table, master carpenter Rozentals shuffling uncomfortably. He stuffed the paper money into the sleeve behind the cover of his pocket calendar, and sorted the gold coins by size, wrapping them in pieces of newspaper, and slipping them into both waistcoat pockets and the inside pocket of his coat. He looked over at his employer with complete trust and submissiveness.

"I think we're done then..." he smiled benevolently.

Sveilis nodded coolly. "Uh-huh..." It sounded abrupt and lofty.

"Thank you very much, Mr. Director... And please don't hold it against me that I pestered you so much at one point. Honestly, I needed it... I really needed it greatly."

Sveilis motioned magnanimously with his cigar. "But of course! You knew it would come..." He reached over, sipped a little cognac, and tossed one of the lemon candies into his mouth.

"Please, Mr. Rozentals..." Lausks, rising to his feet, turned the book sharply to the side. "Sign here... And also here."

Having signed, Rozentals tiptoed back over again. "May I ask... I heard that you sold your new building, which is still under construction."

"Y-yes..." Sveilis was looking at the ceiling.

"Uh-huh...Well, but did it pay off? An unfinished building..."

"It depends, dear Rozentals. It depends."

The master carpenter seemed a bit taken aback by the evident pride and palpable coolness.

"And then... if I may ask... I heard that you had received the order for the construction of the new credit union building?"

"Yes. And I have a new lot of my own – I'm thinking of starting work on it in July."

"Of course..." Rozentals began flattering him even more. "Now you'll have no shortage of credit for certain. I would hope, Mr. Director, that going forward you won't deny me work?"

Sveilis brushed the ash-covered tip of his cigar in the porcelain ashtray. "At this point I couldn't possibly say anything for certain about that. Let's see how it goes... You know, a large project – the master carpenter I choose will need to have resources."

"Well, you know, Mr. Director... I'm not a capitalist, but I've got a few thousand..."

"We'll see about that later," Sveilis said in a cold, raised voice. His face and posture left no doubt that the audience was at an end. Rozentals moved to leave.

Lausks coughed obligingly. "You know, Mr. Director, I don't like that person all that much."

"I don't like him at all!" Sveilis sat up. "When a little while ago... well, I had some minor complications..." Lausks nodded his head indifferently. "There was no escaping him. For those few thousand he chased me down the street. And now he's crawling in here again...You know, Mr. Lausks, I think going forward I won't be getting involved with these kinds of small-time operations. Those who have capital can work in a completely different way."

"Absolutely, Mr. Sveilis. With construction, just as with every other project, there's a certain amount of risk. The more capable and secure the person is to whom you entrust the completion of that work, the more certain you can be of avoiding any kind of unforeseen complications..."

Pauls entered, dressed in a new tailcoat, looking serious and dignified, and announced the arrival of the agent from the motor car depot. He received the sum due to him, signed, and left. The treasurer from the brick factory arrived, received his money, and left. Then Sausums was announced.

Sausums... Sveilis remembered him very well. At first, a member of Brambergis's party, a candidate for auditor, an agitator and a pretty significant loudmouth at the meetings. Now he'd become quite meek. He'd expanded the milk plant, he'd purchased new machines – he probably needed money, possibly something else. So they came, one after another, one meeker than the next. But when he'd had some small difficulty, then he hadn't known what to say, then he was pointing fingers. Aha! Now you see who's smarter and who's in charge! His lips pursed somewhat sarcastically, still reserved and respectful, respectful and cool. Sveilis busied himself with his cigarette holder for a moment, then lifted his head.

"What did you want?"

Sausums extended his hand across the table. "Congratulations, Mr. Sveilis, congratulations!"

Sveilis extended his fingertips, but looked rather doubtfully at the dairyman. "How do you...mean?"

"Well, for the approval of the credit union... I always said that would happen... Where there's such a large majority of votes... and all of it according to the law and statutes..."

But Sveilis knew that already. He had no need to hear it from people like Sausums. He coughed dryly. "What can I help you with?"

"You see, I have this issue..." The dairyman began reaching into his pockets and pulling out all sorts of papers. "Since the number of officials at the credit union will be doubled... You placed an advertisement... My brother's son is from the country... he's finished business school. He's a gifted and hard-working lad, doesn't drink, doesn't smoke..."

"Well, tell him to submit his application to us here at the bank..." Sveilis interrupted him sharply. "I'm not hiring bank officials today. Have him apply and submit his documents – the directors will decide. Tomorrow – today is a Coronation Sunday."

"Of course, of course... But I just wanted to ask if you would put in a good word for him... There will be a lot of applicants, after all."

"Hopefully. We certainly pay our officials enough. We'll select the best from those who apply. We don't believe in nepotism. Good day!" He nodded haughtily and filled his glass.

He took a sip and turned towards Lausks. Something new had occurred to him.

"Tell me... Where is that – Miss Zvaigzne – now?"

Lausks became noticeably redder. "Zvaigzne? To tell you the truth...I haven't kept up with her."

Sveilis smirked as he looked at his secretary. "Now, now? You had such... intimate relations... after all."

"We did, yes..." Lausks became even more muddled. "But then it turned out that we were disappointed in each other. We had different natures... Different world views..."

"Of course, of course!" Sveilis laughed with delight and pushed one of his hands between his knees. He found Lausks's confusion very amusing. "But aren't you at all interested in her anymore? Who does she... work with... now?"

"She was planning on opening a private elementary school – in the workers' district... She is an avid proletarian... But, as far as I now, she hasn't received a permit yet."

"Is that so? But tell me – do you really have absolutely no – contact – with her anymore? I mean, even just occasionally, some nights, do you slink over there still? Well? Better be completely honest..." He found incredible pleasure in watching Lausks squirm and sweat.

"No, honestly! We've parted ways permanently and forever."

Sveilis became quieter and took on a more intimate tone.

"But quite crazy though? I think she's one of those – well, you know?"

Lausks knew. He rather enjoyed flinging some mud at her. "Well, I'll tell you... Anybody who gets involved with her is crazy. A witch, not a woman..."

"I think so too!" Sveilis quickly agreed. "These diabolic hags can suck a man dry like a lemon..."

Lausks didn't have a chance to respond: Kārlis Roblapainis came in. He greeted Sveilis and also shook Lausks's hand in a collegial way. He was so flattered that he even rose to his feet.

"I was at the bank..." Kārlis Roblapainis sat down in the chair offered to him. He put his plush hat down on the table holding it by its brim. "I completely forgot that you're celebrating today." He laughed politely. "Please, did you have a chance to check? Will I be able to get it tomorrow morning? They categorically refused to give an extension..."

"Those seventy roubles? Yes, I spoke with my colleagues. You'll have it. Tomorrow morning, you said."

"Around eleven, if possible."

"Yes, you'll have it...But keep in mind, Mr. Roblapainis: if ever it comes to pass... you'll support us in that newspaper of yours."

Kārlis Roblapainis gestured the unnecessary nature of this comment and said, "There's no doubt about that, Mr. Sveilis. And anyway – our paper will have a direct connection with the Seventeenth Credit Union in the future. Maybe you've heard: two stocks have passed into Mr. Strauss's ownership..."

"I've heard, I've heard..." Sveilis smirked knowingly. "Good day!" He extended his hand towards Kārlis Roblapainis across the table. Just then Tilaks came in.

Tilaks shook Sveilis's hand and returned Lausks's greeting with a nod. He sat down heavily.

"Hot as hell..." He leaned over and looked. "What are you doing? Now you like cognac?" He pushed his head back against the headrest. "Pauls! Bring me a glass of lemonade – with ice. Be quick." He wiped his face vigorously. "Well, how did it go yesterday? All in the clear?"

"All in the clear!" Sveilis laughed as he slapped the box half-filled with paper money and gold coins.

"That's good. And as was agreed: one hundred and twenty thousand, and sixty in cash?"

"Yes. And I still have the unpaid brick and plaster bill to cover."

"Well – what'll that come to for you: one thousand fifteen, maybe twenty? Yes? Well there you go: forty, forty-five in your pocket."

"Good enough." The friends looked at each other and smiled.

"And what about... I left early last night... Did you get an advance for our construction project? Yes? Well, that's just fine then." They both laughed.

"I just stopped in because I was passing by... What did we actually agree: around three, right? From the Baltika – right? How's it going over there? Did you manage to hire a driver?"

"Yes, right away! Nowadays there's no shortage of them. A Russian. Says he's driven in Moscow for three years. Good references."

"But will there be room for everybody? I think it will be a large group. Young Lodziņš and Bebrītis are riding along with me, together with Taube and Ziemelis, and a couple of other fraternity brothers of theirs."

"I'll have my brother and sister... and Miss Caune. Oh yes, Mr. Lausks, you're going too, aren't you? Yes? I doubt we'll all fit. Well, if we don't, we'll get another one. There's no shortage of motor cars..." Just then he thought of something, chuckled and turned towards Lausks. "Listen, just for a laugh, can you get that Miss Zvaigzne to come along too? Sometimes trips like these can get pretty jolly and then...firecrackers like that can come in handy. Well, what do you say?"

Lausks became uncomfortable again and turned red. "Maybe...but I don't know. I don't know her current address..."

Roberts came in, and Tilaks yawned and walked out. Sveilis squinted his eyes and looked at his brother while pulling a face to express his mockery. It was clear that he was once again comfortably tipsy.

"Well, Mr. Assistant Accountant? What do you have to say for yourself?"

Roberts stretched out on a chair and put his legs up on another. "Taube beat me three times in a row. He slaps down those cards like the devil himself."

"Taube? Ye-e-es. Why did you start with the artists? Taube and Fricis, they're the best players."

"Fricis? When he's not drunk. He's staggering around right now! Completely drunk. Andrejs wanted to throw him out."

"Ha, ha, ha!" Sveilis laughed. "Already? Well, the weather's hot, his bald head heats up fast."

Roberts yawned, clasped his hands together above his head and stretched lazily. "Oh – yes... What did we decide then: are we going? Yes? Leaving at three? It's half past two now... You know: I could use a bit more money."

"Again? You got half your salary the day before yesterday, and you haven't even started working yet."

"I start tomorrow. When I work, I'll work... You know, I had some expenses...Twenty-five roubles, if you have it."

"Here's twenty." Sveilis tossed him two gold discs and turned towards Lausks again. "Oh, so you don't know where she lives now? Might be at some institution, right?"

Lausks shrugged his shoulders. "Maybe..." He said, as he laughed obligingly with his boss.

An hour later Lausks retrieved the small empty white box and his boss's briefcase. Sveilis poured the last of the money into two wallets and went out front into the restaurant.

Rozentals and his acquaintances were sitting around the longest table. It was piled high from one end to the other: sausages with cabbage, ham and beer, suckling pig, herring pudding, carafes of spirits, bottles of beer. An incredible racket: conversations, laughter, red faces, hands waving, tobacco smoke and stifling heat. Sveilis nodded and smiled when the somewhat unrefined, tipsy company greeted him. But he turned in a different direction.

Two individuals were getting up from a small square table nearby: a heavy-set country farmer in a homespun brown linsey-woolsey coat and his younger, moderately attractive, slightly chubby wife in a white, brightly patterned calico jacket with a shiny, black belt around her waist, and a headscarf resting on her shoulders rather than her head. Smiling bashfully, they both moved towards Sveilis. The woman was a bit bolder, but the farmer was terrified.

"Good day, Mr. Caune!" Sveilis hoped to drive away their insecurity and to somewhat hide his own with a few loud, energetic words. Devil only knows what they have in mind now. An unsettled conscience made Sveilis extremely nervous. He warmly shook Mr. Caune's hand – which was calloused by work. "Hello, hello. Mrs. Caune!" He shook Mrs. Caune's hand even more warmly. For a moment the three of them stood there awkwardly. "So... you've come to Riga?"

"Yes, yes!" they both responded in unison. And then Mrs. Caune quickly added, "For the milk money... and to bring that girl some things."

That girl... Sveilis couldn't allow himself to show any sign of recognition. Devil only knows what they know... He lifted his hand, instinctively protecting himself in case they were to grab him by the thin collar of his yellow tussore coat, slap him, or spit right in his eyes... He came around and patted down his thin, damp hair. He moved behind the small square table and sat down quickly.

"Please sit. Let's toast to our meeting... Well, why don't you sit?" He lifted his eyes and all of his confusion and fear disappeared in an instant. He began to see the boundless respect, shyness and perhaps even something else radiating from Mr. and Mrs. Caune's faces. Ah! – they don't know, or don't understand, anything! He was a lord to them and remained that way. He smiled benevolently and leaned back in his chair. "Please, do sit – let's drink to our meeting..." He had to reach over and take them by their hands – for some time they absolutely refused to sit, but eventually they did. Sveilis called over the waiter and asked his guests what they'd like.

"We're very grateful, sir!" Mrs. Caune said raising both her arms. "Nothing, we don't need anything! We already ate so much at the coaching inn that we can barely move."

But Mr. Caune was becoming bolder. "What can you do with these women! I'm happy to have one portion...if you, sir, also will."

Sveilis ordered three portions, a shot of spirits and a glass of wine. He laughed – but didn't feel completely at ease. He still wasn't sure: maybe they were pretending to be ignorant simpletons on purpose. He turned their conversation away from any sensitive topics.

"Well – and how is it in the country now? Have you finished planting?"

He toasted and urged them to drink. But Mrs. Caune couldn't hide what was on her mind for long.

"You, sir, have given our daughter so many gifts..."

"Yes... rather a lot." Mr. Caune added, wiping his mouth with the back of his hand.

Sveilis couldn't lift his eyes again. He chuckled, but his laughter sounded constricted and unnatural.

"Not at all... Just a few trifles."

"Don't say that, sir. That gold watch alone must have cost at least fifty roubles. Let alone that bracelet... and that pretty little ring..."

Sveilis looked up again. Yes... That golden glimmer he'd seen a moment ago was still twinkling in their eyes. Naive joy, genuine gratitude, a most heartfelt feeling of gratitude for this generous gift was unmistakably evident in these windblown, sun-scorched faces. What? Why should he feel like a thief or criminal? He liked to make people happy; he made them happy and did good work, that was the kind of man he was!

"Cheers, Father Caune! Cheers, Mother Caune! Let me tell you... I'm not like some of the others. I treat my employees like my very own children. As long as they don't talk back and... behave as they should. I can look after them. Thank God, I have plenty of money... Pauls! Another glass of wine for Mother Caune!"

"Thank you, sir, thank you! I think that'll be enough. If I carry on like this, I'll get completely drunk... And be firm with her, that girl of ours. She has always been a bit headstrong, since she was a child."

"Ha, ha, ha! I never put up with wilful behaviour, none at all! With me it's like this: to those who listen to me, I'm like a father. To those who don't, they're out the door!"

"That's not what I mean exactly...She'll listen – that Milda of ours. She's still a young child... But you must teach her, sir, to work hard and not to waste time. She's still a bit naïve... and there are so many ruffians slouching around this city. Like those around the Jānis Gate where we rode in..."

"Ruffians, you say? Ha, ha, ha! don't worry at all, Mother Caune! She's not as naive as you think... Cheers, Father Caune!"

"That's what I say!" Mr. Caune exclaimed as he beamed with joy, while he gnawed on a bone from the roast. "Studying – that's something the devil himself couldn't get that girl to do. But she might become an apprentice someday."

"An apprentice, you say? Ha, ha, ha!" Sveilis laughed, slapping his knee with his hand and looking around to see if anyone else was laughing. "She'll become a first-rate apprentice, that's for sure!"

"But, sir, be firm with her." Mrs. Caune, clearly flattered, put her hand on Sveilis's. "Work never breaks anyone's back. No good at studying, well then, she needs to get used to working. And is it so hard to sit at the bank for a few hours? Then on a Coronation Sunday or what have you – she gets to sit at home until lunchtime. When do those Sundays come for toilers like us?"

"We..." Mr. Caune repeated loudly. "Filth-waders, tillers: that's what we are. Look how the gentlemen in the city are living nowadays... Cheers, Mr. Director!" He looked around, elated. Could they all see that he was friends with the bank director.

Mrs. Caune poked him in the side with her elbow.

"What are you yelling like crazy for! Strangers – they'll start to make fun of us... You, sir, practically take the place of her father. What can we do, living so far away. Be firm with her. She said...that you're taking her along on some kind of a trip today? A girl like that! And you'll be bringing along only the finest gentlemen."

"I, Mother Caune, am never arrogant towards my employees. My own parents are farmers..."

"Mr. Sveilis?" Mr. Caune waved his hands in protest. "Mr. Sveilis, no no no!" Then turning to his wife, "And what are you blabbering about? Do you think that our girl doesn't know how to behave in the company of sophisticated gentlemen?"

"Behave with them, you say? Ha, ha, ha!" Sveilis could barely contain himself. With every moment it all became more amusing to him. He so wanted to toss in a word or two – so they'd know how things truly stood. With such people you could get away with anything... He barely resisted the temptation. "She certainly knows how to behave with them. And if she stays with me, she'll get even better... Ha, ha, ha! Pauls, another glass of wine for Mother Caune!" Ha, ha, ha, Mr. Caune joined in twice as loudly, and Mrs. Caune tittered more quietly – hee, hee, hee... The three of them were having a jolly time...

Roberts, a bit unsure on his feet, was slipping three bottles of beer into his inside pockets, as he walked by. "Well – get ready. They just pulled up."

The doors swung open and in came Strauss, Bebrītis, and Ziemelis, along with five or six students and other young people. All of them in light-coloured suits with lilacs or other late spring flowers in their buttonholes, all of them already quite drunk and merry in anticipation of the trip. They noisily piled into the buffet and the sound of cigarette packs clattering against it followed in an instant. Waiters loaded beer bottles into baskets, pulled them along the floor, and dragged them outside.

Four motor cars were waiting outside the Baltika, with their engine ticking over. In front was the Torpedo Sveilis had bought yesterday with its bright yellow lights on each side. Made – splendidly-attired but shattered and barely containing herself – sat, slumped in a corner. She couldn't get over the fact that Rodolfs Lodziņš was sitting with friends in the last car, but had barely acknowledged her at all.

Aside from her, there were only two other women coming on the trip: Milda Caune and Little Flame. Milda was sitting in the third motor car, wearing a white silk suit, a bright red band around her waist and streaming down from it, long elbow-length gloves on her hands, and a giant hat with red poppies on her head. She was next to Tilaks, gently smiling while she listened to her companion's risqué quips, and she poked at the front seat's cover with the handle of her red silk parasol.

The Caunes accompanied Sveilis to the doors and were awestruck. Mr. Caune, with a smile brimming with boundless delight, looked again and again at all the motor cars – the glare of polished metal was dazzling everyone there and the smell of fresh paintwork and of soft expensive leather wafting by. Mrs. Caune couldn't take her eyes off her daughter: thin, elegant and refined... like an aristocratic child!

"This is my sister." Sveilis took Mrs. Caune by her elbow and directed her gaze to the pale young lady who was pursing her lips and looking over contemptuously.

"Is that right?" Mrs. Caune looked over. "And that fine young lady who is flirting with that young man over there? Is that his bride?"

"His bride, you say?" Sveilis couldn't keep himself from laughing out loud. "Yes, yes, that's his bride."

Mr. Caune poked him casually in the side.

"But tell me, Sveilis – how much does a machine like this really cost?"

"Climb in, gentlemen!" someone bellowed from the rear motor car.

Sveilis climbed in with a single deft move and sat down next to Made. Roberts and Lausks were in the front seat.

"Vorwärts!" Sveilis commanded and lifted his hat. "Goodbye, Father Caune! Until we meet again, Mother Caune!"

The motors began to sputter. The wheels turned with a hum. The motor car horns blared. One after another, the four motor cars slipped down the street.

"Make way, cruel world!" someone yelled from the last car.

The waiters and a crowd of guests standing in the doors of the Baltika looked on with amusement. One after another they whispered sarcastic comments to each other. Only the Caunes looked on with considerable amazement. Mr. Caune was waving his hat about as he loudly wished them a good journey, while Mrs. Caune waved with her handkerchief and rubbed tears of joy from her eyes...

They drove slowly through the city. It felt so good to sit back in those soft seats with their elastic springs and feel how the warm afternoon breeze caressed one's face and rustled past one's ears... Those with horses stood aside for them at a distance. Those crossing the road ran out of the way in terror and only once they'd made it to the pavement would they turn around and watch the cars pass by. There was anger in their gazes, but also jealousy and awe. It was pleasant to feel the anger and jealousy of others directed at oneself.

Immediately beyond the city limits, just before the last factories, they started to speed up. Now the wind wasn't rustling, but whistling past their ears. The road was less even, it rocked and shook them more. In taking the more abrupt curves, an invisible force oddly pushed them all to one side. All of it was new, strange, and unspeakably enjoyable.

At first it seemed like dizziness. Because of the fast driving - or perhaps because of something else. The wind pushed the dust sideways off the road, and when it came to rest again in heavy swirls, the travellers were already far down the road. The dust settled and only the wide, symmetrical lines dotted with the regular impressions of metal studs showed where the city's gold and culture had reached... The air was clean and clear. The bright blue cooled the eyes; the vast, nearly forgotten, expanse of fields exhaled its warm scented breath. The crops in the pale green fields were already growing high and ruddy strips of meadow empty of flowers rushed by as if in a dream. The trees greeted them by bowing down and bringing their vibrantly green crowns covered with an abundance of new leaves closer to them. Their eyes would catch the sun's glare when reflected from windows on the hill. Across the hill the white, curly-haired head of a boy flashed by as he bounded away and disappeared behind a small dilapidated stable. And then came a valley with a small stone bridge under which shimmered a brown, rocky stream, so narrow that it would be easy to cross with a single step. And then another steep hill where they had to drive through a narrow gap with hawthorn bushes brushing along both sides. And then another expanse of fields with its warm scented breath as well as the brightness of blue sky which cooled their eyes. Hearing their approach, those coming in their direction cleared a path for them. Here and there along the edge of the brush they'd see a disobedient nag shuffling about and an old farmer beating her mercilessly with a whip. A woman jumped over a ditch and stood on the other side; a tiny girl was clutching her skirt and hiding her face in it. Further on in the clover field, three girls were gathering stones. They stood tall on the tips of their toes, shielding their eyes from the sun with their hands, and looked over. Their white teeth flashed as they laughed when the students in the motor car at the rear shouted all kinds of clichéd, risqué comments and blew kisses at them. But that was just for a moment, and immediately afterwards these farm girls returned to their labours. And in their wonder and excited conversation they didn't even notice the stalks of last season's rye poking their hands, or the weight of the stones pulling down their aprons and cutting their waists with their taut bindings.

Four motor cars, happily sputtering, rushed down the white, sandy road. Their passengers were wealthy people, smiling with delight, free of work and worry. It was so good, so very good to realise that there was freedom enough to go for a ride, breathing in lungfuls of fresh spring air, and that everything which surrounded them was just scenery, a setting to aid their visual enjoyment, relaxation and delight.

Roberts fidgeted with a bottle for a bit. Now the cork was out. Putting its neck up to his mouth, he drank eagerly. Having his fill, he handed the bottle over to Lausks.

"Have a drink, colleague!"

Made watched her younger brother angrily. "Yes, just go ahead and get drunk again..."

"Me, huh?" Roberts answered and laughed. "And what of it? Isn't today Coronation Sunday? And isn't the responsibility of every loyal citizen to add to the crown's coffers?"

"Yes, yes!" Sveilis agreed warmly.

"Thank you..." Lausks barely touched the bottle to his lips and handed it back. He wasn't used to it: sweet, bitter, or sour – all these drinks disgusted him.

"Why are you grimacing like a young lady!" Sveilis scolded him. He snatched the bottle away from Roberts and took a healthy swig from it. "Look, this is how you drink!"

Lausks smiled shyly to imply his amazement. In truth, he didn't find anything amazing in all this drinking. He was revolted by it. But there was nothing to be done. He had to get used to it and many other unpleasant things. When you get a salary like this, there's a lot of things you have to put up with. Made had stretched her legs across the entire length of the fairly narrow space – and it felt like she was still trying to stretch them even further. He had to huddle completely over to one side, all the while taking care that he didn't bump into her: his boss's sister. It wouldn't matter if it happened on purpose or jokingly: he wasn't like that. He knew how to treat young ladies, and sometimes liked to joke around with them, but this one sitting across from him looked frozen, or torn apart by pain or cramps. Her chin planted in her breasts, staring at her hands, which she was holding stiffly in her lap, it was as if she'd seen nothing of the drive. Her brothers, who were already rather pickled, couldn't have noticed her strange appearance. Or perhaps she was always like this - Lausks didn't know her very well. He shrugged imperceptibly and huddled over even closer to the edge. A bit on the old side, but not unattractive. In some ways - it wouldn't be so bad... Lausks coughed and shifted nervously in his seat. No change in her expression, not even the flutter of an eyelid.

"Drink!" Sveilis pushed the bottle up to her mouth.

She looked over as if she didn't understand. There was an utter indifference, revulsion, and profound anguish burning in her gaze. Then her hand reached over instinctively and held the bottle. The moist neck of the bottle shared by all the men plunged deeply and awkwardly into her mouth. The brown, sweet, sticky, sparkling drink burst out in spurts.

"Don't drink all of it!" Roberts yelled and pulled the bottle away from his sister. He swirled it around and lifted it up against the sun to look through it. He laughed and shook his head. "Oh you... grousing about our sousing!"

They all stopped in a beautiful, green valley. The motor cars were parked in a row along the roadside. The drivers leaned back and gave their tired hands a rest. The gentlemen crowded around Sveilis's new car and examined it. It was good - it had passed the test... Then they all went to lie down in the meadow, shielded from the wind by a row of white alders and osiers. The grass was only just beginning to sprout. The occasional wilted late season marsh marigold glowed here and along the edge of the half-dry brook. But these city-dwellers had little interest in greenery or flowers. They drank and ate, ate and drank, lolled around in the green grass, wrestled, joked loudly and laughed.

A couple of the students took off their shoes, rolled their trousers up to their knees, and began wading into the brook's silty, shallow eddies. Lodziņš played around more than the others. He was the most drunk or at least, seemed to be. A farmer from one of the nearby houses came over, looked along the bushes, shuffled uncomfortably for a bit, but didn't dare approach.

Made drank and drank. Someone would hand her a drink and she'd drink it; someone else would do the same – and she'd drink that too. It seemed like the sun gradually grew duller, as if a dull blue haze was being stretched across the sky and sinking lower and onto her. She now saw what she needed to see. She would see it at night without even looking. If she turned her back to it, she would still see it. Throughout this trip, this inevitability had never faded from her sight.

She climbed up higher, without any plan or clear intention, and she laid down on her stomach and gazed out at the densely overgrown and ungrazed fallow field, stretching out and dangling her legs indiscreetly, while holding her head in her hands and supporting it on her elbows. Late-season bees wandered between half-open, tiny meadow flowers – a sorrowful hum washed over her a like distant weeping. She felt sad, even heartbroken. She wanted to cry about all that she had dreamt of achieving and hadn't, about all that she had seen and desired, and yet had not found in her life. But her eyes burnt and felt as dry and wide as the brook below – it too had dried out in the harsh spring sun and wind. Just as below, there were some eddies hiding in the silt, but everything that had drawn in upon itself had calmly and solidly come to rest. The heaviness of uncried tears burnt her palms and pushed her elbows down towards the caked, loamy earth. The beastly noise coming from the drinkers – yells, laughter, the clinking of glasses and bottles echoed somewhere close by, without expression, without meaning. Not only her ears, but her entire body and all her senses were filled with this distant unsettling and discomforting noise.

She heard the sound of familiar footsteps. It was him. Made waited, but without particular interest. Each day she would wrap herself with an extra layer of her own deep sadness, like an insect in a cocoon of silk thread. As the thread bound her tighter and tighter, it became difficult to breathe, and the sky, sun and earth became ever hazier. Revulsion and boredom grabbed at her with their cold fingers. It was difficult – so difficult.

Lodziņš was wearing muddy boots with white socks and his trousers were rolled up rather high and in a careless manner. In one hand he had a bottle with a glass slipped onto its neck. He sat down next to her and with his other hand stroked Made's reclining body immodestly. She noticed, but didn't move; she was without anger or offence, only boundless disgust and boredom.

"Well, my sad-faced damsel! What are you lying around like that for?" He let out a long hoarse laugh. A strange, oddly unsettling laugh – without a beginning or end, without a rise or fall.

She heard the same sorrowful note in this laugh that had been buzzing in her ears all this time. She'd heard it for so long already – in the city's walls and in the noise rising up from the street... She turned her head and looked at him.

The face of a sick man – pale, almost blue and sinewy, as if covered with moisture. Beneath the high, modern collar, a white cloth with a cotton layer dotted with yellow spots... But his mouth kept forcing itself into a long, unending laugh.

"Drink, you two, you high-born children!" Bebrītis bellowed from further down in the valley.

"Drink!" Lodziņš topped off her glass and shoved it roughly towards her mouth.

She drank – without particular delight or disgust, in one motion down to the last drop. She turned her head and looked: was he really alone? Where was his bride?

Lodziņš slumped back and drank, gurgling disagreeably in his throat. He drank half the glass and poured the rest out onto the grass. He wasn't interested in drinking; he wanted to sing. Squinting his eyes, slurring his words, without any particular melody, varying his pitch quite a bit, he warbled a German drinking song.

"Oh, the splendour of the fraternity brothers of old!" he was interrupted by the roar of the student choir down in the valley. Lodziņš rolled over onto his elbow closer to Made. The strong smell of wine on his breath wafted into her face as he spoke.

"You're angry at me, yeah? Don't deny it?"

Made didn't shift her gaze and kept looking at him.

"Why didn't you come? I was waiting for you - yesterday and the day before..."

"Why didn't you come..." he was practically mocking her. "So I'm not busy, is that what you think? I'm supposed to just sit with you all the time, is that what you want?" After his sudden flash of anger he suddenly slipped back into sorry cowardice. "But I can come tomorrow, or the day after. I'll come the day after... You'll wait for me, won't you?"

She shook her head.

"No, not anymore... It's too late..." She didn't understand why, but she just knew it was too late now. She couldn't do it anymore. The mountaintop was behind her, the path she had walked had collapsed and was now blocked, but going down she had no need for a path anymore. The angle of the earth beneath her feet, the tremendous heaviness of her indifference and fatigue pulled her lower. Without her wishing it, without resistance, like a loose stone rolling down a hill.

"I'll come over, all right? But don't get all pickled before I get there. Then you..." He leaned over even closer, and whispered something in her ear. Her ears were offended by his outrageous words, but her awareness was unperturbed. She didn't care. An overpowering heaviness pulled her downward. Slowly it got emptier and darker.

"Please, no flirting in public!" Bebrītis bellowed again from the valley.

With a bottle in one hand and a glass in the other, Lodziņš fell back heavily onto the field's edge. But the deep, distant blue of the sky grated in its coldness. He struggled up into a seated position. Waving the bottle and glass about, he kept droning the words of the drinking song, now without any melody at all."

He lurched to his feet and threw the glass away. It came to rest somewhere in the grass shattering with a distant ting. He threw the bottle haphazardly after it. It went spinning through the air. With every twist, dark, blood-red liquid shot out in small, beaded arcs as it poured down onto the ground...

Down in the valley there was a discussion about the little manor Tilaks was planning on buying, and it had been agreed that everyone would have a look at it along the way back.

"City life eats away at a person's health." Strauss declared. "It's been proven that farmers live somewhat longer lives. We need to arrange our lives that way... We need to combine the benefits of city culture with the healthy living conditions of the countryside. Work in the city, live in the country – that's my theory."

"My theory," Ziemelis yelled over him, "is live where you can get better beer."

Taube had not drunk for two weeks: his doctor had forbidden it – his friends were winking at him and slapping him on the back. He was suffering and bored with his teetotalism. He tried not to look as the others poured drinks and drank, and he smiled at the incoherent, uncontrolled rambling of those who were drunk.

"But Mr. Tilaks will build a factory and cover these healthy country living conditions with soot."

"Yes!" Tilaks slammed the bottom of his bottle into his fist with such force that it sent a stream of liquid shooting out of the bottle and across his cuff. "I'll have a hundred hectares of clay there. First rate clay – without rocks, without anything. In two years a brick factory should be smoking away there – with the most modern methods and the newest machines. I've studied the ones they use abroad... As long as the credit union gives me the money..."

"I've said..." Sveilis slapped his chest. "Our banks are community institutions. In the future we'll have to turn more of our attention towards the supporting and growing our national industries... Honestly!"

"Oh, the splendour of the fraternity brothers of old!" Roberts began for the third or fourth time, motioning and smiling to the students prompting them to join in.

Milda and Little Flame emerged from the alder trees with handfuls of sad-looking flowers they had picked. The young men surrounded them in an instant – some taking their flowers, others plying them with wine. The noise grew louder with every moment.

They all got back in and kept on driving.

They sat down haphazardly. Sveilis was now next to Milda. Made was placed in a different motor car. Young, drunken men were sitting around her and across from her. But close up next to her was Roberts Lodziņš; she sensed his arm holding her tightly around her waist and his fingers groping around the front of her blouse. She didn't fight back. That didn't matter anymore...

The sun slid down further. The deep blue of the sky seemed to have turned darker. Everything along the horizon appeared more distinct, had taken on clearer contours, seemed to be more easily and clearly discernible. With the city retreating into the distance, the surroundings became increasingly attractive – the earth was richer and more fertile, there were birch forests and gardens, and more verdant fields of crops. But the city-dwellers were not looking out at the beauty of nature, which they had travelled here to see. Their heads were heavy but their tongues were loose, and their fantasies vibrant. Laughter, shrieking and jubilation so loud that at times it drowned out the howl of four engines and the rumble of sixteen large, studded rubber tires.

They drove on and then stopped again. A huge pub, a mix of country and city construction, a long and formless two-storey building with different porches and other structures projecting off of it. The motor cars were parked in the courtyard. A colourful company composed of country day-trippers and farmers from the surrounding areas descended on them to have a look and be amazed. The gentlemen all walked up to the upper floor. Before driving on to the little manor Tilaks was buying, they had to refresh themselves.

They began to live it up in a way that these rooms had never encountered. As they filed in, Sveilis poured a handful of gold coins onto the buffet and ordered them to serve up what they had. Tilaks and Strauss contributed too. The students paid less, but fooled about, organised, sang and drank more. The long tables filled up with beer, wine and liquor glasses. Bottles that had been started or only half drunk were piled up along the walls. Bebrītis had found a gramophone somewhere and brought it upstairs. The rollicking conversation and laughter were overpowered by the howling and wailing of the records.

Milda and Strauss sat together on one chair, their backs resting against each other. Roberts pulled a pub bench close to them and plopped down on it heavily. A bottle in one hand and a glass in the other, he leaned over towards his old acquaintance. He laughed and looked her in the eyes.

"Well, Milda. Still up on your high horse?"

She stuck her tongue out at him. "It's quite high up. Be careful you don't get dizzy."

"Don't worry about me, worry about yourself. When you fall, then you'll be sorry." He winked towards his brother – his expression and movements spoke louder than words. He couldn't help himself and started to laugh loudly.

"My goodness, how rude!" she said, pushed him away and turned around, but couldn't help herself either and started laughing along with him. She turned back towards him. "Well, pour me some too. Get a grip and serve the ladies!"

Roberts rushed to get a second glass.

"Roberts – Roberts, you devil!" Ziemelis wagged his finger at him as a warning, and added in Russian, "Careful and don't get dirty!"

"What?" Roberts giggled back. "That's my old bride..." He pushed the glass towards her hand and filled it. "Cheers, Dulcinea!"

"Cheers, my sad figure of a knight!" she replied resting her head against Strauss's shoulder, she wiped her red lips with a red silk ribbon.

Little Flame, sitting in the open window, dangled her feet in sync with the rhythm and droned in an off-key alto along with the gramophone.

"None of the girls are as lovely, as those I saw on the hill..."

The tavern's waiters and local farmers were looking in through the half-open door. Noticing them, Lodziņš walked right over with a full glass of beer...

Made couldn't stand it any longer. She couldn't watch him romping around like an idiot, drinking without reason or measure, and avoiding her. She felt she was suffocating in this clamour of drunks. Almost as if she were sleepwalking, she placed her hands behind her back and felt her way along the wall; she came upon a door, grabbed the handle, turned it, and slipped out unnoticed into the other room.

A small room with whitewashed walls and curtains filthy with flies. A small table with its legs jutting out, a single rush chair, and a narrow bed with a striped homespun blanket... She saw it, but she wasn't looking. Like a magnet, her gaze was drawn by the half-drunk carafe of water sitting with a glass on the windowsill. It felt like she'd come here just for that... it felt like she'd known the whole time that there was a carafe with a glass by the window. Just for her.

But then she looked around, as if still searching for something. Had she forgotten something else? But then she heard the noise in the large front room begin to subside. As if the throng were heading out the door. Going home already? She'd completely forgotten that they were planning a trip out to Tilaks's little manor... But what did she care? She sat down heavily on the only chair, looked at the glass, and waited.

Yes... and then he came. She recognised him again from his steps. She didn't turn, she didn't become agitated. She knew that he would come, and that he had to come.

Rodolfs Lodziņš came in – a bottle and glass in hand. She

hadn't seen anybody not holding a bottle or glass all day. Leaning against the door jamb, he stepped over the threshold. He squinted, glancing around for a moment until he caught sight of Made – from his eyes it looked as if he'd been crying. Seeing her, he locked the door and came up to her. His staggering steps sounded strange on that floor. Made didn't care.

Placing the bottle and glass on the table, he grabbed Made under her arms and lifted her up off the chair. Even if he hadn't lifted her, she would have stood up on her own. She gave in to each of his movements, each of his desires. She sat on his lap and didn't resist when his insecure, trembling and still eager hands stroked and embraced her. It had to happen this way eventually, and she'd known that for a long time. Gradually she became excited too, and moved her whole body with his when his hot and hungry mouth tried to kiss her flesh through the fabric of her thin suit. Oh – she already knew his passionate caresses and kisses! They fell across her entire body like pale white coals from head to toe, stealing away her strength and will. She lay in this man's arms as if her limbs were bound. Neither resisting, nor screaming – no, she couldn't and didn't want to. All this time she had avoided him and struggled with herself. Now defeated and attained. Her earlier weariness, disgust and ennui seemed to blow away like drifts of fog. She now found herself in a fresh, free vastness and under an unknown blazing sun as pale white coals dropped across her entire body intoxicating her, almost as if to death itself.

The buttons along her back burst free from their loops with a pop. A hot mouth stinking of alcohol was slurring words into her ear.

"It's nothing... nothing... I'm just... my love!"

Like ringing golden drops these words poured over her heart. My love... How she'd yearned and waited for these words.

My love... She sank back numb into his arms.

"Drink... Drink!" He filled their glasses and they both

drank – once, a second time, they drank as if there was nothing else left to live for.

And then he held her even closer in his drunken arms. He lifted and carried her – breathing heavily from his drunkenness and from the significant weight of her body. He walked, staggering as his dirty boots trampled the clothes strewn across the floor. Swishing strangely, an expensive silk dress dragged behind his mud-caked boots, a gold ring which had broken free, rolled glittering and bouncing, jingling and tinkling, under the bed.

Out of breath, he released her from his arms. She fell down on the bed, bruising her bare elbow painfully. But none of that mattered... She wound her arms around his sick neck and pulled him closer.

"My love... my love... my love..." she babbled senselessly.

When he pushed her away, appearing angry again and somehow disappointed, she looked at the whitewashed wall and everything around her seemed like a whitewashed void. And then her tired eyes finally dropped down and gazed across her own bare, defiled body, and it too seemed to be made of the same whitewashed void. So this is what that joy feels like, that mysterious forbidden golden apple about which respectable people are forbidden to speak even in whispers. So this is what that wondrous pleasure feels like, the pleasure about which poets have written a thousand poems, for whose sake a river of wine, gold and tears flow each day! She'd grabbed a hold of it, drunk of it, wanting to become richer and happier – and instead watched as she lost that last tiny sliver, her only worth, which linked her to life and humanity... She didn't see it... She went over to the table... but she knew it just the same. But that would be lost for her too... for all time... Revulsion and boredom – a hundred times heavier than earlier. Her body shook with silent tears filled with pain and despair.

"Drink." He pushed the glass he'd taken down from the window into her hand and filled his own. "We need to drink and get drunk... So heaven and earth can spin together..."

She heard in his voice the same helpless despair filled with revulsion and pain. She drank – and yet she kept looking at him and for some reason asked him gravely:

"You're not going to marry her?"

"Miss Ziepēns?" He quickly poured more, drank it, and laughed hoarsely. "Crazy goose... What do you expect?" He reached around in his pockets, pulled out a square piece of modern deckle-edged paper and pushed it towards her to see. "Read it! I don't want to... I have to take her! There's no other way..."

She only managed to glance at it, but even without it she would have understood. An engagement announcement... Now there truly was nothing left... emptier and colder...

"Fill it up!" She pushed her glass towards him and drank with great gulps, gagging. And just at that moment she noticed how his eyes were watching her naked body with boundless revulsion and hatred. She leaned down, lifted up her silk dress, and sat down. "Fill it up!" She pushed her glass towards him. She'd been drinking this whole time and hadn't yet become drunk. With every glass she emptied her desire and her thirst only grew. The world had been emptied – it was as empty and dry as an old broken wine glass, her thirst unquenchable like a hot dusty gust of wind spinning heaven and earth together.

Then the bottle slipped from his hand and he collapsed on the edge of the bed. Like a drowning man, he groped at her waist with moist, sticky hands and pressed his face into her thin, rustling blanket.

"What am I to do! What am I to do!" he whimpered as he shook. "I'm sick... I'm at the end... I'll make my wife sick too... What will my children be like!"

Talking about children... and yet he was just a large, weak, deathly ill child himself. Made heard, but didn't listen. Something else had occurred to her. Where his head was laying on her limp, tormented body, something was pressing sharply and painfully. She knew. Saved for this day... Everything happened as it had to.

She pulled it out with a sure hand. A small, brown bottle... The cork came out with a chirp. Its neck clinked against the edge of the glass. An acrid-smelling liquid poured out in a tiny stream into the glass and into the blood-red wine. Made was not thinking about anything anymore. Everything happened as it had to, and as had long been clear to her... To drink and get drunk, and to quench that terrible thirst at last...

She couldn't look... Death was smiling back at her there in that red, iridescent liquid. She closed her eyes... Clink – the cool glass sounded as it hit her clenched teeth... She drank... one swallow... then another. Thinking of nothing and aware of nothing with her eyes still closed, she felt around with her outstretched hand. The sharp edge of the glass hit the snoozing man's skull with powerful force.

"Drink!" she grunted strangely as if she were choking, gasping. Her tongue felt as if it were melting away in a burning flame, as if it were sticking to her mouth. Still her hand held the glass up to the man's mouth – pushing it firmly, forcefully up to his lips, turning, and pouring... He drank, retching, with crazed eyes transformed by fear, and what he didn't manage to swallow dribbled down his chin and onto his shirt and chest. His hand, its fingers outstretched as if driving something away, rose up and then fell back down again... It was too late... It was done...

They both lurched up at once – as if fleeing to each other, as if seeking to be rescued by the other, they embraced and held each other. Two savage, beastly howls, two bodies bound together falling back onto the bed as convulsions continued to shake and shatter them.

Roaring, horns blaring, four motor cars rushed back towards the city.

Roberts was sitting across from Little Flame in the back seat. Holding his arms above the elbows, leaning in closely, whispering something into her ear. A stupid smile was plastered across her face. As the motor car rocked, she kept swaying and with every bump would fall back into the corner of the seat wobbling back and forth. Tilaks was slumped next to her – he was sleeping now. At first he had kept fighting to keep his eyes open, but then they gradually fell shut as his head hung limply onto his chest – the new owner of the little manor and the future major industrialist occasionally snored so loudly as to drown out the thrum of the engine and the clatter of the wheels. Little Flame pushed his hat down over his eyes so that his face disappeared and it looked as if a hat with an upturned brim were slowly sliding down, only to suddenly lurch up before sliding down again. Roberts slipped in his thumb and laughed like mad when Tilaks soft double chin bumped up against his hard fingernail.

The students were sitting in the two cars in the middle. The hoarsely droned songs, shouts and laughter didn't stop there for even an instant. Glasses clinked, drinks spilled onto clothes and stained the inside of the motor car. As empty bottles shattered against roadside verst markers, the cars rushed by, spun after fleeing shepherd dogs, splashed down into muddy brooks and eventually came to rest in half-tilled fields, their exhaust pipes still smoking.

The workers further out in the field dropped their tools, climbed up higher, and shielding their eyes against the late afternoon sun, watched the mad convoy. A tardy sower drove his horse with a harrow to the far side of the field and then, grabbing the halter, held it tightly. The travellers were falling over each other laughing, staggering about, showing off to each other. Three schoolboys jumped over a ditch and, showing their tongues, whistling, and joking around in all sorts of ways, saw off the convoy. A flock of sheep ran helter-skelter across the road and into the bushes – only one small, feeble lamb wasn't so lucky. It flopped down with its head hitting the dust, and lay there for a moment, then lurched dizzily to its feet, and staggered underneath the first motor car... A small bump, like a fist-sized stone – nothing more.

Roaring, horns blaring, the convoy rushed onward. A giant

cloud of dust puffed up into the sky, its grey swirls winding across the fields, and slowly coming to rest again on the ground.

Sveilis was in the front car – a good distance in front of everyone else. The wind was lifting his hat and stealing his breath, but still it seemed too slow. The quickest jolt, the sharpest feeling seemed too slow and gentle for his dulled senses. Faster, even faster... to run across the entire country in the blink of an eye... to hold the entire world within a single breath!

"Faster, you bastard!" Sveilis reached up and shoved the driver in the back with his fist. He grabbed the open bottle with his other hand. "Let's oil it, so it moves easier..." He dripped the wine onto the whizzing rubber tire. Red drops shot off painting the grey side of the car and also hit him in the face. "We need to baptise this new wagon!" Sveilis leaned his arm back and flung away the not quite empty bottle and fell back onto his seat.

"You're crazy!" Milda laughed as she slapped him with her closed parasol across his legs.

"What? Girl!" He pulled away the parasol and threw that out too. "Let it be!"

"You're crazy!" Milda pouted.

"Girl!" He grabbed her hands and clenched them tightly. He leaned forward and shoved the driver in the back with his fist again. "Drive, you bastard!"

Roaring, its horn blaring, the motor car rushed ahead.

A grey cloud of dust was swirling behind him, but ahead the lights were shining on either side. They glowed like two giant yellow coals in the sun. They seemed to stretch out like gold ribbons tempting and fooling those who couldn't keep up.

Dizzy, giggling sweetly, Milda lay lightly against Sveilis's chest.

"Crazy... We'll end up getting killed like this."

She was resting her feet on the empty seat in front. The wind blew back her dress, lifting up its red ribbon, shaking and flapping it about above their heads. The wind howled in their ears and burned their cheeks. They had to close their eyes.

"Eh!" Sveilis grunted drunkenly with delight and gripped her weak, submissive body even tighter. And then bellowed like crazy: "Stand aside! Money's coming through!!"

A good distance ahead a grey horse was ambling down the road. The horn blared without stopping which only served to frighten it. The driver jumped off the wagon, holding the horse by its stirrups, and tried in vain to steady it and turn it around. It reared up launching a cloud of dust into the air. Bursting by at wind speed, those sitting in the motor car only noticed a horse stretching across a somewhat deep highway ditch; a driver in the ditch on all fours dressed in a brown, shiny, fulled, homespun coat; a stout farmer's wife sitting in the wagon in a white, brightly-patterned calico jacket with a black, shiny leather belt, desperately reaching for a small bag on the seat; bundles, packages, and a row of pretzels all strung onto a line were falling from the wagon onto the plants sprouting on the rye field... And then they were past it... And once again the wind was howling in their ears and burning their cheeks.

They drove into the city. Pedestrians ran off the street and onto the pavements, and drivers pulled over to the very edge. Like a black stream, it split and parted, and down the straight, smooth path cleared in the middle, four motor cars raced recklessly. Rules and regulations... Who could stop them or keep them from doing anything? Money's coming through!

Money always has time and freedom and all roads are open to it. Even a person thrown headlong off the road doesn't feel irritated or offended. That's how it was and that's how it had to be. He'd pull out his handkerchief, wipe his face, dust off his knees. Look warmly at the jolly, reckless travellers. He'd hurry to snatch the cap off his head in case he saw an acquaintance in one of them. And look around proudly and with delight, if that acquaintance noticed him and returned his greeting. And would laugh heartily if someone else was run off the road and had fallen down just as he had. But then he'd become serious again and stand on tiptoe watching them drive off. That was money coming through...

The driver pulled onto a straight, wide street. People stood along the sides and watched with amazement. But the middle was clear and smooth. The convoy rushed on roaring – straight towards the great disc of the sun, which burned right in front of them, low at the far end of the same street. In the front motor car, a red silk flag fluttered around the drivers' heads, but the lights burned on both sides. They glowed like two giant coals reflecting the sun. They seemed to stretch out like gold ribbons tempting and fooling those who couldn't keep up...

1913-1914